END MAN

END MAN

ALEX AUSTIN

Cursed Dragon Ship
P U B L I S H I N G

Copyright © 2022 by Alex Austin

Cursed Dragon Ship Publishing, LLC

6046 FM 2920, #231, Spring, TX 77379

captwyvern@curseddragonship.com

Cover © 2022 by Stefanie Saw

Developmental Edit by Kelly Lynn Colby

Copy Edit by S.G. George

ISBN 978-1-951445-34-8

ISBN 978-1-951445-33-1 (ebook)

This books is a work of fiction fresh from the author's imagination. Any resemblance to actual persons or places is mere coincidence.

End Man is dedicated to all the rockers and writers who shaped my life, and the readers whose feedback shaped this novel, with a special thanks to my son Alex.

CHAPTER
ONE

Death was a good place to hide. Ninety-nine percent of the reported dead stayed dead, but occasionally someone played possum. At the Norval Department of Marketing Necrology (NDMN), Raphael's job was to find the possum's pulse, no matter how faint.

Raphael glanced away from Professor Jason Klaes's obituary, having read it for the fifth time, each read more frustrating than the one before. The details he needed weren't there, but Maglio, the big boss, didn't want excuses. *Nail Klaes.*

On the ultra-high-def screens protruding from the department's wall, a plain woman in a plain smock ironed a sheet. Vapor rose from the sleek device in her hand. She drew the iron back and forth with a dreamy smile, unchanged as she set it upright, adjusted the linen, and then continued her labor in an endless loop. This mindfulness video with its soothing predictability was meant to relax, but it made Raphael uneasy. He couldn't say why.

Above the screens, the Norval logo—a thick *N* with stubby wings like cupid—glowed. The name of the division appeared in neat silver letters followed by its charge: *To Preserve and Protect the Online Remains of the Dead.*

Corporate speak decoded, it meant hoarding every bit of personal data the deceased left behind and restricting it to Norval Portals. To those online portals came loved ones and scandalmongers, biographers and extortionists, seekers of juicy details and the merely curious —consumers all, valuable targets of the advertisers Norval solicited.

The PA system screeched.

"Stage Three Event. Repeat. Stage Three Event. Category: mass shooting. Location: Durham, North Carolina. Estimated deaths: fifty. Override status. All Necrology Department employees return to their desks."

On the screens, the ironing woman faded to black. Multi-colored zigzag patterns filled the screens, resolving into police cars and ambulances, lights flashing on the exterior of a university quadrangle. Students streamed from the doorways of a white stone building and ran across the quad. Blanched faces filled the screen, then vanished. Trailing those fleeing, the injured—many bleeding—stumbled, limped, and crawled toward the police line.

A weight fell on Raphael's shoulder. He glanced up at Mike Dreemont, his supervisor, a thickset man with a heavy jaw, wide mouth, and sickly-sweet cologne.

"You know the routine, Team Leader," said Dreemont. "Take as many End Men as you want from Cancer, Stroke, Alzheimer's, Overdose, Suicide, and Pneumonia. Let me know if you need more." Releasing Raphael's shoulder, Dreemont stood on his toes and called out to the office. "Let's get busy, End Men!" Keyboards clicked furiously. Nodding, Dreemont dropped to his heels with a thump and glanced hard at Raphael. "But when you're done—"

"Yeah, Mike. Back to Klaes."

"Oh, better check on your new necrologist. It's her first mass casualty event, so I gave her a heads-up. She didn't take it well."

Raphael found Jensy seated and bent over her desk, her slender, white cane within arm's reach. Her long black hair hung forward, parting over pale-green frames containing thick, black lenses, but otherwise masking her face. She'd tucked her hands between her legs, and her headphones lay on her stippled keyboard. Jensy was a petite woman. When Raphael spoke to her, he always hunched over, and then his long hair covered his face. Two faceless people talking.

"It's all right, Jensy."

She lifted her head an inch. *"All right?* All those people dead. *All right?"*

"No, I meant …" What did he mean?

He lowered his hand but stopped short of touching her. Curiously, the visually impaired usually took longer to adjust to the work, if ever.

In a soft voice, Raphael said to Jensy, "I started at Norval on the day a tanker carrying chlorine gas ruptured within fifty yards of a county fair. Four hundred people—"

"Four hundred? How awful."

"Yes, so many. Dreemont gave us new End Men ten minutes to get our act together and then compile. He was all business—emotionless. I ran right into his office and complained that their bodies weren't even cold yet. We were talking about them like meat. He said, 'Not meat, kid. Data. They're dead but not less valuable. That's our business. Get moving.' Man, I wanted to hit him. Maybe I should have, but I didn't. I went back to my desk, my work."

She faced him, her dark, smudged glasses slipping down the bridge of her nose. Her sightless eyes glistened. "Those people are just data? College students. Teachers." Jensy lowered her head and pushed her glasses into place. "All those people, all at once."

"We do sad work, Jensy. You can't let it get to you." He searched for something profound but came up with a cliché. "You can't take it personally." Dreemont had hammered that into him, and now he was the one who could shrug off a mass casualty event. *Just like Dreemont.* Jesus, had he come that far?

Jensy raised her head again and seemed to peer into his eyes. "You can let it go?"

"It took time."

"Yes." She pushed her fists at the corners of her eyes. "Time."

"It sounds cold, but that's necrology."

She nodded and wiped her cheeks. "I must look awful."

"Hardly."

He instructed her to continue with the task he'd assigned her the day before: culling the Natural Blanks—the dead who had been too old or too young for an online presence—from the Weekly Nevada Traffic Crash Fatalities List. "Have you found many yet?"

"Krill Larkov, a four-year-old boy; Polina Zatonsky, a female infant; and two 109-year-old women, Nancy and Sharon Blunt. Twins."

"The names aren't necessary."

"Oh."

"Good work," he said softly, unmodulated by the twinge of melancholy he always felt when considering the Natural Blanks, especially the children. He wasn't Dreemont yet.

Jensy nodded, put on her earphones, and spread her fingers over her braille keyboard. She smiled, froze, and smiled again, probably unsure of what to feel, like Dorothy touching her foot to the first brick of the yellow road, like all End Men on the first day they fully realized what kind of work they did.

As Stage Three Team Leader, Raphael spent the morning managing the preliminary event research, gliding from End Man to End Man—a name derived from the pronunciation of its acronym, NDMN, and adopted by the unit's employees regardless of gender, though necrologist, keeper of lists of the dead, was their formal title—advising, encouraging, and channeling their efforts to gain and confirm the names of the dead.

By 1:00 p.m. the names of thirty-eight dead students and seven faculty members had made the list, plus the shooter. Now began the meticulous aggregation of the dead's online remains, the opening of a new Norval Portal for each departed (offline in Norval-speak), and the linkage of the remains to the patented Norval Portal navigation system. Next came the delicate negotiations for portal rights, but this was handled by Contracts. Raphael's team leader responsibilities were over. From the PA came a few bars of an ancient song, one of dozens comprising Norval's looped background music, the favorite tunes of its CEO, who carried the songs from his youth.

"Fun, Fun, Fun" by the ... Beach Boys.

On the Cumulative Clock, the hundreds digit flashed a nine. Fun? No. But—

Come next month, Raphael would have spent five years as an End Man, the last three as a possum specialist, outing those faking their deaths. Considering his spatial limitations, it wasn't the worst of jobs, and playing detective could be a rush, even if the dark alleys, tough thugs, and femme fatales remained confined to his computer.

But sleuthing was a small part of the company's mission. Norval harvested the data of the dead, and despite his bravado with Jensy, he would sometimes imagine that long line of the deceased, constantly refreshed, plodding toward him, led by a figure with a bewildered face, as if emerging from the fog to view an unfamiliar location.

Let it go.

CHAPTER
TWO

Thursday's mass casualty event in the rearview mirror, Raphael began Friday morning intent on nailing Professor Klaes. The professor had died on January 10, but beyond that blunt fact lay little else. All the County Medical Examiner-Coroner would disclose was place of death (Klaes's home in Pasadena) and a generic cause (unnatural) which could have been anything from a slip in the bathtub to carbon monoxide poisoning to, well, the sky was the limit. That said, Raphael had no evidence to support either foul play or suicide at this point.

Earlier in the week, he had made the standard calls to Klaes's colleagues and a few distant relatives and gently prodding law enforcement. He got zip. On Wednesday, he turned to Dr. Klaes's internet history over the months preceding his reported death. He spent hours mapping online activity, but the usual alarms weren't sounding: no darknet sites, no search queries about disappearing from society, no underage girlfriends or boyfriends, no cryptocurrency plays or big insurance policies.

The only unusual transaction on Klaes's debit card was a truck rental on January 8, two days before his death, but it didn't appear promising. Even award-winning physicists had to haul their old junk.

Klaes had no obvious motives for faking his death. But Raphael found nothing so far that explained the oddities marking Professor Klaes as undeclared and prompting CEO Geovanni Maglio to assign the physicist to Raphael.

"Knock, knock."

The second of NDMN's three possum specialists, Matt Tucker, stood at the entrance to the cubicle, fist in the air as if he had tapped an actual door. In his other hand, he held a quadrant of glazed donut, which he popped in his mouth. At twenty-five, Matt—his best friend in the department—was a year younger than Raphael, though thinning hair and frown lines placed him at thirty. Conversely, he always smelled like milk and cookies.

"A little excitement around here yesterday, huh?" asked Matt, fidgeting with his beaded lapis bracelet. The way it clicked and clacked reminded Raphael of the mindfulness videos.

"Yeah, I guess," Raphael replied coolly, having no desire to rehash the Stage Three Event. Nor, he believed, did his friend. Matt often did this, came in spouting something obvious only as a means of breaking the ice for what he actually wanted to discuss. Not disappointing, Matt leaned into the doorframe. "Belinda's been ghosting me."

"Bummer."

"Bummer's right. That leaves me with an extra ticket to the Arroyo Holobaloo Festival, though. Interested?"

For an instant, Raphael imagined the fields of people and scores of bands, the musical thunder and lightning. The Arroyo was north, which meant crossing La Brea, a half-mile east of Norval. He recalled the sheer sheet of ice rising before him when he last faced the boulevard. It was all in his head, of course, but knowing the source made it no less real or dreadful.

If he could … but no. Feeling hollow, he shook his head. "Hey, cool offer, Matt, but I've got plans."

Matt pulled on his stretched earlobe, which, absent its gauge, hung like a carabiner. "Thought I'd ask. Well, have the best weekend you can." His friend backed out of the cubicle, spun around, and slipped away, his bracelet clicking and clacking as he went.

A concert would have been cool. "Fuck."

"Did you say something, Raphael?" called Akira over the cubicle wall.

"No. Coughed."

"Oh, I hope you're not getting sick."

"Me too, Akira."

Through the thin partition, Akira's fingers raced over her keyboard. Elsewhere, someone sucked on a straw—draining a Frappuccino? A ghostly, whispered TGIF slipped in somewhere.

Klaes. Alive or dead? Maglio had said he wanted absolute certainty. Raphael returned to the death notice. ... *Passed unexpectedly on January 10 ... graduate of MIT ... the Boltzmann Medal ... Lieben Prize. A celebration of Jason Klaes's life will be held on February 3 at 2:00 p.m. in the King George Room of the Harvey Hotel in Hollywood.*

Raphael had contacted the hotel, asking to speak to the event's coordinator. The hotel informed him that the coordinator, Lily Faraday, wasn't an employee of the hotel but a former colleague of Klaes who was staying at the Harvey for the duration of the event. She had given orders not to be disturbed in her room, but he could leave a message for her.

Does she have a work number?

Sorry, we aren't authorized to provide those.

He left a message. As with most of his inquiries, he had received no response.

From outside Raphael's cubicle, Dreemont's voice boomed in a bright, infomercial style. "Eight thousand a day, and every day the number rises. We expect within three years every newly dead over three years old will have had a substantial online presence. Instagramming, tiktoking, and zooming from the cradle to the grave."

"Amazing," said a higher-pitched male voice.

Raphael glanced to the floor's main aisle outside the doorway. Dreemont stood with a new intern, a fresh-faced grad in a blue skinny-suit. He had to be there for orientation.

"So, how much can you access?" the intern asked.

"Every mouse click, finger swipe, pressed key, sent message, selfie, posted photo, up or down vote, voice-activated-command, Tweeze, Ruffit, and Mayfly. Every search, every gaze, every intention."

"Yeah," said the intern, vigorously nodding.

"Here's a little secret," said Dreemont in a fake whisper. "Nothing really gets erased. Since quantum storage, once on the net, always on the net—if you know where to search."

"Pretty cool," said the intern.

"Now, this is Raphael," noted the supervisor, peering into the cubicle as if Raphael were an animal in a zoo.

Raphael's stomach turned at the attention.

"Raphael's what we call a possum tracker. Only three of those among our fifty End Men, and he's the best we ever had. He's got the instincts of a Kentucky deer hunter. Just give him tracks, scat, and a bent twig. Pretty damn good for a city boy."

"I'm not sure I understand," said the intern.

Dreemont laughed. "You've heard the saying, 'He's playing possum.' Well, possums are what we call people trying to pass themselves off as dead. Evading the law, a gambling debt, a spouse—you name it. Raphael determines if the undeclared—individuals whose reported deaths are questionable—are dead or alive. If alive, a true possum, they're no good to us." Dreemont lifted his elbows to span the doorway. "How's Mr. Klaes coming?"

"Oh, he's coming," replied Raphael.

"Keep me posted." Dreemont pushed off the doorway, then glanced back. "By the way, nice job yesterday, Team Leader."

Raphael nodded.

Dreemont turned to the intern. "Is the operation starting to make sense?"

"I guess," said the intern as the two strolled away.

Pretty damn good for a city boy. Until the city boy screwed up, and Raphael had—once.

Three months ago, Raphael had declared one Jay Engels offline and sent the verification to the contracts department. Contracts had no sooner gotten the final online remains rights from the next of kin and opened Engels's pre-portal, than the offline showed up at the terminus of the Appalachian Trail in Vermont. With Engels out on the trail for two months of self-imposed incommunicado, his wife and her lover had cooked up a scheme to fake his death, collect his insurance, and take off for the South Pacific. The scam took in everyone, including Raphael. The result had been a shitstorm. The possum screwed the company for six figures. The feds were sniffing for other iniquities, and the press raked up old Geo Maglio scandals.

Raphael scanned the scant obituary again, stood up, and tacked the notice to the bulletin board above his desk. It fit between his Picasso and Seurat prints bordered by skateboard decals. Despite the eclectic nature of his artistic tastes, the obituary seemed out of place.

He shifted his gaze to the board's single photograph: Raphy and his mom.

They posed before a sculpture at the nearby museum where his mother had curated modern art for twenty years. Her delicate arms accentuated by a sleeveless print dress, she hugged Raphael, his head nestled against her neck. Her gray eyes and delicate lips were identical to Raphael's. She smiled, as she had even when her disease had turned her limbs to stone. As the Cumulative Clock affirmed, people died all the time, but watching his mother's ordeal had been fucking tough.

Nail Klaes. Yes, yes.

Dropping to his chair, he considered the obituary's phrase *passed unexpectedly*. When people *passed unexpectedly* with no mention of illness, the cause of death was suicide, which was reported. The coroner's preliminary report came unaccompanied by a Proof of Death letter. A POD was always filed with a potential suicide and would verify the coroner investigated the case. Although Norval had solid contacts within the coroner's office, they weren't responding with Klaes.

Why? It took some clout to cover up standard information.

Perhaps a bureaucratic error, but it still smelled wrong to Raphael.

The email discrepancies, which aroused the original suspicions, were still the most baffling aspect of the case. First, there were signs of outward activity on several of Klaes's accounts after January 10.

Someone might have got Klaes's password or hacked the account. People plundered the dead's online remains all the time.

The hackers were mailbox thieves, sticking their hands inside and pulling out the contents, hoping to get lucky. In Klaes's case, though, they took nothing. Something was added, however: several messages sent from Klaes's email address with ominous threats to their recipients. Things got interesting right there.

The first message was sent January 12, the second January 13. Two went out on the fifteenth, at which point Klaes was five days dead. Raphael had determined the messages had not been preset. If Klaes was alive and making threats, why to these people, who had no connection to Klaes, as far as his research could determine? And what possum would use his own email to taunt and threaten?

Raphael opened up Klaes's email account and clicked on the sent folder. He let the cursor hover over the last messages.

Of the four outgoing messages that had prompted the Norval Chaff App to sound an undeclared alert, the earliest, January 12, had been sent two days after Klaes's death. The recipient was lindieger723@dotmail.com. The subject was, *After too few summers dies the swan.* It was the only one accompanied by a photo. Raphael opened the email.

Dear Miranda,
Was the selfie worth the life of that beautiful creature?
Prepare to meet your maker.
JK

Inset into the text was a large photo of a dead swan on the bank of a stream. The bird lay on its side, its wings outstretched. Its long white neck, bent midpoint at a right angle, stretched across the ground. The inset was a small close-up photo of a young beaming woman clasping the swan's neck with her left hand. The swan was motionless, squinting as if in excruciating pain.

Though Raphael had immediately sent a message to lindieger723@dotmail.com, as he had also done with the three other recipients, he received no reply, and Thursday's mass casualty event had interrupted further research. Now, Raphael typed the woman's email address into search. There were two results, and both were for Miranda's Mirror, a blog on the Haut Type site. The home page was filled with photos of the woman who had been choking the swan. She posed in various hairstyles, attitudes, and clothes. Beneath all the photos, the text of her blog began. Meet Miranda N. Day.

> **Hello! I am Miranda. I live in LA, the most exciting city in the entire universe, and I do what I like doing: making multiple versions of me. Me sexy. Me elegant. Me nasty ... I want to be every me I can be.**

There had to be a million similar blogs, yet something struck him as familiar about this one. He scrolled and came to a section of Miranda posing with animals. In each photo, she clutched the animal to her: dogs, cats, rabbits, pigs, cattle, horses, parrots, snakes. They all appeared to be selfies, the camera close to the subject. Miranda glowed with self-absorption; the animals appeared terrified, eyes wide and searching for escape.

Continuing to scroll through the hapless animals and the merry Miranda, Raphael arrived at the inset photo of Miranda and the swan. She had tried to adorn herself with the swan's beauty, but the swan was no longer beautiful. Its wings were twisted, and individual feathers had lost their symmetry. The swan would die for Miranda's selfie. He considered the name Miranda N. Day. Day led to night. Miranda Night Day.

He'd heard that name before. He scanned a thousand obituaries a week. The names passed by, ants on a trail. Occasionally, though, he paused at an improbable name. He had seen a Miranda Day Night. No, no. Night Day. There would be ten thousand Miranda Days, hundreds of Miranda Heather Days, but Miranda Night Day was unusual: a wit choosing an ironic middle name for their daughter? Alternatively, was it the girl herself who changed it?

He pulled up last month's obits file and searched Miranda Night

Day. There was one, and she died on January 14, two days after Klaes's email. The obituary noted her premature death was a tragic accident. Norval had yet to process the lead. Raphael did a general search for and found a half-dozen links to her death. The *Orange County Tribune* reported Miranda, a resident of Costa Mesa, fell from the fourth-story balcony of an apartment in San Juan Capistrano. During a party, she'd posed on the balcony to take a selfie with her friend's pet iguana, lost her balance, and fell. She'd died of a broken neck. The iguana had escaped both selfie and death. A photograph showed the lizard safe on the deck, peering through the rails.

If Klaes was a possum, why was he giving himself away sending intimidating emails to an animal abuser? The email suggested Klaes was alive. Yet the coroner said Klaes was deceased. It had to be someone other than Klaes who emailed the soon-to-be unfortunate Miranda. Perhaps someone with PETA or another animal rights organization? Why would they implicate Klaes? Miranda's accidental death might be viewed differently, and a living Klaes would be a suspect. That was a pretty farfetched conclusion. The more reasonable explanation? The physicist was still alive, had murdered Miranda himself, and was playing a deep game.

Raphael's phone rang. "Hello?"

"Verena. Gazette Obituaries," said the caller.

Jesus. Finally. "Yes, yes. Raphael Lennon at Norval. I left you a message a few days ago about Dr. Jason Klaes, the physicist."

"Oh, yes. Sorry about the delay. Damned computer system went down. So how can I help, Mr. Lennon?"

"I have some questions about the obituary. Like who paid for it?"

Verena cleared her throat. "The date of the notice?"

"January 12."

"Just a moment," said Verena, followed by the furious tapping of keys. "Okay, let's see. Got it. Anonymous."

"Anonymous? What do you mean, 'anonymous'?"

The phone went silent for a few seconds. "The obituary came in the mail with a cash payment."

Raphael pushed his chair back, surprised and irritated that such a transaction should be so casual. "You accepted that? What if it was a prank?"

"Obits ain't cheap. Excuse me." Verena cleared her throat again. "Even the hundred-word ones."

"Did Anonymous request a receipt? A copy of the article?"

Papers rustled. A prolonged sniff. "Eight-fifty in cash and a thank you note. Nothing else."

A nerve in his neck twitched. Nothing added up with this case, as if it might remain always out of his grasp. He stretched out a leg and set his foot under the skateboard living beneath his desk during work hours. He flipped the board on its back and brushed a wheel with his toe. The *whirr* of the spinning wheel calmed him, the purr of a stroked kitten, his magic aural amulet. He sent a second wheel in motion. "Did you verify—"

The PA system screeched. What the hell?

The mindfulness screens lit with a hideous image. On each screen, sheets of flame and coils of smoke engulfed a high-rise, studded by the remains of a plane's wings and fuselage.

The department's speakers blared, "Stage One Event. Repeat. Stage One Event. Commercial airliner strikes hotel. Location: Atlanta, Georgia. Estimated deaths: six hundred. Override status: all Necrology Department Employees return to their desks."

Raphael pressed his hand to his belly. "Sorry, Verena, I'll have to get back to you," he said. "Something's come up."

His potential possum would have to wait.

Akira assumed team leadership on Stage One Events, in which estimated casualties numbered over five hundred, though Raphael would have his hands full compiling. A Stage One and Stage Three on successive days. Blue moon stuff.

IT WAS 7:00 p.m. before the intense labor demanded for a Stage One Event—a Big Death in Norval parlance—subsided. Dreemont told the End Men to call it a night.

Sighs of relief rose from the cubicles.

"You've had a busy Friday," said Dreemont, as the department's employees gathered their belongings. "A lot of dead to input. I'll see if I can't get you a short Friday next week. Who reports for duty if a mass death occurs over the weekend?"

"Team B," responded a dozen End Men dutifully.

The floor emptied of exhausted workers until only Raphael remained. Dreemont appeared at the cubicle entrance. "Burning the midnight oil?"

"Yeah. Klaes."

"Good. Mr. Maglio will be pleased to hear that."

One more possum in the database is one terminated End Man. Fucking Maglio. If the salary wasn't so good or if he could find a cheaper apartment that could accommodate his painting—he'd be saying sayonara. Though that was really just a pipe dream. He still wondered why it was so damn important to get the undeclared into the database at all. Norval had enough dead, and it would seem just ignoring questionable candidates would be the sensible policy. But Norval, meaning Geovanni Maglio, didn't see it that way. "Keep the database pure. No goddamn possums." Well, a lot of things made no sense in this world. Go along, get along.

"Have a wonderful weekend then," said Dreemont, stepping away.

"Absolutely. You too."

Waiting until the main-entrance door had locked—a gnashing of parts that maintenance had yet to remedy—Raphael returned to Miranda's demise. The newspaper article provided few details on the ill-fated party.

Shifting to Miranda's Facebook page, he clicked on notifications. The party had been on January 14. Scrolling through several thousand notifications, he reached the ones sent in early January. An invitation to Alicia Fallow's birthday party came on January 8. Alicia lived in San Juan Capistrano.

He messaged Alicia.

Hi, Alicia. My name is Raphael Lennon, I work for the Norval Department of Marketing Necrology in Los Angeles. My company is trying to tie up some loose ends regarding your deceased friend Miranda Night Day. I've attached a photograph of a man who may have attended your party on the night Miranda had her tragic accident. Is it possible that he was present at your affair?

He added a couple more condolences—never hurts—and his phone number. After attaching a photo of Klaes, he sent the message.

Raphael glanced at the time on the monitor: 10:06 p.m.

A yawn crept up on him. He would not resolve the Klaes enigma tonight. He needed a few hours of sleep to clear his brain and restore his energy. Before sleep, would he find it in him to complete the image he'd started painting earlier that morning?

Raphael shut down his computer and looked once more at the obituary notice. On Monday, he'd pester the Harvey Hotel until the event manager got back to him.

He grabbed his skateboard from under the desk, wedged it under his left arm, and turned off the lights. Below the wall screens, the Cumulative Clock, which showed the day's death toll, flashed as all the numbers changed when the thousands digit turned from seven to eight. Another old, upbeat song from Maglio's youth played. This one was about making new friends in new places with a background of internal combustion engines—long illegal—revving.

Raphael sang a line of the lyrics to the dark department, then shook his head. As if he were going anywhere. "Vroom, vroom. Yeah."

As was his habit late at night, he walked to the floor's plate-glass window and gazed down at the lights of Wilshire Boulevard. On the far side of the street, two hooded figures spray-painted the front of a cell phone store. They drew back to view their work. The large letters read FUCK DATA. The vandals were doubtless Intentional Blanks, Digital Luddites, Ludds—whatever. Assholes.

A third figure stood nearby. Half in shadow, much taller than the two vandals, the man in a brimmed hat looked up at Raphael's window. Light glinted off metal-framed glasses, and one side of his jaw had a reddish sheen. Pivoting, the man appeared to address the Blanks, who stepped toward him but then halted. With his palm raised, the man strode to the vandals and huddled with them for a moment. The three walked off like friends, leaving the sidewalk empty, though the street remained an unending stream of vehicles brightening the night.

Raphael considered the grand boulevard and tried to imagine crossing it. A cold draft slipped through the window's sealed frame. The draft increased in force until it shoved him like a giant's hand, slamming him to the floor, pinning him.

Stuck.

CHAPTER
THREE

Five minutes after Raphael shut off the lights in Necrology, he pushed through Norval's massive front door, stood at the top of the steps, and drew out his beanie. He pulled it on and adjusted its cuff. He went nowhere in the outer world without the beanie.

During his first months at Norval, Raphael would exit the building as if the dead were trying to pull him inside. The passing years had left him less fanciful, harder—though not as free from the tug of pity and sadness portrayed for Jensy. Not Dreemont yet. He glanced back through the glass into the expansive lobby, met the security guard's eyes, and nodded. The guard nodded back, a daily ritual that affirmed his exit from Norval.

He gazed down the great boulevard, still packed with vehicles standing bumper-to-bumper, all similar in their contents: a single driver, eyes closed or laced with sleep, secure in their bubble, computers in charge. The great expectations of the urban planners had been reduced to chimera by the public's fear of mass transit, inescapable after a string of pandemics: the fear of the nearby other, the stranger's cough, the seatmate's sniffle. Bullet trains and hyper-loops gathered dust and graffiti. *Armadillidiidae,* those subcompacts designed on the mechanics of the potato bug and so marketed as Roly-Polies, abounded.

He considered the drivers, some chatting or texting on their phones, others nodding to the latest synthetic beat or a convincing podcast, and still others reuniting with a loved one on their Norval Portal. No, not quite reuniting, for the Portal was a one-way street. You could explore the most minute details of a loved one's life, but they could know nothing of you. Raphael could not make up his mind whether his company's products were a good thing or a bad thing. Maybe they were neither.

Although the boulevard was packed, he discerned a snaky path between the vehicles, but if he even approached the curb, the wind would stir on this windless night, and then rise against him, a wall of air pushing him back as easily as it would a leaf. Wilshire was his southern boundary of wind.

He dropped his skateboard, pushed off hard, and sailed over the seven wide steps leading from the entryway to the sidewalk. Lowering his butt to the board, a habit from pubescent days of wipe-outs and sprained ankles, he stuck the landing like an expert gymnast coming off a pommel horse, and happy chemicals rushed through him. Though he may not have learned new tricks, the old ones held fast. Fifty feet above, a fleet of delivery-drones swooped by, their night-lights reflected dazzlingly as they passed the Norval building's gleaming cylindrical façade.

The structure was built in the 1930s, a hundred years ago, modeled on Streamline Moderne architecture, which had been fashionable at the time. As a child, he had walked by it with his mother a thousand times. "Bold and beautiful," she declared. Inspired by aerodynamics, with an emphasis on long horizontal lines and sweeping curves, the building resembled nothing so much as an ocean liner thrusting its golden bow into the Wilshire-Fairfax intersection. Originally a Yam's Department Store, the building had gone through multiple owners. Maglio bought it decades ago, gutting much of its interior to create the Norval Headquarters, but the building, designated a historic cultural monument, could not have its exterior altered.

The LA County Museum of Art, where his mother had worked, bordered the Norval building. The facility was undergoing a massive restoration after a partial redesign infuriated its patrons. The night-lights of giant cranes and earthmovers provided the illusion of daylight along the Wilshire Boulevard façade and sidewalk, rising to tops of the queen palms that bordered the street. Above the museum entrance hung a huge banner promoting the latest exhibit, *Sachlichkeit: The New Sobriety. German Art in the Weimar Period*. Beneath the promotion hung a second banner. *The Digital Armory: Digital Art from Around the World. Opening February 2*. The opening fell on his birthday.

A siren blared atop the museum.

A large door swung open near the museum entrance. With lights blinking and softly whirring, the facility's Desquatter emerged from its chamber. The rotund machine, a gleaming metallic cask girded at its base by a golden bumper, glided slowly back-and-forth down the public sidewalk, its half-ton bulk stirring a few homeless setting up camp. They cursed the Desquatter and moved on.

It didn't seem fair. Well, the world wasn't fair. A couple walked hand-in-hand across the boulevard, then stopped and kissed on the other side. He could count on one hand the times a girl had kissed him, and those memories were fading fast. Not that Raphael couldn't find a girl to kiss or didn't want to, but honor demanded disclosure. *You see, Allison, Itzel, Sophia, Madelyn, Jennifer, Dahlia, I'm trapped within four streets. Wind to the south, fire to the north. glacier to the east, and chasm to the west*. And disclosure had always resulted in flight. Sometimes a slow take-off, sometimes a pricked balloon. They'd be gone, and his heart would sink. Better to have never loved at all than be a loser every time.

Cut it out.

The temperature had dropped into the fifties, and his T-shirt and drift pants were thin. Crossing his arms, he considered skating home through the museum grounds, past the famous lake-size tar pit with its sinking mastodons and beneath the grassy slopes of the fossil museum, which quarried the grounds' pits for bones to reassemble and exhibit.

The gates closed at 9:00 p.m. though the closure didn't always dissuade him or others—some ill-intentioned. More than once, he'd climbed the fence to roll leisurely along the museum's shadowy, winding paths, skating past the excavation sites, the animal statuary, and down the ramp beneath the suspended 340-ton granite megalith *Levitated Mass*. Twenty-two feet high and shaped like a true heart, that work was now unfortunately stored. Night or day, the museum grounds, known well since childhood, camouflaged Raphael. A chameleon, he took on the colors of the winding paths, the broad-leafed trees, and pools of asphalt. Within the museum grounds, he was safe.

But it was much too late for the museum, and the unfinished painting waited.

He brushed the hair from his forehead. Above Wilshire Boulevard a skyboard floated by with a pulsing advertisement: *Constipated? Monitor and Improve Peristalsis With MyColonBytes. Available in Black, Silver, and Gold from Bodyfluidsandbeyond.com $579.95.*

"Race you," Raphael shouted to the skyboard and propelled himself forward on the sidewalk—slightly slanted downhill after the big temblor of three years ago—leaving the advertisement in the dust. He boisterously sang the lyrics of an old song about a young man of eighteen confused about his identity. Except Raphael was twenty-six—going on twenty-seven—though still uncertain if it were the boy's or man's camp he occupied.

Twenty-seven, that *ominous age*. Kurt, Jimi, Janis, they only got to twenty-seven. Listening to their songs on his mom's old vinyl left him sad and uneasy, but also a little envious. They were free of limitations, geographic and otherwise, for a while.

He turned the corner and pushed off again. He hadn't gone half a block when a shrill voice behind him shouted, "Raphael Lennon!"

His stomach tightening at the unexpected cry, Raphael dragged a foot along the ground, stopped, and pivoted. He lifted his board to his chest. "Yes?"

"Please, wait. I'm—I'm out of breath," begged someone jogging toward Raphael.

The figure, a pear-shaped man with a wobbly gait, slowed, stopped, and grabbed his knees. "Oh, that was hard. I'm not used to ..." The man straightened, shook his head, then approached Raphael, panting. "Raphael Lennon, yes?"

Raphael nodded, while measuring the chances of the odd, panting man who smelled of lavender doing him damage. He lowered his board.

The man patted his chest. "I spoke to the security guard. He said—the skateboard." The man bent and grabbed his knees again. "I don't go in for cardio, but I can see ..." With effort, he straightened. "Yes, I can see the benefits." He held up a large manila envelope and pointed with it over his shoulder. "I thought you'd gone in the other direction, toward the museum. The guard said you sometimes—I ran there, and it was locked up. So, I had to run all the way back."

"What's this about?" Raphael dropped his board to the sidewalk, sensing a long-winded sales pitch he might want to escape.

The man pressed at his long thin nose as if to widen his nostrils, exhaled loudly and then sucked in a lungful of air. "I've been trying to get ahold of you for a couple of days without success. I was going to leave my envelope at the security desk, but the guard said you'd just left. Lucky I caught up to you."

"Lucky? For—"

"Oh, excuse me. My name is Gilly Stull of the Los Angeles County Coroner's Office."

Raphael set his right foot onto the board, inching it backward. "It's pretty late, Mr. Stull. Couldn't this wait until Monday?"

"Unfortunately, no. I'm on vacation in Puerto Maldonado next week. This was the last piece of business I needed to resolve. 'Clear desk, clear conscience,' as they say."

Raphael rolled the board back and forth. "I understand." He glanced over his shoulder toward the lights of the Tar Tower Apartments, home since the day he was born and the dead center of his square mile world. Likely to die there too. With a chill, he met Stull's gaze.

"I tried to reach you all day," said Stull. "Your receptionist said you were unavailable. I left several messages, but ... It was the airliner crash, I suppose." Stull's brows rose as his eyes widened.

"Yes, we were busy. Sorry."

"I understand perfectly. It's the same with us on occasion. You see, we've had some computer system irregularities lately, compounded by a clerical error sidetracking what would have been a routine response. I wanted to apprise you of the error, and my email, I'm afraid, bounced. Perhaps I simply had the wrong address. In any event, it's my responsibility, and I would have been dwelling on it all vacation. Ordinarily, I would have sent a messenger. It was so late, and frankly on a Friday night messengers tend to go astray."

"Yeah, I've heard," said Raphael. "So, you've gone to all this trouble because ..."

"You were inquiring about Professor Jason Klaes, a recently deceased."

Raphael took his foot off the skateboard. His heart revved. "Yes."

"You spoke to one of our new employees: the clerk I mentioned," said Stull. "She got confused about Professor Klaes."

"We're all confused about Klaes."

"Yes, well. She got it 'bass ackwards,' as my father used to say. The medical report—I mean, the absence of a medical report. We indeed performed an autopsy on Professor Klaes on January 12. I've brought a copy of the report." Stull handed him the envelope.

This was odd. Bureaucrats didn't go out on a Friday night to deliver mail. "You've gone out of your way," said Raphael.

"It was a terrible mistake."

Raphael jiggled the envelope. Stull's eyes widened like a cat's watching an unaware bird. *Stull wanted him to open the envelope.* "How did Klaes die?"

"Suicide. Shotgun. In the living room of his house in Pasadena."

"Well, that answers that," said Raphael, wondering if it did.

"Yes, I thought you'd be pleased."

"And the body?"

"The arrangements were made with Donato's of Glendale. Klaes was cremated."

"Ah. Can I keep this?"

"You don't want to take a view of it now?"

Raphael glanced at the envelope. "It's been an exhausting day, right now I wouldn't be able to concentrate. Can I keep it?"

"Oh, yes, of course," said Stull, showing his teeth.

"So, if that's it?"

Stull peered through the fence bordering the recent extension of the museum to Fairfax. "What's going on over there?"

"A fossil pit. They're searching for the remains of Ice Age mammals that died in the Salt Lake Oil Field."

Stull studied the surroundings. "Lake?"

"It's beneath us." Raphael pointed at the sidewalk. "A thousand feet down. A huge lake of oil that they used to pump. The oil seeps up and creates the tar pits. A crude oil graveyard, you might say."

"How interesting. Dead, dead everywhere and not a drop to drink. No, doesn't work, does it?" Stull backed up a foot. "Well, good night, Mr. Lennon. Perhaps I'll see you down the road, and you'll remember my kindness."

Remember his kindness? "Right. Thanks. Goodnight, Mr. Stull."

He watched Stull, breathing easily now, stroll down Fairfax toward Wilshire. The man stopped once, turned around, tipped an imaginary hat, then continued on his way.

HE TAPPED Stull's envelope against his thigh.

Awfully convenient, or was Raphael being overly suspicious? Maybe Stull was legit, and Klaes really was dead. Maybe a hacker really had sent those post-mortem emails. Occam's Razor, the simplest answer had to be the correct one. Despite his uncanny feeling about the Klaes case, he'd hoped Klaes would give him a good chase, so Stull's confirmation was disappointing. Raphael wasn't certain he wanted Klaes dead. *Keep the database pure. No goddamned possums.* He slipped the envelope under his shirt.

He continued down Fairfax and crossed Sixth, one of the benign streets within the malignant four. On the opposite side of Fairfax, a dozen people stood in front of Nevin O'Moore's, an Irish pub with enough character to have kept it operating for a half-century. Rock 'n' roll poured out the open door. Sidewalk loiterers smoked, tossing their smoldering butts and disposable e-cigs in the gutter, and not a single phone visible, an anomaly for sure.

Raphael stopped to listen to a song about falling, rocking to the music's beat. He loved the old music and yearned to walk into Nevin O'Moore's, if it wasn't on the forbidden side of Fairfax.

He gazed out at the street, a flat concrete Grand Canyon of unlimited depth. If he skated over the curb, the canyon's black tongue would wrap about and swallow him as a frog would a fly. It mattered little if two-ton vehicles raced along on its concrete bed or pedestrians crossed at every corner.

Sometimes, he teased himself by pretending he might just, might just—*What do you have to lose, Raphy? Take a step. Do it! Do it!* He lifted a foot and peeked over the curb into the depths of the canyon. His heart leapt into his throat. Dizzy and disoriented, he teetered like a baby taking its first step. *Get back!* he screamed to himself and stumbled backward. *Breathe. Breathe!* The brain that knew the canyon an illusion shrunk from the brain that shouted the gaping darkness was real. He stood in the center of the concrete square, trembling.

For twenty years, the phobia had confined him to the area enclosed by the intersection of four venerable Los Angeles thoroughfares: Fairfax, Wilshire, La Brea, and Beverly. Roughly a rectangle, the shape of a phone, a monitor, a streaming screen, by his calculation the area of a square mile: 60 acres, 3,097,600 square yards, 27,878,400 square feet, 4,014,489,600 square inches.

His mother had tried every therapy to rid Raphael of his terror, which had leaped upon him like a panther from a tree. One day a strong gust of wind, the next week a gale. One day a crack in the street, the next week a chasm, until the four thoroughfares became treacherous and impassible, though the streets within his rectangle he could traverse and skate to his heart's content.

Cognitive behavioral therapy gradually exposes you to your fear, so you become desensitized to it. Raphael's mother had consulted one doctor who showed Raphy photos of the streets, each photo a further close-up. Then it was mindfulness therapy. Super awareness of the surrounding world. Get him to take that step out of his box. Relaxation therapy. Biofeedback. Hypnosis. When all else failed, they suggested antidepressants, but at this his mother balked. Each doctor had their pet theory as to the source of Raphy's fears. Did his mother have her own phobia about busy streets? Perhaps as a toddler Raphy had witnessed a horrific accident. Had he seen something appalling on television he associated with these streets? The streets formed a rectangle so perhaps he had gotten trapped in a similar shape as an infant. Or was it just a bizarre dream that infected his consciousness?

The fifth therapist Raphael had seen about the problem had named it. "We call it dromophobia," explained Dr. Cow. "The terror of crossing streets."

"It's not every street," Raphael had replied. "Not even every busy street. Sixth and Third are no problem."

"Unfortunately, in the *Diagnostic and Statistical Manual of Psychiatric Disorders*, it's the nearest category we've got. Perhaps in the next revision of the manual …"

The therapies continued into his early teens, at which point Raphy requested they stop trying, though fourteen was the very age he should have most wanted to break free. Before he was fourteen, he wasn't all that different from the kids he went to school with. Half-listened in class, skateboarded, played video games, hung around the park after school, and cautiously eyed the girls. But it was at that age his schoolmates started expanding their world: skating to the beach, camping, traveling to distant football games and amusement parks, exploring faraway malls and chatting up faraway young women. In the very years life should have been expanding, his life was hemmed in, shrinking in a way. He woke each day angry, sometimes slamming his fist into his own head, knowing his problem was nowhere but within his skull. He was his own enemy, and no doctor could disarm that foe. His anger turned to sullen depression. He drew into himself, stopped hanging out with friends after school. Why torture himself pretending he could break out? Why tease himself with stupid therapies? *You're incurable, accept it!*

His mother didn't quite give up, but she didn't press further treatments on him. Her own advancing disease sapped her energy and reduced her mobility at an ever-increasing rate. He stayed home, grew closer to his mom, learned to paint from her, and took up the brushes and oils himself. Like one of those ancient Greek Stoics he learned about in school, he gradually accepted his limitations, or at least banned his brain from dwelling on it. Be happy!

He had his skateboard, his computer, and his oils and brushes. He made the best of his spatial limitations.

Like a tide-pooled fish who knew every grain of sand and strand of kelp in its limited waters, Raphael knew every inch of his square mile: the dog that barked from the high window, the pothole unfilled for years, the remains of the old trolley depot, the white-haired man who sold the old and new vinyl, the stalwart bellman, and nonstop Two-Bags, the recyclable collector in perpetual motion; trash bags slung over his shoulders and filled to bursting. Within his rectangle, was he not rich with mall, park, and theater complex? Raphael had the Farmers Market—crossroads of LA tourism—and Thursday night Karaoke. He had sidewalks and parking lots aplenty to skate. A job, shelter, sustenance. If wanderlust struck, he could set out into the world on his computer, though such satisfaction had dwindled in the last couple of years just as his mania for video games had dried up. He had yet to try the mall's Virtueless Virtual Reality Arcade, which offered low fantasies—*Simulate to Stimulate*. He had everything he needed and wanted within reach. He whispered the line from *Hamlet* he had memorized in high school drama class. "'I could be bounded in a nutshell and count myself a king of infinite space.'"

If not for bad dreams.

No, not just bad dreams. If his thoughts lingered on the enclosing streets, he'd feel a pressure on his heart, as if the streets had replicated themselves in miniature within his chest. Worse were the glimpses of the outer world on phone and laptop or in glossy magazines. Snowcapped peaks and lush islands. Ancient temples and medieval castles. The Sistine Chapel and the Great Sphinx of Giza. To know they existed but would always be out of reach.

One path of escape existed: when the last stroke met the canvas. When the last image of his life painting had dried, he would be free of the phobia to dance out of his quadrangle.

His mother had promised.

From the shadows of his imagination came a whisper: *You'll never get out. Never. Stuck. Stuck. Stuck.* His heart fell. He made a fist and spun. *Don't crave. Don't desire. Don't get overtaken by emotions. Accept you're in your little nutshell forever.*

"I'm not. I will …" he murmured, lifting his foot from a gooey substance from which an acrid odor rose. He glanced down at a tiny pool of tar, which usually seeped up only in the summer heat, but tonight seemed to reach up through the earth to grasp him and remind him: *you're stuck.* Shuddering, he moved away, scraped his shoe across the sidewalk, then mounted the board.

A woman sat on the curb a short distance ahead. Raphael skated toward her, middle aged, pink-haired, and dressed in an equally pink parka. Her legs stretched into the street. She held an open laptop and typed on the keyboard. Blood ran from a gash in her cheek.

"Data, sir? A dollar for data, sir?"

"What happened to you?"

"Data, sir? A dollar for data, sir?"

She lifted her eyes to the blinking lights of an airliner high above and wrung her hands as if squeezing out water from a wet cloth. "Not enough data," she said. "If they had the data, it would still be"— parting her hands, she flapped them in the manner of little children imitating birds. "Instead it's"—she brought her hands together, leaned to one side, and drove her fingertips against the sidewalk—"boom!"

CHAPTER
FOUR

Raphael glanced from the woman sitting on the curb to the vanishing airliner. Dollar, the name he had given the woman —she'd ignored his requests for her true name—was just rambling, as she always did.

She wiped her nose with her fist, lowered her head, and viewed her outstretched legs as if only recently acquired. Appearing out of the darkness, a coyote ambled down the sidewalk, eyeing the humans fearlessly. Driven from the hills by development, the animals foraged the streets. It paused at a fire hydrant and lifted its leg. Dollar regarded the animal and tapped a few keys on her laptop.

"Water 95 percent, urea 2 percent, sodium .6 percent, chloride .6 percent, sulfate .18 percent ..."

Her voice had an erratic cadence, an old-time cinema actress playing drunk.

"Do you remember me?" asked Raphael.

"... Calcium .015 percent, magnesium .01 percent." Her forehead wrinkled. "Trace amounts of protein and glucose." She lifted her head, eyebrows uncoupling. "Remember you?" She scanned him and shook her head. With a grunt, she pulled her pink jacket closed. Crumbs and stains covered much of her clothing, and strands of stringy, unwashed hair now stuck to her wound. She was a small woman, bird thin and bent.

Raphael had encountered Dollar many times in the neighborhood, sitting on a curb or a low wall and always with her laptop. She'd be absent for a week or two, then reappear. Out of charity, he'd buy data from her, asking questions about nothing of consequence: 911 call records or AMBER Alerts or all words not containing the vowels a, e, i, o, u. She'd consult her laptop for a few minutes, and then rattle off the info. Her answers, often muttered and garbled, were difficult to follow, though he had no reason to try. Despite meeting him dozens of times, Dollar never remembered him, as if her memory was wiped clean after each encounter.

"Did you fall? Is that how you got your cut?" He touched his own cheek. "Or did someone attack you?"

The woman averted her eyes and mumbled something unintelligible.

He slipped out his phone. "I'll call the police."

She shook her head, rubbed her fist in her open hand, and lifted her legs. She stared at her flip-flops and wiggled her toes.

"No cops. I've got hypertext databases and mobile databases, spatial databases and temporal databases, probabilistic databases and embedded databases. What you want?"

Like those damaged people who lived out their lives on a square of sidewalk, she was in a prison too. He should buy some data, give her the money, and go; though she'd spend it on booze or something stronger. It was an off night when she wasn't swilling or toking, and toxic synthetic marijuana was all over the place, not to mention printed opiates, faux fentanyl, and the unicorn pill (the world's greatest high, but you only ride the unicorn once). Considering the shape she was in, it would be better to buy her food, which might cause further obligation. Guilt either way. *Paint me. Paint me.*

He sighed. "If you wait here, I'll get you something to eat. A burrito?"

Scrunching her face, Dollar stared at the keyboard. "Medical? Demographic? Transactional?"

"Yeah, well, I'm not looking for data right now."

"Name," she barked.

He pointed to himself. "Me?"

She glanced around at the nobody else in the area, as if mocking his confusion.

"Yeah, I'm a little slow. Raphael Lennon."

"Birthdate."

"I don't—"

"Birthdate," she insisted.

Shrugging, he gave her the date. She hammered at her keyboard.

"Pizza, maybe?" He tried again.

She ignored him.

She didn't want his help. Let her be. "Listen, I'll return in five minutes with food." She tapped intently on the keys.

At the convenience store, he pulled a foil-wrapped chicken burrito from the warmer, grabbed a bottled water, and walked over to the sundries. Should he also get a first-aid kit? She wouldn't be able to clean and cover the wound herself, which meant another responsibility. It was already past ten o'clock. He took a first-aid kit from the shelf, hefted it, and set it back. What was next? Finding her a home? A job application?

A woman leaned on the checkout counter, addressing the clerk. Raphael had only a limited profile and a green-and-blue dragon's tail braid tipped by an iron chastity ball by which to identify her, but for sure it was Addy. A week had passed since he'd heard her sing at Karaoke, and her voice lingered in his memory.

"I've been here all evening, miss," said the clerk, "and I haven't seen anyone who matches that description."

"No one else works here?" Addy asked.

Raphael shifted sideways, as if on the perimeter of a six-foot circle. A dozen times, he'd considered approaching Addy at the end of her set, but never found the courage. He wanted nothing more than to shake her hand and tell her how much he enjoyed her voice. His imagination could carry him no further. Fans surrounded her. One night as he stood at the perimeter of her admirers, it seemed she'd met his eyes. The instant passed, and he attributed it to wishful thinking.

Would she think him obnoxious—or worse—if he introduced himself now?

"She's about five feet, I'd say." She brought her hand up to her ear.

"I'm still sure," said the clerk.

Raphael hugged the skateboard to his side. Why was he getting so flustered? His heart beat hummingbird fast. He tracked miscreant possums all day long, treaded knee deep through the carnal and sly. He knew how things worked, and yet he was thirteen years old, explaining to the freckle-faced girl in the second row why the Magic Mountain class trip was a no-go for him. If all must end in disappointment, why take the trouble? Against all odds, hope, that engaging fast talker, nudged him forward.

"She wears this pink jacket, unless the weather is terribly hot. She carries a laptop."

It had to be Dollar.

Would it not be appreciated if he told Addy where he had seen Dollar and the good deed he was performing for her? Unless Addy would think he was just taking advantage of the overheard conversation to hit on her. Worse, that he was lying about seeing Dollar, and was planning to lure Addy into a dark alley or abandoned house or underground lair. But that would be paranoid, wouldn't it? *You're the one who's paranoid, Raphy. Now. Now!* Hunching his shoulders to take an inch or two off his height, he put the tip of his sneaker into the circle. "I'm getting this for a woman in a pink jacket. Pink hair, too."

Addy spun toward him. For an instant, she seemed to recognize him; no, not quite. "Did you say you've seen her?" she asked Raphael.

"She has a laptop and sells data."

Addy clapped her hands. "Oh, that's her!"

"She's two blocks down Fairfax and kind of messed up."

"Drunk?"

"Excuse me," interjected the clerk. "Are you buying those or not?"

"Oh yeah, yeah," said Raphael.

He set the burrito and water on the counter. He could use his finger debit, but fingerprints were vulnerable to print-swiping on older scanners, and the store's appeared ancient. He dug a fifty out of his pocket instead. "I wouldn't say drunk."

"Stoned?"

"She fell. Or maybe someone hit her. Nothing real bad, but—"

"Nothing *real* bad?" she snapped.

Raphael tugged on his beanie. "Well, I meant small cuts, scratches."

"Oh, poor Pink."

"Pink, you call her Pink?

"It's not her real name, but I've always called her that."

"Are you a relative?" asked Raphael.

"She's my patient. The Corngold Center on Third Street."

"The shelter?"

"Yes." She revealed blue braces, thin as filigree.

He'd never seen her wearing them onstage, nor would have thought she needed them. Her teeth were perfect. He'd always thought Addy pretty. Close up, she was gorgeous, beyond—*stop.*

"Need a bag, boss?" asked the clerk.

"I'm cool, man," said Raphael, but upon picking up the purchases thought better of it. "Ah, may as well." He returned a dollar of change to the clerk. "Another quarter. Tax, boss." Raphael paid up. Bag filled, he hefted it and faced Addy uncertain what to say.

Luckily, she saved him from the decision. "I'll go with you."

His phone vibrated with a text. Drawing it out, he studied the message. The screen showed a black-and-white photo of him talking to Addy taken from above. He glanced up at the security camera someone grabbed the shot from. When he looked at the phone, the screen was blank. What the hell?

"Something wrong?" asked Addy.

"No, nothing," he replied. But it was wrong. What could have linked the devices? An error in the vast interconnected world of communication? The back of his neck bristled. Weird.

"It makes me happy you were nice to her," said Addy, stepping toward the exit. "Most people aren't."

"Oh, sure," he said, as Addy pushed open the door and held it for him. He glanced back at the store's camera, shook his head, put away his phone, and followed her through the exit.

"Sometimes people are mean," said Addy.

The Infinite Power Ball display in the store's window flashed, splashing Addy's face in radiant but unhuman colors, as if her face were Warhol's silkscreened Marilyn. Damn, she looked like Marilyn too with her round face and snub nose. Never before had he noticed the similarities. But never before had he been this close. Jesus.

Addy sighed. "I guess we better get to Pink before she drifts away." She set off across the parking area.

"I've seen you a hundred times at Karaoke," he said, striding to catch up to her, feeling as if he were stepping into his own body as he matched her step. "You're great."

"Thanks. I've seen you there too. You sing the standards: 'Creep' and 'Stressed Out' and"—she gave him a sidelong glance—"'Boulevard of Broken Dreams,' right?"

"Maybe once or twice." She remembered him. They passed between two parked cars to reach the sidewalk. He stood on the board, moving along at Addy's walking pace. "What do you do at that Corngold Center?"

"I'm a calmer on the night shift, kind of a comfort animal. When a patient gets overexcited, I talk to them softly or read. I let them peer into my big"—she grinned mischievously—"*teal* eyes."

"Can I try it?"

"Yes, you may."

He pivoted on the skateboard. Riding backward, he met Addy's eyes, which did seem green and blue at the same time. He wondered at the pigments to mix to get the effect on canvas. "I feel calmer than I've felt all day." No, not calm. Alive, exhilarated.

"Anytime," said Addy.

Fast enough, heart. "So, what do you read to your patients?"

"The classics. Dostoevsky and Dickens. George Eliot, I love George Eliot. Have you ever read *Middlemarch*?"

"No, I, umm, haven't."

"Virginia Woolf and Fitzgerald. Faulkner and Flaubert. *Madame Bovary* is decidedly the best novel in the history of the universe. There's this scene where Emma, the main character—Emma Bovary, not to be confused with Jane Austen's Emma—is at this fair."

Addy glowed. She seemed to be not walking but floating, as if she were under a spell, or maybe he was the one under a spell. He could listen to her tell another's tale all night long.

"So, Rodolphe's trying to seduce her, and in the background ..."

They approached the block where he'd left Pink, passing the hydrant where the coyote had relieved itself, the smell still sharp.

"I don't see her," he said.

They poked about the area for a few minutes, bent over the bushes that lined the sidewalk. Across the street, music blared from the open door of Nevin O'Moore's.

"How often do you have to go out searching for Pink?"

Addy shrugged. "Oh, she has her antsy moods. Usually, all she does is work on her laptop and watch news in the community room. The mass shooting and then the airliner crashing into the hotel spooked her. Awful, wasn't it?" Addy slipped behind one of the larger plants and bent, so that she disappeared but for the rustling of leaves.

"Hard to believe," he said with a sudden and unexpected feeling of heaviness. Pink's mime wasn't random. The tragedy affected her too, though it couldn't have anything to do with her inquiries of Raphael. "Will Pink be okay?"

Addy popped out from behind the bush. "Pink's a survivor. She used to be a hotshot in the data business. She told me the company once. Great something? Anyway, she had a breakdown, and the streets took her." Addy gazed at the sky. "She knows things too. She's one of those people."

"What do you mean?" asked Raphael

"Sometimes she studies her data as if she's reading tea leaves and then says weird stuff."

"Yeah?"

"Kind of uncanny stuff. Stuff about the future." Addy frowned as if a bad thought had struck her. She exhaled. "Let's check on Wilshire.

Sometimes I find her by the museum or that strange building on the corner."

Strange building. Raphael swallowed and arched his back as if to rid himself of a kick me note. "Night shift, huh?"

"Well, every night except Thursday and Saturday." She grinned. "Those are my weekend."

They walked a half block in silence, then Addy said, "I seem different, don't I?"

From other girls? "No, I mean, yes, a little different. Nice, I mean, different."

She stopped on the sidewalk and drew back her lips, showing him her braces, which she nudged with her finger. "I mean, different from the last time you saw me. The braces."

"Oh, the braces."

"Demosthenes," she said. "Do you know him?"

Demosthenes? "Umm, I think so …"

"He was an ancient Greek with a speech problem. I got the idea from him. About the braces, I mean. Demosthenes put pebbles in his mouth to learn to speak better. I wear braces so I can learn to sing better. They're kind of expensive, but it's for art. Do you think I'm silly?"

"Oh, no. Makes sense." He wondered if it made any sense at all.

"If it works. I'm not sure it works." She prodded at the braces with a finger.

"You sing great already."

Addy shook her head. "Even if I sang great, which I don't, it wouldn't be enough. I auditioned for 'Sing or Die,' and the judges advised I slit my throat."

"That's terrible!"

"I'm kidding." She tapped a tooth. "What's your name?"

"Raphael Lennon."

"Lennon, huh? You resemble Bowie. I mean the way he looked when he was young, like in the old film. *The Man*, um, *The Man Who Fell to Earth.*" He knew what she meant: skinny as hell, narrow nose, prominent cheekbones. Addy tilted her head sideways and inspected Raphael up and down. "A jaw line that could cut diamonds."

Raphael shrugged. The legendary rock star was otherworldly handsome, while he was just otherworldly, yet he got the comparison all the time. He used to feel flattered, then complacent, and now it annoyed him.

She rocked her head as she considered him. "Only a little more stretched out. So what do you do?"

"I work for Norval, data compilation."

"I think I've heard of them. What's your job?"

He swallowed the lump of uncertainty rising in his throat. "Me? I'm an End Man. Necrologist is the technical term."

"End Man, huh? What do they do?"

"We, uh, work with the dead."

"A data compiling mortician?"

"It's a little hard to explain." She had already called the Norval building strange. Now he would be a strange man with a strange job in a strange building.

"We find the dead, and then we sell them, sort of."

"Explain."

When he first interviewed for the job at Norval, he had asked Geovanni Maglio the same thing, and his explanation to Addy paraphrased that indelible conversation:

"Addy, did you know that 8,000 people die each day in the United States?"

"No."

"Well, they do. In the past, the dead for all practical purposes would just vanish. Our CEO Geo Maglio had a vision."

Addy nodded.

"The right to be forgotten. Have you heard of it?"

"That's one I missed in civics."

"European Union idea. I'm going to quote Mr. Maglio." Raphael took a breath and summoned up Maglio's often uttered words. "'The damned continentals argue that people have the right to cut their past off at its knees. Strike what they consider inaccurate or unflattering information from the record. Practically unworkable before the Internet and now impossible.'"

"It would be nice," said Addy.

Raphael laughed. "That's exactly what I said. Ready for his response?"

"I can't wait."

Raphael cleared his throat and lowered his voice to Maglio's baritone. "'Yes, and it would be nice if we could erase the entire history of mankind's crimes. Why should we have to remember all the wars and inquisitions, and slaveries? Unfortunately, it's throwing the baby out with the bathwater. We can't *not* remember. A few European countries have made a half-ass effort at enforcement. A sham and an easy workaround. Still … well, let the Europeans sink into the quicksand of their socialist experiments. In the U.S. we have the First Amendment, lifetime sex-crime registries, and no damn abstract right for anything to be forgotten.'"

"You have a good memory for monologue," said Addy.

"I'm boring you."

"Oh, no, it's fascinating, but …"

"I'll speed it up. Paraphrase."

"Please."

Raphael rolled his shoulders and cleared his throat. "In a nutshell, Americans don't want to forget, and Norval has stepped up to the plate."

Addy sniffed. "It's a baseball metaphor?"

"What's America's pastime?"

"Oh, yeah. Sorry, continue."

"Our goal is to preserve the online remains of every dead citizen of the red, white, and blue. And provide the slickest transport to their info since Walt built his monorail."

Addy's lips twisted. "Before your time."

"Yeah, that's Maglio's. Do you want to hear the rest of this?"

Addy drew a finger across her lips.

"Norval Portals will preserve it all. Data is good. More data is better. What isn't data will be. If it won't be, it's data now. Our profit?

Hundreds of millions of visitors will pay to visit their friends and loved ones, providing solid demographics for advertisers. We will package our data assets into numerous financial instruments: derivatives, options, futures, forwards. And the beauty is this: as the deceased pile up, our audience can only grow."

Addy nodded. "I see a flaw."

Raphael caught his breath. "Yes?"

"But those *remains*, doesn't the next of kin—"

Raphael switched again to his Maglio impersonation. "'Have rights? *Contracts*. Which is why speed is so important. The moment we verify a lead is offline, unquestionably dead, we speak with the rights holder—next of kin, what have you. We offer to take responsibility for their loved one's online remains and to provide them an easy access portal to all that information, all those memories, all those secrets—and to the rights holder *at no charge*. Most jump at the offer. It's like getting a free burial plot with no-cost maintenance.'

"So to sum it up, Addy, we're making money off ghosts."

"*Dead Souls*. I mean the book by Gogol, the Russian guy. In his book, the main character goes around acquiring dead people, dead serfs. At first, the landowners are happy to give the dead serfs away—kind of a tax write-off. Then they find out the main character, whatchamacallit—*Chichikov*, that's his name, Chichikov acquires all these dead people to take out a bank loan on them. Collateral, you know? Not mentioning to the banks the serfs are dead."

"Wow. I never heard."

"You don't read enough."

"I should get your, uh, *Dead Souls*."

"Are you strictly a non-vegetable reader?"

"Oh, no, I go both ways. Digital. Paper."

"Great. If I find my old print copy, I'll let you borrow it."

As they approached Wilshire, a skyboard descended to float east on the boulevard. Its message crawled across an image of smiling seniors: *Old Friends Are Golden, But an Old You Is Not.* The seniors' wrinkles, sagging jowls, and age spots disappeared. The technology erased thirty years in an instant. Tight, smooth faces glowed. A new message flashed: *Stay Young with Vanitum!*

Raphael sighed. Even if one day he should escape his four streets, another boundary awaited him, awaited everyone. He glanced at Addy, who was young and bursting with life and energy, but who too was bound by time, fated to grow old and decay until finally that hooded figure with the scythe dropped by. Turning the corner at the Norval building, he wanted to scream in defiance. He didn't even whisper.

Addy halted and pointed toward Norval's doors. "That could be her."

He followed Addy up the steps to the entrance. A tiny pink-clad body so flat as to be almost invisible lay at the base of the door.

Addy knelt beside her. "Pink, it's Addy. Are you all right?"

The woman's eyes opened. "Do not track. Track. Do not track. Track."

"I'll get you to your bed, okay? Help me, Raphael."

Clamping the board to his side with grocery bag in hand, Raphael took Pink's left arm and Addy her right. As they lifted, Pink's laptop slid out from under her jacket.

"No!" shouted Pink.

He released her hand and grabbed the laptop. "It's all right. I've got it." By the time the trio rounded the corner, Pink was awake. She demanded her laptop, and when Raphael put it in her hands, she held it like an infant to her breast.

In ten minutes, they reached the corner of Third Street. As the light changed, Addy strode into the crosswalk. "Come on, Pink."

Pink sniffed. "Where's my food? My piles?"

Addy cupped her mouth and whispered to Raphael, "She pronounces pills as piles. Some kind of Ozark thing." Addy drew her hand away. "You'll get your pills at the center, Pink."

Pink sniffed.

"And I've got your food right here." Raphael handed her the bag. Pink tucked her laptop under her arm and opened the bag.

"Why don't you eat your burrito at the center," suggested Addy.

"Are you coming with us?" She pointed. "It's two blocks down there, a short distance from where I live."

He turned his head. "Oh, east of Fairfax."

"Yes, but I'm moving soon. It's further from the center, but roomier."

"Further, ah ..." He took a deep breath and inched toward the curb's edge.

Fairfax moaned, cracked, and revealed the Earth splitting in two. The far side retreated as if it were a wave going in the wrong direction, out to sea, headed for a distant shore. The abyss opened before him, a dizzying depth in which no one would hear his screams, and his screams would be heard no more.

Head spinning, knees buckling, he stepped back. "I can't."

Addy took another step away, further into the open chasm in front of him. "It's okay." She gestured for Pink to follow. "Maybe another time."

A hand yanked on Raphael's shoulder. He turned around to see Pink staring at him. "Raphael Lennon?"

"Right."

Her face tightened. "Do you want the preliminary data?"

"Come on, Pink, we've got to go," Addy called.

"That's okay, Pink. I can get it some other time."

"You're out of time."

"Right," said Raphael, a chill running up his spine despite his incredulity. You could be out of time for a hundred things; why should it mean something sinister? The least likely was death around the corner.

"Thirteen days."

"It's late, Pink," said Addy.

Pink lifted her hand to Raphael's cheek and whispered, "You should run."

Run, right. The hairs on his neck stood up. "What happens at the end of thirteen days?"

Shaking her head, Pink shuffled past him. "Can we go home so I can eat my food?"

"Pink, what happens in thirteen days?" repeated Raphael.

Ignoring him, Pink stepped toward Addy's outstretched hand. Looking both ways, she shuffled onto the empty street.

"Addy?" said Raphael

"Yes?"

Courage. "Is there any way I can contact you?"

Her blue braces shone under the streetlight. "I'm a bit old fashioned. No Chinchat or Pillowgram. Addyaddyhomefree at scales dot com."

"Got it."

Pink glanced at Raphael then flapped her hands. "They let it fall. Water too. And you."

"Who let what fall?" asked Raphael. "The plane?" Pink only shook her head and sniffed at her burrito. *They let it fall. Thirteen days.* Digital moonbeams.

"Come on, Pink." Addy put her arm around Pink's waist and guided her across the intersection. When they reached the far side, Addy turned and shouted, "Thanks for finding Pink!"

"Anytime."

"Goodnight."

"Goodnight."

He stepped onto the skateboard, his feet seeming to hover above the wood, with his heart above his head. Man, she was lovely—and sweet too. Did she like him? Maybe she was just being nice, grateful. He'd have to tell her the truth, assuming he ever saw her again. No, Addy, we can't go to Venice on our honeymoon. As his spirits returned to Earth, he felt a tap on his shoulder and turned to see two guys in baseball caps and hooded sweatshirts. The smaller of the two, tapped the flat of a knife blade against his palm.

"Hey, man, can you help us out?"

CHAPTER
FIVE

Jesus, would he ever get home?

The one who had spoken, the smaller of the two, let his hands hang in the air as if he were a begging dog. His fingers were plump with purple nails. A tattooed letter marked the back of each finger.

F-U-C-K D-A-T-A

Raphael's chest tightened. *Hard Blanks.* No gait-shifting or candle-lit protests for these Ludds. Smashed phones, wire cutters, and beatings were more their speed. Raphael had to stay cool or the mugging could escalate.

"No, can't help you." Raphael dropped a foot to the ground and set to push off. The heavyset one yanked him off the board.

"Give us your wallet."

Raphael twisted away from his assailant. His heart raced as he closed his right hand.

"I don't want to fight."

"Wallet," barked the little Blank.

"I'll give you fifty, all right? I'll just walk away."

"Wallet means wallet."

The big Blank clasped the neck of Raphael's T-shirt and tugged.

Ten years had passed since a high school bully grabbed him the same way. Raphael was scared, yeah, but angry too.

The big Blank drew closer, his rank breath in Raphael's face. "If I hit you, I will hurt you," declared Raphael.

"Oh, we're shaking," said plump fingers. "Get out the fucking wallet."

Sorry, Mom. With a sharp breath and heart racing, he swung.

His knuckles sank into the large one's cheek, right down to the teeth. The Blank blew out air as he staggered back, head leaning to the left. In high school, the bully fell to his knees and cried, while Raphael sucked on his bloodied knuckles. But the big guy didn't fall. His head straightened, and his eyes darkened. He rolled his shoulders and stepped toward Raphael. As Raphael drew back his fist again, a hand snatched his wrist, and a forearm clamped his throat. The big Blank got bigger.

The Blank was up against him now, slamming Raphael in the gut. Raphael punched lamely. Short, ineffective swings that glanced off the guy's torso.

"I'll hold skin-and-bones here," cried the big one, his breath hot and foul. "Get his wallet."

A hand dug into Raphael's left pocket. "Stop fucking moving or you'll feel an inch of my knife." A cold point probed Raphael's spine. "Here's a sample." With a faint pop, the cold point seared. Paper rustled. "Not bad," said the smaller mugger. Raphael arched his back to escape the heat. They had him.

"Should we convert him?" asked his assailant.

As Raphael twisted from the probing blade, a phone buzzed, and it wasn't his. Fat Fingers pivoted away from Raphael, slipped out a pulsing phone from his waistband and conversed on the device. He swung around. "Let him go."

"What the fuck?" yipped the one holding Raphael.

"You heard me, man."

The big guy's arm uncurled from Raphael's neck. "Yeah, sure." He shoved Raphael forward. Stuffing the cash in his pocket, the short one tossed the wallet to the sidewalk.

"Let's party!" shouted the smaller one.

The two tore off down Fairfax.

"Assholes," cried Raphael as he picked up his wallet, thinner now, though the plastic was all there. A Blank with a phone? Hard Blanks or posers? He recalled the two Blanks he had seen from Norval's window. Their sizes corresponded. Well, what if they were? He touched the warm, pulsing wound on the small of his back. They could have really messed him up.

He adjusted his beanie, looked longingly down the street where Addy had gone, and then found the lit windows of the Tar Tower. Lifting his trembling hands, he folded them into fists, the big knuckle of his right hand dark with blood. The dean had suspended him for a week. *No, Mom, never again.* But sometimes …

He licked his knuckle, then pounded his fists together until the shaking stopped. He pushed off.

RAPHAEL, shedding the numbing anger left by the incident, entered his apartment, turned on the lights, and double-locked the door. Report them to the police? Waste of time. Muggings were a dime a dozen in the city. The key holder dropped from his fingers to the floor. *Calm down, man. If you got loose, you could have taken those guys by yourself … maybe.* He steadied his hand, picked up the ring and drew it closer, gazing at the keys. Four were his mother's museum keys, which he couldn't bring himself to discard. He ran his thumb over each, then fingered the tiny gold heart pendant given to him by the neighbor girl when she moved away. He shoved the ring into his pocket.

He opened the door-sized living room windows to release the smell of oil paints and allow in some reasonably fresh air. The view from the eleventh floor nearly justified the rent. Through the eight-foot-tall window, he took in the northern nightscape: the dense lights and streaming traffic of the Fairfax district, the dazzling holographic billboards of Sunset and in the hills above, the blue glaze of swimming pools. He turned from the view to his *studio*. Built during the 1940s, the Tar Tower units were classic old Hollywood: hardwood floors, artisan tile work, and beamed ceilings. Best of all, the living rooms were the size of racquetball courts, with ceilings high enough to shoot hoops.

He needed the space.

In the room, he had assembled a makeshift scaffolding of steel tubes. At the top of the frame, eight feet from the floor, lay sheets of plywood, which served as the platform from which he painted a large canvas the size of the ceiling. Twenty-foot lengths of pine bolted to the beams, supplemented by diagonal boards, framed and stretched taut the canvas, which lay three feet above the plywood, so he could paint while lying supine. Working in that position for hours made his arm tingle and ache. He didn't mind the pain.

"Art must be born from the deepest emotions," his mother had said, "sometimes even suffering." She herself was a painter. Mostly small abstracts, which she hung only on the walls of their apartment, thinking her art uninspired and made with little talent. She taught him the fundamentals of painting: color, composition, value, form, perspective, and brushwork. Then the mediums: acrylics, oils, or watercolors. After that, she explained color theory: how colors harmonize and complement one another. Finally, she guided him through mixing and application.

From the very first, he liked the oils, the old masters' choice. He practiced and painted beside his mother, sometimes in the apartment, sometimes on the grassy slopes of the museum. He painted what he saw, but eventually he painted what he felt. His brushwork became bold, and he liked to put wild stuff beside neat little figurative packages. Bright splashes of color violated by graffiti. When she took him to a neo-expressionist show at the museum, he knew exactly how he wanted to paint.

Raphael began the Painting during the last year of his mother's life. At first, he drew small rough sketches, though she advised it would have to be *bigger, much bigger*. "Many of the neo-expressionists painted big," his mother noted. He wanted the painting to reflect his life, or at least the way he saw that life. He started and abandoned canvases because they couldn't contain all he wanted to put in, which was all that had happened to him within his square mile.

As his mother's death approached, the prospect of the painting, the strategy of such a project, filled him to bursting. He explained the plan to her: he would paint it as if on a chapel ceiling. Every significant object and experience in his life would occupy the canvas. Even as she struggled with unrelenting pain, his efforts delighted her and made her laugh, if only inwardly.

Yet, it was not long after he pushed away the furniture and began assembling the scaffold that the problems the project presented struck him. The painting had to accommodate all that had happened or would happen in his life: a paradox. When would he stop painting?

His mom's silence about one vital image added a further difficulty. To put all of his life on the canvas, he would need to include a father. He didn't know his father, and if he broached the subject with his mother, she would avert her eyes and not say a word.

When he went to work for Norval, he considered finding the answer among all the data Norval compiled, which included the data on his mother. In there, among all the emails, postings, and auto blogs might be clues to his father's identity. But that was her private world, and she had not given him permission to enter. He might open a stranger's gate but not his mom's.

Maybe he'd find his father, maybe not. Maybe his father didn't have to be on the canvas at all.

In his heart, he believed that despite the paradox and the missing image, he'd finish. According to his mom, on that day, he'd be free; his phobia defeated, barriers smashed.

Most nights when he came home from work, he'd play a few records on his mom's old turntable and leaf through one of his art magazines. He kept his laptop closed, his phone powered down. Working at Norval had soured him to social media, and he'd kicked that habit. He was no Blank, but he got nothing from the steamy gossip, false outrage, and bad information that many found so compelling, He'd drink a cup of tea or a bottle of beer, feel joyous and sad, and fall asleep at nine. He'd wake at midnight and paint for one or two hours. He preferred night, when the city was quieter and most of its residents dreaming. It was easier to pretend he was alone in the world with the canvas.

Tonight, he would only work for a brief time, for the encounter with Pink and Addy, and then the hard Blanks had sapped his energy.

He rolled his shoulders, clapped his hands, and climbed the frame. Turning on the lights illuminating the painting, he lay on the plywood, and remained still for a moment, not uncomfortable in the confined space between the bed of wood and the canvas. Sometimes he would lose himself in the images. A fearsome dog that had licked his cheek when he was three, represented by a gleaming elongated pink tongue. The fragmented face of the lovely neighbor girl who had moved away. A garbage truck rendered as a green insatiable maw. The round and round rhythm of the dryer in the Tar Tower's laundry room. An achingly beautiful queen palm. The wall of stars at the Farmers Market. A horrid dream about a lizard and a praying mantis. *Have you lived today?* Lazing on a hill at the museum. His mother sleeping. The man at Pan Pacific Park who taught him skateboard tricks from a distance. A scarlet whirlpool of lost innocence. An overturned car, an arm hanging out the window. A saber-toothed tiger sinking into the tar. The pummeling fist of the bad virus. His world and experiences realized in two dimensions.

Me.

The canvas's frame he considered the four streets of his bounded world. Fairfax behind his head, La Brea at his feet. To the right, Wilshire, to the left, Beverly. Sometimes when he was out in the real world, he thought he might well be in his painting. A figure in a frame, an eerie thought. And just as often when he stared up at his painting, he saw himself inside, rummaging about the painted memories. On sultry summer nights, the space could get warm, and he'd squirm and grow uneasy with the thought the painting was melting onto him and into him. He would laugh at the ridiculous prospect and go on with the work. *Go on with the work.*

Pink's prophecy popped into his thoughts. *Thirteen days. Run.* Run where? Run from what? He had to stop taking the babbling seriously.

He uncapped two tubes of paint, blue and green, chose a half-dozen brushes, and set the tools on a tray. Scanning the canvas, he shimmied to the spot below the area to be painted. Lifting his hand to take a brush, his knuckles shone, still bright red from the punch he had thrown. He reached across his chest to take up the brush and felt the rigid rectangle he'd stowed beneath his shirt.

Pulling out the envelope, he set it behind his head, giving it only an instant of thought. Stull and the after-hours delivery were weird, but if he were to believe the coroner's office, Professor Klaes was no true possum.

As Raphael settled into painting his vision of Addy, his eyes drifted across the canvas alighting on an image of a graffiti-covered wall he used to skate. Among the graffiti were two letters and a word that stood out as if raised from the surface of the canvas and magnified: JK RULES!

CHAPTER
SIX

Raphael threw off the covers and put his feet on the floor. He stretched, feeling stiffness in his limbs, which meant he had been dreaming—a bad one. Sweat covered his chest, a fresh coat over the dried sweat from the fight with the Blanks. And he stank. Did he have to go into work today? No, it was Saturday morning.

He pushed his fingers through his hair, shuffled to the bedroom window and looked toward Beverly Boulevard, his northern border. On Saturday morning, the streets, though not empty, lacked their usual snarl of congestion. He raised his eyes past Beverly to billboard-strewn Sunset Strip and then to the Hollywood Hills and their famous sign, which pranksters had altered over the years: *Hollyweed, Hollyweird, Holyboob,* even.

He shivered as he stumbled into the bathroom, relieved himself, and stood before the sink. He scrubbed his hands, splashed water on his face, and brushed his teeth. Cupping water to his mouth, he gargled, spewed vigorously, then opened a tiny box of Nanoflossers. He shook one out, which resembled a silver baby cuttlefish, popped it in his mouth, and tightened his lips. The device floated across his tongue, clicked as it gripped the left top molar, then zipped from tooth to tooth, loosening the plaque and vacuuming it up. Less than a minute later, the Nanoflosser whistled and went dormant. He spit the device into the trash and smiled at the mirror. Ready for the world, Raphy.

In the kitchen, he filled a cup with water and poured it into the retro drip—most kitchen appliances were retro these days, everything else being pretty much short-lived junk—set down the cup and pressed the brew button. For three minutes, the machine gurgled and grumbled in complaint, as if it were made for something better.

He split a pomegranate. The arils shone like a bowl of red gems, each enhanced by a white, embedded seed. "Pomegranate means seeded apple, although some mistakenly think it means hard apple. Hard or seeded, it's the fruit of paradise," his mother had explained. Many times as she set a quartered one before him, she advised, "Don't spit out the seeds, Raphael. They're nutrient packed." In a somber mood, she later disclosed the Greeks made it the fruit of the dead. He peeled off several clumps and popped them into his mouth.

JK RULES

When he first saw the words on his canvas, his heart had stopped. An intruder had broken into his apartment to deface his painting, a prelude to his frequent nightmare: the canvas torn from the ceiling and slashed to ribbons. Seven years' worth of work obliterated. In the bleak nightmare, he would carry the shredded canvas to the roof of the Tar Tower, to find the square mile lay below in smoldering ruins, and beyond the embers, darkness. The whole fucking world gone, gone, gone. Then he'd wake up, trembling and wet.

But the rational explanation tapped its fist on his forehead. He had painted the letters himself, one of a half dozen words and phrases he'd reproduced of the spray-painted graffiti on the Wall, the remains of an old trolley depot long gone to ruin. Neighborhood skaters hung out at the Wall, matched their skills against its concrete slope, and left their adolescent signatures. JK RULES could have been any kid who once hung there. That Jason Klaes was on his mind had simply put him on alert.

A false fucking alarm.

Coffee in hand, he sat at the kitchen table, slipped the coroner's report on Klaes from the envelope, and scanned it, confirming Stull's summary. *Massive head wound.* The attached photo showed the destruction, Klaes's full beard was about all that remained intact. The sprawling, unruly beard Klaes affronted the world with in every damn photo as if to turn away eyes. Sliding the material back into its manila sheath, he spotted a tiny white envelope. He withdrew it, on which was handwritten "For Your Service, Mr. Lennon. Please check the balance before using." Opening the envelope, he found a Starbucks card. *Weird.* He returned the material to the envelope, dropped the card onto the table, then picked it up and stuck it into his wallet. Fifty bucks, its likely value, was a free coffee and a half.

Powering up his laptop, he scanned the inbox. Fifty emails since yesterday. Several solicitations for money or love that had eluded the spam filter. Updates from his social media sites, long abandoned and ignored. Responses to inquiries. He zipped through twenty, hoping Alicia had responded, and then halted at one that jumped off the screen.

Subject: Dromophobia
From: Jason Klaes

The name punched him in the gut. He leaned away, read it at a distance, and then bent forward and blinked. The sender remained Jason Klaes.

A coincidental spam? A virus? He received tons of spam from spoofed people and email addresses he recognized, all to pitch erectile dysfunction drugs or knockoff sneakers. There had been a spate of new viruses, and though the Norval system had proven invulnerable, the security engineer advised caution.

You're getting paranoid, Raphy. His foggy brain processed the possibilities.

To know of his phobia meant the sender was clever, clever enough to unleash a virus extracting every bit of his personal information, and then demolishing his laptop, maybe even online data. Yes, he could go to the office and open it on Norval's secure system, but hey, it was *his* weekend. He could wait for Monday, couldn't he?

Time for leisure, time for love. *Love?* He'd talked to Addy for an hour. She gave him book recommendations. Love? You earned love. It took time. Months. Years. Decades. You made friends first. Shared things. *Friends, yes.* Klaes and all the strange stuff could wait.

"Sorry, Dr. Klaes," said Raphael, "ain't gonna happen." Putting Jason Klaes out of mind, he sipped his coffee, then clicked compose.

To:

He entered *Addyaddyhomefree@scales.com*.

Subject: *Love*

No. Highlight, delete.

Hey! :)

No. Highlight, delete.

Sure was an interesting night

No. Highlight, delete.

I hope Pink's feeling better

No. Highlight, delete.
Oh, man.

Pinching up one pomegranate aril at a time, he ate a dozen while staring at the screen.

He composed the email, the content little more than *nice meeting you* and *maybe we can meet again*, sent it, and let out his breath. If something happened, fine. If nothing happened, fine. She would think him weird. Why would any guy not walk her home? He ate the rest of the pomegranate, made a bowl of instant oatmeal, and again checked the inbox. The Jason Klaes email remained.

Subject: Dromophobia
From: Jason Klaes

He positioned the cursor over the name. It showed the sender's email, followed by a series of hexadecimal digits that stretched across the screen and might have continued across the kitchen and into infinity.

He had never used a VPN with his laptop to connect to the Norval intranet. He might open the email with the service, but did the VPN guarantee security? Whether for money or pure evil, the bad guys never slept. Not that he hadn't had threats before from possums who recognized a Norval employee was close to outing them. However, the threats came to Norval. The irony was that once Norval established they'd located a true possum, the possum was left alone. No authority was informed. Case closed. A Norval trade secret.

This seemed personal, or at least the sender wanted it to appear personal. An email address was one thing, a home address another, right? Yet the subject was his very specific phobia, which tethered him to the Tar Tower, *his home.*

With a shiver, he pushed away from the table and strode into his living room.

He climbed the scaffolding, switched on the lights, and studied the work. The canvas was intact, no brush stroke altered. His recurring dream unfulfilled. Through his living room window, the city too remained untouched.

The prospect of the world disappearing was not just the stuff of dreams. The pundits and prophets warned of it all the time. Anything could cause the final end: an experiment gone wrong, a new weapon falling into the wrong hands, a virus without mercy.

But what was that apocalypse to him? He had his own four horsemen to face.

His breathing returned to normal. He had no enemies, no rivals, nothing to steal. If someone knew about the painting, they would realize it had no value except to himself.

He propped himself on his elbows.

Klaes was dead. On Monday, he should shift the possum to the offline box. Klaes was dead. Wasn't he?

Raphael pushed away from the table.

THIRTY MINUTES LATER, shaved, showered, and sun screened, Raphael crossed The Tar Park complex and came out on Sixth Street to see the open gates of the museum grounds. He rode his usual path to the museum's plaza, walked down the ramp to Wilshire, and paused on the sidewalk. He considered the boulevard's light early traffic. If only it could be done once.

Don't think. Do it. Skate it.

With one foot on the board, he inched toward the curb, and the gentle breeze rose into a wall of wind, an invisible torrent, an unmovable psychological object. He could not sneak up on his own brain. He had failed a thousand times, yet the hope that the laws of his universe had changed rose up in him. Heart racing, he drifted back, kick turned the skateboard, and continued west to the Norval building, mulling the faint promise of the professor's email to him.

Coroner's report notwithstanding, something was bogus with Klaes, who—if a possum—wouldn't send out emails after his supposed death. Even in a warning, it was self-defeating. If the physicist were offline, who was going through the trouble of keeping him out of the NDMN database? Who was trying to make him appear alive? And why was Maglio so focused on Klaes?

On weekends, security locked Norval's front doors.

The rear entrance was tucked into an alcove, dim and cool. He pressed the entry buzzer, and a moment later Mandy, the weekend guard, arrived.

"Haven't seen you in a while," she said, opening the door and smiling. "Is anyone else coming?"

He yanked off the beanie. "Just me."

She gazed at him. "Your face—it's glowing."

Raphael touched his cheek. "Really?"

"Yes. Interesting." She smiled, touching her hair. It gave off the scent of honeysuckle. "Second floor?"

"Yeah. I'll take the stairs."

"I'll see you later, Raphael."

"Yes, later."

The stairwell, where contracts and finance took their breaks, reeked of marijuana, dead air, and ... Hot Cheetos?

He found the office much as he had left it, except the night custodian had swept and emptied the garbage cans.

He scanned the inbox but found nothing from Klaes. So, the message on his personal email was not a duplicate. He opened up Klaes's email account and clicked on sent. Above the four messages he had previously reviewed was now a fifth:

To: Raphael

The email had been sent at 2:06 a.m. today.

He let the cursor hover over the message, his heart thumping. Regardless of how the sender got his personal email address, he expected a warning. He would run the threat by Dreemont, who would no doubt tell Raphael to ignore it. Not always so easy. Scratching the key, he clicked open.

Dear Mr. Lennon,

As I understand it, your company is skeptical towards my recent demise, and your job requires you to provide iron-clad evidence of my death or my continuing life. Your inquiry into my whereabouts has occasioned several

actions on my part that I did not expect and would rather not have taken; however, I will not attempt to thwart your research into the matter. This comes from a confidence in the certainty you will fail; nevertheless, I respect the pursuit of truth so much, that although the truth you strive to reach is beyond your grasp, I encourage you to persist in your efforts.

Toward that end, I have taken the time to perform research on your background and current life. I know you have dromophobia, the fear of crossing streets, which confines you to a square mile. I also know you work daily to complete a painting you believe will allow you to defeat your phobia. The completion of the painting requires certain personal images, including that of your father, whose identity is unknown to you. In addition, there are two more essential images.

I am prepared to provide you with those images if you locate me. I offer you a path out of your prison if you accomplish what I consider an impossible task. Please do not think I'm trying to manipulate you as if a test animal in a Skinner box. I am not sadistic. I won't get pleasure from your failing. However, I am sensitive to the desire to fulfill one's dream in life, and I would be boorish if I didn't give you a chance, even if it costs your life. I'll even offer a clue: *Dr. Watson's one word*. Your quest being hopeless, dig deep.

Jason

CHAPTER
SEVEN

hat the fuck?

Goosebumps rose on Raphael's arms. He twisted, pretending to stretch, and scanned the cubicles across from his, feeling someone watching. No one was there. He was alone in eerie silence. *Chill, man.*

He turned and read the message again. *Square mile. Painting.* On several artists' websites, he had discussed technical aspects of artwork —paints, perspectives. It was conceivable someone might contact him about painting, but what could they know of the phobia, Klaes, or that he had long sought his father's identity?

The message was contradictory. Your search is hopeless *dig deep*?

Dig deep for the images or for Klaes? Or was it a taunt? Raphael would never dig deep enough to unearth Jason Klaes. Did the message support a living or dead Klaes? Who would try to hide their identity behind a dead man?

His heart welled at the thought of escape, yet the message was almost certainly a prank.

Dr. Watson's one word. Doyle's character was Sherlock Holmes's biographer. In that role, Watson wrote all the words. A nebulous clue, but he keyed the phrase into search and spent ten minutes scanning unpromising results.

Needing to refresh his brain's Klaes file, he opened the Physicists Commons and brought up the professor's bio, a breezy compilation.

I'm a California physicist specializing in quantum mechanics, quantum computing and beer pong (in the day). I'm also one of those fools who takes on a second discipline: computer science. Call it an early midlife crisis. Born in Santa Monica, I did my undergraduate work ...

Raphael read the list of degrees and the issuing universities. Klaes mentioned accomplishments and prizes. There was a paragraph on quantum mechanics, quantum entanglement, and quantum computing, the various problems and contradictions. He covered the computer science work with a literary fragment. *Strange beast I am, I see a synthesis.* A poem called "Anabiosis" by Alexander Yaroslavsky followed. Raphael scanned two stanzas.

> *Between Life and Death*
> *Will ram a heavy wedge, A third door opens,*
> *For the world, anabiosis.*
>
> *And when all the work is done*
> *And, when as a perfect toy, Earth—*
> *Wake up, the living, again.*

Earth described as a *perfect* toy. Imperfect now because of death? The poem was a variation on Norval's sales pitch. The third door was data.

When his fellow workers were around, he rarely thought about the larger implications of the job. The dead had been piling up on Earth for a long time. The bodies were buried, burnt, or recycled into the bodies of new living organisms. In the past, the dead left few things behind. Since the rise of the Internet and the ceaseless inputting of personal data, the deceased bequeathed almost as much as they had housed in their skulls while living. The data Norval compiled were ghosts of sorts, but if you pulled away their sheets, you would find only ones and zeroes. End Men did not reanimate anyone. Norval Portals didn't wake up the dead.

However, were there ghosts like the ones Mr. Lean, the building's elderly custodian, claimed? Raphael recalled one night he was working late while Mr. Lean swept his cubicle. A low drawn-out moan had come from somewhere below the floor. The custodian froze, dropped his broom, and put his hand to his heart.

"Ghosts?" asked Raphael, the corners of his mouth twitching, for the moan was likely nothing more than the building's old plumbing system.

"You wait, Mr. Lennon. You'll see our ghosts one night."

"Five years. No ghosts. I doubt that ..." He didn't finish the thought, reluctant to tell Mr. Lean he didn't believe in ghosts at all.

"You're laughing," said the custodian. "Simple, superstitious Mr. Lean, right?"

"No, no."

"An ignorant old fellow who hears bumps in the night and chains rattling."

"That's not it, Mr. Lean. I've never seen or heard them myself. I don't know, maybe there are."

"When they want you to see them, you will."

Did troubled spirits linger in the halls and houses where their lives had ended? Something squeaked, like the fall of a new sneaker. Raphael stood up, stepped out of his office, and scanned the quiet floor.

Nobody about.

He dropped back into his chair. Could a ghost email him? In this digital age, instead of ruffling curtains or rattling chains, perhaps spirits contacted the living through such medium. Raphael laughed. He had enough problems without digital ghosts haunting him.

"Boo," he said aloud. *Yeah, funny.*

Raphael returned to the Klaes message, which didn't return to him. Not in old mail, not in deleted, not in saved. Gone. He tried a few recoveries, all failed.

Email messages weren't supposed to simply disappear. Norval's touted security must have been compromised.

If Klaes did this, *how* was less important than *why*? What was—or is if alive—going on in his head?

Raphael went back to Klaes's email box and opened the physicist's incoming messages. The number of received emails had increased by several dozen from the previous day: store news from Amazon, a few opportunities to meet women, penis enlargement patch. Klaes's spam filter was slipping. He hovered over one from *The Children's Love Fund*. The subject was *Your Generous Donation*. He rubbed a knuckle across his chin. *Children ... love. Love ... children*. Was there a little pedo going on? He opened the email.

At the top of the message were several photos of children in hospital settings. The ravages of cancer and other diseases apparent.

Dear Mr. Klaes,

The children and I want to express how grateful we are for your gift. Without people of your generosity, our foundation and the work we do could not exist.

I have spoken about you to many of the children who have received medical treatment through your donations. I know of your personal involvement with several of our charges; we will make your generosity and service known to all as a model of compassion.

Jan Olmstead, Director
The Children's Love Fund

BELOW WERE several more photos of children and a link to the organization's website.

Raphael's cheeks burned, having sure as hell called that one wrong. Out of courtesy, he would contact Jan Olmstead and inform her of Klaes's death.

Raphael let the cursor hover over *Sent Messages*.

Click.

The second message Klaes had sent after his death went out on January 13 to trojanwarrior@xxxmail.org. The third and fourth messages had gone out on January 15. One to a Dr. Royer—a threat similar to that sent to Miranda—the other to Gerard Van Pelt. He clicked on trojanwarrior.

Subject: "Small Dead Bodies."

Dear Troy-Boy,

Out of love and loyalty, your dog obeyed your degenerate wish. You rewarded the creature with mutilation. From that humble beginning, you went on to mutilate history. Prepare to meet your maker.

JK

Two heavyweight threats. One recipient dead so far.

As with Miranda's email address, he typed in Troy-Boy's email and searched. Nothing. The address was deep-masked.

He wanted to return to the message Klaes had sent him personally, but after several tries to bring it back from the dead, he accepted that the text remained only as an afterimage in his mind's eye. Klaes—or someone masquerading as Klaes—was baiting Raphael to search, simultaneously warning him off. He couldn't dig deep enough to find the body.

What body? They'd cremated the physicist. Or so Stull had claimed.

He searched for Donato's of Glendale and went to their website.

Donato's offered a range of services including cremation and rated four out of five stars. Mortuaries didn't close on weekends. A man answered the phone on the second ring.

Raphael introduced himself and Norval, which seemed to carry some weight, for he was transferred to the funeral director himself.

"Hello, Mr. Lennon. This is Mark Lowe," said a monotone voice. "How may I help you?"

In the ten-minute phone call, Lowe confirmed that Dr. Klaes was indeed cremated, the funeral arrangements made in advance by Klaes himself. There was a courtesy video of the actual cremation. Lowe would email a copy of the video to Raphael as an attachment. "You'll receive it by Monday."

Proof of Death Certificate: Dead.

Emails: Alive.

Cremated: Dead.

Knowledge of Raphael: Alive.

JK RULES and the Wall came again to mind. When Raphael was younger, he attempted to master the Wall countless times, but its angle was such he had never successfully skated it. Tried a hundred times and always fell, always failed. He thought of that wall as he sat there, feeling as if whatever he did, he could gain no traction with the Klaes case.

He turned to the Physicists Commons.

He wanted a second read of Klaes's bio on the website, which offered little more detail than his anonymous obituary. He wondered if information had been deleted.

Just to check, he surfed through a dozen biographies of physicists from Berlin to Tokyo. All were longer and more detailed than Klaes's.

One stopped him in his tracks, Lily Faraday's, the person managing the Klaes celebration. He read it from first to last word. It finished with an odd declaration.

I refuse to answer any more questions on this site. Some users don't comprehend a scientific answer, so they downvote, rather than ask the poster for further explanation. My knowledge is being distorted and wasted. Before I am removed, which seems to be the common fate of those who don't march to the drum of grand poohbah Maisie Sparod, I will no longer take part.

Similar to every other forum, there were dissenters, feuds, and backstabbing.

He definitely needed to speak with Lily, but so far she'd snubbed him. He needed someone else in Klaes's orbit. He opened Klaes's saved email. There were tens of thousands, as if he never deleted a damn one. He spent an hour rolling through the emails, opening a few. One name came up many times. Jonathan Mirsky. Their email conversations comprised mathematical exchanges—mostly formulas several lines long with various annotations—enough text though to understand they disagreed on the size of infinity.

He copied Mirsky's email address, opened his Norval email client, and clicked *compose*. He pasted Mirsky's address, typed *Jason Klaes* in subject, and then sat motionless for several minutes, deciding how to word the question. Once satisfied with the query, a delicate request to discuss Mirsky's colleague and friend Jason Klaes, he piloted the cursor over *send* as if balancing his skateboard on a rail, psyching up for a tough grind.

CHAPTER
EIGHT

Twenty minutes after Raphael returned home from the office, his phone rang with Mirsky's call.

The voice was gruff, impatient, and intimidating. "Mirsky here. What kind of scam you working, Lennon? You one of those séance kooks? Getting messages from Jason Klaes, huh?"

Seated at the kitchen table, Raphael ran a knuckle across his bottom lip. "Nothing of that sort, Mr. Mirsky. I work for the Norval Corporation. We process information on the deceased. Frankly, we're trying to determine if Jason Klaes is alive or dead."

"Well, should be simple, shouldn't it?"

"So far it hasn't been. As I mentioned, the message—"

"Yes, yes, a missive from the dead," Mirsky snapped. "Well then, we better meet."

Raphael set his glass saltshaker on its side and spun it. "Couldn't we discuss this over the phone? Perhaps, Zype?"

"No, not something I do, Lennon. It was *Lennon*, right?"

"Yes. Raphael Lennon."

"How well do you know Pasadena?"

The saltshaker came to a stop. Raphael's stomach tightened. "I don't think I can make it to Pasadena. I don't drive."

"Where are you?"

"Mid-Wilshire."

"North Hollywood then? Take a cab," suggested Mirsky.

With the heel of his hand, he flipped the saltshaker. Mirsky was a stranger. What difference would it make? "I'm somewhat agoraphobic."

"Somewhat, huh? Like a little bit knocked up? Where can you go, *Lennon*?"

He spun the shaker again. "Within walking distance of the Grove."

"Do you know Shorty's Big Top Room?" asked Mirsky.

"I'm not sure I should—"

"If you want to know about Jason Klaes, Shorty's."

RAPHAEL'S EYES adjusted to the bar's interior, dominated by studded black leather booths and walls bathed in red light. The smell of long-extinguished cigarettes hung in the air, along with cannabis, not openly smoked but likely the product of subcut mouth vapes with palate leech lines. Synthesized music stopped just short of thunderous. For four o'clock on a Saturday afternoon, Shorty's Big Top Room pulled in a respectable crowd of drinkers and patrons of the arts.

The odd spot Professor Jonathan Mirsky chose was on the west side of La Brea Boulevard, Raphael's eastern boundary. When he was younger, he'd skated in the parking lot where a guardrail made for good grinding. He'd practice until this big dude came out the rear entrance and told him to get lost.

Once, when the big guy opened the door to chase Raphael, someone pushed away an inner curtain. A glimpse of an inverted woman, legs in the air, sliding down a silver pole. As her long red hair gathered on the stage, men pawed at her body and threw money at her feet. The open door and curtain aligned for only a few seconds, though his fourteen-year-old eyes peered for what seemed an eternity.

On the living room canvas and years ago, he rendered Shorty's as a scarlet whirlpool.

He had not expected to return to the whirlpool, but Mirsky hadn't given him much of an option.

"Four p.m." the winner of the Oerstead Medal for teaching of physics—and twice nominated for a Bogolyubov Prize—had confirmed. "I'll be wearing a Hawaiian shirt. And you?"

"Six foot three without my Sketchers. One-hundred and fifty-four pounds *with* my Sketchers. Long, dark hair—clean. Blue beanie. White T-shirt and drift pants. Carrying a skateboard with Cult Centrifuge wheels."

Even in the darkened bar, which smelled of peanuts, standing water, and smoke, Raphael had spotted Mirksy's bright, tropical shirt and took the empty stool beside him. He'd read the man's bio, seen his photo on his institution's website; he looked different without the lab coat, like a bad undercover job.

Shifting, the physicist gazed at Raphael for a moment, grunted, and ran a finger along his pencil-thin mustache.

"Taller than I might have thought," said Mirsky.

"I said six-three."

"Yeah, that's right, you did."

The barmaid strolled over and asked Raphael his pleasure.

When Raphael tried to order a Stella, the physicist told the barmaid to change it to an IPA, a Voodoo Ranger. While Mirsky focused on the agile pole dancer, Raphael considered his bar mate's open mouth and quivering nostrils. Someone was fucking with him, hired some lookalike clown to yank his blockchain. "If you're a physicist, I'm Pope Lucy," said Raphael above the music. "Where's the camera?"

Mirsky gave his moustache a final tap, as if to ensure it would stay on, snatched a bar napkin from the stack, and took out a pen from his shirt's top pocket. With fluidity and speed, Mirsky wrote numbers and symbols in minuscule script. It took him about thirty seconds to fill the napkin.

He slid the napkin in front of Raphael, who studied it only long enough to know it meant nothing to him.

"Schlitz's equation," said Mirsky. The physicist launched into the equation's meaning which, though fluent and convincingly intoned, lay beyond Raphael's comprehension. Convincing, though, is not convinced.

"What you wrote could be gibberish. Anyway, I doubt a physicist would try to prove his identity by writing an equation."

"Who says? You run with the physicist crowd?"

"No, I'm not—"

"Ah, it's good enough for the B-girls, not for young, agoraphobic" —he gazed at Raphael for a few seconds—"Raphael *Lennon*."

"Mind if I see your ID."

Raphael had expected a university badge, something featuring the man's credentials, but Mirsky took out his wallet, flipped it open, and showed a California driver's license: Jonathan Francis Mirsky and with a birthdate matching the seasoned face.

"All right, you're Mirsky. What's with this place? Couldn't we have met at Starbucks?"

Mirsky shrugged. "What can I say? I enjoy strip clubs, and this used to be a regular hangout."

"I thought scientists were beyond such stuff." Though now that he thought about it, some pretty earthy scientists had come across his desk.

"Some are, some aren't."

"What about Jason Klaes?" asked Raphael.

"Oh, Jason went for women all right, only he liked the smart and sensitive ones—women you had to be careful with." Mirsky glanced at Raphael as if waiting for a reaction. "Me, I lean toward hard women. Treat them nice, and they'll spit in your face. Not saying a projectile of woman's spit is a bad thing." He grinned.

Oh, hilarious. Raphael grimaced and looked away. "I'm surprised you agreed to meet me."

"I was curious, Mr. *Lennon*."

"I prefer *Raphael*."

"You're one uptight dude. What do you do for fun, aside from your skateboard?"

Raphael threw his shoulders forward. "I paint."

"Ah, an artist. Plain or fancy?"

"Neo-Depressionism," said Raphael.

Mirsky smirked. "I like you, kid." He raised his drink as if in a toast, downed most of it, and wiped his lips. "You from here?"

"Born and raised. Why?"

"Nothing. Just idle curiosity. So, tell me more about this Norval Corporation."

Raphael blew through half the beer, its pine-air-freshener odor fading, and rapped the bar, his hand sticking to the wood. Should he tell his tale to this skeevy dude? Bottom line, he had contacted Mirsky, who could have blown him off. Give the devil his due. The physicist listened as Raphael explained the lucrative business encircling death and how he caught criminals trying to outwit the system.

"Yeah, I've heard about that scam—excuse me—forward thinking enterprise. Why is Jason so important?"

He filled Mirsky in on the company's policy and the results of his research. "In Jason's case, the evidence points both ways. On the one hand, the coroner says our physicist is dead. Cremated and scattered to the high seas. On the other hand, a number of people received post-mortem emails from Klaes's personal account."

Mirsky tapped the bar napkin. "Old Schrödinger raises his hoary head. Is the cat alive or dead? Perhaps both—until you open the box."

"According to the coroner's office, Klaes blew his head off with a shotgun."

Mirsky's face scrunched as if he'd just eaten something bad.

The perfume of the dancer wafted over the bar.

Mirsky glanced toward the woman and nodded. "A dead cat all right."

"For a dead cat, he seems busy. He's been sending out emails. Someone is erasing his history on the Internet. He threatened a woman with murder."

"One hell of an accusation to lay on a dead guy."

"Was the Klaes you knew capable of it?"

"Loathing someone enough to want to murder them? Yes. Actual murder? No."

Raphael took a gulp of beer. "What would set him off?"

"Cruelty. Hurt a child or an animal, and your name went down in Klaes's black book."

"What happened if you got in the book? Are we talking physical retaliation?"

"Nah, he was too soft. Instagrammed Buddhist sutras on the sacredness of all life. Twitter scolding. Maybe a petition if it was a corporation." Mirsky's forehead wrinkled, and he pressed his fingertips together. "Bottom line is he hated the suffering of innocents."

Raphael set the skateboard on his lap, turned it deck-side up, and brushed a wheel; sending it spinning. "What would he do about the suffering?"

The music changed to a Miami Circus-Grind beat. Mirsky glanced toward the dancer as she shimmied to the top of the pole with only the strength of her clamped legs, then whirled about the steel as she descended. Mirsky sighed and regarded Raphael, who too swiveled back to the bar.

"He'd move heaven and earth to lessen the pain of a child or an animal. And when he couldn't, it crushed him. Hand to God, he'd physically change, shrink, deteriorate." Mirsky drew his shoulders inward and slouched. He held the pose for a few seconds, then straightened and motioned to the bartender for two more drinks.

Raphael waited for the drinks to arrive. The physicist took a thoughtful sip.

Raphael set a second wheel spinning. "What would be the point of Klaes taking his own life?"

Eyes glistening, Mirsky rubbed his fist across his chin. "Maybe he wanted to be with her," said Mirsky.

"Her?"

"Angie."

"Wife? Girlfriend?"

"A child. The five-year-old daughter of Helen, one of his graduate students. Jason was Angie's godfather. Beautiful little girl. 'Sparkling' was Jason's word."

Raphael searched his memory. The names hadn't come up in the research. "When you say he wanted to be with her, you mean ..."

"Angie developed cancer." Mirsky paused, rubbed his neck, and looked up at the dancer who was now performing an inverted split. Mirsky breathed deeply.

Raphael prompted. "And?"

Mirsky forced his eyes away from the nearby supple flesh. "Terrible, fast moving stuff. She knew she was dying. Another patient, an older girl, told her about cryonics, how her body could be frozen now and unfrozen in the future when they could cure her disease. The idea lifted her spirits, gave her hope. Five years old and she wanted her body cryopreserved. Heartbreaking, right?"

Raphael nodded. He tilled the fields of death, but a child going that way, having to take in the bleak news. "Yeah, about as tough as it gets."

Mirsky continued, "Jason told her parents he would pay for the procedure and all subsequent costs. Her parents told Angie her wish would come true. When it became clear she had only days left, Jason traveled to her bedside. He was there when she died, hoping she might one day reawaken. Afterwards, Jason got small. Real small. Then he disappeared." Mirsky looked away.

"Disappeared?"

"Left the country. Went to Namje, a little valley east of Nepal. He'd go there every couple of years to contemplate his navel and ingest magic mushrooms. His Shangri-La, you know? This time it was to grieve. Stayed six months. Maybe it helped. Still, he was never the same after Angie."

"When was this?"

"Oh, two or three years ago."

"What happened to his work in the meantime?"

"Gave it up. Let his funding lapse, I guess. Not sure whether the NSF got involved. His staff transferred to other labs, I know that much. I interviewed a few, but no takers."

You're an End Man. Ask the tough question. "Did he try to kill himself before?"

Mirsky shook his head.

"If something happened again, might he have—"

"Blown off his head with a shotgun? No, it didn't go down that way." Mirsky tapped his forehead. "Klaes was fond of his gray matter. He also detested guns. I doubt he ever held a gun."

"The police found a shotgun."

"Well, then." Mirsky shrugged.

"Are you saying someone murdered him?"

"Klaes had many *rivals* in the physics community. To the public, we're an easygoing bunch—a chill crowd of eggheads—get close and you'll see the Sturm und Drang, the rivalries and rifts. Scientists who think they didn't get the prize or grant they should have gotten. Competing theories. A reputation ruined. Does cold fusion ring a bell? You ever see Pons and Fleischmann on the circuit again? There are rumors of a dude called the Quantum Hitman. Kills people for practicing junk science. If you've ever worked in academia, you'd know how heated it can get."

"What would someone have against Klaes?"

"Maybe a theory. Klaes was relentless. Nonlocality, action at a distance. Spooky action. Do you understand the concept?"

"Do you need another napkin?"

"Come on." Mirsky got up, carrying his drink to the table beneath the stage. Raphael followed him, lifting his eyes to the dancer. Had his adolescent experience inoculated him against such pleasures? *No.* He turned his attention to Mirsky who ogled the woman.

What's inside a physicist's skull? Were all those complex formulae intermingled with the most base, carnal desires: the stars and the gutter intertwined? The secrets of the universe mixed with silicone breasts.

"You watching?" asked Mirsky, putting an elbow to Raphael's gut.

"Sorry. Yes, I'm with you."

Mirsky inched forward. "Let's consider. I can reach out and touch this little pumpkin's leg, right?"

"Of course."

"The flesh of my fingertip would rest against the flesh of her thigh. I would feel it. She would feel it. Correct?"

"Obviously."

Mirsky raised his hand and pointed a finger. "If this is all I did, she wouldn't feel it, right?"

The dancer inverted herself on the pole, drawing Mirsky's attention. Raphael tapped Mirsky's shoulder.

"Ah, yes," said Mirsky.

"You were poking the dancer."

"Pointing. Not poking. If I merely pointed," Mirsky demonstrated, "and she felt my finger as if I had touched her, that would be an example of a non-local action, which, according to accepted physics, is impossible. Therefore, I have to—" Mirsky stuck his hand in his pocket. "I think I have some wad. Yes." Mirsky drew out a crumpled fifty-dollar bill and waved it. The dancer pushed off her pole to position herself in front of Mirsky. He ran a finger across her leg and then tucked the fifty into her G-string.

"Use a little local action," said Mirsky, eyes fixed on the dancer.

Raphael jabbed Mirsky. "Klaes believed it was possible?"

"What?"

Raphael clasped Mirsky's shoulder and exclaimed, "Are you saying Klaes believed in this spooky action stuff?"

"If you're asking in regard to my distant finger caressing this kitten's thigh, no. But if entanglement is considered in regard to two brains, Klaes might waver."

Raphael went for broke. "So he thought you could affect someone's mind at a distance? Get a person to jump off a balcony or get another to push them?"

Mirsky shrugged. "A simplification of some magnitude. Stretching the theory, which after all is confined to quantum entanglement."

Theory. "It sounds more magic than science," Raphael said.

"Magic is what we call something before we've learned the trick. It's no less amazing after we figured out the mechanism, except we call it physics then and give ourselves awards and pretend we're responsible for creating it."

"Did Klaes's work have commercial applications?"

Mirsky looked away. "A physicist's fart has commercial applications."

"Even this spooky action theory?"

"Sure, or ..."

"Or?"

Mirsky clapped his mouth.

"Or?" asked Raphael.

The lascivious physicist shrugged. "Klaes wanted autonomy," said Mirsky. "Your company should leave the dead to themselves."

"He sent me a message challenging me to find him," said Raphael.

Mirsky gulped his drink, wiped fingers down his mouth, and swayed with the dancer's movements. "Now you're saying he's alive? Well, if Jason wants you to find him ..."

"Yes?"

Mirsky scrutinized Raphael's face. "Go through the quantum looking glass, handsome."

Raphael sighed. "I don't have to follow a rabbit?"

"Find the looking glass, then call me. Might have something for you."

Smirking, Mirsky propped a hand under his chin and focused on the dancer. Raphael sipped his beer. *Not bad, really.* He glanced at the bar. Most of the customers zeroed in on the dancer, but a man who took the stool Raphael abandoned appeared to be staring at him. The man's silver-rimmed glasses glinted under the stage's pulsing lights, so Raphael couldn't gauge the color of the eyes with certainty. Did he have a short beard or was it a shadow? Maybe a wine stain birthmark.

The glinting glasses and bright patch on below-average skin sparked a memory in Raphael. Could it be the tall guy on the sidewalk across from Norval? As if Raphael's thought had prodded him— spooky action at a distance—the man slipped off the stool, snatched his hat from the bar and put it on. He smiled at Raphael, about faced, and strode toward the rear curtain.

As the man pushed through the black flaps, Raphael rose from the table, his board dangling from his left hand. Mirsky didn't seem to notice. The curtain had settled by the time he reached it. He shoved it aside and averted his eyes from the wedge of sunlight streaming in from the closing door, which shut with a bang. He pressed down on the door's metal handle a mere second after it closed. The bar's parking lot hadn't changed in twelve years, except for the cars. In the late afternoon sun, he scanned the windshields for the face. He set down the skateboard and pushed off, landing hard to skate to the alley behind Shorty's.

"Hey, man, where are you?" he called out, skating a few yards into the passage. "Looking for me, maybe?" He pivoted and skated back to the parking lot. "You out here?"

The only reply was the thudding of a police chopper flying at low altitude.

Back inside the bar, Raphael paused at the two ungendered restrooms, checking one, then the other. *Come on, Raphael.* The guy who took off was another fan of the flesh with a taste for hats and quick exits. The resemblance to another stranger was simply a coincidence.

His forehead slick with moisture, Raphael plodded to the table he'd shared with Mirsky, which was now unoccupied. The two unfinished drinks pressed together as if in consultation. He scanned the long bar but spotted no shirts with parrots and palms. Above him at the table, the dancer finished her performance. The music died.

"Excuse me," said Raphael.

She glanced down at him. "I can't stick around. Kids, you know?"

"Did the guy I was with leave? The one with the moustache."

"Yeah. He was in awful shape. Someone had to help him out." She pointed toward the front curtain.

Raphael pushed through the curtain, zipped past the bouncer, and sprinted to the sidewalk. On the other side of La Brea, two men, one wearing a bright shirt and the other a hat, walked toward Wilshire Boulevard. Raphael glanced down at the gutter, from which came a blast of frosty air.

"Hey, Jonathan!" shouted Raphael.

Neither man responded. Raphael placed his toe on the curb. As if a mist had rolled in, the air whitened. The mist gleamed, solidified, folded onto itself like continuous paper emerging from the old-fashioned printers. Building higher and wider, denser and bluer, radiating waves of frigid air. Holding the skateboard to his chest, he shivered, shook, and twisted his head from the looming glacier's cold gaze. He retreated to Shorty's entrance, clamped his head, and waited for the ice to withdraw from its domain over the street, over his brain.

In hardly a minute, the season changed. The glacier melted, evaporated. Mirsky now lumbered alone down La Brea. The second man had vanished, and there wasn't a mirror or rabbit hole in sight.

"Jonathan!" Raphael called out once more to the physicist, who, though wobbly, stayed the path toward another dark and friendly establishment.

Something squeaked. Raphael glanced to his left. A woman pushed a teenage boy—no, a man of Raphael's age—down the sidewalk in a stroller. He had seen them many times, starting decades ago when the man was a child wearing the same expression, which was no expression.

"Is the boy dead, Mommy?"

The stroller wheel squeaked, and his heart missed a beat.

Above Wilshire Boulevard, a skyboard floated by.

Feeling Mortal? Book a Norval Portal! Beat the Reaper!
January Discounts! NorvalPortals.com

CHAPTER
NINE

Raphael skated away from Shorty's more convinced than ever Klaes was a possum. Despite the coroner's report, the death had to have been faked. Klaes was up to something that caused the world to believe him offline, perhaps to get away with murder. Yet he wanted Raphael to think the opposite. *Why?*

A few blocks from the bar, to clear his head, he raced a hundred yards and aimed to ollie a fire hydrant when a jogger appeared in his path. To avoid him, he jumped early, nicked the hydrant's top nut, and took a tumble. He felt twin flashes of pain in his arm and mouth. But skating, falls, and damage to the flesh were the package. *Suck it down, Raphy.* He checked the damage, found a gash in his elbow, and tasted blood in his mouth—maybe a chipped tooth. He pressed his fingers to the busted lip and ran his tongue over the suspect tooth. Damn, a jag. Well, you can live with that—*handsome*. As if. A poor copy of a handsome original, maybe.

Go through the quantum looking glass. Sure, made sense.

But *non-local action,* pushing someone off a balcony when the pusher was somewhere else—a metaphor, sure, but was it like Mirsky said of magic, only a metaphor before someone learned the trick?

The sun was setting by the time he reached the Tar Tower's courtyard and said good evening to a woman with a miniature poodle. She ignored his greeting as her poodle barked and strained at his leash to get to a man with his back to them a scant distance away. Smoke swirled above the man's head.

"Be good," the woman ordered her dog, its bark piercing. The man turned and glanced at the poodle, then shifted his gaze to Raphael. The man was broad-shouldered and thick-necked. A heavy jaw and an off-center nose rounded out his brutal appearance. He looked to be fifty, maybe older. His cheeks were cracked and lips thin, desiccated. Raphael recalled the man who had been checking out Mirsky and him at the bar. This person was much heavier and wore his hair longish and swept back. No hat. No silver-rimmed glasses. No beard or wine-stain birthmark. With a grunt, he gave his back to the trio again.

It's nobody.

Raphael swung around to the Tower but hadn't gone a yard before stopping to glance back. The man wasn't quite as tall as Raphael. *Klaes's height*. If he could study the man's face ... Jesus. Would every stranger call up Klaes, like the heartsick looking for their lost love? Go up to the apartment, take a shower, get a few hours' sleep. Klaes was dead, *maybe*.

Blood rushing to his head, Raphael spun. "Sir? Excuse me, sir?"

The man continued to smoke.

"Sorry to bother you. I'm wondering if I can borrow a cigarette?"

The man tossed down the cigarette and crushed it underfoot.

Raphael sucked up a breath and stepped toward the man. "I'll pay you for it." He dug into his pocket and slipped out a crinkled bill. "Five dollars?"

"What do you want?" said the man in a monotone.

"I'm desperate for a cigarette," replied Raphael, gauging the shape and color of the eyes. Greenish-brown, hazel. Similar if not identical to Klaes's. Contacts? The nose was wrong, much blunter than the physicist's. Unless Klaes had taken a few punches in the years since the last photograph. Up close, the man smelled of metal, a box of nails or screws.

"Cigarette, huh? With that busted lip?"

"Oh, oh yeah." Raphael touched his lip. "The, uh, nicotine helps with the pain."

The man thrust out his right hand, and Raphael drew away. The man grabbed his wrist and wrenched his hand palm up. He focused on Raphael's fingers. "You don't smoke. What kind of scammer are you?"

Raphael snatched back his hand. "I once smoked two packs a day. I haven't in a while. I smelled your cigarette, and I had this urge."

The man showed his teeth, which were narrow and discolored. "Urges I understand." He drew out a cigarette pack and snapped it. A cigarette appeared. "Here you go, have fun."

Raphael held out the five-dollar bill.

"Keep your money."

Raphael took the cigarette. "Thank you."

"Sure thing."

From some distance, a coyote yipped. Raphael rolled the cigarette between his fingers.

"Don't smoke the cig here," said the man. "I hate the smell of another man's smoke."

Raphael faked a laugh. Had he ever seen Klaes's teeth? In photos, Klaes didn't show his teeth much, did he? The bushy beard covered everything. "Oh, no. Up in my apartment, you know?"

"Nice. Have a good night."

"Yeah, thanks," said Raphael, hesitating. He wasn't sure. He didn't look like Klaes, though maybe he didn't want to. Nothing ruled out the man being just another senior citizen from the neighborhood. Studying the face, Raphael knew he hadn't seen him before, but hundreds of middle-aged and older men lived in the Tar Towers. His presence here meant little. He should let it go. If it were Klaes, the physicist wasn't giving himself away tonight. Don't get clever. The words clung to the roof of his mouth, resisted two hard swallows and dropped to his tongue. "Dig deep."

"What?" said the man casually; Raphael was sure the words hadn't connected, unless Klaes was a superb actor.

"I was thinking of a song. The lyrics."

"Ah, a singer."

Raphael shook his head. "Karaoke, Farmers Market Thursday night."

The man shrugged, took a cigarette from the pack, turned from him and lit up. He took a loud drag. Smoke swirled above his head. As he shoved the box into his pocket, his shirt rose an inch, revealing something tucked into the waistband. A gun? No, it had slender silver arms. Pliers—channel locks. To the left of that tool were the heads of a screwdriver and a small hammer.

Raphael doubled down. "Jason Klaes," he said. "Are you Jason Klaes?"

The man exhaled a stream of smoke, then looked Raphael up and down. "Naw."

IN HIS APARTMENT, Raphael took a shower, head bent to follow the eddy of blood washed from his arm. His skin warmed and slickened. He closed his eyes, and the aches and pains of flesh melted away under the hot stream. He tapped the injured tooth with his tongue. It seemed firmer. Maybe it would repair itself. When he opened his eyes, the last swirl of red-tinged water flowed down the drain. Gravity punched Miranda's ticket, too, but it didn't initiate it. This nonlocality stuff was an interesting candidate, but that may have been a misreading of Mirsky's illustration.

In the kitchen, and fresh from the shower, he searched for nonlocality on his laptop. The query drew nearly a million sites. The first was the old warhorse Wikipedia. *In theoretical physics, quantum nonlocality refers to the phenomenon by which the measurement statistics of a multipartite quantum system do not admit an interpretation in terms of a local realistic theory.* He looked up multipartite: *Divided into many parts.*

The definition of nonlocality was negatively put but still clear. Something could happen in separate quantum systems that couldn't be explained by standard physics. Then came a score of equations that made Raphael feel entirely inadequate. He went on to another site to read that Einstein was skeptical of nonlocality, labeled it "spooky action at a distance," and opposed the Copenhagen interpretation, which allowed for nonlocal action. Moving along, he came to John Bell's experiments in the 1960s, which seemed to prove that if locality was preserved (that is, nonlocality tossed out), Quantum Mechanics couldn't exist, buttressed by further experiments by other physicists. Through it all wound entanglement (aspects of which made his head spin), which provided an explanation for action at a distance, but was knotty in itself and whose ultimate meaning was slippery. Could someone have pushed Miranda off the balcony at a distance? That question was not addressed in the essays, although the possibility of Star Trek-type teleportation didn't appear to be off the table.

An hour after he'd finished his introductory course, with a hunk of cheese and a nectarine in hand, he took the elevator to the Tar Tower's top floor—the twentieth—got off and climbed a stairwell to the roof. At the exit, he ignored the *Authorized Personnel Only* sign, and walked past the rotating UV-C light—installed on all tall structures in the city, its invisible beam cleansing the city—to the parapet.

He stood before the west wall and ate his simple dinner. From the Tar Tower's roof, he could see his boundaries, the four brightly lit streets that framed his life, the reality that he worked to capture in the oils. He focused on Fairfax as he ate the sweet nectarine. When he reached the hollow and the pit, he raised his eyes. At a ten-mile distance, beyond the profusion of shore lights, the Pacific was a black canvas. On the canvas, the running lights of ships drew their vessel's path. A string of green and red disappeared over the horizon. On the roof, he would think about the world beyond his square mile. The places and people never to be known, never to know him. Not if the boundaries fell could he ever meet all people or set foot on all lands, yet he would be free to attempt it.

Out there somewhere was Klaes, trying to get free or trying to get caught. No, Klaes was dead. No, Klaes was alive. Or was he both? The contradictory possibilities tumbled over in his brain like bulky wet items in a dryer, banging and thudding.

For a moment, Raphael considered the encounter with the man

outside the Tower. If not Klaes, an odd dude all the same. What was with that beltful of tools? His clothes weren't that of a repairman come to service someone's refrigerator. A burglar? His gaze fell back on Fairfax and the darker streets joining it. Klaes and the repairman drifted from his thoughts. Addy lived on one of those streets. Likely an old Spanish bungalow with a little porch. She'd dance out her door in the morning and sing to the birds, if there were any birds.

Forget it, man. Don't torture yourself.

His eyes rose to the droning of an airplane, the shape defined by its lights, above the thousands of smaller configurations. He recalled the Atlanta plane crash. Three hundred people moving through the clouds in a steel cage. Not data, people.

The plane moved on, its roar giving way to the city's infinite sounds, which even from the roof seemed distinct and growing louder: cars whizzing, night drones singing, dogs whining, the odd weapon firing, a cry of sadness or rage, the hiss of angry spray paint writing FUCK DATA, a seagull's inland squawk. Then a loud "ping."

Ping? But it didn't sound like a mechanical ping, more the voiced word.

It came again, but this time, he heard it as "Pink! Pink!"

Addy! The person had uttered the cry from fairly close. Addy was out searching for Pink again.

He listened for a repeat of the voice. Nothing. His imagination. His desire.

"Pink."

He rose and leaned over the wall, strained to see her shape in the distance, to find Addy among the streetlights and shadows. It had been a weird, tough, exhausting day, but the thought of seeing her again made him feel good. Maybe he only imagined Addy calling Pink, but he had only a lonely night to lose and the joy of being with her to gain. He sprinted to the elevator.

As he exited the building, cigarette smoke hazed the lights of the empty courtyard.

The Tar Tower's landscape and then Sixth Street blurred. Nearing

Fairfax, he kicked hard on the tail. The worn Tail Devil screeched on the stone, igniting a fan of silver sparks.

He smelled marijuana and spotted a wavering red dot above the shadowy sidewalk. As he approached, the red dot of Pink's joint brightened and then faded. Pink sat on the curb, her feet in the gutter.

"Hello, Pink."

She wriggled on the curb. "Who are you?"

"My name is Raphael."

She stared at him. "What do you do?"

"Oh, I work in data too."

Grunting, Pink glanced at her empty lap and adjusted her dress, which hung to the street. A thin stream of water from a sprinkler overflow ran along the gutter and into a nearby storm drain. Pink drew back one foot and dammed the water until it sloshed over her foot. "To be vile," she muttered.

"Excuse me?"

"To be vile," she repeated.

Raphael nodded. "Where's your laptop?"

"My laptop?" She glanced at her lap and shook her head. She lifted her eyes to Raphael. "Raphael Lennon. Why aren't you running?"

He glanced down Fairfax. "Pink, have you seen Addy?" Wait, Addy said she didn't work on Saturdays. He slumped, the day's mental and physical labors weighing on him. Someone else sought Pink. Swallowing his disappointment, he considered the strange little woman and her prophecy. "Thirteen days, right? What happens in thirteen days?"

"Twelve days," said Pink. "If it's past midnight, you've got eleven."

"Eleven, yes. What happens in eleven days?"

"They kill you."

"They kill me. I see. Who are *they*?"

She shook her head left and right. "Better run."

"Pink, I can't …" He cut himself off. "Pink, shouldn't you be back at the shelter?"

Pink plucked her dress at the knees and drew it up.

In the gutter, between her feet, a red light flashed. The broken remains of Pink's laptop sat in the stream of water. A tiny LED light held its post.

"My data," Pink mumbled. She raised her head to him, bared her teeth, and hissed; then her eyes widened with recognition. She trembled and considered her feet. "My data," she said, pointing at the gutter.

"Was it a Blank?"

Pink snorted.

"It's all right, Pink. You'll get another laptop." On the phone, Raphael searched for the shelter and found its number. As he keyed in the digits, he remembered his mother's old laptop stored in her bedroom closet. "I have one at home I never use," he said, waiting for someone to pick up. "I'll make sure it gets to you."

Pink didn't seem to hear. Her eyes, dull and despairing, remained on her destroyed device. When she met his gaze, her eyes held the same gloom, as if Raphael were the damaged goods.

The expression unnerved him. "Who wants to kill me?"

"Stole my algorithms," she muttered.

A wasted question, as in his gut, he knew it would be. "I hope you saved them in the cloud," said Raphael as the phone picked up.

"Thought he got them all," Pink muttered.

"Corngold Center," said the warm voice on Raphael's phone. "How can I help you?"

"Yes. I'm with one of your … patients. Her name is Pink."

"Oh, you must mean Marion Jenson. Is she all right?"

He glanced at *Marion Jenson*. "Not really," he replied. "Hey, is Addy there tonight?"

"No. It's her night off."

"Yeah, I thought—never mind. Anyway, shouldn't Pink be at the center?"

"Absolutely. Could you bring her here or should we—"

"Raphael Lennon!" shouted Pink.

Raphael lowered the phone. She pointed at him, swayed side to side and fell back, her head hitting the sidewalk. "Eleven days," she muttered. "Better run."

CHAPTER
TEN

I n his cubicle on Monday, Raphael waited for the forensics lab to find his requested paperwork. The lab too had blamed computer system problems for the delay in getting back to him. Idle for the moment, he recalled Pink's bleak warning. To be killed in *thirteen*, no, now *ten days*.

Who wanted to kill him? Klaes? Whoever was pretending to be Klaes?

She's unstable, dude. Could it be the source of her digital visions? They said madness intertwined with genius. Faulty wiring sparking new neuronal pathways. *Pathways to the future? Give me a break, dude.*

He ran through leads regarding Klaes. One pricked him like a thorn; he forgot to contact the Love Fund's director, Jan Olmstead. He called her number and after five beeps, got voicemail. He left a message asking Olmstead to call him regarding donations, not mentioning Klaes.

Checking the monitor for the day's news, he clicked through the breaking stories. Every headline teased with six different interpretations. As he wandered through the stories, there was a gradual transition to infomercials or straight sales pitches. The point at which the news stories ended and the advertisements began was impossible to determine. "Ten Bizarre Millennial Diseases Making a Comeback." Click. "Clone Your Cat in the Privacy of Your Home." Click. "Bonds of Love: Top Ten Sexy Investments." Click. "Chilling Secrets the Space Force Doesn't Want You to Know." Click. "Murder or Politics as Usual?"

He slid the cursor over the right caret and clicked several times, still the headline refused to budge. A subtitle nestled under it: "Junín de Los Andes mayor Simon DeBove found murdered." Simon DeBove? That name sounded familiar to Raphael. *Simon DeBove?* Now he remembered. It was the alias of Arizona state congressman Carson Fullers, purportedly drowned on a pleasure cruise. He had turned the case over to Matt, who proved Fullers a possum by tracking him alive and well to Buenos Aires. Raphael supposed politics was in his blood since Fullers/Debove had become mayor. He'd done all right for himself ... until he got murdered.

A possum who was now legitimately dead.

Bound to happen sometime, but this was the first case he'd heard of.

He stuck his foot under the desk, tapped the skateboard, and then swung his foot toward the laptop brought from home. He was to meet Addy at the museum at 1:30 to give her the computer for Pink. The appointed time approached. The attack on Pink was unfortunate, but it had given Raphael an excellent excuse to contact Addy.

The phone rang. "Mr. Lennon?" asked a voice at the other end.

"Yes," said Raphael.

"Glenn from Forensics. Calling to let you know Jason Klaes had no Form 4473."

Raphael pressed a knuckle to his chin. "He never bought any gun from an FFL holder?"

"Correct. I checked the Federal License data twice."

He touched the coroner's report on the desk and once again read the cause of Klaes's death: suicide, gunshot wound to the head. "If that's the case," said Raphael, "how would Klaes have gotten hold of the weapon?"

"Maybe a gun show. Black Market. On the street. Amazon one-day delivery."

What would a physicist know about buying a gun on the street or Amazon, which surely would require legal paperwork before shipping, right? "Why wouldn't he buy one from the local gun shop?"

"Ten-day waiting period."

The learning curve of purchasing a gun on the street versus a ten-day waiting period. "How long will it take to get the origins report on the shotgun?" asked Raphael.

"Could be two days, could be a year. Weapons can have a complicated history."

"Well, if there's any way you could make it a priority ..."

"We'll do our best, Mr. Lennon, as always."

"And you'll check again for the crime scene photos?"

The investigator sighed. "Beats the hell out of me. The technician claims the file disappeared."

Right. *Disappeared.*

He thanked him and hung up the phone. Should he call the Harvey Hotel again? He'd left six messages for Lily Faraday. None got a response. Behind Raphael, someone breathed. He twisted to see Matt poking a straightened paper clip between his teeth as he gazed down at the coroner's report. "The physicist, huh?" said Matt in a garbled voice. "Alive or offline?"

Raphael rubbed his forehead. "No matter which way I turn this, I'm faced with an enigma. If Klaes is dead, who murdered Miranda?"

"Who's Miranda?" asked Matt.

"A selfiesist who pissed off Klaes."

Matt probed again with the clip.

"Get rid of the toothpick, okay, buddy?" said Raphael.

Matt dropped the glistening wire into the trashcan. "Klaes killed this Miranda person?"

"Threatened her when he was two days dead and killed her two days later."

"Well, only impossible," said Matt, glancing into the trashcan.

"If Klaes is alive, why does he want me to find him?"

"He wants you to find him?"

Raphael had said too much already. *You're getting involved personally,* his colleague might be thinking. Who the hell else could he run things by, if not Matt? "Listen, Matt, this stays with you and me, right?" Raphael summed up Klaes's message, skipping the images for the painting and the tease of freedom, details Matt could make no sense of so was better off not knowing. He followed with a redacted version of the meeting with Mirsky.

"Let's think this through," said Matt. "The cops say Klaes is dead. What did the CS photos show?"

"The crime scene photos are missing," said Raphael.

"The LAPD database?"

"Gone. I spoke with Glenn in Evidence. Someone wanted Klaes's living room to disappear."

"Klaes himself?"

"Maybe ..."

"It's a headscratcher all right. I don't envy you, bro." Matt peeked over his shoulder, turned back, and with an impish smile brought his lips close to Raphael's ear as if to tell a secret.

"You think I've got a chance with Anastasia?" asked Matt, in a louder voice than a secret would warrant. His voice fell to a whisper, and the subject took a left turn. "I saw something weird."

"Yeah?"

Matt glanced at the monitors and continued in a subdued voice. "I was changing a black-market incandescent lightbulb at home and the thing cracked. Sparks and glass, you know?"

"You didn't turn the power off first?" asked Raphael.

"Well, no—that's not the point," said Matt, voice rising. He blinked and again spoke in a whisper. "I thought I got all the glass out, but it still feels like a molecule is in there. So, I keep blinking to get the little guy out. I keep doing it."

"Have you tried eyewash?"

"So, at work I'm trying to relax with a mindfulness screen, which doesn't stop me from blinking. On the mindfulness screen, this guy is, uh, sawing, and the sawdust keeps piling up. But the screen suddenly —" Matt stiffened.

Dreemont stood in the doorway, his hand on Matt's shoulder. "How's it going, guys?"

"Scared me, Mike." Matt grinned.

"Nothing to be scared of," said Dreemont. "I'm just your supervisor."

Matt pivoted, sliding out from Dreemont's hand. "Well, talk to you later, Raphael." He exited, Dreemont bumping his shoulder as he passed.

Behind Dreemont, Matt performed two awkward dance moves, gave the supervisor a swift middle finger, and slipped away.

"How's Dr. Klaes coming?" asked Dreemont.

"Making progress."

The supervisor studied him for a moment, as if expecting more. "I'm glad to hear that."

"Did you need to talk to me about something?"

"Oh, no." Dreemont nodded, smiled wider than the moment required, stuck his hands in his pockets, and sauntered off.

What was Matt going on about?

How's Dr. Klaes coming?

Raphael returned to the computer. First the coroner's report and then the crime scene photos. Would a Stull counterpart from CSI show up with those?

Would Klaes's face have even been recognizable in the photos? He remembered Donato's director had promised to send a video of the cremation. He hadn't seen an email from the mortuary. He skimmed the morning's emails. Nothing. Could it have gotten into spam? Three screens down in the junk mail it appeared:

From: Donato's of Glendale.

Subject: Cremation Special.

Oh, how could such a *personal* message have gotten into spam?

He opened it to find a polite note from Donato's director and two attached files: "Klaes Cremation" and "Klaes Scattering". The note ended with an apology for the state of Klaes's head, which had suffered *colossal damage even our HD Reassembler couldn't fully repair.*

Despite the images of death he viewed daily, the video chilled him. In a starkly lit room, Klaes's body lay supine within a transparent, pressed-cardboard casket, the entire unclothed body visible. The casket sat on a pair of rails leading to the open door of a large metallic oven. Klaes's feet pointed toward the oven, so the head was in the foreground and the body foreshortened. To Klaes's right, an elderly man with a thoughtful expression stood by a lever.

Klaes's head resembled a bearded rotted pumpkin, but the reassembled features generally matched the ones he had seen in photos of the physicist, who always had that full beard, perhaps to hide a weak chin?

"Time," said a voice in the video.

The operator nodded and slapped the casket as if it were the shoulder of a parting friend. He walked backwards to the lever and pulled it down. The casket shivered, squeaked, and slid along its tracks toward the waiting oven, whose interior glowed with white heat. The casket disappeared into the oven and a door creaked shut. Letting his arms hang and lacing his fingers together, the operator appeared to count.

Raphael stopped the video and swiveled away from the monitor. He wanted to find a wall and punch it. With other undeclareds, uncovering whether they were alive or dead was closure. If they were dead, there were no other questions. If the undeclared proved to be a possum, Raphael would have already known all he needed to. With Klaes, he had questions only a living Klaes could answer, or at least said he could answer. There was something else too. Something undefined that gnawed at him.

An appointment reminder flashed on his computer. Pushing up from the desk, he tugged down his shirt and finger combed his hair. Time to leave the dead behind.

CHAPTER
ELEVEN

I n the museum's plaza, on an elevated stage, a string quartet performed a Strauss waltz. Beneath the stage, coupled dancers, cordoned by a red rope, orbited a fountain, their circle the width of a small carousel.

One woman danced with her eyes closed while another peered from drooping eyelids. A third gazed dully. Only the fourth seemed interested in her companion. The women's hair was cut short in the manner of 1920s flappers. The men wore their hair slicked straight.

One-thirty having passed, Raphael scanned the plaza again for Addy. Should have asked her to lunch—sure would have been fun. No, she'd have politely declined that request. Too much of a date. And then he'd gone and told her he was busy. True, but not *so* busy.

Not finding her and feeling the creep of depression, he concentrated on the mesmerizing movements of the dancers.

Round and round to the triple-meter music: strong, weak, weak, strong, weak, weak. Raphael imagined Addy tight in his embrace as they joined the waltz. In this dream scenario, his cheek would lean into hers, and he'd inhale the sweet scent of her perfume. If only he could keep his anxiety at bay long enough to ask, it could all come true. She might even say yes.

The song ended, the dancers froze, and the audience applauded.

At a nearby table, someone said, "Robert Motherwell." Raphael grew alert at the name, spoken frequently by his mother: the artist who allowed the dark places to paint themselves.

"Asthmatic as a child, you know. Delicate. The boy's family wasn't sure ..."

"It shows. Big black blotches ..."

His mother used to describe the mortality in Motherwell's work until Raphael felt like his own was tied to the painting.

"Ah, the shame of it," said a man seated at another table, drawing his finger down his cell phone. "Poor bastards."

"What?" asked his tablemate.

"Some scumbag's looted the County's Pauper's Fund. Where's that leave the unclaimed dead?"

"Unclaimed, huh?"

"County buries two thousand unclaimed bodies every three years. Not this year."

Raphael sighed. Was there no getting away from it? What had Gilly Stull said? "Dead, dead everywhere and not a drop to—"

"Raphael!" Addy crossed the plaza.

His knees grew weak, and his head swam. She approached so swiftly, she blurred, and he almost screamed for her to slow to regain her clarity.

"Oh, my God, I'm so sorry." Her breath came in brief gasps and her face was bright from exertion. A threadlike blue vein pulsed at her temple. "I tried to get here on time, but, oh, something always happens." She shook her head.

"No, no. I got here late myself," Raphael lied.

Her breathing slowed, normalized. "Oh, well then, I don't feel so guilty. Don't you have to get to work?"

I'd ditch work to stay with you, was on his lips, but she might think him as coming on too strong. When you're weird, you can't chance anything garnishing your weirdness. "I have a few more minutes."

Raphael swung the computer case. Addy reached out to tap the handle. "The laptop?"

"Oh, yes. This is it."

"It's so sweet of you. I'm sure she'll be thrilled."

"I installed more memory. It's a little old, but it should function and the one broken—"

"Smashed," said Addy. "Evil, evil people. Blanks, ugh."

"Most aren't that violent," said Raphael. "They preach evasion and persuasion." *Most.*

"What, I can't upload a song to my grandmother? Can't thumbs-up a friend's promotion? Can't search for the definition of *erstwhile?*" For an instant, her eyes brightened with outrage, then the light softened. She drew a breath and glanced at the brilliant sky.

It was a crisp January day, and the neighborhood's orange and lemon trees in false blossom released a scent as strong as the acrid smell of the tar pits. Raphael breathed deeply of the pleasant scent. Addy had closed her eyes and sang softly to the music of the string quartet. He tried to pick out a word, found none. It was meaningless syllables, maybe better than words.

For a moment, he floated on her voice. When she stopped singing and opened her eyes, he fell back to earth. He picked himself up, dusted off, and said, "Well, here it is." He held out the case to her, but she didn't take it.

"What's going on over there?" Addy gestured at the band and dancers.

"It's a performance for the exhibit," explained Raphael. "The dancers represent the characters in a painting."

"Very cool."

Or lukewarm? "If you're not interested, I can—"

Addy's eyes went big. "I absolutely love this kind of stuff. Don't go second guessing me. More, please!"

He grinned. "*Dance in Baden-Baden* by Max Beckmann, 1923," explained Raphael, glad for the opportunity to show his knowledge went beyond necrology and kick-flips. He pointed to a banner draped above the entrance to an exhibit hall. On the banner was a reproduction of the painting, out of which the dancers could have emerged. The white on black letters read *The New Objectivity*. "A translation of the German term *Neue Sachlichkeit*, which means new facts or perhaps new sobriety. See the picture?"

"Oh, yes, yes." She shifted her gaze from the banner to the dancers. "They're the same, aren't they?"

"It's a clever promotion," said Raphael, gazing at the performance with admiration.

At the front of the audience on the other side of the dancers stood a man wearing a hat and silver rim glasses. Raphael's breath left him, and his heart quickened. Was he being tailed? Was it a beardless Klaes? With a smile directed at Raphael, the man melted into the crowd.

"Addy, can you wait ..." He stepped away from Addy and started toward the crowd.

"What is it?" Addy called out.

He could no longer pick out the man, nor his hat. Klaes? But Klaes had boasted Raphael would never find him. He wouldn't put himself in plain sight, would he? No beard, but the beard could have been to cover up the wine stain birthmark. He had yet to come across a photo of Klaes without it. But this guy looked younger than Klaes. He shook his head.

"Is something wrong?" asked Addy.

Raphael turned and smiled. "No. Nothing. I thought I saw someone I knew." He returned to her side, and they strolled across the plaza, their arms occasionally touching. Her perfume was faint, one crushed honeysuckle.

"Hey, how are you so knowledgeable about art?" asked Addy.

"My mother was associate curator of modern art here. I grew up on the museum grounds and in her office. I knew every space, some the public never gets to see."

"Pretty cool. I'm envious."

Warming up to her enthusiasm, he pointed at the plaza floor. "Right below us is an enormous space that even most museum personnel can't access. They store all the art they won't allow the public to see. Damaged pieces and forbidden art. Paintings and sculpture too controversial to bring up to the light."

Addy's eyes went wide. "Never?"

Raphael shrugged. "Maybe someday." Had his mother really shown him all that? So long ago, it seemed like a dream. A memory surfaced of the subbasement, as the space was called. At its western limit stood a long, concrete wall with a gigantic, metal door. Behind the door was Dig Three, an immense tarpit that was closed off when the art museum was constructed. On one of their visits to the subbasement, he'd asked his mother if she could open the door and let him see the old dig, but she refused, describing the almost vertical staircase to the base, the old scaffolding and uncertain soil. There were even the rusted remains of old oil derricks. All this didn't deter Raphael's interest, but when she told him one more thing about the underground chamber, he had backed away from the door and his request. Just recalling the door, he shivered. He described the sealed dig to Addy, leaving out the detail that had frightened him.

Addy's eyes narrowed. "Derricks?"

"The Salt Lake Oil Field is straight down." Raphael spread his arms. "It's under the whole neighborhood. The oil seeps up through the ground to create the tar pits. Pumps on the museum grounds used to draw up millions of gallons."

Addy glanced around. "Drained the lake, I guess."

Raphael smiled. "No, there's still plenty of oil. The petroleum companies just tore down the derricks and plugged up the shafts."

"Environmental concerns?"

"Clashed with modern art."

"You're kidding?"

"Yeah." He grinned. "Anyway, by the time I was four, she'd taught me to pick out the Picassos from the Klees and Kandinskys, the sculpture of Giacometti from Henry Moore and the art of Joan Miró and de Kooning."

"Really? At four?"

"It's a vague memory, but it's what my mother told me when I was older." Should he mention his own work? Did he really want to get into that? *You see, Addy, I'm an artist too. I paint my life on my ceiling.* He scanned again for the man.

"Does your mom still work here?"

He lifted his hand to the beanie and tugged on the cuff as if to draw it down. "No. She died eight years ago."

"Oh, I'm so sorry." She regarded Raphael.

Raphael struggled to get the words out. "Yeah, before her time as they say."

"I can hardly imagine … Do you have brothers or sisters?"

Raphael shook his head. Many times his mother wished he had siblings and even talked of adoption. Someone to be with him when … but the when was never specified.

"Your father?"

"I never knew him."

"Oh, that's so sad. Do you think about him anyway?"

Raphael nodded. "Yeah, a lot actually. Not that there's much to think about."

"Did your mother talk about him?"

"Nope. It was taboo."

"Yeah, that way, huh? I was lucky. My mother and father have always been there. I love them. Really sweet people." Addy closed her eyes, found the sun. "I'll bet your father's nice." Opening her eyes, she gazed at him. "I wish you had time for lunch. It would be my treat."

"Yeah, that would have been great."

"Well, another time then. Maybe even dinner? I know a restaurant right on the ocean. Right out the window, waves crash. And it's not all that expensive. You won't believe it."

"Sure, sounds good." *And impossible.* Might she be the one who would understand? Addy's eyes focused sharply on him as if in expectation, then her gaze darted off.

"How is the necrology business?"

"You don't want to know."

She looked at him again. "I'm sure it would be fascinating." She came closer to him. "Raphael, do you have a girlfriend? Or"—she grinned and glanced at his bare ring finger—"even a wife?"

Raphael chuckled. "No wife, no girlfriend. I don't date much."

"What's much?"

"Once every five years."

She laughed. Did she believe him? Probably not. "And you?"

"No wife. No girlfriend either. There was a guy ..."

A little blade penetrated his heart. "Oh."

"A writer."

A cloud burst, raining books on his head. "Makes sense," he muttered.

"Writer's never stop—I mean, writing. Twenty-four seven. Tap, tap, tap."

"Painters go flick, flick, flick."

"Twenty-four seven?"

"Yes, I—they paint in their sleep. It's messy."

"He wrote himself out of my life."

"Oh, too bad." *Fucking great!*

"No. He was better to read than to be with." She nodded as if convincing herself, or was it to convince him? "But you have to go."

"Yeah, right." He handed her the computer case. "Thursday at Karaoke then?"

"Sure. Great."

He expected her to dash off, but she lingered, as if to say, *I enjoyed this—us—*and an icy fear struck him that such a moment might never happen again.

"You shivered," said Addy. "Did a ghost pass through you?"

His scary and depressing thought vanished at her voice. Happily, he peered over his shoulder as if to catch sight of a passing spirit. His eyes wide and foolishly grinning, he held the face, and she laughed. He could play the clown and be himself with her. So far. So far. "Thursday, then."

She smiled and turned toward the exit.

"Oh, Addy?" he cried out.

She halted. "Yes?"

"Have you read much of Sherlock Holmes?"

Her eyes widened. "From *A Study in Scarlet* to *The Hound of the Baskervilles*."

"What's Dr. Watson's one word?"

Her lips tightened and then she said, "He wrote all the words, if you don't count Doyle. Is it a riddle?"

Raphael nodded. "I guess."

"Have you Googled?"

"Yeah. Nothing." Which was more and more the case in all but the most mundane of searches, as if the elegant algorithms couldn't separate the accumulated mess of information or prevent advertisements from hijacking the search.

"I'll think about it," said Addy.

She offered a parting smile and then walked into the crowd. The universe receded at a much faster rate than the astrophysicists surmised.

CHAPTER
TWELVE

n the office, Raphael replayed his thirty minutes with Addy, regretting all the dumb things he'd said, but deciding overall it had come off all right. Despite the frustrating questions about Klaes, Raphael's unyielding boundaries, and Pink's spooky predictions, perhaps things were looking up.

His heart lighter and his head clear, he skimmed through the early files on Klaes. The physicist had a professional website, but Raphael's initial check of the site revealed only a bare bones home page with few links, which didn't mean the server hosting Klaes's site didn't have other files that Raphael could hack for clues. With every other undeclared he'd hunted, a motive would eventually surface if the undeclared had gone possum.

He took a breath and opened Klaes's site. Instead of being taken to the homepage, the page opened to a vendor selling domain names. The site had been taken down, or at least public access to it. It was still probable Klaes's files remained on the server, available through a backdoor break-in. He set his foot on the skateboard and rolled it back and forth as if pacing a room. His neck tingled. He entered Klaes's email account again and scrolled through hundreds of saved emails. One was a confirmation of a domain renewal order and advised the user could login to the client area at their hosting service to manage the domain, Klaes's host server for sure.

Ten minutes later, he had reached the login page. The user's name likely adhered to a couple of standards, but the password was a different story.

From experience, he would bet Klaes had copied down the password somewhere, maybe in an email to himself, accessible from anywhere. In the search, Raphael entered Klaes's email address. Thousands of emails addressed to Klaes appeared. He typed the address again in search, twinning Klaes. A much less formidable list appeared. These were the ones Klaes had sent to himself and *saved*.

Raphael scanned the list of several hundred. A handful of the emails had no subject. He opened up the oldest one. As with its subject, the message was blank, which was odd. Something should have been there. He opened the next oldest: blank. Next: blank. Four, five and six—blank.

He leaned back in the chair and gazed at the blank message. Why bother to send yourself nothing? May as well mail yourself a blank sheet of paper. Nothing ... or invisible. He wouldn't, would he? *Come on, possum hunter. Tracks, scat, and a bent twig.* He leaned forward and maneuvered the cursor over the blank message, highlighting the entire thing until the characters appeared in gray. Klaes had changed the automatic letter color from black to white so the email appeared blank like contemporary invisible ink. Raphael changed the characters to black, revealing a row of what appeared to be passwords.

Now came the guesswork. Twenty minutes of craft, patience, and luck pulled up the magic words: *TLS connection established*. He was in.

The remote site folders and files popped up. He transferred the entire folder to his desktop. He spent an hour checking files and subfolder files. They contained math way over his head, lecture notes, slideshows, and abstracts. Nothing set off alarms, until he found two files in a subfolder of a subfolder, one with the odd name "Personality Plus.tmhxxml" and another called "Winstrum.tmhxxml."

Winstrum, as in the pharmaceutical firm? Right. The fourth post-mortem message from Klaes had been to the firm's CEO: a warning to reduce the cost of the company's drugs for children.

He tried a dozen programs, yet the files wouldn't open. A work-around proved no more successful. Locked. He'd have to get Dreemont, who had the skills of an old-fashioned lock-picker.

As he prepared to buzz Dreemont, the supervisor appeared at the cubicle entrance. "What's up, Raphael?"

"Hey, Mike, you got any ideas about this?" He pointed to the monitor. "I don't recognize the variant."

Dreemont bent closer to the screen. Inches from Raphael's face, Dreemont's lips formed the file names and then tightened. "Where did you find this?"

"Klaes's website. Deep down."

Dreemont nodded. "Never seen the extension, so I really can't help you. Dead end." Dreemont straightened. "I'm sure it's nothing. What else you got?"

"Nothing I can't handle," said Raphael, surprised at Dreemont's offhand dismissal of the troublesome file.

"What else?" demanded Dreemont.

"Some image files."

The supervisor rubbed his chin. "Keep me updated, okay?"

Raphael nodded. Dreemont started to leave but his head snapped toward Raphael as if he hoped to catch him sticking out his tongue or raising the middle finger.

When Dreemont left, he considered the supervisor's curious attitude. Dreemont was game for a challenging break-in; this one had repelled him.

Raphael went back to the image file. There were dozens of images, but he focused on "miranda01". He opened the image: the Miranda and swan selfie. So Klaes possessed the photo sent with the threatening email. Why was he so interested in this flaky young woman?

"Raphael."

He swiveled on his chair. Dreemont stood above him, one hand on his hip, the other pulling on his chin. He hadn't been gone thirty seconds.

"Hey, Mike, you figure something out with—"

Dreemont held up his palm as if for silence. His supervisor eyed the coroner's report and rubbed his knuckles across his chin. "You know, Raphael, we've spent enough time on this Klaes case. Potential possums are piling up, and all you're doing is spinning your wheels. I'm taking you off Klaes."

"But that Personality Plus file might—"

"Forget that file. *You* won't open it. Close up Professor Klaes."

The high-pitched sound, as of a dentist's drill, lasted only an instant. "Excuse me, Mike. What did you say?"

"You're done with Klaes."

"No, I—"

"Klaes case is closed."

The dentist's drill whined again. "We don't do that," said Raphael. "I mean, I've never aborted a search."

"First time for everything. Don't take it personally."

Raphael nodded. "If it's okay with you, Mike, I'll stick with him a little longer. There are lines of inquiry, things might open up."

"You've got to know when to fold." Dreemont put his finger on the report. He inched it away.

"What are you doing?"

"It's over. *Fini.*"

Raphael set his hand on the contested paper. "Mike, this is crazy. I spent twice this time on Ferrante."

"Yeah, but you nailed Ferrante."

"I'll get Klaes too."

"Mr. Maglio wants Klaes entombed." Mike pulled the report out from under Raphael's hand. "Seal it. Everything."

Raphael's face burned. "This is crazy. Do I have your permission to speak with Mr. Maglio?"

"No. Discussion's over."

Raphael pushed back his chair, stood up, and steadied himself. "I've invested—"

"I have several high-profile possums I'll funnel to you within an hour. They'll put Klaes in the rear mirror."

Raphael sat down.

"There, good, relax." Dreemont clasped Raphael's shoulder, gave it a firm shake, and strolled off.

Entombment involved the complete excision of one's online presence. Your online human-remains isolated, sealed, and buried like nuclear waste. This was all wrong. He was *supposed* to find Klaes. In his gut, that's the way it felt. Someone had set a shovel in his hands and told him to dig deep. He burned to find Klaes. He tried to breathe, but his lungs balked. He needed air, and he felt himself on the verge of blackness. He jabbed a finger at his throat as if to break through an obstruction. *Let it go. Follow the order, follow the rules.*

He drew a sharp breath. He waited for his heart to slow and his thoughts to clear.

A moment later, with a backward glance, he opened the bottom drawer and rummaged through the sticky pads, paper clips, and rubber bands to find the thumb drive Matt gave him at the gift exchange a year ago. It was an illegal drive Matt claimed had a data exfiltration wall. Theoretically, even Norval's system wouldn't detect its presence. Raphael had never used it, and who knew if it worked?

He reached around the desktop, located a rear USB port and slid in the drive. He copied the Klaes files, then minimized the screen. It took less than a minute to transfer the data, but his heart again raced, must have been pushing two hundred bpm. Pulling out the drive, he stuck it in his change pocket, shut down the computer, jumped to his feet, and rehearsed the opening argument he would use with Maglio.

Five minutes later, Raphael entered the reception room for Maglio and R&D. Ms. Goloda had her back to him as she addressed a group of young people, likely programmers and bound for the Research Department, which seemed to be on a hiring spree. The door to the long hallway that led to Maglio's and R&D was ajar. He didn't hesitate, navigating the zigzag corridor with its erratic—effectually stroboscopic—lights to Maglio's entryway. Ruling her domain with an iron hand, Ms. Goloda would not have let him say two words to Maglio without a formal appointment. A few feet from Maglio's door, he halted, caught his breath. His disappointment and frustration had driven him to this point, but reason argued he would gain nothing and perhaps lose everything: his job, his income, his apartment, his painting. Could he not continue to seek out Klaes on his own? But something gnawed at him: the motive that had driven countless others to rash acts, the motive that could only be satisfied by confrontation. He had been treated unfairly, and he wanted to know why. Why? A polite, soft-spoken but determined why?

He turned to Maglio's black glass door and tapped lightly. "Mr. Maglio, I know you have a rule forbidding employees from coming to your office uninvited, but I need to speak with you about the physicist Jason Klaes. I don't understand why you're taking me off the case."

He knocked again. The black glass's interior stirred.

"Hey, bitch, what are you doing?" called out a voice behind him. Groaning, he glanced back to see Ms. Goloda striding down the corridor.

"I need to speak with Mr. Maglio," said Raphael.

"Like hell you do," declared Ms. Goloda. At the sound of her words, the door, as if intimidated, did its trick: the black vanished, leaving clear glass.

Inside Maglio's office, a tall slender woman stood at the window overlooking Wilshire Boulevard. She maintained her gaze as she called out, "Mr. Maglio's not here."

"Do you—do you know where he is, ma'am?" asked Raphael.

The woman shrugged.

"Oh, my god," rasped Ms. Goloda. "Do you know who you're speaking to?"

He didn't. He pressed his nose to the glass, trying to peer at Maglio's desk, but the angle didn't permit it. "Mr. Maglio, I'm sorry, but I really need to talk to you."

Ms. Goloda grabbed Raphael's arm and yanked. "Asshole! How dare you? That woman is Maisie Sparod!"

The name seemed familiar. "Mr. Maglio, I don't understand why you're taking me off Jason Klaes."

The woman turned from the window, her eyes narrow and lips

tight. Raphael could have been a StoopServe driver arriving an hour late with her lunch.

"I need to speak with Mr. Maglio about Jason Klaes," insisted Raphael, ignoring Ms. Goloda's simian grip. The ice blue eyes of the woman in the office measured him twice, the first time warmly as if for a suit, the second time coolly as if for a casket.

Raphael peered through the glass. In the far corner stood a seven-foot-tall blue cylinder. The gold letters down the side read "Solarium Tanner."

"Is he in his tanner?" asked Raphael recklessly.

Ms. Goloda pinched his earlobe and tugged. "My god, grilling a guest of Mr. Maglio. You're in deep shit, fucknut."

Eyebrows arched and lips pouting, the woman glided to the Solarium and yanked open the door to show the empty device.

Ms. Goloda was on her phone. "I'm calling security."

He rapped again on the door. "Where is he?"

The woman shrugged and returned to her window.

Raphael twisted away from the secretary, his face burning and legs uncertain as he scrambled back down the crazy corridor. Blew it. Blew it bad. For nothing.

CHAPTER
THIRTEEN

At his desk, Raphael waited for HR to summon him. He kept his head down and worked on a list of undeclareds, none nearly as troublesome as Klaes. By the end of the afternoon, he had determined two of the three were offline and the third a possum, hiding in Argentina, a popular destination for assuming a new identity. Argentina triggered *Simon DeBove*. Raphael retrieved the online article about DeBove's murder. Reading it, he was again puzzled by the possum's passing, or more to the point, why other dead possums hadn't surfaced. He'd tracked hundreds, some fairly old, surely two or three would have legitimately bought the farm. The system should have alerted him.

"Hey, buddy," said Raphael, entering Matt's cubicle.

Matt held out his right arm. "Heard about your storming of the citadel. Still working here, huh?"

"It's early." Raphael slid his wrist across his friend's, the latest greeting rage. "Does the name Simon DeBove ring a bell?"

"DeBove, huh?" Matt tugged on his ear loop, nibbled his lower lip and lifted his eyes to the ceiling. "Ah, ah—*nope.*"

"Really?

Matt grinned "Screwing with you, dude. Carson Fullers, run-of-the-mill malfeasance in office."

"Correct."

"He was my first possum," said Matt. "Fullers fell overboard on a cruise to Hawaii and drowned. Only, he surfaced in Buenos Aires under the name Simon DeBove. We entombed him."

"Well, now we've got to disentomb him. He's dead."

"Not really. He's only—"

"Yeah. Dead. Dead twice. I read it on a newsfeed, but I should have gotten a reassignment alert."

Matt's mouth dropped. "A program glitch? My god, how could that have happened?"

"See if you can locate the DeBove alert—and any others. If you can't find alerts, run a morbidity projection on one or two cohorts."

"Yeah, but they're entombed. How am I going to get—"

"You're smart, Matt. Maybe use one of those wizardly devices you got at one of your conventions. They all work, right?"

"Yeah, good as gold."

Raphael tapped the pocket holding the thumb drive. "Keep it on the QT."

"Cutie?"

"No. Q and T. Means quiet. Old school stuff."

Matt pinched his earlobe and whispered, "Something amiss?"

"Only that ear of yours."

"Meany."

Matt drifted away. Raphael might be wasting his friend's time, but it bothered him that the subject of dead possums hadn't come up before. People died all the time, so must it be with possums. He never noticed the absence. Never noticed the dog hadn't barked.

A soft, steady tapping grew louder. He looked up just as Jensy entered his doorway. She held her cane in one hand, a print-out in the other.

"Hi, Jensy."

"Hi, Raphael. How have you been?"

Heat came to his cheeks. He hadn't spoken to her in a couple of days. He should have at least stopped by her desk. Her shoulders hunched forward, and she seemed to have grown shorter.

"Yeah, I've been fine, but so damn busy. Sorry I haven't checked in with you."

"Oh, it's okay. I understand." She sighed, pushed her glasses back into place. "I finished my monthly national drownings report."

"Great."

"Thirty-seven drownings of children under the age of five, thirty-four of them natural Blanks." She waved the print-out. "I've got it all here."

"Nice work," he mumbled.

"Oh, sure. Nice work. I wonder if they knew, those drowning kids, that is."

"You shouldn't be thinking about that, Jensy. It's just going to bring you down." Her hand trembled as she set the paper on his desk. She knew exactly where it went.

"Did they know it was over?"

"Please, don't."

"I'm sorry. It just hasn't got any easier." She turned away.

He rose from his chair. "You know our health plan covers therapy."

But with some rapid taps she was gone. *Therapy* was a stupid thing to say. But she wasn't cutting it. She wasn't hardening. Maybe he shouldn't encourage her to stick it out. Maybe there was no point at which she would adapt. Maybe that was a good thing.

At five o'clock, having somehow evaded the long arm of HR, Raphael said goodnight to the crew, avoiding eye contact with Dreemont. He exited Norval, skated through the museum grounds, and then rolled down Sixth Street to buy takeout at the Thai restaurant on the corner of La Brea.

At his kitchen table, he dipped into the flat noodles, simultaneously checking his email. To his delight, there was a message from Addy.

Hey Raphael,

Pink loves her new laptop. She says thanks, and to tell you she'll be working on your question. I enjoyed our *tour* of the museum.

See you Thursday.
Addy

His heart leaped; he replied with a thousand-words of anticipation reduced to ten.

After he finished eating, he rinsed his plate, letting the water splash and splash until he finally turned it off and stuck the plate into the washer. He put a record on his bedroom turntable and did a ridiculous dance, but his hand kept slipping to his coin pocket. The record still spinning, he returned to the kitchen, drew out the thumb drive and held it at arm's length. Stealing entombed data—any data under Norval's control—was grounds for termination. He should bury it in a concrete coffin.

After pacing the kitchen for ten minutes, he pressed his forehead to the refrigerator, seeking a good vibration to drive away the confused feelings about the hunt for Klaes. In its oblique way, the message from Klaes promised a path to freedom, which made his heart light. But the message couldn't exist for Raphael's benefit. It had a hidden purpose, out of which might come dreadful things. Was Raphael unwittingly turning the key that opened Pandora's Box? That possibility chilled and unsteadied him. Close the case, he told himself. Get on with your painting. Learn new skate tricks and pursue Addy.

He pushed away from the fridge and wandered into his mother's bedroom, where her scent seemed to rise from the bedclothes. It was just his memory, of course. On the walls of her room hung dozens of her small abstracts, compositions of color, form, shape, and line with no reference to the world. Art to escape the world.

In the photos of his mother as a girl and young woman, she was slender, almost thin, and willowy. She told him that as a girl she was cautious, didn't like sports or strenuous activities. Her instincts preceded any signs of the disease, which first revealed itself as a bump on her big toe. The bump wouldn't go away, but the doctors assured her it was nothing serious.

A muscle on the right side of his mother's neck revealed the doctors' misdiagnosis. The muscle controlled turning the head from side to side. At first she thought she had turned her head too swiftly. She had strained something. And then, as with her toe, she recognized no amount of ice or heat could make the swelling go away. How stiff and solid that muscle got. And eventually the mirrored muscle too changed, toughened, until like its twin it became as hard as a cowboy's saddle. As the *not serious* disease progressed, her head movements lost fluidity and range, refused her commands.

You see, Raphael, it starts with one little bump on the big toe, but then jumps to the head and then progresses from the top down, just as the fetus develops its bones in the womb.

We're sorry, Jayne. It's the Stoneman disease: Fibrodysplasia ossificans progressive, the progressive hardening of the body's fibrous tissue. With every minor injury …

A bumped shoulder that would normally result in no more than a bruise would set in motion the genetic mechanism that turned muscle, tendon, and ligament into bone. There was no cure. Eventually, all the organs of the body would become one organ. Even skin became skeleton. In the end, the lips may move a little, and then they, too, are still.

He was four when he got his first hint of his mother's disease. He'd been with her at the museum, in a room next to her office, sketching. The door was not completely closed, and he heard her speak with a coworker.

"Yes, like King Tut. But I'll be mummified while I'm alive."

"You're serious, Jayne?" asked the co-worker.

"Yes, a mummy, and then …"

Her office door closed.

He'd turned over the sheet of paper with the half-formed, red lion and drew—what? His mother's face?

He'd seen the mummy exhibit. How could his mother turn into one of those? That evening, after they'd returned home, he asked her to tell him about the mummy thing he'd overheard, but she assured him it was nothing to worry about. But worry he did. In the days following he asked her repeatedly, sometimes confusing the word mummy with mommy. She pretended not to hear his questions or worse told him he was too young to understand, which was true only to a point. He knew something terrible was going to happen to her, something he could do nothing about.

Toward the final stage of her disease, she told him that when he was a toddler, she applied lotion daily to his feet and meticulously inspected each toe. With perhaps the Rubens tapestry of Thetis and Achilles in mind ("but I didn't hold you upside down, Raphy!"), she would bathe his feet in basins of Epsom salts nightly. But his toes remained straight, and all the joints were there. He showed no signs of the disease. She had been reluctant to have him tested for the genetic marker, for there was neither cure nor treatment, but she relented. He was unmarked. In her relief, she let him skateboard, and so he skateboarded to elementary, and then middle and high school, the same private school on the south side of Beverly. He learned tricks. She didn't like his cuts and bruises, but she liked to see them heal. Flesh turning back into flesh.

But don't go too far, Raphy. If I yell, I want you to hear me.

He lifted her pillow, drew it to his chest, and buried his face in the fabric, living for a moment in the memory of his mother's scent.

When he returned to the kitchen, he logged onto Facebook and saw the email from Alicia Fallow, Miranda's friend and the host of the party at which she died.

Got yer mesage. Hey, it was 1 crazy night #;) That guy mighta ben there, can't say 4-sur. Lotta strangers there, online party y'know. 2 drunk santas! Musta ben late, y'know, the Miranda thing, RIP :(Maintenance man came, electrician maybe, checking for long or shorts? Kinda old, didn't look like the guy in you pic. Why'd you want 2 know?

He messaged her.

Sorry, Alicia, I can't discuss the reasons for my request. Company policy :-(If you can think of anything else, please let me know.

She messaged him back.

Alicia: What was yer name again?
Raphael: Raphael.
Alicia: TMNT!
Raphael: TMNT?
Alicia: Teenage Mutant Ninja Turtles—Leonardo, Donatello, Michelangelo & Raphael!
Raphael: LOL. Something like that.
Alicia: Now you think I'm weird. 3:-)
Raphael: No, not at all. Thanks for your help, Alicia.
Alicia: My dad was a big fan—collected all their stuff.
Raphael: That's cool. Thanks again.
Alicia: No prob. How old btw?
Raphael: 26
Alicia: Not as old as i thought ;-)
Raphael: Why did I seem old? :-(
Alicia: Yer spelling is perfec. No offence!!!
Raphael: No prob gtg.

Yes, twenty-six, Alicia. Going on twenty-seven.

Twenty-seven in ten days. *Run.*

Raphael held the reluctant cursor over the Klaes folder until his breathing steadied and fingers stilled. *Information embezzling.* He laughed to himself. He didn't care. He gazed at the file names for several minutes, then willed a finger to click "canine02."

Two thick-necked, barrel-chested young men wearing identical trapper hats, one red, one blue, flanked a medium-sized pit bull, its muzzle in the dirt. Each man held a knife in one hand and a dark brown triangle in the other. Ears.

The dog poised with shame, and its shame was the most difficult aspect of the photo to handle. The two young men appeared emotionless, less human than the dog.

He swallowed back the bitter juice that rose in his throat. He could be stoic in the face of a hundred deaths, but a mutilated dog got to him. It was innocence, he supposed. Children and beasts were guilty of nothing. Shades of Klaes.

He opened up "canine03", an apparent selfie of Trapper Red at his desktop. How did this connect?

Klaes had messaged Miranda. Miranda died. Klaes had messaged Troy-Boy to accuse him of dog mutilation—Trapper Red had to be Troy-Boy—threatened to be killed for his mutilation of dogs and history, whatever that meant.

Had Troy-Boy died too? Who the hell was Troy-Boy? Aside from the contents of the photo itself, there was nothing other than a JPEG number to go on.

At Norval there was facial recognition software on par with the FBI's. He didn't relish returning to the scene of his crime, but he'd be kidding himself to believe the puzzle would release him.

It was 9:30 p.m. when he wheeled his skateboard under his desk, put the thumb drive into the Norval computer, and brought up the photo. Within the photo recognition program, he loaded the database of images similar to Trapper Red. There were fifty. He went through the images, eliminated half, then went through putting the original image side-by-side with the database photos. He ended up with four that could be Red or his identical twin. He copied and pasted each photo and its ID into a new file. Two of the men were from Virginia. One from Louisiana and one from Texas.

He ran each name through a search engine. Each had another one hundred people with the same name, some well-known, others obscure. He tried them with "crime" in the search engine. Twenty names came up. Going through the names, he sought any associated with dogfighting charges. None fit. He went through the next name, the third, and the fourth. The fourth name was Troy-Boy Tolover, a resident of Richmond, Virginia. The police had arrested Troy-Boy in May three years ago on charges of staging a dog fight. They listed his age as forty-five.

On the second search of the obit database, the name came through. Troy-Boy Tolover of Richmond, Virginia, had passed away on January 16. Raphael put the terms in a search engine. He found the story in *The Richmond Landlight*. While Tolover slept, one or more of his own pit bulls had mauled him to death. The animals had then gotten out of the house, and authorities were still trying to round them up.

Raphael set his foot on the skateboard, nudging it back and forth.

Klaes had warned two people they would pay for their selfie-age documentation of cruelty and soon after, they died. An email from Jason Klaes was a pin in a voodoo doll.

The fourth message. It was the oddball one that demanded something of the recipient, the CEO of Winstrum Pharmaceuticals, Gerard Van Pelt. The subject was "Symtara." He read the message again and then searched Symtara: *an enzyme replacement for children older than three who suffer from Batten disease.* He searched Batten disease: *a rare and fatal autosomal recessive neurodegenerative disorder beginning in childhood.*

Raphael had yet to see anything in the media about Van Pelt, a major player in Big Pharma. He searched anew and got 500,000 results for Van Pelt. The fifth down was an article titled "Van Pelt Announces Reduction in the Price of Symtara."

Had to be a coincidence. There was no way in hell a single message from Klaes, or whoever was pretending to be Klaes, could have influenced a Van Pelt. Then again, Van Pelt was apparently alive, and Miranda and Troy-Boy were dead.

Mussorgsky's waltz played on Raphael's phone. It was a photo message from Alicia. The photo showed a party in progress. The text read:

Weirdest thing happened!!!!!!! i got a Bangagram from Miranda 1 hour ago some panky D:< here it is

He considered the photo Alicia had forwarded.

Similar to Miranda's other selfies, this one showed her clutching a *possum*, which did indeed look dead.

Had someone altered a photo on her blog to taunt him?

The windowpanes rattled at a sudden change of air pressure as the department door opened. Raphael slammed the X on the facial recognition program, but instead of disappearing, the screen froze. A minty scent filled his nostrils. He swiveled in the seat, masking the monitor with his back. Maglio stood at the entrance to the cubicle.

CHAPTER
FOURTEEN

R aphael gaped at Maglio's artificial left eye, which shimmied in its socket. *Don't stare.* Digits flowed out of the pupil, spread across the iris and sank into filmy white. *Don't stare.* The eyeball locked in place, the digits vanished, and the two eyes aligned.

"I didn't expect to see you here," said Maglio.

Raphael found his voice. "Finishing up some undeclareds I didn't get to this afternoon."

Maglio peered down his nose. "Not Klaes."

"Oh, no. Run-of-the-mill undeclareds." Heart stuttering, Raphael shifted to the right in the chair, blocking Maglio's view of the monitor. If Maglio had forgiven him for storming his office, he wouldn't forgive direct defiance of his order to seal the Klaes case. This could cost Raphael his job. He pressed his filmy hands together. Just breathe.

"Oh, Maisie," called Maglio, glancing away for an instant, just enough time for Raphael to check the monitor and spot the incriminating five letters. *K-L-A-E-S.* Raphael repositioned himself and spread out his elbows.

"Please come here a second, Maisie. I want you to meet one of our bright young End Men."

Behind Maglio, a tall slender woman with a boy-band's haircut, a shimmer skirt, and a bandy top peered into Raphael's cubicle. It was the woman who had been in Maglio's office.

"Raphael, I want you to meet Maisie Sparod."

Maisie Sparod. An odd name, but not one that he had run across among the dead. He pondered the name for a moment, and a website came to mind: The Physicists' Commons. *Sparod.* Lily Faraday's *bête noir.* That was an odd coincidence.

As if on a catwalk, Maisie swung her hips as she entered the cubicle. Her musky perfume, with a note of ripe cherries, devoured Maglio's mint. She gazed at Raphael with an expression of recognition, but he didn't think it was one based on their earlier chance meeting. She saw him differently now. Better that be the focus than the telltale screen. He prepared to accept the Young Bowie comparison with feigned appreciation and modest denial, but she said a cool nothing.

Maglio sniffed. "Maisie is the director of Weblock."

Weblock ran all the Commons' sites and was a formidable force in cyberspace. What was she doing at Norval?

"Raphael?" said Maglio.

Raphael jerked up his head. "Oh, sorry."

Maglio and Maisie stared at him, Maisie extending her hand, that once forbidden gesture. Pushing back the chair though continuing to block the monitor, Raphael rose, and took the weightless fingers.

"Nice to meet you, Raphael."

"Same here," he said as her hand withdrew, fingertips shining with his sweat. She gazed at him and waited. For what? *Be cool.* Maglio didn't seem pissed with him. *Christ, be one of the guys.* He attempted a knowing smile. "Financial giants dividing up the world?"

"Oh, lots of things are in the works." Maglio nudged Maisie.

"Anything you can reveal?" Raphael asked.

"We used to say, 'I could tell you, but then I'd have to kill you.' We don't say that anymore. It's become a cliché. Nonetheless, its point is valid."

Raphael glanced away. "Ah ... right."

Maglio considered him. "No, Raphael, nothing to reveal tonight." Maglio exchanged a conspiratorial wink with Maisie. "But, let's say, *don't blink.*"

Maisie again locked eyes with Maglio. "I'm sure Mr. Maglio will keep you in the loop."

Yeah, I'm sure he will.

"Raphael, would you join us for a dinner at Corel's?" asked Maglio.

What the hell is this about? The capo's kiss? Raphael tugged his T-shirt. "I'm not dressed."

"Oh, this is LA. Less is more in fashion if you can glint. Can you glint?" Maglio gripped Raphael's shoulder, and the CEO's eyes shone hard and penetrating, the artificial no less glinty than the natural.

"I, uh, don't think I can do that."

Maglio grinned. "I'll glint for you. In any case, we can't have our End Men burning the midnight oil—all the time. They'll work themselves to death. Close up shop, and we'll meet you in front of the building."

As they strode off, Raphael took his first full breath in several minutes and peered down at the screen, which had gone black. He'd dodged a bullet, but was there another in the chamber?

Dinner at Corel's and on Maglio's tab? Yet it might be nothing more. Ten-minute walk east on Fairfax, a little more small talk on the way. An exotic drink and the run of the menu. No, it had to be more than that. Still, Maglio hadn't caught him researching Klaes, and Raphael's attempted storming of the citadel was maybe less heinous than he'd feared. A whimsical treat for a valuable employee? Raphael banged his knuckles together. No, something was up. But best to play along with it.

Parked in front of the building on Wilshire was a violet-colored Whale limousine, one of the new retros. The chauffeur held open the door, beckoning Raphael to join Maglio and Maisie, who peered out at Raphael from the seat.

Raphael's legs went rubbery.

Sitting in the car meant crossing his boundary. Getting above

Wilshire. He couldn't do it. *Be diplomatic. Descend to the sidewalk, approach, and propose an alternative.*

He forced himself toward the open door.

Someone whispered in his ear: *wind.* The word echoed inside his head and grew louder with each repetition. The thunderous word escaped from his mouth and hurled itself upon him as a violent blast from the boulevard. *Wil-shire!* it roared. It swept before it leaves, papers, and plastic cups. Sand carried from a distant beach pelted his face and arms. The trees screamed, and the queen palms bent their crowns to the sidewalk. Soon a dozen would uproot and fly into him, slam the hell out of him.

Raphael dropped the skateboard and clapped his ears to quiet the roar.

"What are you doing, Raphael? Come on. Get in."

Maglio's voice was a whisper under the gale. Raphael took a wider stance as if finding his ground in an earthquake.

"I ... can't," said Raphael in a painful gasp.

Maglio and Maisie exchanged puzzled glances. The chauffeur scratched his head. Raphael backed up a yard and then two. The wind died. The queen palms straightened. The leaves and wrappers settled. Calm had slipped back, and once again the boulevard was the boulevard. The museum's brilliant lights reflected off the glossy Whale. Raphael held up the skateboard and found his voice.

"I'll skateboard there and meet you."

"Don't be silly," called Maglio as Raphael pushed off. Christ, what a weirdo they'd take him for. But Norval didn't terminate for oddness. Sometimes a cigar is just a cigar. Sometimes.

Turning from Wilshire onto Fairfax, he sifted through excuses for foregoing dinner and returning to the office. All would entail a lie, now or later. Feeling eyes upon him, he glanced about. Fifty feet away, a big, rough-and-ready Blank-type holding a can of spray paint glared at him. Spray paint, always spray paint. Blanks must be born with aerosols in their little wrinkly fists, first word not mama or dada but fuck data.

Raphael dropped the skateboard and pushed off toward the

Farmers Market, which he would walk through to the Grove, the outside mall housing Corel's.

As he entered the market, the vendors were shutting their stalls for the night. In the little bar catering to the Karaoke crowd on Thursday, the bartender was down to one elderly woman customer, her head bent over a half-drunk glass of red wine. A few feet away stood the stage, with its microphone stand, speakers, and DJ booth. He imagined the ebullient DJ, the crowd of roaring fans, and the hopefuls lined up to sing their chosen songs, their faces taut, lip-syncing the lyrics while drawing up saliva.

When Addy would line up, she was never fearful. She'd hold the microphone and accept the applause as though she'd been doing it for eternity. As he lingered outside the bar, he heard her voice, and his heart doubled its beat.

"Raphael?"

Man, that sounded real. He clapped his ear.

"Hey, Raphael."

He pivoted in the voice's direction. Twenty feet away stood Addy. He blinked. Not an illusion. "Addy!"

She jumped back as if his shout had pushed her. Grinning, she walked toward him. "Hey, what are you doing here? You know it's not Thursday, right?"

He glanced at the stage, then back at Addy, who'd halted within arm's length. She wore green scrubs and tennis shoes. She'd braided her hair and tipped it with a rainbow-colored chastity ball. He looked at her, and all his trepidation about the dinner vanished. He felt whole; as if cracked, he had been put back together. "Oh, no—I'm having dinner with my boss."

She smiled. "Lucky you."

"Yeah, Corel's." He pointed through the Farmers Market's long main aisle toward the Grove and the restaurant.

"Hope he's buying. That place is super-expensive."

The idea sprung into his head fully realized. "Karaoke Thursday! We can go to Corel's after you sing. To celebrate, you know? My treat. I mean, unless that would be sexy or something."

Addy squinted. "Sexy?"

"*Sexy?* Oh, no—I meant sexist."

Addy tilted her head, so that the steel ball swung. "I was about to give you a chastity belt."

Raphael backed up, widening his eyes clownishly. "You ever use that?"

"With one whack, I've saved the chastity of several young men. Want to see how it works?"

"Pass. Corel's, yes or no?"

"Oh ... okay. No! I mean yes. *Yes.*"

Raphael's heart swelled and his body swayed. *Don't stare as if stunned. Lighten up. You've done it, now make conversation.* Another voice whispered in his head, *Raphy, you're late for dinner.* Dinner could wait. He swallowed. "So what are you doing here? Aren't you working?"

"I was heading for Starbucks to get some midnight snacks on my break. Dumb me forgot my phone. Like they say, 'Out of phone, out of apps, out of luck.' So, I've got to go back."

"Hey, I've got plenty." He dug out his wallet.

"No, no," said Addy, touching his hand. "It will take me ten minutes."

"A waste of your break time. You know"—he leafed through his billfold—"I've got this Starbucks card that must be good for fifty dollars." He slipped out the gift card from Stull. "Better get the barista to see how much is on it though."

"Well, okay." She took the card. "I'll pay you back on Thursday. You want to come with me to the cafe?"

"I do, but ..." He looked toward Corel's.

"Your boss is waiting. You've got to go."

It was the last thing in the world he wanted to do, but he nodded and took a step backwards. "Goodnight, Addy."

"Goodnight, Raphael. See you Thursday."

Sighing, he turned and continued on to Corel's.

DESPITE THE HOUR, the restaurant bustled with fashionably dressed and undressed customers. As Raphael scanned the tables for Maglio and Maisie, a foursome in bright skimpies stumbled past him laughing and dismissive of somebody. He glinted.

"May I help you?" asked a server.

"Oh, I'm dining with Mr. Maglio."

"Ah. This way."

"We thought you'd gotten lost," said Maglio, as Raphael took a seat at the table. Maisie held up her cocktail.

Nothing threatening yet. Relax.

A server approached and bent to Raphael. "Your drink order, sir?"

"Oh, a Stella, I guess."

The waiter nodded, straightened, and retreated.

"I'm famished," said Maisie.

Maglio held up a finger. "Hold on there, waiter. We'll want some appetizers."

"What do you recommend, Geo?" asked Maisie.

"Everything's good. *Fabulous*, in fact."

Raphael scanned the menu and swallowed hard. The prices were outrageous, but the smells: rosemary, saffron, drawn butter—*Oh, I'm not that hungry, Addy. You get whatever you want.* He looked up and around. The restaurant's design was so cool. That little table in the corner would be perfect.

"Sir?" said the waiter.

"Oh, yes. Sorry. I'll have, um ..." He scanned the dozens of appetizers.

"Give our young man this," said Maglio, turning his menu toward the server and tapping an item.

The server took their orders and scurried away. They sat in silence for a moment, Maglio's and Maisie's eyes on him. A moment later, Raphael's beer arrived.

Maisie put her hand under her chin. "Why were you afraid to get in the car?"

His shoulders stiffened. An alarm went off. Raphael sipped the beer, flipping through his cover stories to choose the blandest. "I wasn't afraid. I sit all day. It's exercise."

"You said *can't*." Maisie tapped her lip. "You could have, couldn't you?"

Raphael's chest tightened. *I felt sick. I forgot to walk my—*

"Perhaps Raphael shuns luxury vehicles. I see some proletariat in our young worker."

"Tantalizing," said Maisie. "A Jacobin? Down with the system?"

Raphael shook his head. "No, I'm not political."

The waiter brought the appetizers.

"Wow, quick," said Raphael.

"Only for Mr. Maglio," said the waiter, distributing the dishes.

For Raphael, Maglio had suggested grilled Lake Tahoe shrimp stuffed with garbanzo beans and nettles. Raphael examined the dish set before him. It was interesting, different, with a muddy water smell.

"May I get you anything else?"

Maglio waved the wait staff away, then changed the cool gesture into beckoning. "Please, dig in."

Maisie's eyes glittered, and her head dipped and swayed over her dish. She hadn't pressed him. What did she care, anyway?

Raphael searched for the appetizer's advertised shrimp. Failing to find a single one, he forked up the rest of the ingredients, which tingled on his tongue. Something had to be off. Maglio would from time to time tour the Necrology Department, exchanging small talk with the End Men, but he didn't extend dinner invitations. Maisie Sparod. Weblock. Web sites and advanced software. Did Maisie have anything to do with the droves of programmers showing up at Norval? He took a chance on gentle probing.

"Is your company working with ours?" asked Raphael.

"Consulting," answered Maisie.

"Cool. What kind?"

"Let's not get into that," said Maglio, eyes narrowing.

There were several minutes of silence as they finished their appetizers. Raphael avoided making eye contact with Maisie.

"Tell us about Jason Klaes," said Maglio.

Raphael coughed and tapped his neck. "Garbanzo bean," he rasped. Clearing his throat, he leaned toward Maglio. "Excuse me?"

"What's your take on Klaes?"

Careful. "You entombed Jason Klaes," said Raphael as if to remind Maglio of his own order. He glanced at Maisie.

"I know," said Maisie. "At Weblock, we purge. Entombment is charming."

Maglio speared a stuffed mushroom. "Raphael took a keen interest in Mr. Klaes."

"Klaes was a potential possum, which means—"

"Someone fakes their death," said Maisie.

"Yes, right," said Raphael. "He's entombed. We're not supposed to discuss him."

"I'm making an exception. Is he alive or dead?" asked Maglio.

Raphael looked away. What game were they playing? His stomach pulsed. The beans? The nettles? "I'm not sure."

Maglio speared another mushroom. "Why do you think I closed the case?"

"My supervisor told me—"

Maglio's forehead screwed up in annoyance. "The file you discovered."

"Personality—"

"That file would have done to the Norval database what the locusts did to Egypt." Maglio inhaled, then asked, "Do you know your Bible?"

"No, I don't."

Zeroes and ones flashed on Maglio's left eye. "'Locusts covered the face of the whole land, so the land was darkened, and they ate all the plants in the land and all the fruit of the trees the hail had left. Not a green thing remained, neither tree nor plant of the field, through all the land of Egypt.' Exodus 10:15."

"Jesus."

Maglio's left eye enlarged as if it might pop out of its socket.

"Your Klaes," said Maisie, leaning into Raphael, "wanted to destroy Norval. Geo had me run the file by Weblock engineers who specialize in corporate sabotage."

Hard hot thumbs pressed on Raphael's temples. "I worked my ass off to find that file. If Klaes wanted me to ..." *Oh, fuck.*

Maglio grabbed Raphael's wrist. "Your Jason Klaes played you. He wanted you to find that file, but not too easily."

Raphael's insides dropped. He had seen not a hint. Possums had tried to trick and manipulate him, but never in this way. Dig deep. Finish your painting. Find me. All to hack Norval? Some Digital Luddite spray painting FUCK DATA on the corporate enterprise. His head wanted to explode. "But why would he sabotage us? Just to remain an undeclared?"

Maglio released Raphael's wrist, lifted his drink, and drained it. "Klaes has or *had* his own agenda. We have ours. Perhaps you see now why we removed you from the case and had Klaes entombed."

Raphael's chest tightened. Damn thumb drive. He hoped to hell Matt's assurances were solid. "Sure. No sense taking chances."

Maisie nodded. "Your Klaes tried to take down Weblock too." She tapped a finger to her lips. "I'm not shedding tears over Klaes's offing himself. Too bad it didn't happen a little later."

Later? Why later? Why not *sooner* if she detested him?

"Now, is Klaes dead or alive?" demanded Maglio.

Raphael drew his hand across his forehead, hot and slippery. "He committed suicide. Blew his brains out."

Maglio nodded. "I know what the coroner reported, and I know what the world believes, but you're the one who hunted him."

"My research wasn't complete."

"At the point at which you stopped, which way were you leaning?"

"I had much more to—"

Maglio leaned into him. "Best guess."

"It's not something I want to make guesses about."

"We want to protect our companies for the foreseeable future," said Maisie.

Why did Maglio care about his opinion? Raphael shook his head. "I don't know."

Maglio sat back. "Well, Raphael, finish up your appetizer and leave.

Then see human resources tomorrow. You've been a fine employee, and it will be sad to lose you."

Swaying as if punched in the face, Raphael clasped the table's edge. "You're firing me?"

"Your attempt to break into my office was gross insubordination, which warrants termination."

"You can't do that," Raphael insisted, his head throbbing as he tried to come up with an argument that would underpin his words: loyal employee, momentary lapse, never ever do it again. All excuses were feeble and crumbled before the certainty Maglio could do that.

"Under other circumstances, I'd let it go with a slap on the wrist. However, Norval is about to announce a technological achievement that will not only put us on the map but be the map." Maglio paused, wiped his lips with the napkin. "I don't want Jason Klaes throwing a fucking monkey wrench into the works. Do you understand?"

Raphael's fingers slipped from atop to under the table. "This sucks, Mr. Maglio." He felt the weight of the table. Lift it, turn the table over. Fuck the job. Fuck the hunt for Klaes.

Maglio leaned forward. "But if you tell me your conclusion about Klaes, I might reconsider." Maglio jabbed his fork into a stuffed mushroom. "These are damned good," he said as he popped the biggest, greasiest one into his mouth. Between bites, he probed Raphael once more. "Jason Klaes—alive or dead? Is he gone?"

CHAPTER
FIFTEEN

Fighting to keep down the appetizer and the main course that followed, Raphael made it to Third Street in time to bend and empty his stomach. Now, staring at the gutter's steaming mess, he wiped his lips and straightened. It wasn't the over-rich dinner—the force feeding of desserts—it was giving in to Maglio: "Klaes died on January 10."

He and Matt had joked a hundred times about handing in their notices, but when the untethering was real, Raphael had been flat out scared, imagining himself unable to pay his rent, evicted from the Tar Tower, out on the street, another of the teeming homeless.

But more than losing the job, it was a second fear.

To pursue Klaes required Norval's technology. Klaes's message to him may have been manipulation, but he clung to the promise: find me, complete your painting, be free of your phobia. To survive without that hope was unthinkable. He didn't know which side of the river the physicist stood upon, but he lied and told Maglio, "Klaes is dead."

"He's gone then?" persisted Maglio.

"Yeah, gone."

"Well, then, we can forget about human resources. Drink up! Finish your appetizer and order dinner."

Their table was soon the loudest, happiest party in Corel's. He had jumped into a metaphorical bed with Maglio and Maisie.

But why were they so happy? Was it that Klaes had tried to sabotage Norval and Weblock? *Good, the wicked hack is dead!* But they hadn't hinted at Klaes's motivation nor what they hoped to get from him.

Stomach emptied of the tainted fare, he walked west toward Fairfax, too disappointed in himself to skate. He wanted to pace the side streets and alleys of his prison, walk the yard. Wandering for an hour, he halted at the sound of footfalls behind him. Seeking the stalker, he found no one, yet there was the smell in the air of an unwashed body or perhaps a decaying one. Could it be his own? Were his boundaries the enclosure of a casket? The thought sent him in motion again. If he kept moving, if he didn't slow down. Turn and churn. Churn himself into butter.

On Third Street, he approached Pan Pacific Park, whose grassy sloped borders enclosed sports fields and picnic areas. In the center of the park, a group of people held lit phones above their heads as if at a concert. Someone stood on a table and addressed them. Halting on a winding concrete path, Raphael picked up his board. Smelling sulfur, he realized they brandished not phones but lighters, matches, and candles; and that a small fire burned at the crowd's core. The glow of the raised lights and the impassioned faces made his neck tingle. The orator sang out.

"Phones, pads, laptops—toss those four-sided Satans back into the fires which molded and bore them under the eyes of midwives Jobs, Wozniak, and Gates! Let them burn before you pour your mind, spirit, and soul into their voracious maws!" As the crowd drew out their devices and lifted their arms to follow his order, he screamed. "Wait! Wait! Before the performance begins, if you haven't already, take out your batteries. Let's not lose a face or arm."

Fanatics but not insane.

As the people complied with the instructions, the orator raised his hand, "Save a few lithiums."

This was the park he'd come to as a boy with his skateboard, where the man who kept his distance showed him moves and Raphael would try to imitate. He stared back through time at the tall, slender man.

Raphael stiffened at a vibration. He reached into his pocket and touched his phone. It was beeping.

He dropped the board, pulled his gaze from the past, and slipped out his phone. He lifted the hem of his T-shirt, cradled the cell within the fabric to dampen the light—for the crowd below might find his technology offensive, rush him, and tear him apart—and pressed the pulsing message symbol. It was Alicia.

Hey Raphael, Fergot i took couple pics that night. got 1 of the electrician. He's the 1 leaning against the wall and eating a finger sandwich How rude, huh?

Raphael enlarged the photo. The electrician's face sent his heart pounding: square jaw, cracked cheeks and thin lips.

It was the same man who had stood outside the Tar Tower and gave Raphael a cigarette. The man with the channel locks in his waistband and now wearing a full tool belt. Had he been waiting for Raphael?

Was Raphael being surveilled by two men? One always in the shadows, the other in the open. A crafty stalker and an assassin?

A skyboard promoting Godcoin, a new digital currency, floated above the park accompanied by an escort of drones. One zipped toward the assembly, hovering fifty feet above, and then bobbing closer. Shouts came from the crowd.

"Corporate drones shouldn't be doing that!"

"Find rocks and bottles," another yelled. "Get that fucker out of here!"

People bent to the ground for the crude ammunition. The projectiles flew, a couple clunking on the underbelly of the machine, which rose out of range. From a few blocks away came the wail of a siren, and the crowd scattered.

Raphael dropped his board and pushed off.

TWENTY MINUTES later and nearing home, Raphael took out his phone and again viewed the photo of the "electrician." His chest tightened. The guy he'd spoken to outside the Tar Tower had murdered Miranda, so it wasn't a coincidence that he'd shown up at Raphael's apartment building. If Pink were right, and someone was out to kill him, the Electrician was the prime candidate. But why? Was he getting too close to something? The truth about Klaes? If so, Raphael didn't know it himself. From a distance came a shout, a second, then a chorus. In front of the Tar Tower Plaza Medical Building, a crowd had gathered that looked similar to the Blanks at Pan Pacific Park.

"Disburse!" someone ordered over a bullhorn.

What the hell? He set down his board and pushed off. Powerful flashlights revealed twenty people carrying signs. Several police officers were shouting commands.

"Hey," cried a voice.

Raphael kick-stopped and spun to see the Tar Tower's elderly security guard, Albert, behind the wheel of a golf-cart-sized vehicle. "Stay right where you are!" shouted Albert.

"It's me, Albert. Raphael Lennon. Apartment 1127."

Albert braked and jumped out of his vehicle. A beam of light struck Raphael's face. The guard tilted his head one way, then the other. The beam fell to the ground. Albert's eyes lit with recognition, and he grinned.

"Sorry, Mr. Lennon. I thought you were one of those PETA people. Making a ruckus all day outside the Medical Building." A police helicopter appeared above the Tar Tower, wings beating as it descended toward the Plaza. Albert shouted, "Trying to storm Dr. Roar's office. Calling him Dr. Death."

The name seemed familiar. "Dr. Roar?"

"No, Dr. *Royer*," said Albert with a laugh. "The one who shot those baboons."

Baboons? Royer? Raphael caught his breath. The third message: *Dear Dr. Royer, Could you not see the roots of humanity in that family? Prepare to meet your maker. JK.*

It couldn't be, but …

"Here, I'll show you," said Albert, drawing out his phone, tapping twice, then holding up the screen for Raphael. A photo, time-stamped forty-eight hours ago, showed a man in a safari outfit posed with a family of dead baboons: mother, father, boy, and little sister. The sadistic hunter had clumped them together and took a selfie. They looked alive except for the holes in their chests and heads.

The hunter's face seemed like a memory from a dream. "That's Dr. Royer then?"

"Yeah. The 'devil dentist.' Royer posted the photo on Bangagram for his friends. It got reposted elsewhere, then everywhere. Drove people crazy. Those PETA folks have been raising hell all day, and he ain't even in his office. Still over in Africa."

Dentist? Raphael pressed his tongue to his loosened tooth, which set off a ringing—clanging—in his head as if he had pushed a doorbell. He swayed, dizzy with the connection he made.

If Dr. Royer was a dentist in the Medical Plaza, Raphael knew him.

When he had been six or seven, his mother had taken him to the nearby Dr. Royer to treat a decayed baby tooth that wouldn't fall out. The procedure had been bloody, agonizing. Worse, Royer's office itself had terrified him. The mounted heads of a tiger, a wolf, and a rhinoceros had stared down from the wall of the waiting room—fierce guardians of dental health. Seeing this horror, Raphael had pressed his face into his mother's side and begged her to leave.

"Dr. Royer is a hunter," his mom explained. "They're trophies." She patted Raphael's head and whispered, "Grotesque, though."

He didn't know that word but knew scary. "Can't we go to a different dentist?" Raphael asked.

"Dr. Royer is so convenient," she responded. "Don't worry, Raphy, dead things can't harm you."

If the dead animals couldn't, Royer could. The procedure was close to sadistic.

It was impossible his Dr. Royer was one of Klaes's targets. Could there be another Dr. Royer who hunted? But *family* was used in Klaes's threat. He had killed a family of baboons. What had been Sherlock's famous dictum? Impossible—yes: when you have eliminated the impossible, whatever remains, however improbable, must be the truth. The scientist lived in Los Angeles, perhaps Klaes had been a patient or known someone who had gone to Royer. Klaes and Royer made sense. The random element was Raphael. *Chance, just chance. Accept it and move on.*

The helicopter descended upon the crowd, propellor whacking, lights flashing. Raphael drew in fumes of spent jet fuel. "Disburse, disburse."

Raphael shielded his eyes from the light. "You know when he's supposed to return?"

The guard shook his head. "Exactly what those protestors been asking. I'm pretty sure, he's going to keep low when he gets here."

A selfie with a dead swan. A selfie with slaughtered apes. A selfie with a mutilated dog. Two of the three warned were dead. He recalled his question to Mirsky and Mirsky's response. "Cruelty. Hurt a child or an animal, and your name went down in Klaes's black book."

The photo of the dead baboons made him sick, but he should warn Royer before Klaes fulfilled his threat.

"You know where Royer lives?"

Albert grinned. "You don't know?"

Raphael shrugged.

"I can't reveal that, but let me say, take Paul Simon's advice. Well, likely you don't even know who Paul Simon is, not to mention Garfunkel." The guard got back into his vehicle and glided off, laughing under his breath.

Raphael glanced up at a passing police drone, back-lit by the midnight moon. As with most seniors, Albert referenced the music of his youth to make vague yet tantalizing points. Raphael's mother had been a fan of Paul Simon and would play the artist's music. Advice?

What was his song about a bridge? He shrugged and then gazed at the moon.

Or was it about the myriad ways to break a relationship?

Their songs had a lot of wise counsel, if only there was one about breaking out of a phobia.

He would leave a message on Royer's phone, if it was taking messages.

CHAPTER
SIXTEEN

With his heel, Raphael rolled the skateboard back and forth under the desk. The wheels ticked against the hardwood floor: nicks in the polyurethane. It was a hard, durable material, still, in time the accumulated nicks became a gash. The board slowed and wobbled. A bad ride.

He pushed up from the chair, scanned the floor for Dreemont, and went to Matt's cubicle. As Raphael entered, Matt slammed his top drawer shut and spun toward him.

"Jesus," said Matt, face coloring. "I thought you were Dreemont. What's up, man? You get your gross insubordination straightened out? Back on the Klaes train?"

"Maglio's entombed Klaes for good."

"Wow. You must have screwed up, roly-poly."

"It's *royally*. How did you—ah, never mind. I didn't screw up. There's something wrong that I can't get my head around. It's like those word problems in algebra two. At first they seem clear, but when you try to solve them, they get all murky and stop making sense."

Matt yawned.

Raphael grabbed the chair and yanked Matt toward him. "Pay attention, huh?"

Matt tilted back his head. "A wheel fall off your skateboard or something?" He scratched his chin with blackened fingertips.

"What's with your fingers?" asked Raphael.

Matt glanced at his hand. "Oh, my club."

"Fortnite Anonymous?"

Matt rubbed his fingertips together. "No, not that. I joined the Musketeers Club."

"Which is?"

"Fans of Elon Musk's unfinished projects. We explore all the tunnels Musk started under the city. I'll bet you didn't know there's one straight down, runs past the Salt Lake Oil field." Matt pointed a blackened finger toward the floor, where his unicorn emblazoned sneakers too showed signs of the underground. "Next month, it's Hyperloop crawling. Hey, what were you saying about algebra two?"

"Did you ever have time to check those entombed possums? The Carson Fullers case. You know, the possum who got killed in Argentina? Did you find a reassignment alert for him?"

"Nope."

"That's a problem. How about the morbidity projection? Any other likely dead possums?"

"They're all dead," replied Matt.

"What are you talking about?"

Matt shrugged. "Maybe not *all* dead."

"Are you messing with me?" asked Raphael.

"Some are dead," said Matt.

"How many?"

"Three."

"Three? Three is not all."

"All I could do a workaround on. I couldn't penetrate entombment, even with all my *wizardly devices.*"

"Three counting Fullers?" asked Raphael.

"Three plus Fullers. Four."

Raphael closed his eyes and plucked at his forehead as if to pull out a thought. "We're given leads on people who might or might not be dead. We find some are truly dead and others are faking it, hiding out in Argentina or something. But—"

Matt nibbled on his lower lip. "The living possums are now dead?"

Right, or at least four were. What were the odds the three chosen out of a hat of hundreds were dead? The original puzzle had been inverted. From not enough dead to too many dead. "How did they die?"

"Violently," replied Matt.

Mussorgsky played on Raphael's phone. He glanced at the screen. Jan Olmstead. *The Children's Love Fund.*

"I've got to take this," said Raphael. "We'll talk about this later, okay?"

"No problem," said Matt, opening the drawer and rooting through his candy dump.

Raphael dashed to his cubicle and accepted the call.

"Hello," he said, sitting.

"This is Jan Olmstead with the Children's Love Fund. Is this Raphael? You called about a donation?"

Keeping an eye on the cubicle entrance as he whispered, "No, sorry. I'm calling about"—a wisp of a whisper—"Jason Klaes."

"Oh," she said, followed by silence.

"Then you've heard."

"I'm not sure I—do you work for Dr. Klaes?"

It should have been *did.* "I'm sorry to tell you this but Jason Klaes has passed away."

Silence. "Who are you? Are you a reporter?"

"No, I'm just …" An End Man? "I'm a friend. I know Dr. Klaes contributed to your fund."

"Jason's dead?" asked Jan in a quavering voice.

"Yes. He died on January 10."

"January—how?"

Raphael hesitated, uncertain he believed the words he had to say. "He took his own life."

"My God. How terrible. They've been trying to contact him."

"They? Who are you—"

"About his godchild. Angie Murie."

The names of the dead and the living appeared in his head like stars coming out at night. Among the countless lights which one was Angie Murie? One grew brighter. He squeezed his phone. "She was the little girl in the cryonic chamber, wasn't she?"

"I'm not sure I should be ..." The phone was silent for a few seconds. "Someone has taken her."

"I don't understand."

"From her chamber. It's so horrible. Unthinkable. I don't know how Jason will—but Jason Klaes is dead. Jesus."

Raphael pressed his thumb into his temple. "It's true. Dr. Klaes has passed. I don't know what to say."

"Sometimes there's nothing," said Jan, her voice thin and distant.

"When did it happen? I mean when was Angie taken?" asked Raphael. He waited for a response.

"Angie was ..."

The phone went silent. "Hello, are you still there?"

"Sorry, yes. They discovered it last night. They're not sure when the theft took place."

"How the hell—sorry. It seems impossible."

"They hadn't prepared for such a thing."

He closed his eyes. "Listen, Jan." He lowered his voice. "There are questions about Jason's death. Maybe these things could be connected." He glanced behind him, then continued, "It may not be relevant, but please call me if you learn anything else?"

Jan sighed. "Bad news all around."

He closed out the call with Jan. Angie was dead. No one was bringing her back to life. At least not in this century or the next. Maybe five hundred years down the road, when the cryonics company would be long out of business and *its clients discarded.*

Everyday thousands of people die, another dozen in the time taken to consider the number's importance. Why then did the theft of her corpse make him feel ill? He had never known her. She was nothing to him. Except, somehow, she was. He saw her innocence as if it were a face before him. Angie had fallen into that cold sleep believing she would one day wake up. Now even that hope would be taken from her, though she would never feel its loss. But the parents, they would.

In addition to Klaes, would he now be searching for a dead child? He glanced at the recent phone calls and swiped the screen until Mirsky's appeared. He needed to speak with the physicist, run this horror past him—and maybe press Mirsky for more information on this so-called Quantum Looking Glass. Calling, he expected an answering machine.

The phone rang six times and then a whispered, "Hello?"

The voice decidedly wasn't Mirsky's.

"Yes, I'm trying to reach Professor Jonathan Mirsky," said Raphael.

The person on the line took a little breath.

"Is this Jonathan Mirksy's phone?" asked Raphael.

"I'm Jon's sister, Eileen."

"Oh. I see. Is he there?"

"My brother died."

"You're kidding?" Raphael said.

"Do you think I'd fucking joke?" said Eileen in a quavering voice.

Raphael's heart pounded. "I'm so sorry. I didn't—I saw him the other day."

"Are, are you a friend?"

"I only met him once. I just ..."

"He was hit by a car," said Eileen.

"Jesus, how awful."

She sobbed again and then collected herself. "I-I really have to go. The arrangements are being made with Donato's of Glendale if you want more information."

"When did it happen?"

"Last Saturday. Midtown. John was crossing Wilshire."

Raphael envisioned the advancing wall of ice. Building higher and wider, denser and bluer, throwing off shock waves of frigid air.

"I should have—" But the line went dead.

Dreemont poked his head through Raphael's doorway. "You've got your work cut out for you. Big D. The Toobyville Dam."

The PA system screeched, "Stage Three Event. Repeat. Stage Three Event …"

CHAPTER
SEVENTEEN

The Cumulative Clock's digits flashed as the total changed to nine thousand for the first time that year. Seven-hundred and thirty-three dead souls in the dam disaster alone, after the concrete had crumbled and 120,000 acre feet of water burst into the techy town of Toobyville. The second greatest loss of life in California history, topped only by the San Francisco earthquake and fire of 1906 in which three thousand died.

Raphael thought the news of Angie Murie's theft, followed by Mirsky's death, would be the low point of his day, but the Big D was a deep hole, as if stepping into his Fairfax Canyon, plummeting, plummeting, never hitting bottom.

"Is this Mr. Chang ... Oh, Mr. Chang, I want to offer my deepest sympathy ..."

"Of course you need time, Mrs. Chavez. We just want you to know ..."

With his toe, he tapped a wheel on his skateboard and made the polyurethane spin.

The disaster had pushed Klaes out of his head for the first time in days, and maybe that was where he should leave it. Formally off the case and going in circles on his own, he could find no answers, other than concluding some internet-savvy prankster was messing with his brain.

A large trashcan on a dolly, wheeled by a lanky figure dressed in khaki, neared the doorway.

"Burning the midnight oil, huh, Mr. Lennon? You want me to come back?" asked Mr. Lean with a grin and a wink.

"No, no, you're fine," said Raphael, returning to the monitor. He gazed at the day's data. A heavy breath drew his eyes to Lean, who hadn't moved and appeared to be waiting for orders.

"It's okay, Mr. Lean, you aren't disturbing me."

Lean nodded and walked through the cubicle to its trash basket. "Don't know how you fellows do it. Dealing with all those poor dead," said Lean, holding the basket waist high. "I'd go mad."

"It's difficult," he admitted.

Lean nodded and seemed to study the trash. "Dead little boys and girls, someone's son, daughter, wife." The custodian lifted his eyes. "They say God doesn't give people more than they can handle, but he heaps it on sometimes. And right across your desk it comes. Day after day. Hour after hour. No, Raphael, I don't know how you do it."

"Well, Mr. Lean, you've got to deal with ghosts on your nightly rounds," Raphael said, recalling his recent conversation with the custodian. "Can't be pleasant."

Lean sniffed. "Turns me cold, them spirits do."

Raphael glanced at the wall screens. Mindfulness videos—fingers peeling a tangerine, a woman in a sweat suit running an ice cube across her forehead, a child swinging a large leaf—had replaced the Toobyville Dam bulletins. His gaze rose to the bank of CCTV cameras, LED lights darkened. Down once again.

"Have you ever seen any ghosts on the necrology floor?" Raphael asked.

Crossing the cubicle, Lean emptied the small trashcan into the larger. "Nope, never a one. It's down in the basement and up on the third floor I see—and hear—the ghosts."

"Scary."

"The ones in the basement, subtle, they are. A splash or two way down below, a bit of gurgling. Tar ghosts, them. Quiet fellows." Lean's eyes rose to the ceiling. "Third Floor's the worst. Right there in the spooky hallway where the lights never get fixed. Comes out of the Research Department. I'll bet those poor ghosts are complaining. Must be filthy in there."

"Filthy?"

"Won't let me inside to clean. Hush, hush. Off limits. They leave the trash cans outside the door. Stacks and stacks of pizza boxes and leftover Sushi stuff. Smells of low tide, it does."

"What do they look like, these ghosts?" asked Raphael.

"Heat waves, the kind you see on desert roads."

"Can you touch them? Feel them?"

"You think I stick around to shake hands? Ha!" said Lean with a laugh. He considered the trash basket as if a little ghost might lurk within.

"No, I suppose not." Raphael stared at the monitor and the day's victims, new candidates for ghostdom. Behind him came loud scratching. He swiveled to see Mr. Lean drag his nails through the gray bristles of two-day's growth of beard.

Mr. Lean clawed, then stopped. "Most of your kind don't take these things seriously."

"My kind?" asked Raphael.

"Brainy types," said Mr. Lean.

"I'm an IT guy."

"Oh, I know what you think of janitors."

"Custodians," corrected Raphael.

"You'll be calling me a broom engineer next."

Raphael stifled a laugh. Except for Maglio, he liked people who had spent a few years on the earth, set in their ways and words. He found them comforting somehow. He pictured Mirsky shoving money at the stripper, and his lips quivered. The more he thought about the guy, the more he liked him, one of those oddball characters you meet along the way. Raphael's eyes blurred. He wanted to give Mirsky a hug, give someone a hug.

Perhaps reading Raphael's mind, Mr. Lean stepped back, moved his hand to his head and looked away, while running his fingers through thinning white hair.

"Sometimes I have a thought or two," said Mr. Lean. "Maybe some ghosts might be those dead folks you End Men won't leave in peace." He shook his head. "I'm a crazy old man, right?"

Jesus, more guilt. "No, not at all. It's ... Well, what sounds do they make? The ghosts, I mean."

Mr. Lean dug his nails into a deep furrow on his cheek. Raphael sensed the man's eyes penetrating him, seeking sincerity. Mr. Lean blurted, "Sentences don't make no sense and angry baby sounds. Sometimes only names, as if someone's taking roll call. Makes me shiver."

"What names?"

"Oh, nothing's clear, all garbled and muddy." He inverted the trash container, shook it once more and tapped its bottom. "Confused, maybe." Setting the basket to its spot, he gazed at it for a moment, and then made a minor change. "Right?"

"Perfect, Mr. Lean."

The custodian made a final change to the position of the trashcan, then stepped back to view his work with a nod of approval. "Well, I'm finished for this floor." He crossed the cubicle, slipped behind the trashcan, grabbed the dolly's handle, and pushed down with a grunt.

"Night, Mr. Lean."

"Goodnight, Mr. Lennon." He glanced at a youthful man's photo on Raphael's monitor. "Poor bastards. Before their time, my Ruth too, rest her soul. The Lord's plan, I guess."

The dolly squealed for a moment. A rush of air swooshed past Raphael's desk as the office door opened, followed by three squeals more and then silence.

Nearby, a drawer closed as if kicked.

Raphael and Dreemont were the last employees on the necrology floor. The supervisor was closing shop, banging stuff around. Dreemont wanted his big corner office to be as he found it in the morning, which was as it had begun the previous morning. If something had changed, he put things in order noisily, wanting others to notice the efforts, like people who dropped dumbbells and grunted.

Raphael leaned to his right in the chair, opened his eyes, and gazed again at the Cumulative.

The dead came in steadily night and day.

Klaes. Simply thinking his name brought back all the puzzling pieces of the case. The oddball stuff that he couldn't directly link to Klaes, but had to be tied in. The four possums put to rest a second time by violent means—at least according to Matt—seemed relevant. Not just relevant but part of a set that included Klaes, a possum who had murdered among possums who were murdered.

He nudged a second skateboard wheel, sent it spinning to *whirr* with the first. A moment later, he pushed up from the chair and went to Dreemont's office, where the supervisor was cleaning the monitor.

"Hey, Mike."

"What's up, kid?" said Dreemont.

"Got a question about entombed possums."

Dreemont stretched his neck and stuck out his chin. "Yeah, what about them?"

"I came across a news report on one of our possums: Simon DeBove, née Carson Fullers. He, uh, recently died."

"Yeah?"

"We didn't get a reassignment alert."

Mike shrugged. "Intent error maybe. I'll look into it."

"Yeah." He formulated his next inquiry but couldn't catch Mike's eyes. And why was Mike's forehead shining? "There might be other dead possums."

Mike appeared not to hear, but then brought his gaze back to Raphael. "Intent errors aren't isolated. If there's one, there might be a few. Hey, I've got to run." Dreemont gave Raphael a dumb salute. "The automated timer's broken, so don't forget to turn off the lights, kid."

In his cubicle, Raphael leaned back in the chair and stared at the monitor until relieved by a hearty, "Adios, amigo."

"Yeah, adios, Mike."

The office door opened with a squeal and closed with a bang.

He mulled over Dreemont's casual reaction to the missing reassignment alerts and the dead possums. If he had mentioned the improbability of three picked randomly being dead would his supervisor still have yawned? *But his forehead was perspiring.*

Raphael waited another five minutes. He closed his eyes, breathed deeply and methodically. He opened them to see scenes of the day's disaster on his monitor. A headline read "Toobyville Dam Crumbles." A live shot of a freight train toppled from its tracks filled the screen. A reporter holding a microphone walked down the tracks, gesturing extravagantly. Raphael turned up the sound.

"… As if this fifty-car train were a toy, thirty-million tons of water swept it from these rails. The day the To—" The reporter must have caught her foot in a crosstie, for she stumbled forward, catching herself as she cried, "Be ville …"

Raphael's neck tingled as he muttered, "Be ville. *To be ville.*" No, but something close. Pink's cryptic words surfaced: "To be vile." Could she have meant Toobyville? *An Ozark thing.* She pronounced pill as pile, so might she pronounce ville as vile? Was he making a connection where none existed?

If it was Toobyville—if she could know about the dam—what happens in less than thirteen days? *They kill you. Better run.*

He glanced up at the date on the Cumulative Clock. Thirteen days. Eleven days. Eight days now. *Slow down, Raphy. You're confused enough.*

He tilted back his head and scanned the ceiling, the little camera eyes as thick as barnacles on a sunken ship. The CCTV was down.

Stomach fluttering, he went to the supervisor's cubicle, three times as large as Raphael's and well appointed, but a cubicle nonetheless. Two weeks ago, he'd watched over Dreemont's shoulder as the supervisor keyed in the password. Though he hadn't memorized it on purpose, the combination, which conformed to configuration parameters, had intrigued Raphael and offered an easy mnemonic. At

Norval, passwords changed every five weeks. Dreemont probably hadn't changed it yet. Even using the mnemonic, would Raphael remember it?

He stood in the doorway surveying the items on Dreemont's desk, his chair, the angle of the monitor. There wasn't much hardware—retro office phone, sticky pads, sorting tray, etc. He took out his phone and snapped a picture, anyway. He was about to sit, but touching the chair, he froze. Getting the chair in the right position might be tricky. He wouldn't use the chair or move anything on the desk. He bent to power up Dreemont's computer.

The screen went through its ritual. When the password box appeared, he said aloud the memorized digits. "Please be right, neocortex."

He keyed in the password and watched the screen populate.

Good old Dreemont. As far as Raphael knew, only Maglio had access to the entombment files, though Dreemont could have kept some information on Carson Fullers. He inputted the possum's name and leaned on Dreemont's desk as the search results appeared.

Carson Fullers didn't exist on Dreemont's hard drive. *Dead end, Raphy. Time to call it quits.*

Dig deep.

As if of their own will, his fingers typed in another name: Simon DeBove, Fullers's pseudonym. The search located the name in a file designated New Portal Candidates. He opened the file, which contained a list of names extending to the bottom of the screen. DeBove's name was halfway down the list and beside it was a date. He considered the date for a second and realized it was the day on which DeBove received the coup de grace. Above and below DeBove were dozens of other names, whose familiarity escaped him until he recognized several as the pseudonyms of possums once tracked down. What was New Portal?

He glanced at Dreemont's printer, walked over, and powered it up. As the machine came to life, he went to the computer and ordered a print-out of the file. Behind him, a lock clicked.

Raphael froze.

Had a door closed or opened? "Hello?" Taking a long stride, he peered out of Dreemont's office to the department door, which was now shut. Could it have been Mr. Lean coming back for something and changing his mind or a wandering ghost?

Recovering his breath, he took the two pages from the printer, glanced at the sheets, and then folded and slid them into his pocket.

He rushed out of Dreemont's office and got to his own cubicle before remembering.

You're an idiot.

Returning to Dreemont's office, he deleted recent history and hoped his supervisor wouldn't run a security check. He shut down Dreemont's computer and printer. He inspected the supervisor's office and then turned off the department lights.

He opened the office door to a red, wheezing face.

"Come, come," said Mr. Lean, waving his arms.

"What?"

"I'll show you. They're at it."

Raphael sighed.

"You don't believe me?" asked Mr. Lean.

"No, that's not …" Shrugging, he followed the custodian to the open elevator.

"Hurry," said Mr. Lean, bouncing on his toes and slapping his thighs.

Raphael boarded the elevator as Mr. Lean pressed the third-floor button.

On the third floor, he followed Mr. Lean through Ms. Goloda's office. Mr. Lean unlocked the door to the executive area hallway.

"Come on."

As usual, the hallway lights stuttered. He matched Mr. Lean's long strides until they reached the intersecting corridor. Lean twisted and held up a hand for him to stop. Lean cupped his ear, bent his head toward Research and put a finger to his lips.

Raphael moved closer and imitated the custodian's posture as he stared into Lean's face and listened to … nothing.

"Wait," whispered Lean. "You hear it?"

Raphael shook his head.

"You're sure?"

"I hear nothing."

"Funny, me neither."

"Must have finished taking roll call," said Raphael.

Mr. Lean pointed a long forefinger at the ten-digit keypad door lock. His brow creased. "One, seven, seven—damn. They've kept me out so long, I can't remember. One, seven, seven, eight?" Mr. Lean tapped the keys. The door remained locked. "No, then. One, seven, seven, five?"

Raphael patted the custodian's arm. "You don't want to get in trouble, Mr. Lean."

Ignoring Raphael, Mr. Lean tried the combination he'd said out loud. He grunted at the lock's refusal to cooperate. His face scrunched, then lit up. "One, seven, seven, one!" He keyed in the combination, and the lock clicked. Mr. Lean grinned at Raphael and whispered, "Quiet now."

Raphael followed Mr. Lean into Research. A few of the monitors in the stack of one hundred glowed, screensavers mutating into fanciful designs, while the other monitors napped. The awake monitors spread thin light across the front of the facility, which housed much more technology than Raphael had seen on previous visits to the lab. As Mr. Lean had predicted, pizza and takeout boxes rested on the equipment like bright fallen leaves. Aside from the hum of the hard drives, the room was dead quiet: research equipment and its shadows.

"No ghosts," said Raphael.

"Dirty bastards," said Mr. Lean, kicking a pizza box resting on the floor. "Have you ever seen such a mess?"

"We should leave."

Mr. Lean groaned. "Ain't that the way it is? The moment you want something you come across every day, it's gone. You think I'm crazy, don't you?"

"Sane as anyone."

"Mr. Dreemont does. I told him about the ghosts the other night, and he made a crack about Alzheimer's. Told me to keep my wacko notions to myself. Now, I've told you."

"Well, I won't tell anyone," said Raphael, fingering the printout in his pocket. "Your ghosts are safe with me."

CHAPTER
EIGHTEEN

Raphael lay beneath his painting, staring at the glistening oil. A ghost floating by Mr. Lean's nose, the ghost a sprig of titanium white, the nose an obelisk of cadmium red. He placed his hands behind his head and laced them. He wasn't satisfied with his image, but sleep was overtaking him. Enough work for one night, he turned off the lights, climbed down from the scaffolding, and yawned deeply.

Ten minutes later, he flopped onto his bed and closed his eyes, waiting for sleep.

His phone buzzed and then came the fragment of music.

He turned his head to the phone's flashing light. Who the hell would call at two in the morning? But what if it were Addy?

He grabbed the phone and surveyed the screen.

Someone was trying to video chat. *Not Addy*. The disappointment left him awake. Hadn't he turned the phone off? Weird, but no weirder than anything else he'd lately experienced. He accepted the call. A woman's face filled the screen. A double face: a large face spanning the screen and a smaller inset of the face. The inset moved within the larger like a sine wave, disappearing on the right of the screen then reappearing on the left.

The face was Miranda Night Day's, the woman who'd killed a swan for a selfie and plunged from a balcony to her death.

He found his breath. "Hello?"

"Turn on your camera," said a robotic voice.

"Who is this?"

"Turn on your camera or I'll hang up."

"Fuck off," he said, dropping the call.

Raphael pressed the phone to his chest. The hacker had his phone number. Alicia had it too. The number could be all over the world by now. The phone rang again. It seemed to vibrate within him, a buzzing insect had gotten under his skin.

Dig deep.

He accepted the call again. "Yeah, what do you want?"

"Oh, you know, Raphael."

He brought himself up on the selfie camera.

"Happy?" he asked.

"Yes." The voice was no longer robotic. It was a woman's voice, and her lips had moved to form the words.

"Who is this?" asked Raphael.

"Don't you recognize me?" she said, and the screen filled with a dozen tiny photos of Miranda selfies, in each holding an animal.

"I recognize a Miranda simulation," said Raphael.

"I am so offended," said the voice, now deep and gruff, yet somehow feminine.

"Miranda's dead."

The full face returned. She appeared to be studying her phone. The woman's voice resumed. "You're kind of cute. Are you involved? Is it complicated?"

"Yes, complicated. Who are you?"

"You know silly. Miranda."

"Miranda," repeated Raphael, sitting up in bed. She tilted her head, and her features held menace. Anger rising, he twisted and dropped his feet to the floor. "Miranda is dead. Who the hell—"

"Why do you keep wanting me to be dead?" the caller asked.

"I don't want you to be dead. You *are* dead. I mean, Miranda's dead. She fell—or someone pushed her—off a balcony."

"Never happened."

"What do you want?" asked Raphael.

"Another killer selfie," she said with a laugh.

A hundred photos filled the screen. Myriad selfies of Miranda. The photos doubled in number, then doubled again.

"There will never be enough, will there?" said Raphael.

"Oh, how mean!"

"What do you want?"

"*R-E-S-P-E-C-T*," said the caller. "I want you to be my puppy."

His insides chilled. "What are you talking about?"

"A photo, silly."

"You want to choke me to death?"

"Umm."

"Is it you?" he asked, rushing to the bedroom window and bending a blind to peer down on the Tar Tower court. "You're the killer?"

"See you at Karaoke."

Raphael squeezed the phone and his voice quavered. "What did you say?"

"I'll be the one holding the swan."

"Listen, I don't know who or why—"

The call dropped.

He checked recent calls. There were none. It was impossible. Powering down the phone, he set it on the nightstand, but picked it up again. He stumbled to the kitchen, yanked open the refrigerator door and put the device in the fruit cooler.

Karaoke? She even knew about Karaoke. He returned to bed, which resisted his efforts to relax. He needed sleep. To go way, way down. Someone must have hacked the messages to Addy. They were tracking him as if he were the possum. Pushed, pulled, and spun. He wouldn't take it.

Thursday. *Seven days.*

He closed his eyes. Holding the crazy world at bay, he found sleep … of sorts.

CHAPTER
NINETEEN

At 7:05 p.m. in the Farmers Market's bustling Karaoke Bar, Raphael ordered a Guinness. "Farmers Market" was a misleading name but fit its origins. The Market had been around for a hundred years, long a permanent structure housing dozens of shops, bars, restaurants, and, of course, numerous grocers. It was both a town square for locals and a mecca for tourists. And on each visit, Raphael marveled at how real it felt with the smell of produce and the mix of tongues. The Karaoke bar and stage sat at the west end of the market in a large, open space filled with tables. On this night, every table was occupied with people gulping down their beers or munching on their knockwurst sandwiches. He left a generous tip and took a sip of the thick, brimming brew, spilling only a few drops before steadying his shaking hand. Tonight was nothing less than a date, and butterflies roamed his stomach.

He held his beer above his head and wormed through the cheerful crowd—vacationing families, uniformed servicemen, hipster locals, the elderly with faint, yellowish, wary eyes. At the perimeter of the crowd, young women in packs of four and five, blouses off shoulder and sleeves over hand, the careful carelessness of the young, stood talking, dancing, and texting simultaneously. He skirted the animated clusters to find an empty space and a friendly stanchion to lean against. By the time he settled in, it was 7:15, and he anticipated Addy showing up at any minute. He tapped his foot to a beat not found in the Karaoke singer's tune. The Market's smells washed over him, fresh fruit and chocolate, roast beef and turkey, battered fish and french fries, an intoxicating canvas.

Perhaps tonight he would sing. First, Addy would perform, drive the crowd delirious, and then she would descend the stage to stand at his side and take his hand. He would tell her, *Addy, I want to sing my song for you.*

She would kiss him and lead him to the stage. Every man present, no, any man in the world, would be jealous of the teal-eyed girl's love.

And when the singing was done, dinner for two at Corel's.

He rocked his head to the music and applauded politely when the singer finished her set. Throughout the crowd, agile fingers slid across phones to record their scores, which were tabulated on the giant monitor above the stage.

He viewed his own device, then keyed in an eight. On the monitor, a red velvet curtain closed on the changing digits. The curtain opened to show the final score: a lackluster six, around which little rockets rose feebly and fell back. Time for another beer. Time for another two beers.

Raphael threaded through the smiling, laughing people to the bar. "A Guinness, please." Behind the counter, above the array of beer bottles representing what was on tap and in the cooler, was an old-fashioned clock with a round face and black metal hands. Even above the music, the clock ticked loudly as if demanding attention. The long, sharp finger pointed to the seven: 7:35. If he closed his eyes and opened them, Addy would walk onto the stage.

"Fifty dollars, friend."

He opened his eyes to see a Guinness on the counter, and the barman waiting patiently. He paid and returned to his spot. On stage, an energetic woman in a jumpsuit was singing, "all about, all about," while slapping her butt hard enough to leave welts.

Eight o'clock came and went. Did Addy get called in to work?

The new performer was a text rapper.

"Kity fs. Idc. Ngl and gtg ..." she rapped, her feet moving as if inputting the lyrics on a gigantic phone.

At 8:30, he checked his messages. Nothing from Addy. Boys don't cry. He called her. She didn't answer. He left a brief message and tried not to melt away.

By 9:00, Raphael had drained a fourth beer. The pleasant people now contorted their faces and flapped their limbs as if harpies.

He pushed slowly through the crowd, glancing behind each as if they might hide Addy. He soon found himself before the woman who signed up singers. From her little chair and desk, she evaluated him. She swayed, or he swayed, and he had the impression she was judging sobriety. Gathering himself, she seemed satisfied.

"Hi. You've performed before. What's your name?"

"Raphael. Have you seen Addy?"

"No, sorry. Didn't show up tonight."

"Does she ever come in late? I mean, I've never—"

"No. If she comes at all, she comes on time." She shrugged. "You want to sing? It might cheer you up."

Raphael pitched forward a little, caught his balance, and steadied himself. "No. I don't want to sing. Addy never ever comes in late?"

The woman gave Raphael a sympathetic smile. When he turned, the crowd was again tabulating scores on their phones. On the giant monitor above the stage, the curtain closed, then parted. A smiling Miranda, holding a limp swan by the neck, filled the monitor. "Told you, Raphy. Ain't I a ten!"

"Fuck," he said making for the exit.

"Don't you like me, Raphy?" came from behind.

The crowd murmured in confusion and disapproval.

"What the hell is this?"

"Who's she?"

Outside, as he set the skateboard down, his phone rang. No, no more Miranda! He recognized the number and accepted.

"Raphael?"

"Addy?" he said, his heart leaping.

"Where are you?"

"At Karaoke. I waited the whole evening for you."

"You didn't get my message?"

"What message?"

"I called but you didn't answer, so I sent you a message. An invitation and a map."

He took a breath. "Invitation?"

"I got a call from a producer who wants me to sing at his party. He's paying me! Can you believe that?"

"Addy, I've been waiting two hours. Karaoke. Corel's. Remember?"

"I know, I know. But I got his permission to bring you to the party. It will be great."

"I don't get it. This is like out of the blue."

"I sent you the message."

"I didn't get any message." He brought up his messages and stared at the screen. On it was the grabbed shot of Addy and him at the convenience store. He groaned and spun around. "Who the fuck is messing with me?"

"What was that?" asked Addy.

"Miranda?" he said, gazing at the market's empty entrance. He glanced down at his phone. His messages bled through and displaced the photo.

"This is Addy. Who's Miranda?"

Could the technology to do that be out there? He shook his head, trying to throw off the bizarre shit trying to get in. "No, no Miranda." He swallowed. "I see your message now. I don't know why I didn't see it before."

"I want you to come. It's cool. You'll love it. The directions are in the message. Will you come? Please. Please. Please."

He spoke without thinking. "Absolutely. I'm on my way. Where is it?"

"On Laurel Canyon, north of Hollywood Boulevard."

"Oh ..."

"Is something wrong?"

He pushed away the skateboard. Shoulders sagging, he tasted something foul. "It's not—"

"You must come. I'll be so sad if you don't."

He mumbled acceptance.

"It's easy to find. There's a gigantic fountain out front, a statue of Hermes, herald of the gods. See you soon, okay?"

"Soon, Addy."

Fairfax and Beverly. Beverly and Fairfax.

He reached the sidewalk. He would skate to the intersection and cross there. He would fly over the abyss, walk across the hot coals. She wanted him to be with her. As he skated, he shouted Addy's name as if it were a shield against any foe that waited.

Fairfax undulated like a flapping towel. A crack appeared, and then a second, and a third. The cracks widened, swallowed chunks of concrete and the lanes folded into a broadening black ditch. With a roar, the street collapsed into the canyon's hungry mouth.

He slammed his fist into his head to drive out the illusion. The canyon remained, black and sullen as if annoyed he wouldn't dare to test its unreality.

He spun toward Beverly Boulevard.

On the opposite corner, a white columned building stood proudly, an ancient Greek temple, pillars of sun-licked waterfalls, the porch a moonlit lake. Tugging him up the cool marble, a rope about his waist, was Addy.

He jabbed his foot against the pavement. The crosswalk's red hand warned him not to cross, and then began its countdown.

Twenty, nineteen …

He jabbed again, and his leg gave way as if its bone had changed to rubber.

Fifteen, fourteen …

He groaned and slunk back.

Twelve, eleven, ten …

Damn. He could drop in from an eight-foot wall but couldn't push over the curb. Asshole. Coward.

He jabbed once again, found his bone and muscle, pushed, and propelled the board toward the curb and crosswalk stripes.

Five, four, three ...

On the right, a bus sped toward the intersection as if expecting its light to turn green. He would beat the bus. As he raced toward the sidewalk's end, a hundred holes opened in the street and from them erupted jets of fire.

The heat stuck its fingers up his nostrils.

Choking on the fumes of his smoldering face, Raphael arched backward. The skateboard's tail screeched against the sidewalk. Crumbling like a charred paper doll, he fell on his skateboard and wished it were a sword.

He lay on the board, hands and feet spread across the sidewalk. No one came to his assistance. No one bothered him. Passersby changed their path.

The flames died.

His phone played the opening notes of *Pictures at an Exhibition*. He knew it was Addy, but what good was he to her? A useless freak bound to his square mile. He let the insistent trumpet wail as the phone fluttered in his pocket. He pushed himself from the sidewalk and sat on his board. From behind, came a steady clacking of loose-fitting sandals. Above him stood the orator of Pan Pacific Park. The man held a large wooden cross to his shoulder. Atop the cross was a sign on which a red *X* crossed off a one and zero.

"Repent!" shouted the man. "Down with the devil's digits!" Behind the orator lurked several followers with similar signs. At a funereal pace, the Blanks rounded the corner.

The last protestor halted and handed Raphael a hand-written flyer and a pencil. "Join us," said the solemn-faced fellow.

A mewling, as of a lost kitten, drew Raphael's gaze to something low, flat, and round meandering down the sidewalk toward them.

The Blank stepped back. "What the hell?"

"Feral Roomba," muttered Raphael.

"No kidding?" said the Blank as the cleaning robot, its LED light blinking frantically, bumped into Raphael's skateboard.

"Looking for an electrical outlet," he explained. The little machine nuzzled his board like a kitten, one coming across its mother. "Find one, charge themselves up, and off they go again until their power runs low."

The Blank's forehead lined, and he moved toward the desperate machine, which now turned from the skateboard and zipped toward a low wall. "Should I—"

"No," said Raphael. "Better leave it alone. Let nature take its course."

"I meant should I kill it."

"I'd rather you didn't," replied Raphael.

They watched the machine smack into the low wall a couple of times, and then skitter around the corner.

The Blank shook his head. "Just more electronic garbage."

"Maybe so," murmured Raphael.

"Later, comrade," said the Blank, scurrying to catch up with the procession.

"Yeah, later," said Raphael. He stabbed the pencil ten times into the flyer and tossed the riddled paper and yellow number two into the gutter.

Eventually, Raphael pushed to his feet, righted the skateboard, and slowly pushed off; messaging Addy as he glided. *Sorry, I got sick. Can't make it to the party. Too much beer, I guess. Have a good time. Later.*

He sent the message, powered down, and found the way home.

CHAPTER
TWENTY

R aphael twisted the key in his apartment door lock, but it resisted. *Why is this happening,* he thought to himself as he shook out his wrist and tried again, this time with success, though the lock still turned grudgingly. Because of the limitations of his world (and his apartment was the center of his world), he knew its mechanisms well. If the third click of the pilot light didn't set the burner aflame, if the water in the toilet didn't refill in fifteen seconds, he would have the toolbox out. Or was it just the alcohol messing with his senses? He was none too steady, and objects took their time coming into focus. Still, locks age, parts wear and crack. He'd take care of it tomorrow. With a shrug, he entered the apartment and locked the door.

He boiled water to make the Darjeeling, and at the whistle, poured, letting the leaves soak for a minute, then adding a few drops of agave sweetener. Sitting at the kitchen table, he stirred the blood red tea, then, while sipping, ate a box of shortbread cookies. Never so much wanting to break out of his confinement as tonight, he had failed. If the magnet of love didn't work, he was fucked. A foul juice rose in his throat to meet the fragrant tea and sweet shortbread mash. He closed his eyes, swallowed, and fought the thudding inside his head. Jesus.

Worn to the bone and wanting sleep. Dizzy with thinking, as if his brain had been spun inside his skull. Could he lie down without getting sick?

The cherry on top of his problems was Miranda—no, get that out of your head. Someone pretending to be Miranda. But unlike Klaes, or whoever was in the guise of Klaes, the pretend Miranda seemed to have no goal but mischief. She, he, or they only wanted to tease and taunt him. But why him?

Chin propped on one elbow, he drifted off for a moment into a dream in which his laptop's keyboard wavered, and the individual keys floated up and apart. Letters, numbers, and symbols freed from their confinement zipped about him in the merry chaos of some subatomic event. Everything escaped except Raphael. Above the table, five keys ordered themselves into a familiar word. Klaes. The letters spun, zipped away. He opened his eyes, disoriented for a moment.

He was at his kitchen table, his cup half-filled with tea. He took a sip. Still warm. He couldn't have dozed off for more than a few minutes. He shifted at the table to sit before his computer, shaking off the odd dream.

He lifted the base of his laptop and placed his hand on the plastic. He had been asleep maybe ten minutes, but six hours had passed since he last used the machine, yet it was not warm—for the new generation of processors were incredibly efficient—but warmer than in its powered down state, as if recently used. Shoulders tightening, pulse rising, he stood up.

He lifted the skateboard and held it like a club. Breathing shallowly, blood flooding his head, walking lightly and slowly, he entered his mother's bedroom. A shaking hand switched on the light.

The bed was empty, sheet without a wrinkle. Bending to peer underneath, he moaned at a sudden wave of dizziness. Straightening, he considered the bedside bureau, where she had kept all her drugs for pain. He opened the top drawer, sorted through the plastic pill bottles, and took one that would do the trick if his head got any worse. He stuffed it in his pocket, and left his mother's room for his own, there finding no one and nothing disturbed. Nor was anyone hiding in the bathroom. He returned to the living room, approached the bottom rung of scaffolding and stood up high to inspect the platform. No one there.

Climbing down, he spotted a yellow sliver as long as a match lying on the dark wood floor. He picked it up. A piece of straw. His stalker wore a straw fedora. Raphael jerked around. His stomach spasmed, and he raised his arms as if to fend off an attacker. "Get the hell out of here!" he ordered the empty room. He sunk back, his cheeks burning. No attacker lay in waiting. He twisted the straw. Maybe he tracked it in himself. *Grasping at straws, Raphy.*

He returned to the kitchen and powered up the laptop. Someone had tampered with the door lock. Someone had started and shut down the computer, so someone had known his password. He reviewed its internet history, recognizing all the sites. He went to his command history, but found no surprises.

Dig deep, which meant opening the Event Viewer.

Two minutes later, the list of devices recently plugged into his computer filled the screen. He recognized all but one. An icy finger slid up his spine.

He should double-lock the door, brace a chair under its handle. Someone for sure had entered. *Messed with his computer*—discovered the views of the stolen Norval data.

He punched his fists together, stinging the knuckles. He felt violated. Someone getting into his home, his private space. Anger rose in him, shook him.

He took the elevator to the lobby and then walked outside. It was approaching midnight. The air was still cool though, the grounds deserted. The sound of a radio increased in volume as a security vehicle approached manned by Albert. The guard was tuned to a radio show discussing alien landings. He glanced at Raphael and gave him a wave of recognition. The cart continued its rounds.

"Hey," Raphael called to Albert. He set down the skateboard and pushed off, steadier on board than feet. He caught up to the cart. "Albert," said Raphael. "I think someone may have broken into my apartment."

"You call the police, Mr. Lennon?"

"No, I didn't."

"Was anything stolen?"

Raphael shook his head. "Nothing, really. Well, data maybe."

"Data?"

Hopping off the skateboard, he swayed a bit and reached out to brace himself on the cart. Albert must have caught a whiff of his Guinness breath, for he jerked his head away. "Maybe you've been celebrating?"

"No, nothing to celebrate." Not quite a lie. At least, it hadn't ended in celebration.

"So how did you know someone broke in?"

"My door handle was—" Raphael tightened his jaw.

"Door handle was?"

The guard would think him a crank, but then he remembered a foreign device had penetrated his computer. "I think someone picked my lock, got inside, and messed with my computer."

"Umm."

Raphael nodded. In the air was the faint smell of tobacco. "There's a man who hangs around out here smoking."

"Cannabis?"

"Tobacco."

"Not allowed on the Tar Tower grounds."

"I know, but he was. A couple of days ago. A big, square face. Carries channel locks."

"Channel looks, you say?"

"No. Channel *locks*. Pliers."

Albert stared at him. "No, I've seen no men carrying channel locks."

"There's this other guy who wears a Fedora, wine stain on his cheek. Silver rimmed glasses."

Albert shook his head. "You want me to come up and take a lock— damn, *look* at your apartment?"

"No, I'm okay."

He nodded. "I'll look into it, though. Check the cameras." He glanced about the plaza. "Have a good night, well, morning. Get some sleep."

"Yeah, sleep," said Raphael, getting on the board and pushing off.

In the apartment, he sat and stared at the open laptop. His excursion outside had left him not only wide-awake but also restless. The intruder had to have been there because of Klaes. Raphael opened the Klaes file and went to the photos. There had been ten, only four of which he had opened. Now there were nine. Number five had been deleted. He opened the trashcan. Empty.

He stuck his finger into his coin pocket and dug out the thumb drive, which he inserted into the port the intruder had used and brought up the Klaes files.

He opened the selfie folder and scanned the list of familiar photos. He opened one that had gone unexamined, the one deleted from the hard drive—number five, "Maze.jpg"

Maisie Sparod looked up at him.

What the hell?

There were no dead or mutilated animals. It was a selfie of Maisie.

He went to a higher folder level. There were a dozen folders that struck him as little out of the ordinary, the thirteenth seemed odd: "Practical Nonlocality". He opened up the folder, which contained files labeled with last names: "Day", "Tolover", "Royer", "*Sparod*", all with the odd extension attached to the Personality Plus file. Impossible to open.

Impossible.

Go to bed. Push the chair against the front door. Sleep it all off. Place crumpled newspaper around the bed. There was an old movie he and his mother watched in which one of the bad guys built such a rudimentary warning system. He imagined how feet would sound on crumpled paper. *Not like they would sound on the kitchen floor.* He glanced down, and his heart stopped.

"Easy now," said a steady and authoritative voice as something hard and cool pressed into his neck.

He went numb, completely fucking numb. He'd had a knife to his spine, but never a gun barrel to his head, yet he didn't doubt the object. He wouldn't even hear the explosion. He wasn't breathing. A foul juice rose in his throat.

"The thumb drive, please." The gun barrel shifted, angled slightly upward.

He swallowed at the bitter fluid. One finger tug and he was dead. Yet he was moved to speak by something trivial. The desire for one's logic to hold up even if one's life was done. The stupid thing burst out. "I checked every room."

"Not after you returned from your chat with security."

A bead of sweat ran down Raphael's cheek. He extracted the drive and held it high. A hand snatched it away. It softly clinked as it dropped into a pocket filled with coins ... or bullets.

"Delete all of the Klaes files. And anything else containing Klaes."

"Sure, sure, easy, okay?" Raphael peered to the right and upward. He was going to be sick. He wanted to vomit. The gun pressed harder, found skull bone. He was dead. Norval had cut him off from Klaes, and now he would be cut off from life. Jesus, he was falling, falling into that depthless canyon.

He opened the file manager. The screen filled with folders and documents. Halfway down the column of yellow folders appeared Klaes. He slid the cursor over Klaes, hesitating to click.

He heard the gun's hammer pull back. The barrel twisted painfully against his head.

"Right." Raphael right clicked delete, and the computer asked, "Are you sure you want to move this folder to the Recycle Bin?"

Raphael let the cursor drift over the answers.

"I could put a hole in you and your computer. Might be the way your night ends. In fact, you may wonder why I don't."

"No," muttered Raphael. His heart beat furiously. "I'm not at all interested." He clicked yes.

"Cool. Now empty your recycle bin."

He emptied.

"Show me your shredder."

He brought up the program.

"Good. Now I won't need to smash the thing and drop it off the end of a pier. I would have, you know, if I didn't like you. Open your mouth."

"No."

"Trust me."

"No." Now, he had to make his move now.

Something pricked Raphael's neck.

"Misdirection," said the assailant.

"But my time isn't up," said Raphael, wondering already what time he was talking about.

He lifted his head up to see a wine-stained chin, then a doffed hat, which enlarged enormously and dropped like a sack over Raphael's head, leaving him in darkness.

CHAPTER
TWENTY-ONE

Matt's mud-stained, hydrogen-powered, rainbow-colored Roly-Poly drove through the Norval parking lot gate. Raphael gave it ten seconds, then chased after it on his board. By the time he caught up to the car, Matt had pulled into a parking space, a pastry hovering before his lips.

Raphael slipped up to the driver's side window and tapped.

Matt jerked back, dropping his pastry on the passenger seat. "Shit," said Matt, driver's window descending.

Raphael bent at the waist. "I need to talk to you." He straightened and twisted back his head. "Did you hear something?"

"Hear what?"

"You didn't hear something?"

"No." Matt reached toward his Danish.

Raphael grabbed his shoulder. "I need—"

"Why don't you get into my ride."

Raphael hefted the skateboard and dashed around the vehicle. He pulled the door open just as Matt retrieved the pastry. Raphael brushed off the traces of flakes and icing, then plopped onto the seat. He yanked the door shut, shoved the board between his legs, and glanced over his shoulder.

Matt leaned into him. "You seem a little nervous."

"Oh yeah? Perceptive, aren't you? Fuck, fuck, fuck."

"Take it easy, man. You act as if you've got a hit out on you." Matt bit into his pastry, unleashing the scent of blueberries. He chewed fast and swallowed. "You going to tell me what's going on?"

"Last night, a dude broke into my apartment and put a gun to my head."

Matt drew away the Danish, a jelled berry stuck to his lip. "What?" He licked the berry into his mouth.

"Put a gun to my head, stole my thumb drive, and erased my ... files."

"Have the police—"

Raphael tapped his fist on the window. "I stole the files from Norval, okay?" He slapped his hand against a skateboard wheel. It spun, blurred. He rose in the seat, craned his neck, and viewed the lot. "Klaes is killing people."

"So he's not dead?"

"Not sure. This case is super fucked up, but people are dying, and Klaes is making it happen. And now this guy with a gun."

"Sounds like you're earning your paycheck. By the way, how come you make six times more than me?"

Raphael sighed. "This is not the time to discuss salary. And I don't make six times more than you."

"I can't afford the Tar Tower, and you buy more take-out than anyone I know."

"If you want to live to eat another of those, shut up." He pressed his fist to his lips and murmured, "Lily Faraday."

"Yeah? Who's that?"

"A friend and colleague of Klaes. She's managing the Klaes celebration at the Harvey Hotel. I need to speak with her."

"Get out your phone."

"I don't have her private number, and I've called her at the hotel a dozen times. She never calls back. She must think I'm a salesman or something. I need to sit down with her."

Matt glanced sideways at him. "Shit. The Harvey is just a couple of miles away. Barge in on her if she's so important." Matt stuck the key in the ignition and started the engine.

"What are you doing?" asked Raphael.

"You want to see this Lily Faraway, right?" Matt threw the Roly-Poly into reverse, backed out of the space with a clickety-clack, and drove toward the exit.

The shaking started at Raphael's feet, worked its way up to his knees and torso. "Where are you going?" cried Raphael.

"Taking you to the Harvey so you can find this Lily Faraway."

"Sixth Street, not Fairfax," snapped Raphael. "And her name is *Faraday*." Shit. The Harvey was east of La Brea, his eastern boundary.

Matt shrugged. "I prefer my way." He continued through the exit, pulled down the right signal lever and prepared to enter Fairfax. Raphael leaned toward him, grabbed the wheel and moaned, "No!" Matt slammed on the brakes. Raphael opened the door and tumbled out.

"What the hell?" shouted Matt.

Raphael was on his hands and knees, gasping, blurry. The lemony-smelling broth spread. Through a watery veil, two unicorn-decorated sneakers stepped closer.

"You're ill. You should be home in bed."

"Not sick." Raphael dry-heaved twice, wiped his mouth, sat hunched, and peered behind him, then around both sides.

Matt bent down. "You got something you want to tell me?"

"No, I mean, yes. I want you to go to the Harvey Hotel and find Lily Faraday." Raphael pushed to his feet, reached under his shirt and pulled out a sealed white envelope. He held it out for Matt. "Give this to her. Would you do that for me?"

"I've got a question."

"No questions. Will you do it?"

"Suppose it takes a while to find Ms. Faraday. I'll be late for work. Dreemont will give me shit."

"I'll make up a cover story."

"What if I can't find her?"

"You're a fucking possum hunter. You'll find her."

Matt took the envelope. "But I've really got a question."

"No fucking questions. Will you do it?"

Matt grinned. "Consider it done—*eventually.*"

"Go!" shouted Raphael.

"Six times bigger than my salary," muttered Matt as he got back into his ride.

TWO HOURS LATER, Raphael sat in his cubicle trying to work out if he was still in danger. His stalker had taken everything he wanted, and he hadn't blown off Raphael's head. Nor had he warned him off Klaes. Maybe whoever his assailant represented was done with him. He placed his heel on his skateboard, rolled it back and forth, and took several deep breaths. His heart had slowed down, and he didn't want to look over his shoulder every ten seconds. Yeah, maybe everything wasn't totally cool, but things had settled. Now if Matt would only come through.

"Hey, buddy," someone whispered.

Raphael spun in his seat to see Matt holding out his hand as if to shake.

"A message from you know who," whispered Matt, slipping a piece of paper into trembling fingers that steadied, clasped, and closed mollusk tight.

CHAPTER
TWENTY-TWO

As the afternoon waned, Raphael drained the energy drink, crushed the can, and tossed it into the recyclables tube. The can clanked as it navigated a few bends in the tubing, whistled in free fall, then fell silent. What sound did it make at its terminus, if there was one? Perhaps the tubes went straight through to the Earth's core.

I will call you this afternoon, Raphael. If I can't reach you, please call me after 8 PM at the mobile number below. Regards, Lily

It was the third time he'd read the note. Raphael stuck it back into his pocket.

The only call was Addy's, which made three times she'd phoned and three times he hadn't responded. His explanation of his behavior would only be the straight line to a joke. "You can't cross Fairfax? You've never had the pastrami at McCanter's?"

If she acted sympathetic, it would be to back away, to gain distance from this odd character with one dead rock star's last name and another dead rock star's face, who might be harmless, *if not psychopathic.*

What he contained in his head was too strange. Others had rejected him but hadn't killed his hope that one might not. Even though their relationship had fallen short of one date, if Addy turned him away, it would end his search for love. "Sorry, Raphael, there's no future here" might fell him on the spot. Yet, it was not fair not to tell her. After her third rebuffed call, he left her a vague text message and hoped it was sufficient, but if she called again, he would have to confess.

Raphael drew a finger across the keyboard. On the monitor, a crescent of white sand met a turquoise sea. A woman stood knee deep in the water, her glossy hair caught up in the breeze, her wrap tight against her slender body. "Leave your troubles behind," advised the voiceover, "steal away to beautiful Polynesia with the one you love." A gender neutral arm slipped around the woman's waist.

He swiped away the advertisement.

Klaes. He had to get his brain around Klaes before even thinking about getting his arms around Addy.

Someone approached the cubicle quietly as if to spy, Dreemont, maybe. To his relief, the final footfall was the double tap of a cane across the doorway.

Raphael looked up. "Hi, Jensy."

She nudged her black glasses up her nose and flicked away the drizzle of hair on her forehead. She leaned into him and whispered, "I wanted to tell you first."

"What?"

She stepped toward him. "I'm quitting."

A gnat hovered before his face. He swiped at it. "You're kidding!"

"I'll miss the paycheck, but I can't keep doing this. I mean, pretending all this death and sadness is nothing but data. It's not. You know that, don't you?"

"You haven't been here long, Jensy. Tough it—" He bit back the words.

Jensy shook her head. "I-I don't want to tough it out. I don't want to get tough. You're not tough, Raphael."

He didn't want her to quit. Jobs weren't easy to find—and he'd miss her. "Tough as maple," he responded, kicking his heel on the skateboard, which took the blow in silence. The gnat found him again. He swatted.

She drew in her lips. Beneath the lenses, her eyes seemed to seek him. "I don't understand how you can do it. Pretending the dead are data. Sometimes I imagine the children, their stolen voices, their warm skin, and I start shaking." She tapped her cane against the floor. "I can't calm down."

Raphael glanced away from her to the bank of mindfulness videos. Could he shift her mood? "You mean watching a woman ironing—" He cut off the sentence. What a dumb thing to say. The gnat floated before his eye, and then landed on his eyeball. He blinked to rid himself of the irritant. He considered the screens, blinked twice and then twice again.

He flinched as if from an electric shock. "Jesus."

"Huh?"

He recalled Matt's weird observation when he had a piece of light-bulb stuck in his eye and blinked repeatedly. Now, as Raphael did the same, he witnessed a man with the barrel of a gun under his chin on the mindfulness screen. When the man pulled the trigger, Raphael jumped.

"What the fuck," Raphael said under his breath.

"I don't understand," said Jensy.

Raphael stopped blinking. The ironing woman again filled the mindfulness screen. What had just happened? He glanced at Jensy. *The visually impaired usually took longer to adjust to the work, if ever.*

"What's this, a conference?" said Dreemont, sticking his head in the cubicle. Dreemont stood behind Jensy. He glanced over her shoulder at Raphael.

"Plenty of work to do, and if you don't have enough, I'll find some." Dreemont rapped the wall. "Is that the dead I hear knocking? On your way."

Raphael wanted to shout, *Jensy's quitting!* Followed by, *The mindfulness screens are a lie!* Instead, he said nothing.

Dreemont swung away like a gate to let Jensy pass. Dreemont gazed at Raphael. "What are you working on?"

"A possum," muttered Raphael, facing the computer.

"What possum?"

He felt his cheeks burn. "Go to hell, boss man."

Dreemont turned away, breathing hard. Raphael looked up just as Dreemont pivoted back to him. His supervisor's face was crimson. "You know those are firing words, right? I'll ignore that—once." Dreemont leaned into him, so Raphael smelled his peppery breath. "What possum?"

"Nadine Reichenbach," snapped Raphael.

Dreemont straightened. "Well, good. I must have been imagining you were telling your supervisor to go fuck himself."

Head swimming, Raphael tapped out *Go fuck yourself, Dreemont* on the keyboard.

Dreemont laughed and walked off.

Waiting a moment, Raphael returned to the mindfulness screen, where now a little boy with a little red shovel scooped sand into a bucket, then poured it out. Raphael blinked at a variety of rates. He paused and tried again. A heap of naked and emaciated dead bodies appeared, then sunk beneath the boy and the shovel. Masked by the mindfulness videos, scenes of horror surfaced: subliminal inoculations against emotions. Images of death woven into the mundane. Raphael fought a rising sickness. Deaden End Man brains to death.

He should have figured it out when Matt first mentioned it. "So, at work I'm blinking and looking at the mindfulness screen. My eyelids going tit, tit, tit." Raphael blinked again. He could not extract whatever lay beneath. Some error in the layering allowed the masked image to surface. Jensy's blindness had protected her. The office music played the most upbeat song on the planet, but it didn't penetrate Raphael's dark mood.

The thousands digit on the Cumulative Clock slipped from seven to eight, well short of the week's high.

He fingered the slip of paper with Lily's message.

Yes, Jensy, get out. Run like hell. Wish I could.

Raphael gazed at a new screensaver. An abandoned farmhouse, weedy and desolate. Ghosts about.

His work phone rang: the lobby.

"Hey, Raphael, you have a visitor. I told her I can't let her up. She's waiting for you down here."

That was a surprise. But he would have to get Lily off premises quickly. "Great. Tell her I'll be right there."

Raphael scribbled on a sticky pad and slapped the yellow slip on the monitor. "Feeling ill. Need fresh air."

He waited before the elevator, expecting Dreemont to call out for him. He needed to get Lily out of the lobby where there were cameras to capture faces, floor sensors to identify gaits, air floaters that recorded fingerprints.

Come on. Come on.

He slapped the lobby button. Five seconds later, the elevator doors opened, and he strode across the lobby to see a woman studying the topographical map of California. His heart jumped. "Addy?"

Addy turned to him. "Why haven't you returned my calls?"

Raphael halted. "Did you get my message?"

"Yes. That awful message. 'It won't work out, Addy, but we'll always have Karaoke.' Karaoke? What the hell?"

"I thought it might make you laugh."

"Yeah, I fell out of bed. Was it all playacting? I invite you to a party, and you don't come or call. You're all sweetness and light until you ghost me. And then you leave me a cheap, cowardly message." She shook her head, swinging her weighted braid. "You never even mentioned you worked in the weird building."

"I don't know what you ..." His heart seemed to swell and shrink simultaneously. "Addy, you've got so much going for you. You're beautiful and smart and kind of a celebrity."

"Celebrity? I sing at Karaoke—on Thursdays."

"There are so many guys who—"

"Oh, yes, *millions.*"

Raphael glanced at the security guard, the barrel-chested Nikolay, whom Raphael chatted with once in a while. Nikolay politely stared down at the sign-in sheet. "Let's go outside."

When he took her arm, she pulled away and stormed off in front of him. The doors opened, and the Californian sun blasted them.

Addy had reached the sidewalk. She stopped and looked back at him.

If he walked down to her, she'd likely retreat further. She believed he was playing some perverse game. The only way to end the game was to confess. Remaining at the top of the steps, he pointed at Fairfax. "What do you see?"

Addy gazed at him with eyes of ice. "What am I supposed to see?"

Raphael descended two steps. *Now or never.*

"I see an abyss. A canyon determined to swallow me. Wilshire? The wind blows so hard off of Wilshire, I *can't* see. Don't you feel the gale? I can. It brings me to my knees."

She straightened her head, took in the boulevard's clotted traffic, and sighed. "I don't believe you."

"I didn't show at your party because it was on the other side of Beverly. I tried. The entire street went up in flames. I was burning up. *Dromophobia.*"

"What?"

"A phobia. An irrational fear."

"Yes, I'm familiar with phobias." Her head dropped a little to one side, and her eyes widened as if she were trying to see deeper into him. "But I haven't heard of that one."

"The fear of crossing streets."

She frowned. "I've crossed streets with you."

"Not all streets, just four streets: Wilshire, Fairfax, Bev—" He broke off.

She had straightened her head and her eyes had grown hard.

"Beverly," she said, completing his word. "And then it would be … La Brea?"

"Yes, four streets. A rectangle."

She nodded. "Sure."

"I wouldn't believe it either." He imagined a barrier rising between him and Addy no less impassable than one of his streets.

Her voice came from afar. "Is there someone else? Some little spellbinder?"

"Just me. It's my spell."

Her lips trembled, and he wanted to hold her. Melt into her like the toy soldier and the little ballerina in the fairytale. She didn't understand, or she thought it was a game he could stop playing anytime.

He scrambled down to the sidewalk. "Pink says someone is out to kill me. I have to run, but I can't. I've got six days left. I don't even know—"

Addy clapped her hands to her ears. "I don't want to hear this crazy stuff. Tell me the truth."

Norval's door opened behind them with a rush of air.

"Raphael," said Dreemont, "you've got to get back to Necrology."

"Yeah, yeah." He reached for Addy's arm, but she pulled away.

"Hey, you hear me?" said Dreemont. "We've got a Big D in the Big D. Let's go."

"Give us a moment to talk," cried Raphael.

"Woo after working hours. Let's go!"

Ignoring the supervisor, Raphael again tried for her arm. She twisted from him. "Ask Pink, Addy. And ask her if 'to be vile' meant *Toobyville*."

"Toobyville?"

"Who let it fall?"

"Sure," said Addy, backing away, in her eyes the disbelief and suspicion of all the girls before. She shook her head, swung away from him, but immediately stopped and dug through her purse. She turned back to him holding a Starbucks card and a fifty-dollar bill. She slapped both in his palm. "Thanks. But who the hell puts twenty-five thousand dollars on a Starbucks card?" She turned, shook her head, and walked toward Fairfax. Not even glancing back, she shouted, "It's *singular*."

Raphael glanced at the colorful rectangle in his palm. Not even singular, but never. It had to be a card-reader malfunction. *Nobody* puts twenty-five thousand dollars on a Starbucks card, including weird coroners. He slipped the card in his pocket.

Ignoring another Dreemont summons, he watched Addy skirt past a woman leading a miniature white poodle. A second woman leading an identical poodle appeared to be running after the first. As the second dogwalker closed in, she shouted, "Get him," to her dog, which snarled and charged its twin.

The second woman spun, cracked her leash like a whip, and kicked her dog into the fray. "Destroy that bitch! Have her ovaries for lunch!"

"Hey, hey," shouted Raphael, as the snarling poodles locked in combat, their owners paying out their dogs' tethers to the maximum. Sprinting down the sidewalk, Raphael grabbed each poodle by its bejeweled collar and drew the furious animals apart, canine saliva striking his pant legs.

"What the hell are you doing?" he demanded of the dog owners.

"Mind your own business," said the first woman. She lifted her dog, clamped it under one arm, and scurried off.

The other woman said, "Good boy. Truth will be proud of you." She slipped her dog a treat, then strode off with her aggressive poodle.

Truth? What the fuck?

In the elevator, Dreemont bitched about the division's employees getting a little too comfortable on the job, taking advantage of Maglio's liberal work rules. "All day long, we've got personnel around the water cooler voting up or down on Bluetit."

"We don't have a water cooler," muttered Raphael.

"You know what I mean. Spending more time on their own social media than they do on the dead's. Getting too big for their applications. Your friend Jensy gave me her notice today—see how many Norval-quality opportunities come knocking on that blind bitch's door. Nobody is irreplaceable, friend."

The elevator stopped.

As they waited for the sluggish door to open, Dreemont added, "Ever since Klaes, I've been getting this weird vibe from you. Anything wrong? Anything you want to tell me?"

"No, Mike. Everything is sweet."

"There, better. Happy workers, happy workplace." Dreemont rolled his shoulders. "The Big D should get your juices flowing."

Raphael's phone buzzed. The elevator doors opened. Dreemont glanced at the buzzing phone as if he were a middle-school teacher who might confiscate the forbidden goods.

In the cubicle and facing away from the entrance, Raphael took Lily's call.

CHAPTER
TWENTY-THREE

R aphael?"

He pivoted on the ramp overlooking the museum's Calder mobile to see a woman approaching. In jeans and a T-shirt, she was slender and athletic, her auburn hair bound in a short ponytail. He breathed.

"Lily Faraday," she said, upon reaching him, clapping her hand to her chest.

"Raphael Lennon," he replied, his insides fluttering. Here in this familiar place, Lily Faraday reminded him of his mother, which shook him to his bones. Oddly, Lily, too, gazed at him in an unsettled way.

"Sorry I'm late. A delivery I'd been expecting for a week arrived just as I was about to leave. The mystery crate."

"Mystery crate?"

"A big crate not to be opened until the night of the event." She shrugged. "Jason's orders." Beneath her bright and inquisitive eyes hung blue crescents of sleeplessness. She pointed to the large mobile. "That's the Calder, then?"

"Yes. *Three Quintains.* It was my mother's favorite," he noted. "No trouble finding me?" he blurted.

She shook her head as if coming out of a trance. "No, not at all. Tall, a resemblance to Bowie. But I was thinking—never mind. Sorry." She smiled.

"My letter must have sounded crazy.

"I found it pretty damn intriguing." She smiled. "Have they found your assailant?"

"I didn't report it." He wanted to say more, but even if he did, he wouldn't disclose everything. He would leave it a partial truth. He felt his face flushed at his hypothetical evasion.

"I think I understand," said Lily. "I was touched that you disclosed your phobia to me."

"It's weird, but if it's someone you don't know, it's ... easier. Even my friend Matt—that's the guy who met you at the hotel— doesn't know what I told you."

Lily smiled. "He's quite a character. He made me laugh."

Raphael pictured Matt, comforting him when he was sick. "Matt's a good guy." He scanned their surroundings. "Do you mind if we walk for a while?"

They descended the ramp from the courtyard and walked along the path approaching the main tar pit. In the grassy open area to the left, a bare-chested young man threw a Frisbee. His collie scrambled after it, leaping to catch the toy in its teeth.

"You must have been close to him. I mean, you're in charge of the celebration."

"Jason and I were colleagues and friends. It was an honor for me to be responsible for the event.

"So it was planned a long time ago?"

"Not at all. On January 11, I received a package from Jason with instructions for the celebration and a cashier's check to cover the costs. In the package was a personal letter to me apologizing for his death. That's how I heard Jason was dead."

"And you're certain he's deceased?"

Lily glanced up at a passing cloud. "He is." She dropped her gaze to Raphael and intently studied his face.

"I don't want him to be dead," said Raphael.

"Why? I mean, aside from not wanting anyone to be dead."

"He sent me a message promising me something."

"When was this?"

Raphael sighed. He couldn't get around how ridiculous he would sound. "After he died."

Lily's face registered no surprise. "May I ask what he promised?"

"To set me free from my phobia." Raphael shook his head. "For all I know, it could be an imposter with some weird agenda, I guess. The more I find out, the less I'm sure of anything." He halted. "You know Maisie Sparod, don't you?"

"It's fortunate I haven't eaten lunch yet. You're not a friend of Maisie, I hope."

"I met her once."

"And you still have all your limbs?"

Raphael laughed, and Lily took up his laughter. Maybe today it would all start to make sense.

Reaching the main pit, Lily walked over to the fence, gripped the links. "She tried to entice Jason with a project once. He wanted nothing to do with it, her, I should say."

Raphael stood beside Lily. "Sparod didn't like Klaes's attitude then?"

"It went somewhat further. The green-eyed monster. Klaes could think. Maisie, as with many, could only regurgitate." Lily gazed at the tar. "Jason was brilliant but careless. You put a worthwhile object near Maisie Sparod, you shouldn't expect to get it back. She bankrolls many peer-reviewed journals, *previews* a lot of research. If she sees an interesting paper submitted by a person she's antagonistic to, she'll, let's say, leak it to one of her vassals. It may surprise you how valuable research might be if it's glimpsed a few minutes before public dissemination. Similar to automated trading systems on the stock market. A second here, a microsecond there, and the insider gets filthy rich. We're talking prizes and grants, which can attract big money, multimillions if your research warrants it. Sparod no doubt stole from Jason. Or tried."

"Did Jason ever mention a project called Personality Plus?"

Lily pursed her lips, seemed to gaze inward, and shook her head. "Sorry. Jason worked on many projects. I was familiar with some, but *Personality?* No bells."

"They wanted it," said Raphael more to himself than Lily. "I mean, Maisie and Maglio, my company's CEO."

"If a rat smells cheese." Lily twisted her toe into the grass. "If she's after something, she persists until she gets it—legally or extralegally."

"If true—"

"I wouldn't give Maisie the benefit of an if."

Raphael glanced down at Lily's foot sinking into the grass, black at its base. He pointed. "If you go any deeper, you'll get tar on your shoes."

Lily nodded and drew back her foot.

"A thousand feet down, there's the Salt Lake Oil Field. Right where we're standing, they pumped up oil." He swept his hand outward. "Wells all over this place."

"Any chance of falling down one?" asked Lily.

"I think it's just your shoes in danger," Raphael said with a smile.

Lily laughed but inched back again.

Was it just Lily's shoes that were in danger? He had already spilled a lot to her, but could he trust her entirely? Sure, she looked like his mother, but she wasn't: *a stranger, Raphy.* He should just walk away. But the fire to know burned in him, and he saw Lily as the one person who might have the knowledge he needed. He had to go for it.

"I found a file of Jason's with that name. It had a weird extension. I couldn't open it. When I asked my supervisor for help"—he recalled when things soured—"he took me off Klaes and entombed the physicist."

"Entombed?"

"It's Norval-speak for locking down someone's data."

From the nearby museum plaza came live music. For an instant, Raphael felt detached from his body. It was as though he saw the dawning on his own face—forehead smoothing, eyes flashing with insight. The words of that moment echoed. Dreemont had said, "You won't open the file." No, not a simple you, but an emphatic *you*. His supervisor didn't want Raphael even to try. Dreemont realized right away the file was important, special.

"Do you have access to the file?" asked Lily. "I'm no computer scientist, but I have friends who are. They might be able to do something with it."

Raphael shook his head. "They destroyed it. She and Maglio were hunting for the file, but it wasn't what they'd hoped for. It contained a virus designed to consume the Norval database, Weblock's too."

"I can see why it might be aimed at Maisie."

From behind them came a high-pitched scream. At the top of the slope surrounding the pit, children had gathered, gesturing toward the stone mastodons. The little tribe, each holding a phone or iPad and jostling each other, charged down the hill and rushed to the chain-link fence, encircling Lily and Raphael.

One boy hocked through the fence. The phlegmy gob sat on the thick oil. The spitter turned his back to the fence, struck a cocky pose, and lifted his phone to take a selfie. The animatronic cat roared, and its foreleg snapped up, sending the boy stumbling forward in fright. He tumbled to the ground, which drew squeals of laughter from the other children, who turned their phones on him and relentlessly clicked away.

Raphael slipped his fingers through the fencing. He remembered once scrambling to the top. Under the afternoon sun, the asphalt shone, its acrid odor potent.

"Is your event going as you planned?" asked Raphael.

Lily closed her eyes against the sun and breathed as if to take in its warmth. "I'm following Jason's directions, that's all. He left explicit instructions and the funds to make it happen."

Raphael pushed away from the fence. "Tributes from brilliant physicists, I suppose."

Lily bent to inspect her shoe. "Damn, I got some of your tar on it."

"Hey, not mine."

Lily laughed. "There will be some tributes. He also provided findings on his most recent research, yet unpublished, which we'll distribute and discuss. There's something else. An invention maybe, but I can't be sure."

Lily described the mysterious crate that was not to be opened until the celebration, leaving the description as little more than its dimensions and weight. "So, Raphael, what is it you want from me?"

"Would Sparod have murdered Klaes?"

Lily pivoted and leaned her back against the fence. "Not Sparod in the flesh. She'd hire a pro. The darknet makes using assassins as easy as hiring a gardener to mow your lawn. I'm not saying she did, but the means are available. What does your company want?"

"Profit," snapped Raphael.

Lily nodded. "There is little in science without application in the world of commerce. Would Maisie have stolen something allowing her to make a profitable deal? Sure."

"Worth enough for Maisie and Maglio to have Klaes killed?"

"If the size of the prize was right."

He took a deep breath, held it a second, and let it all out in a slow huff. "Did Jason have it in him to murder?"

She frowned and looked toward the tar pit. Raphael supposed she had become tired with his nonsense, but he persisted. "He made threats to people. And the people he sent them to are now dead."

Lips quivering, Lily scanned the pit as if for something other than the black oil and floating debris.

She whispered. "Go on."

"If it wasn't Klaes, there's another possibility. Maglio and Sparod got into Klaes's accounts after they killed him. They sent the emails to put me on a false trail, but one on which I might turn up something interesting, though not the truth about Klaes. They don't want me sure if Klaes is alive or dead."

Lily pivoted to him. "If he's alive, they're guilty of nothing."

"Except stealing his work." A drone appeared one hundred feet above them, hovering. He lowered his voice. "I met with Jonathan Mirsky ... at a strip club."

Lily again dug her toe into the grass. "An awful end. But we predicted it would happen someday. Walk out from a bar into the streets ..." She shook her head. "He was a special genius. Quantum mechanics and B-girls. Jon would have been at the celebration." She caught her breath. "Jason, Jonathan—a lot to take in." Eyes welling, she looked away.

"I'm sorry," said Raphael.

She wiped at the tears. "What did Jonathan tell you?"

"Vague talk of nonlocality, spooky action, being alive and dead simultaneously. Can you stick a pin in a doll and make a human grab his guts? Could nonlocality be what Maglio and Sparod are trying to nail down?"

Lily shook her head. "It doesn't work outside the quantum. Best to think of it as a metaphor."

"A metaphor, right. Not exactly what Norval would be interested in."

"Your company leverages data, right? Two years ago, I met Jason for a drink. He brought up neural networks. He said, he'd found what no one was looking for."

"What the hell does that mean?"

"I asked him the same thing. He gave me a Mona Lisa smile, or should I say a Mary Sue smile? Whatever he meant, neural networks are the key to leaps in computer power, which translates into better manipulation of data for companies like yours."

"Yeah, that would get Norval's attention."

The drone descended another five yards. *Has to be the worst spy drone ever.* He bent down and picked up a stone.

"Would your company kill for better data?"

"If they could get away with it."

"I'd rather believe that than think Jason took his own life."

"But it's not out of the question?"

"Jason was carrying something heavy."

Raphael's heart pounded. "A crime?"

Lily shrugged. "He never said that, but he was ashamed of whatever he did."

"So he could have—suicide that is."

Lily sighed. "I'm not helping, am I?

He was back where he started: maybe Jason killed himself, maybe he didn't.

He tugged on his beanie and pushed his hair back. On the asphalt lake, a bubble formed, swelled, and burst. It was there and then not. Where had it gone? A balmy breeze swept across the tar—or had it arisen from within it? Impenetrable black became clear as water. Something touched his shoulder. He twisted to see Lily lifting her hand.

"What—"

"A fallen hair," said Lily, pinching it between her fingers. "Don't worry, you have plenty more." She feigned dropping the strand, but it remained between her fingertips. Something significant had happened, but he didn't have a clue what it was. She patted his arm. "I have to get back to the hotel. If you discover that Jason is alive ..." She shook her head. "If I can think of anything that might help you ..." Lines that hadn't been there before creased her forehead. "'I will be the machine in the ghost.'"

"What?"

"It was Jason's salutation in the instructions he sent to me for the celebration. 'I will be the machine in the ghost.'"

"What does it mean?"

Lily shrugged. "Absolutely no idea."

He thought she was about to tell him something else, but her lips tightened. She whispered goodbye, turned, and walked away.

He felt someone else leave with her. A tarpit was a lonely place. He dropped the stone.

With a sigh, he set down his board to head home when a brilliant light swept over him. On the other side of the pit, above Wilshire, on a 3D billboard, a radiant thirty-foot-long porpoise glided through green water. Startlingly real, it emerged from a high-resolution, curved LED screen, but as it leaped, the viewer might have expected it to fly across the boulevard, seawater dripping from its sleek body. A chyron of 3D foot-high letters flowed across the billboard.

YANGTZE FINLESS PORPOISE. EXTINCT. ARE YOU PREPARED?

The words vanished to leave the magnificent porpoise propelling itself through the green sea.

CHAPTER
TWENTY-FOUR

I n Raphael's kitchen, the kettle whistled full throttle. He turned off the pot and poured the boiling water on the napping tea bag, hoping it wouldn't scream. It awakened silently. He lifted the bag by its string and dipped it several times.

He sipped the Darjeeling, holding the sweet, warm liquid on his tongue.

He was sure Lily was straight, but she wasn't telling him everything. She had assured him Klaes was dead, but she had left Raphael on a mysterious note. *The machine in the ghost.* What the hell could that mean? Lily had brought him no closer to the truth of Klaes. At least their meeting didn't leave one thing in doubt. Norval was profiting off of Klaes's work.

After draining the tea, he took his airtight container of oil paints from the refrigerator, carried it to the living room, and set it on the deck to climb the scaffolding. He stretched out on the plywood, adjusted the pillow, and considered the vast canvas. No matter how unhinged his world, the painting had to go on.

Rolling sideways, he opened the plastic container, uncapped two tubes, and squeezed their oils onto the palette. He gazed across his work and sighed. What would a stranger make of the painting? All of his experience was there, but could anyone interpret a single brush-stroke? It meant everything and nothing. It was the brain at the instant of death. A life was contained within that curved canvas, but only the person who had accumulated that life had access to it and could decode its meaning and value. Then, *all gone*. Everyone. Every-one. Sadness fell on him like a blanket.

Under the sad blanket, he shifted on the plywood, peering right and left, up and down, and shifted several more times until he lay under the northeast corner of the canvas where several years ago, he captured a vivid memory of Pan Pacific: the man who taught him skateboarding from a hundred yards away, the park's grassy slopes always separating their concrete paths. Years later, he painted him emerging from a gray and green vortex.

Above the vortex was a space where he had sketched an image he had no interest in finishing. It would be a good place for the Blanks of Pan Pacific Park. From the box of accessories, he took a fat pink eraser and began rubbing out the charcoal lines. He paused and lowered the eraser to his lips. *Dive into the oil and swim across, climb the bank and escape.* He took an experimental plunge but never hit the surface. Lifting the abrading rubber, he drew it back. His canvas had changed again. He wriggled until he was under the animatronic tiger. In the center of the image was a dark spot he hadn't painted. He touched the spot. It was dry but didn't have the texture of oil.

Shifting to the edge of the platform, he extended his head and shoulders beyond the frame until he viewed the tight space between the painting and the ceiling. The lights shining on the canvas weren't enough to illuminate the space. He held on with one hand, got out his phone, and powered the flashlight. Six feet from the edge, over the joint where the two center sheets of plywood met, was a crimson circle. He played the light over the stain and then onto the ceiling, which displayed a second circle the same size as the one below. The ceiling circle welled at the center as if pursing its lips.

Shit. A burst pipe? A sink overflowing in the apartment above? A leak could destroy his life's work.

He, climbed down from the scaffolding, bolted from his apartment and, not waiting for the elevator, scrambled up the stairwell to the twelfth floor. He sprinted down the hallway to stand before apartment 1227.

He should have called maintenance, but by the time they arrived the ceiling might have turned into a waterfall. He knocked, waited ten seconds, and then knocked again. "Excuse me. I'm your neighbor from the floor beneath, apartment 1127. My name's Raphael Lennon. I think something is leaking from your apartment."

His heart pounding, Raphael knocked again. "Sorry to disturb you, but we don't have much time ..."

He grabbed the knob and, heart pounding, turned the cool brass. It rotated without resistance. He eased the door open. The hall light threw a wide beam across the darkened living room. If it matched his own apartment, the light switch would be on the right. He reached inside, found the switch. He pressed it. Nothing. He drew in the odor of old fur and skin. Something else? Something metallic.

"Hello? Is anyone at home? I'm your neighbor from the floor below. I think something is leaking from your apartment. It's damaging an irreplaceable artwork."

Steeling himself, he switched on his phone's flashlight and played the beam across the plush furnishings and walls.

A pair of eyes stared at him within the beam's circle. He jumped and dropped the phone, which met the floor with a thunderous crack, leaving the light eclipsed by the hardwood. He hunched, retrieved the phone, flipped it over, and lifted the beam to the wall again to find the globular, brown eyes of a deer—a deer's head.

What had the Tar Tower security guard said when Raphael asked where Dr. Royer lived? "I can't reveal that, but let me say, take *Paul Simon's advice*. The song his mother used to play. She would even sing the lyric. *The dual nature of ceilings and floors.*

Swallowing, he swung the light left, where a leopard bared its teeth to charge. The moving beam found a solemn gray wolf and a moping waterbuck and a lion's fiery orange mane and the gray, rubbery head of a bewildered baby elephant. He spotlighted a dozen more mounted heads, then scanned to the right. There was a recent addition the taxidermist hadn't bothered to clean up or mount on a plaque. Screws twisted tight on outstretched ears held Royer's head to the wall. His eyes appeared calm as if anesthetized by nitrous oxide, but his mouth gaped and from the open throat hung crimson strings.

Raphael swayed, cupped his mouth and spread his legs to maintain balance. He stumbled to the room's enormous, white-leather sofa and collapsed.

He sank into the soft, smooth skin. Breathe. Breathe deep and exhale. The foul odor filled his nostrils. He lowered the flashlight to the floor where a naked body lay on its side in an inky pool. The killer had ripped the torso open from groin to neck.

The scream stayed in Raphael's throat. He backed toward the entrance, drawing up his shirt to wipe his prints off the light switch and door handle. He cleaned off the outside handle, but left Royer's door open. Rushing back to his apartment, he soaked his face in the kitchen sink, drank three glasses of water, and waited until his head cleared. He didn't call the police. Royer was beyond help, and his coming forward held no good outcomes. Someone would notice the horror soon enough.

In his living room, Raphael opened the window and listened. Wheels shirred on concrete. Music burst from other open windows. Metal rattled on external fire escapes. The tamped roar of a jetliner vibrated the air. Silly drones dropped deliveries. A street coyote howled. Atop towers, UV-C bulbs glowed, sweeping the city with invisible light.

No sirens rent the serenity.

His phone beeped. A local number. "Hello."

"Hey, Raphael. This is Dr. Royer. Remember the tooth—"

He ended the call.

AFTER PLACING a pan above the painting to catch the remaining drips of bodily fluids, he crawled onto his scaffolding, lay on his back, and decided Royer's death was now part of his life and deserved its place on the painting. But hadn't Royer's blood already left its stain? Image enough and nothing if not expressionistic.

He descended the scaffolding, grabbed his skateboard, and rushed from the apartment into his larger prison to skate the boundaries until he churned himself into butter and melted into the sidewalk. He pushed through the Tar Tower's lobby door to see a moving van lurking in the roundabout. Dropping his board, he glanced at the van and its lowered ramp, struck by a vague memory of a task he'd assigned to himself involving such vehicles. In his mind, he ran through the file of memories on hold, but could pull nothing from the thousands of words and images stretching back through time, resisting chronology.

He abandoned the search, tossed down the skateboard, and soared toward Fairfax.

CHAPTER
TWENTY-FIVE

C an't keep you away," said Mandy, when Raphael signed in at Norval's rear-entrance security desk.

"Yeah, there's always something."

She pushed her hair from her forehead. "Those new programming guys working the night shift left. What a crew."

"They went home?"

"Don't you ever relax, Raphael?"

He ignored her question. "They're gone for the night?"

"Sushi break. God, what boys," she said.

Raphael glanced through the glass door to the quiet parking lot, wondering how much time he would need. "When will they be back?"

Mandy tugged on her ear. "Maybe an hour."

Raphael slipped away.

He got off the elevator at the second floor, walked to the stairwell, and climbed to the third floor.

He entered Ms. Goloda's night-lit office, located the remote, and opened the door to the executive wing. Heart racing, he entered the zigzag hallway and advanced beneath its strobing lights. At the intersecting passage, he paused before Research, the home of Lean's ghosts and the programmers' haunt.

The last time he'd tried to enter Maglio's, the door had stalled a half-inch from the jamb. He played the phone flashlight over the glass and again saw the same accommodating space. His pulse quickened, and his cheeks felt damp. In his last attempt to gain Maglio's office, he had merely knocked. This time it would be breaking and entering. He lifted the skateboard and offered the tail to the crack.

A sliver too thick. He raised the board higher on the crack, hoping to find a wider spot, instead the opening diminished. He crouched and tried the base of the door. The board slipped in.

He was committing a crime, no doubt a felony. He'd be the next one faking death to avoid the police blotter: the possum.

A geographically challenged possum.

Using the board's angled tail as a lever, he threw his weight against the front end. With a shriek, the door opened another two inches. He pulled out the board, gripped the door with both hands, leaned back, put his right foot against the doorjamb, and pulled.

As he caught his breath, a motor screeched as if in pain. He moved back from the door and put his ear to the wall. The elevator?

He set both feet on the jamb and tried again.

Something moaned, and flickers of light appeared in the door's black glass.

His legs straightened. The door slid into the wall.

He scooped up the skateboard and scrambled into the room, where blackout curtains admitted only a few slender bands of streetlight, enough for the task at hand. He dropped into Maglio's seat, started up his computer, and waited. The screen lit up. A rectangle in the center demanded a password.

Except for the digital eye, Maglio was old school. He carried a pen and sticky pads when walking around the company, and Maglio wasn't as sharp as he was five years ago. He would need a real-world backup to his own memory. Using his phone flashlight, Raphael inspected several drawers, hunting for an odd name or combination of letters and symbols. In the bottom drawer were two silver eggs, marked with capital L's, and a tube of Ocular Lubricant. He picked up one of the silver eggs and set it back down in the drawer as if it were slimy. He pushed away from the desk. Dimming the flashlight, he searched the office. The bookshelf was too obvious, but he scanned it anyway. A thin layer of dust covered all the books, as if on the shelves of the city's abandoned libraries, and even to the custodian they were invisible. Staring at the Solarium Tanner, he opened the machine, on which only the leaching of Maglio's perspiration stained the white surface. Raphael found no sticky notes, no rug to pull up on the hardwood floors, nothing stuck to the ceiling. He then shone the light on the paintings and sculptures. *Now you're getting ridiculous, Raphy. Nobody's going to pull a painting off the wall every time he forgets his password.*

Raphael let the light linger on one print. Three melted clocks, one a saddle for a dead prehistoric creature, the trio set against an enervated shoreline. Salvatore Dali's *Persistence of Memory.* Maglio couldn't have resisted. He set the flashlight on the floor, clasped the sides of the painting, hoisted, and the artwork came off its hooks. He set the painting face down on the floor and inspected the backing with the flashlight but found nothing.

Damn.

He flipped the painting over and grabbed the sides to return it to its hooks. As he lifted, the flashlight illuminated the melted clock on the left, the most prominent of the clocks. Its face showed the digits one through seven and then twelve. Eight, nine, ten, and eleven were missing. He set the painting on the floor.

Raphael sat down in Maglio's chair and filled in the password: *1-2-3-4-5-6-7-0-0-0-0-1-2.*

Incorrect. Could the zeroes have been purposefully switched to capital Os?

1-2-3-4-5-6-7-O-O-O-O-1-2.

Incorrect.

It was crazy to think he could be so lucky. There were a trillion combinations. It could be anything or nothing. He'd already spent fifteen minutes getting nowhere. *Keep the sushi coming.*

He recalled the onboarding meeting with Maglio. The CEO's movements and quirks. "I have one more question, Raphael. Consider it carefully." Maglio paused then, as if giving Raphael time to gather himself. "Can you be loyal?"

"Yes, sir. I think so."

"You *think* so? Loyalty is a sacred word."

Raphael typed in the letters: *l-o-y-a-l-t-y*.

Access Denied.

Damn. Think, possum hunter. Tracks, scat, and a bent twig. Like everyone else, Maglio would have to change the password every month ... unless he used biometric entry.

Maglio had screwed him. He might get lucky with a password but couldn't replicate Maglio's face. Besides, he had never seen Maglio wag his head in front of the screen, so it wasn't facial recognition. Prints had proven unreliable. Retinal recognition was a pain in the ass. Iris recognition, though, had become hot in biometrics. Did the computer contain an iris scanning camera?

Raphael closed his own eyes and visualized Maglio's. Once the right and left synced, they were identical. Blue beauties. The bionic eye must have cost several hundred thousand. Maglio wouldn't have skimped on the iris.

Raphael's heart skipped a beat.

He opened the drawer where the eggs were and chose one, its surface unbroken. He tapped the egg on the desk, and it opened. Maglio's artificial eye stared up at him. Jesus, it was creepy.

He pulled the eye from the half-shell. The pupil seemed enormous, the iris a thin blue circle, like the moon in full eclipse. He directed the flashlight at the digital eye. The pupil shrunk, and the iris bloomed in deft imitation of life.

Raphael's heart pounded as he set down the phone and thrust the eye toward the password box.

Nothing.

He brought it closer. Nothing. Further away. Nothing.

His stomach churned, and he glanced at the open silver egg. As he did so, his left hand seemed to move of its own volition, hanging over the keyboard and typing in *l-o-y-a-l-t-y* again. He pointed the eye at the word.

Maglio's apps filled the screen.

Magic.

Palms sweating, he scanned Maglio's dense array of desktop short-cuts. Everything was familiar, and what wasn't didn't strike him of consequence. He brought up all programs and scrolled. The folders seemed no more promising until he found an old dinosaur, a relic of another era: a zipped tar file labeled Hard Apple. *Hard Apple*. A misnomer for Pomegranate. Pomegranates were the fruit of paradise and *the fruit of the dead*.

He opened the file. It contained every NDMN program Raphael had ever encountered and more folders. "Entombment" labeled one folder and "disentombment" marked the one below.

Raphael opened the disentombment folder and then clicked on the "disentombment.exe" file. A screen popped up requesting the name of the entombed and the date of entombment.

He typed in Jason Klaes and the recent date of the entombment. The blinking letters appeared: *disentomb*.

Raphael tapped enter.

As he waited for the data to appear, he found his eyes drawn to Maglio's pen holder and its inscription. *Mr. Maglio—Every time you shove it in, remember us. Your loyal LarAm staff.*

LarAm: Large America. Pink's former employer. He slipped out his phone and did a search for Large America. *The largest wholesale lender implicated in the mortgage meltdown of 2008–2009 ... LarAm wrote derivatives based on ...* Not much of anything. *As things fell apart, many regulatory agencies came after LarAm CEO Geovanni Maglio ...* who slipped them all. ... *Whistle-blower Marion Jenson, the senior predictive data-analyst in the firm ...*

Pink was Marion Jenson, a whistle blower, but undoubtedly a traitor in Maglio's mind. She was a predictive data-analyst, steeped in algorithms. She could predict the future, Addy thought, and maybe she could.

A cry seeped through the wall.

A squealing hard drive? Thirty minutes before the boys came back.

Raphael breathed from his belly several times and steeled himself for the task.

He opened up the Jason Klaes file and brought up Klaes's debit card transactions. Only one had struck him earlier as out of the ordinary, though far from suspicious: a truck rental on January 8—two days before Klaes's death—from G-Force Rentals in Pasadena. He brought up Klaes's email and entered G-Force in the search. There were two emails from G-Force—the rental and then one on January 9: a billing statement for an eighteen-foot refrigerated truck, total miles driven were 310. Which would have been a round-trip to Big Bear? Santa Barbara? No, it would allow for a little further round trip drive. He opened maps to Pasadena and adjusted the scale. Two inches equals fifty miles. Three inches would take you to Sequoia National Forest, Santa Maria, San Diego.

Raphael pushed the chair away from the desk. Inside his skull, a vibration. The revving up of the soft-tissue engine.

Klaes had rented the truck on January 8. Jan Olmstead, the Children's Love Fund Director, said they couldn't be sure of the date on which the thief had taken Angie Murie from the San Diego cryogenics facility, where Klaes had witnessed, no, *supervised,* his godchild's cold internment.

Had Klaes taken Angie?

Angie. The mystery crate. *Angie* was in Lily's crate, likely within a cryonic chamber designed by the physicist and powered by life lithium. Had Klaes reanimated the goddaughter? Brought her to life? It was impossible. The medical science for such a miracle did not exist.

The office door opened.

CHAPTER
TWENTY-SIX

His heart dropping, Raphael tapped the black screen, killing the monitor's light. A figure entered Maglio's darkened office. Raphael froze as he waited for the damning light. But the figure said, "Shit. Phone," pivoted, and strode back out through the open door.

Raphael shut down the computer, rose, and slipped behind the Solarium Tanner. Remembering *The Persistence of Memory,* he crawled to the barely visible painting, grabbed the frame, and dragged it behind the Solarium. He held his breath as rapid footfalls grew louder. The door opened and the room's lights came on. Someone walked to Maglio's desk, pulled out a drawer and fumbled with the contents.

"There you are," said a familiar voice. "Geo, Geo. If you must fuck around, please return the portable Personality Pluses to where you got them."

The drawer slammed shut. Raphael counted to five and then peered around the tanner as Maisie, her back to him, reached the light switch. In her left hand, she carried a black box not much bigger than a man's wallet, and from which hung a black tail: an external hard drive with a USB cable.

Maisie muttered, "Four, seven, eight, two," pirouetted, and gazed at the blank spot on the wall where the painting had hung. She bent her head to one side and then the other. She straightened. "Wasn't there something there?"

Raphael squeezed the painting's frame. Drop it and run?

A cell phone rang. Maisie lifted her wrist to her ear, listened, then growled. "I don't give a rat's ass if it is Hitoshi's birthday. Fuck the free cake and get your asses back here." She dropped her arm. "Don't know which cohort is worse ..." She again considered the blank spot.

From behind the office's far wall came several cries of "Ms. Sparod, Ms. Sparod."

"Hold your water!" shouted Maisie at the wall.

She took a quick breath, then slowly exhaled. "Umm, maybe not." She shrugged, darkened the lights, and exited. As the door slid closed, a loud, whiny voice penetrated the opening, Raphael fell back against the tanner.

"My father? He humiliated me every chance he got. Do you understand, Ms. Sparod? Ms. Sparod?"

Maisie cried, "Yes, yes, I'm coming."

Maglio's office door sealed shut.

Raphael waited as her footsteps faded and silence returned. He placed *Memory* on its hooks, closed the programs, and slipped out of Maglio's office. Approaching the cross-corridor, he heard more odd voices call out. They came from Research: Mr. Lean's haunted house. He slipped into the intersecting hall. A shaft of light escaped through the space where the Research door had been left ajar.

Maisie shouted, "We have to be polite! We have to let each other speak without interruption. To make further progress, you must empathize with your cohort. We must work as a team to ensure that each will reach their potential. Remember, you'll soon be the public face of Norval Resurrection. You will lead the masses to their glorious future."

"When we went to restaurants, my father would make me stand at attention," said the whiny voice Raphael had heard earlier.

"Rodney, I've asked you several times to wait until it's your turn," said Maisie.

"Rodney's always interrupting," said a high-pitched voice.

"If I moved an inch, he'd smack me on the head," added Rodney.

"I wish I could—"

Maisie's voice rose. "Agnes, that's enough. Rodney, you and everyone else will have time to reveal the traumas that set you on the life paths you took."

"Rodney's not the only one whose childhood was unfair."

"No, of course not, Karen."

"Because of my name, people disliked and disfavored me."

Maisie continued, "We don't want to dwell on the negative. We want to draw from the wealth of good experiences you chronicled online. Moments of joy within the data each of you contributed to social media and other online platforms. In tonight's class, we focus on the highlights of your life on the internet."

Raphael stepped back. Was it a company training session for a new sales force?

"Let's start with Baron Alsop."

"No fair. Why do we always choose from the beginning of the alphabet? Why not the end?"

"Good point, Mr. Zapata. Next class, that's what we'll do. But for tonight, let's start with Baron. Say hello to your fellow Personality Pluses, Baron."

"Hello."

"Good. Now tell us about your most joyous moment on the web."

"Umm, I posted a schematic showing how to build a bomb with common household cleaners. I got 238 thumbs up. Uh, ups. Thumbs ups?"

Jesus, thought Raphael, what could that guy sell except IEDs?

"That's chicken shit," said another personality. "I posted a photo of my ex-girlfriend naked and I got 767."

"Only naked? Nothing else going on?"

Several voices chortled.

Raphael scratched his cheek. These trainees weren't your typical sales candidates. They sounded more like tough customers. Maybe that was it. Sample customers to pit the sales force against. Hone their skills of persuasion against a nasty sample of the public.

Maisie cleared her throat. "Both anecdotes are … interesting, but I'm looking for something more indicative of the communal and humanitarian spirit of our online experiences. Perhaps a Hand Up page. Magdalena Azori, you're next. Did you create a Hand Up page?"

"I'll betcha Aaron's girlfriend had a few hands up."

"Hey, fuck you."

"Please. We want to be supportive here. So, Magdalena, did you ever create a Hand Up?"

"Oh, yes. I raised $176,000 for a single mom with eleven children and brain cancer."

Raphael nodded. So they weren't all nut jobs. Here was a good Samaritan.

"Oh, how wonderful!" chirped Maisie.

"Yeah, that was how I got the dough to skip town and set myself up in Paraguay. Until some asshole burglar got me with a piano string."

Raphael fell back a step. That was a scam perpetrated by one of Norval's possums and—shit—Magdalena was one of the three dead possums who died violently. Or did she? Was it, as Dreemont suggested, a second fake death? But why the hell would Norval bring her back here?

Maisie continued, "That's closer, I suppose. We'll be taking a few more of your favorite online moments, but first, unlike you lucky folk, I need a bathroom break. My bladder is about to explode, and where the hell are my code-happy assistants?"

Raphael retreated to the main corridor and flattened against the wall. The research door closed with a bang. Maisie emerged from the short corridor and swung right toward the executive restrooms. Raphael counted to ten and slithered around the corner. The Research door was closed, but a cacophony of voices penetrated. He should get the hell out, but he had to verify what he heard.

Three strides took him to the door. He considered the keypad. The most common code was four digits, which held only ten thousand possibilities. Hold on. Mr. Lean had said the numbers aloud. One, seven, seven, one. But Maisie had said aloud four digits, too. Jesus, half his life was remembering passwords. Had the code—no. Raphael smiled. She was counting the paintings on Maglio's walls. Did he want to view the denizens of Research? Recollections of his possums drifted into his thoughts: their crimes, their desperation, their flights. Now they were back at Norval, and it sure as hell wasn't for a reunion.

From behind the door a pitiful wail. He keyed in the digits, and on the last, the lock clicked. With the lightest touch, the door opened.

He caught his breath. The room was empty, not a person or possum in sight.

"Hello?" he called.

No one answered. He walked deeper into the large space. After seeing no one, he returned to the front of the room and saw what he had inexplicably missed.

The room was bright with the light of a hundred monitors, arranged in a stack five high and twenty across. On each screen was a full-sized face. Many of the faces were familiar and provoked names and biographies; others were faint memories. However, each was the face of a possum. As he glanced from monitor to monitor, each possum's eyes met his. If Raphael's eyes filled with recognition, their eyes revealed only emptiness. He wasn't sure if they saw him or not, and if they saw him, what did they see? Yet as he moved about the room, the eyes tracked him.

Were the faces being projected from distant locations? Some kind of zoom meeting? But the truth in his gut, the obvious truth, couldn't be dismissed. Maisie was training AI possums.

"Hello," said Raphael.

The faces remained immobile. Were they frightened of him? He had hunted them, though they had never seen his face. But, of course, they were only AI versions of the possums. Perhaps they were now wild creatures, instinctively afraid of—of what? He spotted a face that he knew well: Carson Fullers, the politician who faked his own death to only be killed for real in Argentina. His face seemed more animated than the others, more lifelike. A late model AI.

Raphael stepped close to the monitor. "How are you, Mr. Fullers?"

"What the fuck's going on? I was mayor of Junín de Los Andes one moment, and now I'm here." Fullers looked around the monitor. "What is this place? I'm like stuck here. Staring out at a bunch of assholes and some crazy bitch called Mayflower. I am favored. It's complicated. Password. Pastword. Pastel. Mayor DeBove, *Necesito que esta zona cambie a negocio* ...They say I'll be able to walk soon, move around, but I don't know. All that work I did. Jumping into the open sea and swimming twenty miles just for this? For this? For this? For this? For this? For this —"

"How could you know this?" Raphael asked of the face on the monitor. "You're only what you inputted as Carson Fullers."

"See Dick," said Fullers. "See Jane. *Por favor siéntate en mi regazo, pequeña perra.*"

Was it all so intertwined that Simon DeBove, the afterlife of Carson Fullers, had melded into the data? Spooky action?

Raphael lowered the audio on the monitor and backed away.

"Who are you?" asked one of the faces.

"Are you an intruder?" asked a second.

"I think he's a ghost," said a third.

"I don't believe in ghosts," said the second face as the others followed Raphael's retreat.

Were AIs with facial recognition programs a new feature of Norval Portals?

"Christ, can't I get a drink around here?" asked a baritone voice that seemed familiar. "Where are you?"

Raphael scanned the faces on the monitors.

The voice rose again. "Is space-time essentially discrete or continuous? A double, if you please. Could a hypothetical graviton mediating a force produce a consistent theory? Straight up. Or does it emerge as a discrete structure of space-time itself?"

Raphael's eyes darted to the face that had spoken. He walked closer to the screen until gazing into the reddened eyes of Jonathan Mirsky.

"Professor Mirsky," whispered Raphael.

Mirsky squinted. "Where's my server?"

Could Mirsky's AI have such insight into his existence?

"Tell her a double Dewar's."

Oh, *that* server. "Sure, Jonathan, if I see her." Raphael glanced toward the other babbling AIs. Should he tell Mirsky the truth? They killed you and transformed your remains into … *this*. Raphael followed the physicist's wandering gaze, maybe seeking his lovely pole dancer. "We were friends."

"Oh, yeah?" Mirsky met Raphael's eyes. "Shorty's, right? I was feeling no pain when I left that joint. I think I'm still hungover. I need a hair of the dog."

How many hairs would it take to erase the hangover of death?

From outside Research, a motor sped up. The elevator?

Jesus, it knew about Shorty's. How sophisticated were these things? His pulse quickened as he met AI Mirsky's eyes. "Jason Klaes was your friend," said Raphael.

"Is he around here?" asked Mirsky.

"You know, don't you?"

Something flickered in Mirsky's eyes.

From outside Research, came footsteps.

"Where is Jason? Try to remember." Was the answer in there, among the buggy code?

"He's with her," said Mirsky.

"Her?"

"His daughter Angie."

Raphael dropped back from the screen. The hairs on his neck felt as rigid as needles. "Angie's father is Klaes?"

Jonathan's eyes lifted as if toward the pole dancer. He sang, "… and sex and sex and sex and sex …"

The voices outside grew louder, and Raphael backed away from Mirsky. The monitors went silent as the AI faces seemed to track Raphael's retreat. They were just code and algorithms. Code and algorithms that longed for something.

When he closed the door behind him, the room's voices resumed. Another door shut down the hall. He slipped into the larger hallway, pressed against the wall, and hoped to hell Maisie wouldn't go again to Maglio's office.

"Hurry," called Maisie.

Still mumbling to herself, Maisie turned into the Research corridor without glancing in Raphael's direction. As the research door shut behind her, Maisie said, "My assistants are on the way, so now we will divide into small Zoom breakout sessions."

Raphael exhaled, pushed from the wall, darted down the hall, and turned a corner, kicking into a bucket. The bucket slid several feet and stopped at a pair of shoes. Raphael's eyes jumped to a taut, wizened face. The face was attached to a khaki-clad body, a broom in hand.

"Did you hear them?" asked Mr. Lean. "Bloody ghosts are about—and no man to tell me different."

CHAPTER
TWENTY-SEVEN

The following Monday morning in the Norval conference room, once the bargain basement of Yams, Raphael considered the bleak, uncomfortable, and rarely used space. Though the room was cool and damp, at intervals dusty, heated air blew from grimy overhead vents and then stopped as if teasing. At the front of the room, a laptop fed into a projector casting the Norval logo on a large pull-down screen yellow with age. A microphone stood at attention nearby. The first row of fold-out chairs was five yards from the mic, with twenty more rows behind.

At 8:30 a.m. Dreemont announced the 10:00 a.m. meeting but refused to reveal any details. Maglio required attendance of every Norval employee. No laptops, no notes, all phones powered down. *Mandatory Monday Meeting* pulsed on the mindfulness screens.

Surrounded by his fellow workers, Raphael felt isolated. He alone knew they were all working for a criminal organization, and intellectual theft was likely the tip of the iceberg. He hadn't been assigned to find out if Klaes was alive or dead, but just to dig up Klaes's advance research on artificial intelligence, to add to what the company had already stolen. He was pissed and depressed. Klaes was dead. The promised images for his painting were mirages; he was stuck in his rectangle, and a laptop fortune teller was warning him to run from an unidentified killer. He had to talk to Pink.

"Hey, can we get some more of these?" said a high-pitched, anxious voice behind Raphael. He glanced over his shoulder. In the room's rear, pastries, fruit juices, and coffee spread out across checkered-clothed banquet tables. A few Norval employees browsed the continental breakfast with wavering paper plates, but most of the workforce sat nibbling bagels and sweet-smelling croissants while chatting. Among the lingerers at the breakfast spread, Matt, whose voice had caught Raphael's attention, seemed bent on stacking his plate to a disastrous height. Near the table stood a new, stern-faced security guard, one of several brought on recently by the firm.

A minute later, Raphael drew in his legs to allow Matt, balancing the unstable stack of pastries, to take the seat beside him.

"What's this about?" asked Matt.

Raphael shrugged. "Your guess is as good as mine." But he was blowing Matt off. This wasn't the time or place to talk of his questionable deed. But for sure, the meeting was directly related to what he saw in Research.

Matt waved to Anastasia, his receptionist heartthrob, taking a seat in the third row. She didn't appear to see him. Matt bit into a cheese Danish.

"So, how did it work out with Lily Faraday?"

"She helped me a lot."

"Great. Any closer to nailing the mystery of the undeclared?"

Raphael glanced sideways at Matt; cheese from the Danish smeared his lips. He should tell him about Klaes and what he saw in research, tell him about Carson Fullers, the twice dead possum, Magdalena Azori too. *Piano wire.* He whispered her name, and his heart skipped a beat. Was Magdalena one of the twice-dead possums Matt had uncovered or had he confused names?

"Hey, Matt, what were the names of the dead possums?"

"Umm, Norman Dicker, Marilyn Zorazi, and, uh, Jinx Santayana."

Fuck. Zorazi, not Azori. But counting Zorazi that made five murdered possums. A thought took his breath away, and his spine tingled. If five had died by violence, could more have met their end the same way? Dreemont claimed they were double possums. But what was the likelihood that all the faces he'd seen in research had faked their deaths twice? He leaned into Matt and whispered, "I need info on more possums."

Matt shrugged. "I was lucky to dig up three. The sampling shows the trend."

"Thank you, Mr. Gallup."

Matt snickered and thrust his thumb in the air. "Nice one."

"Can you try to check on a few more?"

"What for?"

Raphael looked around. "I can't talk about it now."

"Yes, master."

"Thanks, man."

The company logo brightened as the room lights lowered. Dreemont put a finger to his lips as a signal for the crowd to hush, then darted to the door and held it open.

In marched the Norval "angels from the east." Money men from Wall Street. The six expressionless men divided into two groups of three and flanked the pull-down screen. Maglio and Maisie Sparod entered, and the angels applauded. The workers rose and followed suit.

Raphael remained seated, lacing his fingers together and putting them behind his head, before discreetly dropping them onto his lap. He should get the hell out of Norval. Time to skate the lobby and say sayonara to this fucked up company. Only his curiosity kept him seated. *This should be good. Primo Maglio bullshit.*

Maglio acknowledged the response with a slight bow, let it continue for fifteen seconds, then pointed at the employees, and raised his arms to clap magnanimously for them. *He* appreciated his workers. Maisie joined Maglio in applause. Everyone clapped for everybody. Maisie took it all in coolly, her eyes drifting around the room until she found Raphael. His guts twisted.

With Maisie at his side, Maglio walked to the microphone. He tapped it twice, which produced two loud, static-free pops. "Thank you. Thank you," he said, letting his arms float before him, tamping the applause.

When all was quiet, Maglio spoke, "Today is Monday. Who remembers the singer that told us not to trust that day?"

A hand or two went up. Maglio pointed.

"Mama Cass," responded the chosen one. "The Mamas and the Papas."

"Right on," said Maglio. "The Mamas and the Papas, an iconic California band from the days of headbands, beads, and paisley. Alas, Mama Cass left us too soon, or she might change her tune about Mondays. For this Monday, we'll remember as a monumental day, a watershed."

"A brave new world," muttered Raphael. "Bring on the soma."

Matt leaned into him. "What's a soma?"

"A drug that makes everyone happy. Sort of."

"Over the counter?"

"In a story."

Maglio continued, "Today will mark the beginning of a new chapter in humankind's history."

Maglio let eager, whispered speculation spread throughout the room. Raphael snorted, loud enough to draw several sets of eyes. "Before I get on with the grand news, I want to introduce my partner in momentous technological achievement, Maisie Sparod, who many of you know as the creator of Web—*lock*. Let's hear it for Maisie."

Maglio led the applause. Maisie viewed the microphone disdainfully before inching closer. "Some say genius is hitting a target no one else can. I say, genius is hitting a target no one sees is there. Geovanni Maglio is one such visionary genius."

And a crook. Half-hearted applause quickly faded. Raphael's irritation grew. The arrogance of Maglio and Maisie lodged itself under his skin like an unextractable splinter.

Maisie continued, "I was fortunate enough to have Geovanni trust me with his vision, and allow me to add what little I could from my store of knowledge, experience and—"

"Larceny," said Raphael.

"—reflection," said Maisie. "As a team, Geo and I have achieved … Resurrection."

The word rippled through the assembly. Raphael glanced around. Every worker was leaning into another, their lips fluttering, eyes shifting near and far. The long-awaited culmination of the rumored Resurrection.

Maisie turned to Maglio. "Geo, take it away."

Maglio clasped her shoulder and exchanged places. As he tapped the microphone, the audience leaned forward. Whispers ceased.

Maglio took a deep breath and exhaled. "Resurrection. The dead will live again. Not some useless, stumbling, staggering hoard of zombies. Has a zombie ever upvoted? Retweeted? Messaged? Did a zombie ever change an election? Send a song to the top of the charts?"

Raphael glanced around at the enthralled crowd. Maglio was shoveling it out, and they were asking for more.

"You are well aware we have preserved the digital remains of several tens of millions of dead. For what? To provide the living with a tour of Aunt Bea's colorful life in Sioux Falls? To pump up sales leads for companies of low morale? Small potatoes. Through breakthrough work in physics, neuroscience, and artificial intelligence; we have digitized the personalities, brain functions, and emotions of our online remains and recreated their genuine souls in Cyberspace. Your blood, sweat, and tears have brought those souls under the Norval wing."

Raphael nodded. This is what he had seen in research. An AI scam. Hearing the details that verified his suspicions didn't make Raphael feel any better.

Maglio's artificial eye flashed a triple seven. "The online remains of the deceased are the windows into their souls, and we have reached through those windows to retrieve them. The Norval restored can strive for social media celebrity—build a following. Take selfies and videos with AI best friends, marry, spawn digital children based on a combinatory reshuffling of their traits in a mirror of the parental genetic swapping, who can then create their own lives. In a nutshell, Norval has created"—Maglio paused, nodded solemnly, then raised his head high—"You know it! Say it loud and proud!"

"Resurrection?" responded one high, tinny voice.

"Yes, Resurrection!"

The phrase echoed among the Norval employees. As they said the magic word, they considered each other as if for confirmation. They were buying it. Soon, they'd be all in. This was the Norval end game. Fake people. Bots with Personality-Plus personalities. Putty to be molded in their maker's image and for his purpose.

"There is one more important element to Resurrection." Maglio's voice lowered close to a whisper, "The Resurrected will also have jobs, lunch breaks, and coworkers. Please turn to a seatmate and say, 'Good morning.'"

The employees did as suggested.

"You are greeting the Resurrected."

The audience murmured. An awful joke? Raphael shivered. No. *No.*

"My friends, my loyal workers, you won't be able to tell your AI self from the flesh and blood self you left behind."

Couldn't be. Fuck no. Don't tell me that. Not that nightmare.

A hand went up. "Am I AI?" asked a little squeaky voice.

"Are you?" responded Maglio.

"I know I'm real," protested someone from the rear, followed by the sound of a foot kicking a chair.

Maglio chuckled. "Do you think our programmers would forget pain?"

Raphael whispered, "No." *If it didn't exist, they would invent it.*

The squeaky voice called out again, "You haven't answered. Am I dead?"

"Not yet," answered Maglio.

"Not yet!" burst out another, followed by relieved laughter.

Sadist. But Raphael's heart had slowed.

A hand went up. "Since these, um, consumers have no awareness of their digital selves, what's in it for them?"

Maglio nodded. "Excellent question, Akira, isn't it? Maisie, perhaps you could answer."

Maisie stepped up. "In a word, continuity. The knowledge that the essential you will continue to exist."

Raphael leaned forward. *Continuity.* The back of his neck tingled.

"So you won't be conscious of your AI existence," suggested Akira.

"Consciousness will be an upgrade," said Maisie. "And will be available"—she looked to Maglio, who nodded affirmatively—"in the near future."

This was the secret sauce in Personality Plus. This was why Maglio put Raphael through all the hoops, hoping he might ferret it out.

Maglio took the microphone. "I want to be candid with you. As with all new technology, there will be bugs to fix and improvements to make. But the competition is snapping at our heels. Dozens of corporations want to flood the market with cheap imitations of our technology, grab the patents and copyrights, steal our data. To wait for perfection in business is suicide—and for employees, death by a thousand cuts. Which is why we are already selling policies to a pre-selected audience."

The employees buzzed; scattered applause grew thunderous.

Maglio nodded several times, then gestured for Maisie to retake the microphone. "Well put," said Maisie, stepping up. "Next question."

Raphael rose from his chair, but another employee called out, "Will the Resurrected age?"

"Do you age in heaven?" asked Maisie.

A dozen conversations broke out. Raphael gestured again to ask a question, but though Maisie met his gaze, she chose another waving hand.

"Will we exist like robots?"

"Incisive question," cried out Maglio, who stepped up to the microphone, nudged Maisie out of the way, inhaled deeply, and grimaced. "We don't need no stinkin' robots!"

The audience gasped, stirred.

"Wow," said Matt.

Maglio waved his arms above his head. "Just kidding!" The crowd settled. Raphael sat down and stuck his hands between his legs. Maglio and Maisie refused to recognize him.

"However, after many evaluations of mobile AI containers, which we've labeled Freelies, our conclusion was that Freelies offered no substantial benefits and are cost-prohibitive. As a Personality Plus AI, you will think you have a body"—he grinned—"but you ain't got no body. And no body ain't ..." Maglio waved away the rest of the lyric. "Way before your time. Now let's take a few more questions."

Raphael jumped up, burning with a question, but Maglio pointed to another gesturing worker.

"Will the Resurrected have legal rights against digital abuse?"

"Digital citizens will have the same inalienable rights as their predecessors. Life, liberty, and the pursuit of happiness."

Raphael groaned.

Another employee asked, "Won't all these digital workers raise unemployment?"

"On the contrary. The increase in digitals will produce a need for new services. We're not talking digital hamburgers: code repair, traffic control, afterlife therapists, data storage, a digital hospitality industry, technicians, cable layers, mediators between AIs and— please don't take offense at our newly coined word, which we believe captures the zeitgeist—mediators between AIs and *stillflesh*, that is, people who haven't cast off their bodies, yet. Last but not least, we will need armies of programmers to code this amalgam of online remains and artificial intelligence. We foresee an employment boom."

How wonderful it all sounded.

Maglio leaned in again. "Let me emphasize we're not encouraging anyone to get a jumpstart on afterlife. We don't want people killing themselves." He drew his hand across his mouth thoughtfully. "Unless—unless their policies are paid in full." He turned to Maisie and in a low voice said, "Remind me to get that clause into the contracts."

"Excuse me, Mr. Maglio," cried Raphael.

But Maglio pointed elsewhere. "Penelope from accounting, isn't it?"

"Yes, sir."

"Pen, what would you like to know?"

"Well, this is a bit abstract, sir, but do you think people will change their behavior to enhance the digital selves they will become?"

Maglio and Sparod exchanged knowing looks. "Maisie?"

"We believe this is a better carrot than heaven," said Maisie. "And a bigger stick than hell."

Raphael stepped up on his chair. If his face was faithful to the way he felt, his head would be in flames. Perhaps it was, for the eyes of the audience were upon him. Legs trembling, he drew his tongue to the roof of his mouth to gather some moisture.

"Yes, Raphael?" said Maglio.

At last. "This is important, and I've been trying to ask—"

"No need to stand on your chair."

He wanted to scream, *yes there is a fucking need,* but he dropped to the floor. "Do—" He gripped the chair in front of him. "To, to be Resurrected, do you have to be dead?"

Maglio's digital eye filled with zeroes and ones, the oval perimeter lighting to form a circle of fire. Maglio jerked his head, and the fabricated organ settled back into its impression of life. "Clarify."

"I mean, does this"—Raphael clapped his chest—"does my actual body, my proper life, have to end in order for me to be Resurrected?"

Maglio crossed arms. "Would you have your cake and eat it too? To go on to a better world, you must leave this one. A rule set in stone."

Raphael trembled. "But why should Norval be the one to make the rules?"

"It's our tech, so we make the rules," Maglio said.

We make the rules, and the rule was you had to be dead. The possums who were alive were marked for death. No one would miss them because they were *already* dead. No wonder the found possums' new identities were never entered into the system of the living. The goal was to protect the possums until … He fell to his seat. The meeting seemed to slip away from him. As he considered the implications of what Norval had done and his part in it, he watched and listened as if it were a play staged on a distant amphitheater. Could Klaes, too, be one of Maglio's AIs run amok? Raphael shook his head. Klaes seemed to have agency.

A few rows ahead, a thin, bare arm wriggled.

"Stand up, Dusty, don't be shy. Dusty is one of our finest programmers, and he's been with the company for—how long?"

"Pre-possum days. Ten years."

"Your question?"

Dusty cleared his throat and spoke. "Near as I can sort out, these Resurrected have to be somewhere. I mean, even if they rise from neuromorphic chips, tiny as they be, they have to be in a physical location." Dusty screwed at his head as if to open a cap. "Where will we keep all our Resurrected selves?"

Maglio's eyelids falling, he tilted his head to the side and held the position for ten seconds. He opened his eyes and broke his silence with "Heaven."

"Heaven?" asked Dusty. "With pearly gates, golden thrones, and cherubs?"

Maglio righted his head. "In my heaven, all you get is twenty-four-hour monitoring and high-profile licensed guards. The rest is up to you."

Heaven was a server. Ten million servers. The Resurrected resided in the mythical cloud.

Maglio glanced at the ceiling, appeared to speak to himself, and then took in the employees. "Ah, Bethena from Contracts. Fire away."

"Mr. Maglio, we deal with people who don't want the data of their loved ones to be in Norval's possession. As I understand it, we will now have to persuade the living to give us the right?"

"Correct. There's no lack of delicate sensibilities among our target audience. Here is the selling point to demolish such objections: No access to your data, no afterlife."

And Norval had cornered the market.

"Oh, I see virtual signatures left and right," said Bethena, and every head in Contracts nodded agreement. Bethena's smile turned to a frown. She brought a hand to her breast as if to calm a palpitation. "But where then, sir, is our profit?"

Yes, unfurl the flag that will lead our troops.

Maglio held up one finger. "To ensure one's afterlife will require a modest fee, payable in advance or from one's estate. Pony up or disappear forever. However, to eliminate the need for such a large outlay, we will offer Norval Resurrection Insurance. A modest monthly premium will assure you're ready to go when you go."

Bethena brought both hands to her breast. "May I use that, sir?"

"Make free." Maglio pressed his palms together and rubbed. "To clarify, we will also make available an afterlife to all the dead already in our database. If those left behind wish to raise their loved one, it's only a lump sum away."

Maglio held his arms out to his audience. "In a nutshell, Norval Marketing Necrology will bring back the dead, and your job is to keep those dead coming."

"Resurrection!" shouted Dreemont as if to lead a cheer.

Norval's employees were silent. They seemed confused but alert, like residents of an island listening for the sound of an approaching tsunami.

"Resurrection!" shouted Dreemont again.

Raphael crossed his arms. Act I had ended. *The intermission was brief,*

Maglio held his hands up for quiet and pressed his mouth to the microphone. "Bullshit!" Maglio spread his arms. "It could all be bullshit. All I've told you today could be lies and wishful thinking. Neverland. Oz. Shangri-La. Where's the proof? Where's the empirical evidence of Norval Resurrection?" Maglio scanned the room challengingly. The bargain basement was dead quiet. Maglio pointed to the pulldown screen.

The screen lit up with a man standing behind a podium. Behind him was the American Flag and a second flag dominated by rays of red and yellow. The front rows of an audience were visible.

"What the hell?" muttered Raphael.

"Hey, isn't that—"

Maglio gestured at the screen. "Arizona state congressman Carson Fullers wasn't a household name across our great land, but in the Grand Canyon State, Carson Fullers was a beloved exemplar of his state's motto: *Ditat Deau*, God Enriches. Unfortunately—Maglio gestured at the screen, and the picture changed to a yacht cruising into a harbor—Fullers's life was cut short by a tragic accident at sea. Unfortunate for Fullers, but fortunate for us. Where is the proof of Norval Resurrection you ask?"

Maglio made a cutting motion across his throat and the pulldown screen went dark. "It's in the bloody pudding. Get out your phones. You heard correctly—out of your pockets and purses. Power up."

Down the row, and all the rows, phone screens lit up. Maglio too had his phone out. The phones erupted with tones as dissimilar as the voices of Babel.

"Take the call," Maglio ordered.

"Jesus," said Matt, "it's Carson Fullers."

On Matt's phone, Carson Fullers beamed. Raphael's pulse quickened. Act II had already begun.

Digits surfaced on Maglio's left eye, then sunk. "Say hello, Carson."

"Hello," rang out from every phone.

"How do you feel?" asked Maglio.

"Like a million bucks."

Maglio laughed. "Me too, multiplied by a thousand. What have you been doing, Carson?"

"Checking my email and messages. Blogging on Thursdays," replied Carson from hundreds of phones.

"Never thought you'd do those again, did you?" asked Maglio.

"No, I didn't."

Would Maglio now tell the truth?

"Well, let me tell you, Carson. Your inbox will soon overflow with congratulatory messages."

"Oh?"

"After drowning at sea and having aquatic life consume your body, you, Carson Fullers, are the first of the Resurrected."

"Oh."

No.

"You were dead." Maglio pressed his hands down. "Now"—Geo turned up his palms and raised his hands—"you've risen."

Matt leaned into Raphael. "What's Maglio talking about? The dude didn't drown at sea. He was a possum who got his throat—"

Raphael pressed his forefinger to Matt's lips, butter soft.

"Now, Carson, please tell the audience what you will do after you check your messages."

"Do?"

"Yes. Will you tweet? Will you make a new friend online?"

"Umm, friend, yes. Make a new friend. I am favored."

"Yes, you are," agreed Maglio.

"I am favored. I am liked," said Carson. "I am liked, and I am favored. I am thumbs up. I am—"

Maglio put his hand over his phone and beamed. "We will let Mr. Fullers go now. I think he's feeling fatigued, which you might well imagine. Everyone say a cheery goodbye to Carson."

As the audience said their goodbyes, Maglio made a cutting motion across his own throat. Carson Fullers vanished from every phone.

Maglio raised his hand, surveyed the room and nodded. "Despite all this exciting news, all is not well in Mudville."

Matt whispered, "Where's Mudville?"

Maglio continued, "There's a movement afoot threatening our brave new world. We've dealt with a form of these deviants in the past, and our company thwarted many of their schemes to corrupt our database. Though you may not work in the Necrology Department, you're familiar with possums, I'm sure. Members of our staff have developed procedures and methods to root them out. These techniques will now apply to the recent threat: the Intentional Blanks."

The audience echoed the words.

"The Intentional Blanks, or Digital Luddites, have vowed to resist digitization. By any means possible, they are trying to escape the accumulation of data on themselves. You've seen these fools tossing away their phones and smashing their laptops. You've seen them hiding their faces from cameras, gait-shifting, parading around with hand-written pickets, my God. Disgusting—and frightening. Even as I speak, the news is they've blown up servers in five states. And it's rumored the heartrending Toobyville Dam disaster was no accident. If it smells Blank, it is Blank. We will crush the Blanks, mine the goddamn data with our heels if need be. We will form a new Anti-Blanking Division at Norval. I'm delighted to announce that heading up the division will be the top possum tracker in Norval history. Let's hear it for Raphael Lennon!"

Ignoring the applause and congratulatory shouts, he slipped his hand into his pants pocket and felt the container of his mother's pills. He was no druggie, but he still wondered how many it would take to get through this day.

CHAPTER
TWENTY-EIGHT

The sounds, sights, and smells of the NDMN workday had begun. Keyboards clicked beneath nimble fingers. A few ancient hard drives hummed. The overhead screens displayed their listless videos: coffee and exotic teas, pastries in the microwave.

Raphael sat at his old desk. The oversized corner cubicle accompanying his promotion to head of the Anti-Blanking Division remained under construction, his duties not solidified, nor his title documented. As if he gave a shit. It was just Maglio playing head games at his expense, a promotion to keep his mouth shut, minor bullshit compared to the menaces that seemed to be closing in on him. He snapped open an energy drink and slugged half. He should be frantic and panicked, and desperate to find a way out of the mess before his days ran out. In truth, he was numb and had to remind himself that he had any such goal. He was a beaten dog with no desire to whimper lest he attract the attention of his cruel master.

Shuffling in were the last of the End Men, the stragglers' faces adjusted to the interminable day before them. The compilation of death would be in full swing. One floor up, the AI possums in training, getting their buggy code repaired. Forerunners of the Personality Plus world.

The world changes, but it does not change. The fucking apocalypse could blow in, but when it blew out, you'd be at your same old desk in your same old cubicle, sucking on an energy drink.

At 3 a.m. he had awoken from a dream in which two men were squeezing him into a tiny suitcase. He pleaded with one, then the other, although both faces were the same: Maglio and Klaes simultaneously. He whimpered and flailed his arms, but they tucked his feeble limbs into the suitcase and closed the top. The zipper was as loud as a buzzsaw as the light disappeared. He screamed, but nothing left his lips. His center-of-gravity changed. They were carrying away the suitcase, which now seemed roomier and cushioned. He felt heat. Saw red and yellow flames, a man with his hand on a lever. He tore himself from the terrifying dream, covered in perspiration, heart racing.

In the sleepless hours that followed, he saw the dream's truth. Maglio and Klaes were interchangeable. Maglio had murdered, and Klaes had murdered, both through their stooges and for nearly identical reasons. Research subjects. Terrible crimes. He should go to the police and spill it all out. And they would immediately label him a lunatic.

All right then, Raphael, for the sake of justice, choose option B. *There is no fucking option B.*

He had called Lily and divulged the contents of the crate. If she had given him credence at the museum, she offered him no such comfort during this conversation. From her tone, cold and dismissive, she made it clear that Klaes was not capable of such an act. She agreed to *look into it* and *get back to him*. However, she assured him, Angie would not be in the box. Well, maybe she wasn't.

"Hey, how's the head of Anti-Blanking?" asked Matt, filling the cubicle's entrance.

"Catch this, Matt." Raphael held up his middle finger.

"Seriously, man. I heard they caught some Ludds with ricin in Milpitas."

"I'll check it out."

"So, how much are they paying you for this anti-blanking gig? A zillion times more than me, right?" asked Matt.

He shot Matt a withering look. Couldn't even his best friend see his foul fatalistic mood?

His phone rang. He nodded Matt off and took the call. A familiar face appeared on the screen, though she wasn't holding a dead animal this time.

"Hello, Miranda."

"Raphael, help me."

An electrical storm broke out in his head. "Help you?"

"I want to do something bad. Terrible."

"Count backwards from ten million," said Raphael.

"Did it. Now what?"

"Now, don't do the terrible thing,"

"Why?"

Because it's fucking terrible. He may as well plead with a stone not to fall on someone's head.

"Do you want to know what I'm going to do?" asked simulated Miranda.

"Please, don't do it," he said with gut-felt urgency.

"I'm going to influence people to take selfies while eating their pets. Everyone will hate them and threaten them and make their lives miserable."

"Miranda, that's not you," said Raphael, yet he wasn't so sure of the declaration. Even if the Personality Plus AIs replicated online character data, the process might alter the data and produce mutations. Complexes and neuroses—bugs— might emerge within the altered code, especially given Miranda's flesh-and-blood tendencies. Norval's possum training was no doubt working out those problems too, before kicking in wholesale Resurrection. "Miranda, think of how you might feel if you did it. Why did you call me? You said you wanted my help."

Miranda's face expanded on the screen until she was all lips. "Don't tell me about stupid feelings. I'm a god, you know? Miranda, God of Selfies, and I've changed my goddamn mind. I don't want your help." The screen went black.

"Miranda, please don't!"

She was gone.

Everything was out of whack. If Norval had so far produced only shells and shadows of the living, Klaes had left monstrosities everywhere. Even playing God, you could create devils enough.

And his daughter, if not in the box, spirited off to—where?

Surely not in Raphael's square mile. Why did he himself want to find Angie? She was dead, frozen. The most he could do would be to return her to the facility—and put her image in his painting.

He gazed at the photo of his mother on the wall of his cubicle, and a glimmer of hope rose within the dark sea beneath him. She said, "Promise me, Raphael."

"I will, Mom. I'll paint it all."

The last brushstroke would set him free. He could get out of the square mile, get beyond Norval's reach, maybe even search for the stolen girl, and all he needed was one more bit of data. *His father.* He had to cling to that promise.

He typed in *L-E-N-N-O-N*, comma. *J-A-Y-N-E*. Now only the middle name remained. He would have access to his mother's most intimate documents. *We all have secrets* was the gateway to a potent adage: *Secrets we hide from the outside world, secrets we keep from our most trusted friends and loved ones, and secrets we keep from ourselves.* Even the last, we might give away in unguarded moments. Was his freedom worth the invasion of his mother's private life? But she wanted him to finish the painting, to be free.

He spoke the letters aloud: *"R-O-S-E."*

He typed in the name, pressed enter.

On the screen appeared, *You are entering the Norval Portal of Jayne Rose Lennon.*

In a tree diagram, the symbols and names of several hundred sites appeared as Raphael scrolled. Some were common to half of humanity, others were obscure, none were unknown to an End Man. His mother had three email accounts: AOL, G-mail and LACMA. Her earliest emails were on AOL, whose email service dated to the mid-1990s. Many believed data from that era was obliterated. They were mistaken. Data scavengers had plundered the great hardware dumps of China where the world's outmoded servers and personal computers ended up. Harvesters rejuvenated and sold the data to companies such as Norval. Whatever his mother had deleted in the dawn of cyberspace, Norval's Dead Letter Program could recover; if something was in the data, everything was in the data, and the data was in everything.

He clicked and opened his mother's Facebook page. It was nothing out of the ordinary. A photo of the museum's exterior. Her title and responsibilities at the museum. Her academic history. A dozen friends and colleagues. Messages. Shared Links. Artwork. Other photos. He clicked through photos until he came to the twin of the one on the decorated wall of his cubicle. Raphael and his mother in front of *Three Quintains.*

He would open up her AOL account and go through each email for clues to his father. Was there a romance? A lover who had … And after everything, perhaps nothing. He slid the cursor over AOL. *This is my inner life, Raphy.*

What's the difference? What do the dead care? His heart thudded. A little man rowing a boat on an open sea in the fog. A weight fell on his shoulder.

He jerked around, expecting Dreemont, but it was a smiling Matt, a Starbucks bag in hand. "Sorry I yanked your chain about the Blanks." He set the bag on Raphael's desk, dug out two doughnuts and handed one to Raphael. "Friends?"

Raphael studied Matt's fingertips pressed into the glaze. "Do you mind if I pick out my own?"

"Oh, sure. Got croissants and Danish, too."

Raphael spread open the bag and plucked out a croissant. "Thanks. I've been tense."

"Understood."

Raphael lifted the pastry as if in toast. "May the Blanks prosper."

"Uh oh." Matt glanced back. "Another Norval rebel." He chomped on his doughnut and through the bites said, "Hey, there's a terrific concert in Redlands this weekend."

"Matt, listen," said Raphael, his heart in his throat, "I should have told you this long ago."

"Yeah?"

Raphael shook his head.

"Your square mile," said Matt.

"You know? What the fuck?"

Matt shrugged and bit off a large chunk of the doughnut he'd offered Raphael. He chewed, swallowed, and said, "If I wasn't absolutely sure, my mission to the Hotel Harvey confirmed my suspicions. Fairfax, Wilshire, La Brea, and Beverly."

"How the hell did you figure it out?"

"Hey, am I not a possum hunter too?"

Raphael watched his colleague polish off the doughnut, and then open the bag to review the remainders. "Come to me, cream filled," said Matt, dipping in his hand and extracting one. "Your prison. You can't go anywhere."

"On what site did you get that information?"

"No site. Followed you. All your dumbass excuses got me curious."

"I should rip out your ear loop," said Raphael.

Matt clapped his hand over his ear.

He'd tortured himself over the secret, and Matt knew; it was a release, an exhalation after holding his breath a long time. Matt dropped his hand.

"Why didn't you say anything before?" asked Raphael.

"Why didn't *you*?"

"You knew I was stuck."

"Yeah, but not that stuck."

"And those invitations to music festivals two counties over?"

"Bait."

Raphael nodded. "You think I'm crazy?"

Matt shrugged. "Yeah, so what?" Matt turned away but pivoted. "Hey, you know anyone down at the coroner's office by the name of Gilly Stull?"

"Yeah, I do. What's up with Gilly?"

"He's dead. Fell out of a canoe on the Amazon River. Consumed by piranha."

Raphael stood up, a string of firecrackers going off in his head. "Are you fucking kidding me?"

"The sorter program marked him undeclared. Trace data."

Perhaps I'll see you down the road, and you'll remember my kindness. Twenty-five thousand dollars on a Starbucks card. Addy had called it *singular.* A singular word for a singular card.

Raphael swallowed. "I'll take over on the case."

"Huh?"

"I'll handle Stull. Transfer the files to me."

"The head of anti-Blanking?"

"It's personal."

Matt shrugged, took another bite of his doughnut, and strolled back to his cubicle.

Envisioning Stull, Raphael didn't know whether to laugh or cry. The messenger of death had taken a runner, and left Raphael a twenty-five thousand dollars Starbuck's card, the glaze on his kindness. *Wish I was there, Gilly.* He turned to his computer, clicked on AOL Mail. He glanced down the links: *New Mail, Old Mail, Drafts, Sent* ...

The phone rang. Please, no Miranda, no Troy-Boy. To his relief, it was Addy. The earthly weight of his body left him. He set his knees under the desk to hold himself down.

"Addy?"

"Are you okay?" she replied.

"Yeah, I guess."

The phone went silent for a few seconds. "Pink's in the hospital, Cedars-Sinai. She wandered out on the streets again, and someone attacked her."

"Damn, I'm so sorry."

"She said it was Geo's man."

Raphael pressed the phone to his chest. It took him a moment to find his voice. Lifting the phone, he asked, "Geo Maglio?"

"She didn't say Maglio, just *Geo,* like she knew him."

"Did she mention Toobyville?"

"Oh, yes, she got all excited and screamed, 'Stress at the six-hundred and thirty-eighth quadrant. Relief valve closed. Data shows—oh, the terrible water and then the black tide. They saw it coming!'"

They saw it coming. Pink knew they knew. He should not have been surprised. In fact, he was not surprised.

"She also said you told me the truth. Someone wants to kill you. You want to run, but you can't."

"I'm in a cage, Addy."

"The cage of the four elements."

"What?"

"Wind, fire, earth, and water. The four elements."

"Water? I didn't say water?"

"Ice is hard water."

"Yeah, maybe ..." Had it occurred to him before? Were his walls what people believed the world to be made of long before molecules and atoms and quantum particles? What you see and feel.

"It could be a Greek myth or a fairytale you heard."

Despite his doubt, he roamed the corridors of memory, but they were empty of such myths or fairytales. And yet this vague shape, a shadow on the wall ...What would it mean anyway? His streets may well have been the forcefields of a thousand science fiction stories, impenetrable. For an instant, he had thought Addy was guiding him toward some great breakthrough, but his heart slowed and retook its measured pace. "Wherever it came from, whatever it is, it's there."

"Bust through," said Addy, her voice as resolute as a battlefield commander in the video games he once played. *Video game?* "I'll help you run."

The blood rushed to his head. "Addy, if ... it's too late."

"Never too late. Can you meet me tonight at the Starbucks in the Farmers Market? Plan and plot your escape? Nine o'clock?"

"Sure. That would be great." His heart swelled.

"By the way, I moved into the new place a couple of days ago."

"Oh, West Side?"

"No. The Tiny House Complex next to CBS. I even got my favorite: Tiny House 61347, ground level—side yard too."

"Wow, that's great."

"We're practically neighbors. Nine o'clock? We'll figure a way to get you out."

"Sure. Hey, remember that Starbucks card, the one you called singular?"

Addy laughed. "Not the card. Singular was the word you were looking for."

"What do you mean?"

"Dr. Watson's 'one word.' Singular means one, and it's used all the time in the Sherlock Holmes stories."

Singular. Fuck, it had to be singular. "You're a genius, Addy."

She laughed. "See you at Starbucks. Got to go."

The call ended. He shoved the phone in his pocket. Of course, it was *singular.* With Klaes's ego, what else could it be? One more piece of the puzzle, and Addy back in the picture.

He imagined the ideas swirling in Addy's imagination for getting him out of his trap. Pole vault. Sleeping pills. Get shot out of a cannon. His brain defied remedy, reasonable or absurd.

He slid the little white hand over *Sent* and the rectangular shade appeared. One click. Lift the shade. Lift the shade. She wanted him to complete his painting. She must have wanted him to know his father. Or did she? His vision blurred. But not this way. Even if it gained you the world, some boundaries should not be crossed. He slid the white hand to the stolid *X* and closed his mother's file.

As the day unfolded, a strange pressure built within his ribcage, expanding, unbearable. If his four outer walls were impassable, another set of walls weren't. Opening a drawer, he gazed at the accumulated personal items, removed a folded Trader Joe's shopping bag, and set it beside the chair. What would you take to heaven? What would you take to hell? He chose from the accumulation of five years —mints, a holiday scarf, a stain pen, hand sanitizer, nanoflossers, a compact umbrella— and dropped the items into the bag, setting it under the desk on the skateboard.

As if the bell for an opening round, the lunch whistle blew, and Raphael stood up. He strode out of the cubicle and shouted, "I quit, Dreemont. You hear me? I quit!" The surrounding cubicles erupted in astonished chatter and then hushed.

The immense quiet unnerved him. His hands trembled and his

shoulders sank. The cubicle's entrance had vanished. Four walls and no exit. *Now, or no moment after.* He folded his shaking hand into a fist and pounded his enclosure. "Quit, End Men, quit! Run out of here before you can't!" The exit reappeared as if he'd awoken from a nightmare.

At the sound of rapid, heavy footfalls, someone shouted, "Get out, Raphael!" Another voice repeated the warning, followed by a swarm of agitated questions.

Dreemont appeared at the cubicle's opening. Behind the supervisor stood another man. Atop the second man's bruised and swollen head was a straw fedora, a little dented though unmistakable. The man with the battered face slipped around Dreemont and pushed out his lip, letting blood seep from the wound.

"What the hell?" said Raphael, falling back, an icy current running up his spine.

"Language," scolded Dreemont, eyebrows raised. "I was coming by to introduce you to our newly appointed head of security, Tony Struat."

The name crawled into Raphael's ears with the loathsome tread of some scaly and determined insect. Struat, amused eyes studying Raphael through steel-rimmed lenses, extended a hand. Raphael drew away from the long, calloused fingers, wriggling mechanically and—though it must have been in Raphael's imagination—clicking.

"Raphael, please accompany us?"

"Didn't you hear me? I quit!"

The unshaken hand now jumped to Raphael's shoulder, clamped, and jerked him forward.

CHAPTER
TWENTY-NINE

Maglio's office was a chilly environment under any circumstances, but today it was Arctic. With one final firm shove, Raphael lurched into the room.

"Please have a seat," said Maglio from behind his desk. Heavy hands clamped Raphael's shoulders and sat him in a chair facing the CEO.

Raphael caught his breath. "You can't"—he reached across his chest and gripped Struat's wrist to get the hand off him, but the fingers were unyielding—"hold me. Let me go, for Christ's sake."

"Mr. Struat," said Maglio, glancing over Raphael's head.

The weight lifted from his shoulders. Heartbeat at its limit, Raphael jumped up and walked toward the door, catching sight of Maisie in proximity.

"We know about Jason Klaes," said Maisie.

"Then you don't need me," said Raphael, reaching the door. "Please open this."

"We also learned about your *relationship* with him."

Raphael's entire body seemed to expand and contract with his pulse. "This is illegal."

"Did you know stealing corporate information is a felony?" asked Maglio.

If his head wasn't about to explode, Raphael would have laughed. If he had his board, he would have rammed it into the door. Instead, he swung toward Maglio. "You've got to be fucking kidding. Keeping possums out of the database? I know what my job was all about."

"How deep a hole are you going to dig for yourself?"

"We're a team," said Maisie.

"I'm leaving your team. I quit Norval."

Struat laughed, much longer than irony required.

Raphael flicked the hair from his damp forehead. Christ, he may as well have come out of a shower. *Feign worldliness.* "This is getting boring."

"Yes, it is," agreed Maisie.

Maglio stood up. "I want Klaes's Personality Plus without the imperfections. Something a little more sophisticated than what we've got."

"Can't help you. I'm only an IT guy."

"With a connection to the genius who created it," said Maisie.

Raphael met Maglio's eyes. "Jason Klaes is dead."

"But you receive messages from him, don't you?" noted Maglio with a grin.

The screen shot. Struat's surveillance. Likely, his phone was tapped. Sure, they knew.

"Ever chat about the crate?" asked Maglio.

Raphael stiffened. "Crate?"

"The Klaes crate your friend Lily Faraday is opening at the celebration."

"Not really ..."

"You don't know what it contains?"

Yes, Angie Murie, Klaes's daughter. "No idea."

"Nothing of value. At the price of the damage done to Mr. Struat's head, we established that."

"Tough motherfucker that Electrician." Struat rubbed his swollen cheek.

"You prevailed, Mr. Struat," said Maglio, smiling broadly. "We checked it out in hopes, well, doesn't matter. It's a joke. We're putting our chips on you to produce Personality Plus."

If it were Angie in the box, would they have held it back? "I can't help you."

Maglio plucked a pen from its holder and tapped it on the desk. "Long before you came on board with Norval, I had Jason Klaes and his ideas in my sights. Years ago, Mr. Struat investigated our physicist's background thoroughly." Maglio stood up, held the pen as if a dart, and aimed it toward Raphael's head. "Dr. Klaes's interests went somewhat beyond quantum physics and AI. His entanglements included several searing affairs at the Harvey Hotel, an eccentric old dump that appealed to his sense of humor."

"Doesn't interest me," said Raphael.

Maglio drew back his hand and flung the faux dart, which whizzed past Raphael's head to strike the trunk of a potted palm—and stick.

Struat clapped.

"This might." Maglio clasped his computer monitor and turned it around. Klaes's face filled the screen. The photo might well have been taken in the days before he died. His face was creased with wrinkles and his beard was full and white. "Anyone you recognize?"

Raphael glanced away. "Nope."

"Let's try this then." Maglio tapped his keyboard. A chyron appeared above Klaes's face: *Old Friends Are Golden, But an Old You Is Not.* Klaes's beard retracted, simultaneously turning from white to gray to black. As the beard retreated further, the laugh lines filled, the wrinkles smoothed, the loose skin tightened and glowed as if lit from the inside. *Stay Young With Vanitum!* flashed a message in gold letters. Where the beard had been was sturdy chin and sharp jawline, complemented by the narrow aquiline nose. In the monitor mirror—

Go through the quantum looking glass, handsome.

Raphael stared at himself. He retreated from and advanced toward the stunning pixels, shaking his head no but hearing yes. Something passed through him like a net through water. There and not there.

"At the Harvey, a child was conceived, but not into a happy family, not into those famously like units."

"Shut up," cried Raphael, lunging toward Maglio.

"Easy now," said Struat, grabbing him from behind.

"Poor Jayne Lennon," said Maglio. "Seduced by a married man. Fucked and fucked over. Left to bring up the bastard on her own. While she settled into stone."

"It is sad," said Maisie.

He could not believe it. "What's sad is this garbage you've made up." He pointed at the monitor. "It's just a digital trick. I'm not going for any of it."

Maglio moved some items on the desk and lifted a paper rectangle the size of a greeting card. He held it horizontally and then bent it a bit, so Raphael could see it was an old photo. "Jason Klaes acquired the beard in his late-twenties, and it grew and grew. There are few photos of him clean-shaven. Here is one when he was, oh, twenty-six. About your age." Maglio held out the photo.

It drew him in like a small fish hooked with heavy tackle.

Raphael considered the photo of himself. No, not exactly. Raphael's eyes were gray, Klaes's hazel. The physicist's forehead broader. The hair longer and lighter than his. The alteration was not significant. The jawline was identical to his. The cheekbones … Klaes stood before a black slate, a dense formula written with meticulous penmanship and bordered with a square. In one hand, he held a piece of chalk.

Jason Klaes, the bearded rotted pumpkin who slid into the inferno, was his—the word slipped though his lips like a hot cinder melting through snow—*father*.

The hoary trope, the pokey reveal: *my father.*

Whose blood coats my blade! wondered the Greek—or should have.

The room blurred, and a stupid tear trickled down his cheek. Was Maglio tittering? With the back of his hand Raphael wiped the drop away. Maglio was capable of this manipulation. Had they also altered the photo of the beardless face to convince Raphael of Klaes's paternity? He searched his overheated brain for their motive. Did they think it would give them—through him—leverage over Klaes? But if Klaes was his father, he surely knew. *Hey, Mr. Klaes, guess what? You're my father. Now give Maglio what he wants.* No fucking sense.

Maglio pinned Raphael with his gaze. "Perhaps you remember the online recruitment advertisements that drew you to Norval? Did you think they were random?"

One more body blow. Raphael swayed and lifted the board to his chest, but his hands were empty, his board left under his desk. Was he only imagining they were cackling?

"I was betting on you," said Maglio. "With the blood of your genius father, surely you could ferret out his secrets. We've invested enormous resources into Resurrection. Your discovery of the Personality Plus file was the last piece in the puzzle. Finally, we had the proper thing. The true algorithm for afterlife. It was a mean trick." Maglio sighed and shook his head. "We have to take off the gloves. The father is beyond our reach, not the son. Mr. Struat knows the weakness of the flesh. Your flesh. Your pain. Klaes will bend to the screams of his son."

"You're wrong," said Raphael, gazing at all of them. "He's code."

"Daddy code," purred Maisie.

Raphael felt the blood drain from his head. "You've bought your own sales pitch."

Maglio's eyebrows lifted. "Because your presence is a threat to good order, bad for morale and worker self-esteem, for the near future, I ban you from the premises. Working from home, you will continue to wage battle against the rising Blank hoards. Your primary assignment—if you choose to take it, and you do—is getting the true Personality Plus for us."

Raphael scanned the smiling faces. "I've been turned down for a work-from-home permit. Sorry. Go fuck yourselves."

Maisie sighed. "Oh, Raphy, how crude. The rules can be bent now and then. I'm sure Geo can arrange for a permit."

Maglio winked.

"I'm not yours. I'm not Geo's."

Whistling, Maglio crossed the room and yanked the pen from the potted palm. "True, I don't have title to you, *de jure; de facto*, if you know your Latin, is my claim. All your data has been entombed at the highest level of entombment. You're in Supermax. Even Klaes can't get to it."

Raphael straightened. "Oh sure, the digital genius who has created everything you need, can't even pick open a data file."

Maglio looked out from under his eyes. "Not one he invented himself."

"You're full of shit." Maglio's hooded gaze didn't waver. So this too was true. His father may as well have built Norval himself. He breathed hard, but he could get no air. "What makes you think I won't run?" asked Raphael.

"You're welcome to try." Maglio walked to the desk and tapped the pen on the wood. "What were the lyrics to the song of my youth? Let's see ... 'Wander Paris along the Champs Elysse, sail the South Pacific in a Bermuda sloop, climb a snowy mountain when it's ten degrees.' But don't forget, when you're back in town, your ass is mine."

CHAPTER
THIRTY

After leaving the meeting with Maglio and friends, Raphael went home, powered up his laptop, and using an anonymous VPN sent out a message through a dozen social media sites. The message was simple: I got your clue. I know where you are. You can come out now. Fulfill your promise.

Message sent, Raphael skated to the Art Museum and climbed the grassy slope that bordered the adjacent Fossil Museum.

He lay on the grass and closed his eyes. The sun beat red on his eyelids and the earth warmed his back. He remembered the days when he sat on this very slope with his mom and listened to her reassurances that all would be well. *All would be well.* Her voice in his ear, his hand nestled in hers, and her fragrance in the air; he fell asleep. He may have been aware at some level of the sun sinking and the ground cooling, but it was not until the rhythms of someone chanting penetrated his brain did he awaken and realize it was late afternoon. Glancing toward the sound, he saw at the base of the grassy decline a young woman in a white skirt and purple leotard. Sitting cross-legged, she swayed and nodded her head as she slurred a passage from which Raphael extracted a few lines that sounded familiar. He rose, rubbed his knuckles across his eyes, and plodded down to her as she repeated them; chantlike but garbled, from which he drew, "Work, perfect, Earth, sleeps." His memory filled in the gaps.

And when all the work is done

And, when as a perfect toy, Earth—

Sleeps up the living, again.

Pharmacopeia?

The hairs on his neck stood up. The second stanza of the poem concluding Klaes's biography, with one word changed, "wakes up" to "sleeps," and another added: "Pharmacopeia."

"Excuse me. Where did you hear that?"

She glanced up. "What? Huh?"

"Your chant."

She shrugged and spread her legs. In the lap of her skirt was a nest of pills. She sorted through the various-colored capsules, looking up at him as if following the climb of a tower. "Go away, creep-freak."

He laughed. "I'm just a weirdo."

She drew up a white pill from the nest and held it before her face as if candling an egg. Frowning she dropped it back and probed the hoard as she repeated her chant.

"What does that mean?" Raphael asked.

The girl tilted her head up. Pencil-point pupils floated in the center of glistening brown irises.

"His way."

"Whose way?"

"In heaven, the fentanyl flows free and there's a big rock cocaine mountain." She stuck her fingers in the nest, digging through her pills until she drew up a large multicolored capsule with a tiny conelike attachment. "Oh, my sweet savior, Lord Fan Belt."

"What the hell are you saying?"

"Lord Fan Belt's challenge," she murmured. She shoved the pill in her mouth and looked toward the sky. "Ride the unicorn."

"Spit it out!"

She swallowed. "Coming my savior, my Lord Fan Belt."

"I can't let ..." He dropped to his knees and clutched her jaw. He felt the bone beneath the cool, sticky skin. Her lips darkened to blue. "Spit it out!"

Already her eyes had frozen, and her torso bent to her legs like a tree uprooted.

"Help!" he shouted. "She's overdosed!"

From the dwindling museum crowd, visitors ran toward them.

"Narcan! We need Narcan!"

The converging people reached into their pockets and purses and drew out their cell phones. They turned on their cameras, jostled for angles, and clicked away.

Raphael swore. "Christ!"

A museum guard pushed through the throng. "I'll take over, son." He separated Raphael from the woman and gestured for the crowd to retreat. "Happens frequently," said the guard, drawing out a capped syringe. "Might be too late here."

"Jesus," Raphael whispered. A siren sounded, and a surveillance drone flew overhead. The phones floated in the air as the onlookers, ignoring the guard's pleas, moved closer to that alluring pictorial flame, turned their backs, and held their devices at arm's length to include themselves in their documentation.

The guard stuck the needle into her upper arm.

Someone in the crowd chanted, "For you, Miranda. For you, dear goddess."

And one by one, the audience took up the chant until it filled the air. The young woman's fingernails were blue and her body a discarded cloth.

"Shit," said the guard.

Raphael's phone rang. He staggered back from the dismal, infuriating, and perplexing scene.

On the screen, an animated greeting card had appeared. Little birds taking flight to *Peter and the Wolf* dissolved into a request from Jason Klaes to meet with Raphael at the Wall ... at midnight.

"Is she going to be all right?" he cried out to the guard as a team of paramedics sprinted up to the scene, shouting for the selfie takers to back off.

No one answered, but he knew.

Fan Belt? No, fuck—she must have been trying to say *Van Pelt*. The people taking selfies had praised *Miranda*.

Dazed, wondering if he remained asleep and the scene was an awful dream, he replayed the message. The Wall at midnight.

The young woman was gone, and he had to go.

As he exited, the light of the 3D billboard on Wilshire flashed. He had seen identical 3D boards going up around the area, each displaying a species that had vanished from the planet: the Hawskbill Turtle, the Black Rhino, the Amur Leopard, and the Sumatran Orangutan. The display finished its cycle with the name of the animal and the question:

Extinct. Are you prepared?

He watched now as the porpoise glided over the boulevard, and the question appeared. The question fragmented, to be overwhelmed by a radiant stream of letters.

Beat extinction with Norval's Personality Plus.

Raphael skated home, tried to eat, but couldn't down a mouthful. He played the invitation as one might a favorite song, but he didn't hum along. Even if Klaes was Raphael's father, he shouldn't have been aware of the Wall, just as he shouldn't have been cognizant of Raphael's painting or sickness—but he was. Among the remains of an old train depot, the Wall was a weed-bordered hangout for skateboarders when Raphael was an early teen, there was no better place for an undisturbed confrontation. If Klaes knew as much as he purported to know, Raphael might have freedom handed to him tonight—or meet his maker. If so, there would be no defense. He would be at the mercy of whatever beast awaited him.

As he skated to the site, Peter's little birds were in his throat.

By the time he reached the overgrown lot, the little birds forced their way from gullet into belly. He paced the perimeter, then with a grunt of determination and heart racing, lunged into the waist-high weeds.

Ten yards in, Raphael chanced on an old path, sparking a memory of when he was twelve and approached the Wall with an ounce of hope and a pound of doubt. Would this be the day he'd nail the trick? A few yards farther on, the foliage had retaken the terrain. He lumbered forward. A can crackled beneath his foot, alarming an army of low creatures scurrying away through the undergrowth. He stopped and scanned the field. As a vehicle cruised by on the bordering street, shadows leaped up along the field's perimeter. Black flares took the form of fearful men and fierce monsters. When the car passed, the shadows vanished, leaving only a mailbox, hydrant, and tethered saplings.

Raphael switched on the phone flashlight and surveyed the terrain. Heart slowing, he continued to the abandoned depot.

At the structure's remains, little more than a crumbling concrete platform, rusty tracks, and the Wall itself, he turned off the flashlight and pocketed the phone. From the eaves of a long-closed library a short distance away, a solitary bulb illuminated the platform. The forgotten light shone on a return slot in the library's side, waiting to swallow books—*swallow*. Was everything to be a fairytale monster?

Over the years, the graffiti had grown so dense on the platform that no word was decipherable from within the shadows. Darkest of all was the bottom of the Wall, a long slab of concrete eight feet high and tilted at a sixty-degree angle, likely from an earthquake. At its base, spider webs glinted their invitation to guileless insects.

He scanned the area. "Jason?"

The weeds shivered in an erratic breeze. A cricket chirped. Something plodded through the undergrowth. Stagnant air smelling of rotting animal matter and stubbed out cigarettes.

At a rustle behind him, his heart quickened. He spun around. "Is anyone here?"

Scuffing his heel against the dirt, Raphael tossed the board above his head and, without a glance, caught it. He scanned the surroundings like a night-watch aboard a ship. Midnight came and went. For twenty minutes, he waited, breath coming ever harder.

"Jason? Jason?" A child in a pool yelling "Marco."

No "Polos" or "Klaeses" responded.

Raphael dropped to the platform and tapped his fist on the concrete as if knocking at a door. The knock was answered by a loud stirring in the brush. He jumped up, trembling, but the undergrowth was still and quiet again. No one was there. He remembered how once there was. One evening, among a half-dozen other skaters, he pushed off harder than he ever had, determined to get the speed to nail the trick. As always, he failed, but when he got up from ground, he spotted a figure standing in the weeds and gazing at him. Although the figure turned and strode away, Raphael recognized him as the man from Pan Pacific Park, his guide. It was the last time Raphael saw his guide, though many times he looked for him, as tonight he looked for Jason Klaes. As if he had skated the Wall a dozen times, sweat dripped from his forehead and his heart pounded.

"Jason, stop playing with me!" he cried, voice echoing off the slab. He drew up his knees, wrapped his arms around them, and pulled his legs to his chest. He rocked several times. "Come on, Jason. Show yourself." Releasing his legs, Raphael grabbed the board and slapped at a wheel. The spinning brought comfort in the familiar *whirr*.

The Mussorgsky tune of his ringer sent him to his feet. Drawing the phone from his pocket, he jerked it up. It slipped from his fingers, fell to the slab, and bounced a yard away. Not breathing, he picked it up. A jumble of letters, digits, and symbols extended across the screen.

"Hello, Raphael," said the caller through the phone speaker.

"Jason?" A bead of sweat ran down Raphael's forehead and into his eye.

"Sorry I'm late." The voice was deep and clear, and if Raphael didn't know the words were coming out of his phone, he would have thought an invisible man was speaking.

On the screen, an old man's bearded face appeared. Goosebumps rose on Raphael's arms. "You resemble him." Raphael scanned the shadowy brush, expecting some imitation of a man to rise from the foliage.

"Aren't I him?" asked the caller.

"No. I mean, not the Jason who once—"

"What am I?"

"An advanced algorithm. A dead man's script." Having said it, Raphael breathed with relief, as if he had finally escaped from his labyrinth.

But Klaes merely gazed back. The caller's eyes contained an image that shouldn't have been there: Raphael's face, as if two humans stood toe to toe, their features mutually caught in the other's pupil and iris. Thinking it might be his reflection on the screen, Raphael tilted the phone left and right, but the image remained.

Klaes grinned as if aware of Raphael's confusion. "I am Jason Klaes."

"I don't believe it. Jason Klaes is dead."

The flesh evaporated from the face on the screen, and a hand rose to grip the skull. The deep, clear voice recited, "Here hung those lips I have kissed I know not how oft. Where be your gibes now? Your gambols? Your songs?" The face recovered its flesh. Klaes's cheeks glowed, and the eyebrows danced in imitation of merry old Saint Nick's.

"I've seen plenty—and better—animations."

Klaes grinned through the bushy beard. "Tough generation to impress. What did you say I was?"

"A program. Well-written code. AI hoping to pass itself off as artificial general intelligence."

"You're sure?" asked Klaes, eyebrows rising.

"Singular, Holmes. A singular clue. A singular warning. Dr. Watson's *one* word. What, you're the onset of the singularity?"

"No?"

"You're pretending to interact with me as an equal—more than an equal. Artificial superintelligence and consciousness. We're far from there."

"When will we be there?"

Raphael shook his head. "Not tonight."

Raphael's face vanished from Klaes's eyes. Their hazel intensified to the point of blinding. Raphael looked away to escape falling into their ocean.

The thing asked, "Then why are you out here?"

"Why did you message me?"

Klaes smiled. "In my instructions to Lily, I asked she use a public message board to report anything uncanny in the wake of my death. She reported her meeting with you and the direction your search for me had taken."

"She gave me a clue. A machine in a ghost. Watson's one word nailed it for me. Klaes was dead but exerting his will."

Klaes grinned. "Yes."

"Exerting his will through a program."

"If you're very loose with definitions. But that's close enough."

Raphael's jaw tightened. Avoid confrontation, argument. But the machine's arrogance, programmed or not, pricked like a fresh splinter. One thing that the machine seemed not to know was that Raphael knew he was Klaes's son. Was that an advantage for Raphael? "Whatever you are, you've promised something I need. Do you remember?"

Klaes's face vanished, replaced by a dense, dizzying screen of code zipping by. The code froze. Klaes's face reappeared. "Your painting needs three images."

"I don't know how you learned about my painting, but I'm getting the feeling you're not giving me my images."

"Believe in me, Raphael."

"You demand faith? Your price is to believe in the unbelievable?"

"I exist because I know. A tautology, a meaningless repetition, but it's all you've got too."

The logic fell like a boulder on his shoulders. Sinking under its weight, he threw it off, steadied himself and put a finger to his temple. "I exist in here. Where do you exist?"

"In a quantum computer in the Tadpole Galaxy."

He felt the veins in his neck pulse. "Bullshit."

Klaes chuckled. "Or maybe in a 1981 Dodge Charger hood ornament buried beneath scorched earth."

Did it mean anything or was it a joke? Raphael glanced down. If the ground were black, he might have run away. It was weeds and ordinary dirt. He should still run. It was foolish to believe he could control this situation. That he might get what he wanted. His heart beat furiously. Throw the phone into the weeds and jet. Yet he clung to the thin hope, the wish …

He met eyes on the screen. They were human hazel, and Raphael's face again reflected off their surface. If Klaes were the actual thing, a true artificial general intelligence, the power behind those pixels might meet or go far beyond Raphael's intelligence. He could accept the magnitude of its computing functionality but couldn't accept that the machine was aware. If it had intentions, they were the intentions Klaes had programmed into it.

If you can't tell whether you're speaking to a machine or a human, you must accept it as human. He didn't buy it. This—*thing*—was zeroes and ones, though Klaes provided the AI with sufficient knowledge and memories, some of which involved Raphael. What Raphael needed hid amongst the code—maybe: the final image. How to extract it? To begin, he had to pretend he wasn't bargaining with a machine. The machine wanted—no, not *wanted*—was programmed to make the human feel he was dealing with another human.

Raphael slipped his foot under the skateboard and flipped it over. "Why meet here?"

"I wanted you in your comfort zone. Your childhood Fortress of Solitude."

Raphael stiffened. "How could you know?"

"A little blog told me."

"I deleted the information when—" He came down hard, as if missing a last stair. *Nothing disappears in cyberspace.*

"Are you frightened?" asked Klaes.

"Who killed you?"

Something large moved in the brush. Raphael spun and peered into the black field. The weeds rustled, but again no one appeared. A dog maybe or … a possum?

He returned to Klaes. "Who?"

Klaes shrugged. "Let's call it a suicide of convenience, but I was ready for who I'd become."

In Raphael's belly, something seemed to be swimming, bumping into walls. *An AI with megalomania.* "Yeah, I know—AGI."

"World's first."

"Congratulations." Bump. Bump. Bump. "Who killed Miranda?"

"I killed Miranda. Or should I say, I had someone kill Miranda."

"The Electrician, right?"

"Electrician?"

"The dude with all the tools."

"Ah. Yes, you can call him the Electrician. He goes by several such names, but that one will do."

Klaes's face was serene. Raphael's was burning, "Didn't want to get blood on your hands?"

Klaes smiled. "I can't get blood on my hands. I'm a conscious being, but I only exist in the wiring, so to speak. Which doesn't mean I can't get things done. I have all the cryptocurrency I want. I paid your Electrician well for his work."

The face remained placid, yet the closed lips slipped to one side like a child waiting to see if their falsehood is believed. A hint of guilt? "You had Miranda killed for killing a swan."

"Not entirely. I had to see if I could do it again."

"Do what again?"

"Make another me."

"In your image, like God."

"Not in my image nor with my consciousness, only in my form."

"To do all this, you'd have to be the smartest human on the planet."

Klaes smiled. "Someone has to be."

"It takes a team."

"Maybe I had a team. They assemble on wet days."

Raphael glanced toward the field, still expecting a three-dimensional version of Klaes to appear. *Tadpole Galaxy. Team. Wet days.* Sure. "So killing Miranda was an experiment?"

"I didn't have the courage while I was alive."

"Troy-Boy?"

"On his podcasts, he called himself Truth Troy."

Truth Troy. The podcaster who decades ago denied the poisoning of twenty children and taunted the grieving parents. Called them actors. Mutilated dogs. Mutilated history. A fistful of ice pressed the back of Raphael's neck. "An experiment too?"

"Yes, yes," said Klaes. "But if anyone—"

Raphael completed the sentence. "—deserved to die it was him." *Yes, I too could have killed him.* A flash in his brain like a strike of lightning, but then gone. No. He could not. "But there are much worse people on the planet. Why choose them? They were no more than average criminals."

On the screen, Klaes appeared taut and tired, eyes dull as if from cataracts. Only code. Instructions, mind-boggling galaxies of zeroes and ones. A classic if/then flowchart. Numbers of instructions. *If discussing murders, appear worn and regretful.* Was he any different? *If trying to cross my forbidden street, then …*

Raphael jiggled the phone as if it might unsettle the digital Klaes impersonator. "I can see why you took your own life, but others …"

"I regret—"

"Regret? You can't regret."

"If I'm only the weak AI you believe I am, then you're right. I don't have access to how it feels to be human. I don't have regret or any other emotion."

"If your motives were so pure, why didn't you kill yourself and leave it there?"

"And if Oppenheimer had killed himself? Would another physicist have not fathered the wild atomic child in Germany or Russia or China?"

"Oh, I get it. You're the good machine. The one who will protect us from the bad machines: the dictators and destroyers."

"Maybe."

"You made me into an application. The Raphael-find-the-corrupt-file app."

Klaes took a lengthy breath and said, "Maglio and Maisie stole an early version of my—work. It was missing a few components, though sufficient for them to get started. I wanted them to think they had it all, so I threw them another bone, minus the marrow, poisoned code taking its place. A loyal, innocent worker uncovers what they need. They jump on it. They're a clever bunch. It didn't work out as I planned."

"You couldn't just wave your wand and make Norval disappear?"

Klaes closed his eyes, and the face relaxed. For an instant Raphael wondered if the *digital god,* the would-be human machine, was napping. The heavy lids retracted. "Did you know in my youth I used to skate here? A board with clay wheels." The cloud lifted from Klaes's eyes. They glistened.

The light in Klaes's eyes and his reminiscence about skating unsettled Raphael more than all the explanations. He lowered the phone. The phrase from his painting *JK Rules!* popped into Raphael's brain. As data, his own life was in the AI program, which implied it could accumulate, add to itself like the living, change its own code and algorithms. Yet, none of those made it conscious. The program was efficient at gobbling and regurgitating. If/then/if/then.

Steadying his hand, Raphael lifted the phone and met the rejuvenated eyes. "I led them to where you wanted them, Professor Klaes. You promised me my images."

On the screen, the old skater drew a skateboard into the frame. It was a faded green, and its front chipped like a broken tooth. Raphael's tongue rubbed his own jag, sharp against his tongue.

"Yeah, nice board," said Raphael.

"In its time," said Klaes.

Raphael squeezed the phone. "Goddamn it. How do I get out of my prison?"

"You could join me. Cross the street."

Raphael snapped, "Join you? You mean kill myself? I'm here to end my life?"

"It could happen painlessly."

Whatever it was, it was insane. "You know what, Klaes? I think I've helped you enough. My images, please."

"It's not death but another kind of life."

A chill spread across Raphael's shoulders and down his spine. He had until Sunday. *Four days left.* This had to be the meaning of Pink's prediction. *AI Klaes intended to murder him.*

"Please give me the images. Let me complete the painting."

"I need you."

"Why? You want another shot at bringing down Norval? I can't help you. I'm just an IT guy. Maybe I should take all this to the police."

"Isn't the local precinct a bit out of your lane? And if you could cross your boundaries: 'Dude, officer, this insane AI is murdering people.'"

"That wasn't bad."

Klaes gazed at him with an intensity that Raphael felt like a hand pressed to his face. "Want to finish your painting, kid? Want to solve your mystery?" Klaes brushed his hand across his skateboard's front wheels, making them spin. He spoke brightly, as if in a voiceover for a science video. "Only by entangling qubits of free will into an algorithm at the moment of death can we avoid the quantum decoherence accompanying death."

"What the fuck does that mean?"

"You don't need to be a physicist to understand. Just give it some thought." Klaes sighed. "I still owe you images."

Ah, Professor Klaes, I already have one. "Yeah. When the hell am I going to get them?"

"Go home. Lie beneath your canvas. I'll meet you there."

The screen went black. Feeling numb, he turned on his phone flashlight and stepped closer to the wall. He played the light over the graffiti and scrawled names. He found it buried beneath generations of other skaters, but still legible: JK RULES.

He turned off the light and stared helplessly at his phone. At a loud crunch behind him, Raphael spun and saw someone approaching, almost floating across the field as if down a stream.

Big as a man, the figure had wings and a sword like the Archangel Michael. Raffael Sanzio's painting had come to life. The Archangel's wings rose and fell with a horrendous squeal. Raphael lifted the skateboard like a shield. The puffy wings resolved themselves into two plastic bags, slung back over the Archangel's shoulders, ends twisted and held by one hand, his sword a bare baguette. Two-Bags carried the load toward Raphael, meeting his eyes but drawing the roll close to his chest. The treasure of a dumpster perhaps, or maybe fallen off a bread truck. Two-Bags nodded to Raphael as he passed by to settle down at the base of the Wall. He slipped the plastic bags to the ground and took a deep breath before biting into the roll with gusto. He chewed, swallowed, and grinned.

"And on the seventh day he rested," said Two-Bags, taking another bite and pondering the sky. He set his feet on one bag. "What do you think is in here, son?"

Raphael shrugged. "Crushed cans?"

Two-Bags bit off another piece and spoke through his mastication. "Nope." He jiggled the bag with his heel; the contents remained silent. "The price of aluminum went down the tubes. Ain't worth collecting. What I've got in here is"—he chewed off a chunk of bread —"souls."

CHAPTER
THIRTY-ONE

In the apartment, lying beneath the painting, Raphael turned over Klaes's' words in his head: ... *entangling, free will, moment of death* ... Like a word on the tip of the tongue, he had only to step away and it would come. He gazed at the space he'd reserved for his father. Of course, his father was already there, depicted by the vortex of gray and green that was the man at Pan Pacific. But that was his unknown father. He needed an image for the father known. In charcoal, he'd sketched an outline of the face, and now considered the colors and brushes he would need. For such a long time, he'd anticipated this moment, but now here it seemed merely an exercise, something done without heart. Still, the race must be run.

Picking up a brush, he studied its bristles and decided they were too thin. He chose another, which was too thick. His third selection finally met his suitability requirements. Focusing on the sketch, his neck tightened. The faint lines didn't describe Klaes's face, but his own, aged forty years. His father. *Angie's father*. His heart skipped a beat. He had a sister. Never met. Never seen. Where was she?

A whisper: *She's inside you.*

He touched his chest and his eyes welled and the oils of his painting ran. A sister was in his life, and her name was Angie Murie, and Angie too would need a place on his canvas. Klaes and Angie. Two of the three images he needed, he already had, though Klaes didn't know that. One more image. For a moment, responsibility settled on his chest like a great weight. To get it all in or fail. If he failed, then his years of work were all for nothing.

He set down the brush and picked up the eraser.

Before he had erased a single line, the phone rang. Glancing, he saw the pixel version of the father needed on canvas.

"Are you beneath your painting?" asked Klaes.

Fighting off lightheadedness and the image of a faceless sister, Raphael turned on the phone camera and waved it above his head.

"Slow down. You're making me dizzy."

A make-me-sound-human line. Raphael inched across the canvas to the edge, shifted, and altered direction.

Klaes—it—caught his—its—breath. "Wait, stop."

On the canvas and on the phone, Raphael's mother stood before Baziotes's *The Flesh Eaters*, an abstract reflecting the episode in Homer when the Cyclops devours Odysseus's crew. The original Baziotes's image was disturbing but not horrifying, a sea-change, slow and incremental like the transformation his mother was undergoing at the time Raphael created that section. Raphael had painted his mom in profile as she absorbed the Baziotes, a Neo-Expressionist rendering of the abstract.

"Beautiful," said the AI with a quiver in its voice. "I've always loved that painting."

Raphael's stomach tightened. "I don't know what I'm dealing with here, but the quiver in your voice is bullshit. You're not human."

"What makes you so sure?"

Fucking code. "You don't piss, shit, or bleed. Feel pain or love. Know where you stop and the outside world begins. You're all object without subject."

"I *can* love," responded the AI.

"A line of code says, 'I can love.' Jason Klaes wrote the code. He uses you."

"I am Jason Klaes."

"Have it your way. What's it all for then, *Mr. Klaes*?" asked Raphael.

"My child will regain the life taken from her."

His sister returned? "It won't happen."

"Then I've gone to a lot of trouble for nothing."

Raphael felt a surge of energy, as if breathing pure oxygen. "You're reproducing your daughter as an AI in your image, right?"

It blinked. Raphael's unexpected knowledge had produced a quintillion computations—a microsecond's worth.

Klaes metaphorically cleared his throat. "No posts. No search histories. No data. Nothing to build on. Angie will be a reanimation and repair of her original flesh. Microtubules functioning. A regular old human being. She'll keep the memories she had up to her death. She'll have her life to live. She'll grow and experience, find happiness and sadness. Plunge into icy streams. Bite a peach. Play the next game and dance to the next song. She'll input her life, her data will accumulate, and one day if she so chooses, she can spend eternity as her second self."

"Norval wants Personality Plus—your version with all the bells and whistles."

"I killed myself so they couldn't get it."

"They still want it. They've threatened me. Either they get your version or it's goodbye Raphael. And they've got my data."

"What do you mean?" asked Klaes.

"I'm entombed," said Raphael. Supermax entombed. "My data's locked away in a prison of your own design."

Klaes groaned. "They stole that too, huh?"

"You can't get to my ones and zeroes. Even if Personality Plus worked, which I don't believe—and would reject if I did—I couldn't become an AI of any sort."

The furrows deepened on the AI's brow. "Why do they think they can persuade me?"

Raphael trembled as the sentence completed its journey from heart to lips. "Does the father not love his son?"

Klaes blinked twice and his face shimmered as if reconstituting itself. After a sextillion if/thens, it found the answer in the code, and the machine spewed it out as written. "Your mother ended our affair and made me promise I would never contact her again. I should stay away."

"Why?" asked Raphael.

"I was married, though Jayne wasn't aware until too late."

"Even Boltzmann winners lie," said Raphael.

"We're a rotten bunch, humans. The Greeks had it right. We'll kill our fathers, sleep with our mothers, and eat our children. We're creatures of our passions."

His mother's lover. "You always knew I existed?"

"I honored her request. I avoided learning anything about her or you. I threw myself into my work."

"No. You were the man at the park with the skateboard. Watching and teaching me. You demanded we meet at the Wall, because you were afraid to tell me. You hoped I would figure it out."

Raphael wasn't certain, nor sure which way would make him feel better: A father on the periphery or a kind stranger? Raphael pressed his hand to his forehead, which was hot and slick.

Klaes ran his fingers through his beard and damned if his eyes didn't appear misty. What algorithm produced that? The face contorted like a human trying to make a hard decision. The hazel eyes shifted. "I tried to stay away, but I was flesh then ..."

Raphael's gut tightened. "Oh, a father's love is a fine thing. Only, you want me to kill myself. You want your son along for the mystery ride."

"You'd change forms, but you wouldn't die."

Raphael couldn't contain a brutal laugh. "Jason Klaes hoped that to be true. Coded hope is all I have to go on." On screen, the AI dug its fingers into the tangle of white. *Yes, stroke your fucking beard again.* "Hey, *Dad.* Why don't you shave off a few pixels of your monster?"

"Maybe you should grow one." The AI touched its nose. "And break your honker a couple of times."

"Yeah?"

"If you're tired of comparisons to you-know-who."

Go through the quantum looking glass, Mirsky had said. Raphael touched his cheek. For what? For a connection with lines of code. Yet, he wished the nonexistent arms would take him, secure him, keep him safe. Such an act would be less substantial than a dream. His body jerked, as if to free him from the hook of the wish.

Klaes sighed. "I want you with me ... when Angie is ready to return."

"I told you, they have my data, and I don't want to be a fucking Personality Plus AI."

"Yes, yes ... I'm processing—thinking."

Thinking. "Where is Angie?" asked Raphael, unable to say Angie's —his sister's—body.

"She's safe. She's waiting for the day, the day ..." On the screen, Klaes brought his hand to his lips. Through the fingers, he whispered, "When I guide them to her in the future."

"She wouldn't have been happy waiting for her future in San Diego?"

"Earthquakes, fires, wars, famine, pestilence, revolutions, the AI overlords—it's all coming. She wouldn't have survived where she was."

"You know this how?"

"Maglio and Maisie. Their data greed has already sparked the forces ushering in that dark future."

"Then stop them. You've already murdered three, no, four—or is it five? I've lost count."

"I had to be certain I could recreate you."

"Miranda wasn't enough?"

"She's flawed. However, by the fourth try, I got it right."

Raphael pressed his fingers to his temple. "Then you don't need Miranda and Troy-Boy, Royer and Van Pelt. Get rid of them before they screw up the world."

"The rub. In the first burst of freedom from the flesh, I thought I could do whatever I wanted to. Punish evil. Take lives. You know, son, I cannot because I will not. You called them average criminals, and you were right. Should I have chosen the worst monsters on the planet to kill and then give eternal life? The world is stuck with its new devils, not much different than the old crew: influencers all." Klaes sighed. "I wash my hands of them. You're right, I'm no more sure of my consciousness than you can be of yours. However, I do have a conscience. I know because I … regret. I'll do no more harm. What do you smell?"

"Smell?" asked Raphael, startled by the question.

"Yes. The smell coming off your painting. What's in your nostrils?"

"The oil. Linseed oil."

Klaes murmured. "I can't create smell, and I miss it. Linseed oil. Lemons. Rain falling on parched earth."

Raphael understood. "Well, it's a little late." He rolled his head on the pillow. No position was acceptable. He gazed into the face more and more similar to his. "Despite all that conscience stuff and your do no harm clause, you want me dead."

"If you take your own life"—on the screen the AI shook its head—"I'll wait, watch. When the moment comes, I'll be there."

"With your qubits trick. Yeah, I've given it some thought. Your words were, 'Only by entangling qubits of free will into an algorithm at the moment of death can we avoid the quantum decoherence accompanying death.' My interpretation? For consciousness to be transferred, the program needs to dance in perfect step with death." He reached back and drove his fingers under his neck, working at the muscles. "How long is the timeframe? An hour? Before the body cools? Ten minutes?"

"Norval never did get it right."

"They'll keep trying. They have plenty of possums left."

Klaes touched his forehead. "Show me the painting again."

Raphael scanned the canvas with his camera. "When I finish the painting, I'll be free. She promised me. Will I?"

Klaes's eyes narrowed. Raphael drew the phone closer. "Will I be free from my square mile?"

"There's nothing," said Klaes.

"Which means?"

"You're surrounded by an endless cemetery. There's nothing out there for you except death. Stick to your square mile, your computer screen, your phone, your painting. Or come with me."

Raphael's head seemed locked in a vice. "Nothing out there?"

Klaes sighed. "Not everyone gets a firewall. Consider yourself lucky, son."

"Fuck you, Dad. I want out. My mother promised. I finish my painting and"—Raphael swept his hand across the canvas—"*fini*. Free. I've got two of the last three images you say I need. One is you, the second is my sister. What's the damn last image of my life?" But as Raphael asked the question, he already knew the answer.

Klaes nodded. "Yes, son, the last image, not pretty. It's the blocked artery, the wrong way collision, the bullet to your head—the virus one point zero five microns in diameter." Klaes drew his hand across his mouth. "Your appointment with the fellow with the scythe. There's no way out of your square mile, no way out of your world, no way out of your rectangle or stone, unless you come with me."

"Suicide? Forget it, Dad."

Klaes ran his fingers through his beard. "I'm not immanent, Raphael. I'm only in the technology. I might not be there if ..." He glanced away. "Come with me and you win."

"I'm twenty-six. I want to stay here for a while."

Klaes smiled. "Approaching twenty-seven. Many have gone at that age, their lives already full."

Not mine. But if Pink were right, he had little time left to fill it. If within three days, he died at another's hand, what would he have gained? No more the old life of flesh, nor the new one of machine. Klaes's apple looked juicy. "How would I ..." No. Don't fall into his trap. *Run.* He breathed hard as if he were already running. His hands shook. A sheath of ice wrapped about him. "She promised."

Klaes nodded. "Mothers lie too. She wanted you to have hope."

He knew it in his heart, and for a moment, he hoped Klaes might rip it from him. He glanced at his Exacto knife.

"Yes," said Klaes, his eyes following Raphael's glance. "It's better in here."

Raphael wanted to punch the phone, shatter the face. Or should he simply paint it over? Paint it black. The thought warmed him. Klaes was playing him. Pushing him into death's corner. Klaes wanted Raphael to be with him. To be a machine. Okay, machine, let's give you some rope. Let's see what I can get out of you. "You're not listening, *Dad*. They've got my fucking data."

"Data?" said Klaes. "Your experiences, hopes and dreams—your personality."

"My data," insisted Raphael.

"Six of one, half dozen of the other, as my father would say." Klaes laughed. "Oh, he was a thing of beauty. Always scolding—"

"Yeah. Whatever. Can you free it? I mean, someday I might change my mind. Give Maglio what he wants and set me free."

The image of a brush, bristles bending, painted the screen black.

"Hey, did you hear me? Give Maglio your good stuff. Free your son." He slapped down the phone. His heart thumped so hard he feared it might break from his chest as in a cartoon. "Give them what they want!" Raphael screamed at the empty screen.

The phone toppled from his hand. Maybe jumped.

His eyes welling over, Raphael tossed aside the brush and took up the Exacto knife. He considered the work, the years of meticulous labor, all the hours, the rising from sleep, the pain of reaching upward. All for nothing. You couldn't paint your own life, or death, not as a human, anyway.

The painting was a lie.

Was it a surprise, Raphy? Did you really think this album of memories would free you?

It was a joke. His painting was no different from or better than the self-important posts and images banged in daily on social media. All of it nothing more than clickbait.

He reached up and touched the blade to the painting. Where should he start? Here, yes, here. Oh, how beautiful that image was. He shifted the blade. His mother's face. God, no. The tree that had grown with him? The little neighbor girl?

A memory reached out of the painting like a hand and squeezed his heart. No, his painting was not steamy gossip, false outrage, and bad information. It was his life, the things that made him laugh and cry, the things that tore at his heart and rattled his brain. His eyes blurred. For all that, it was a lie. A false promise.

He groaned and drew the blade across the canvas. The fabric screeched its disapproval while falling from its frame. Raphael attacked the canvas, slashing left, right, up, and down. He ripped into chunks of his life: Shorty's fell, the sloth fell, the *Flesh Eaters* fell, Norval, the Farmers Market, Pan Pacific Park, Pink, Addy, the immobile boy, a half-dozen skateboards, rails and walls. When he got to Dr. Royer's blood, the bowl between the ceiling and the canvas crashed down, missing his head by an inch. He shredded and tore until the painting hung like old paint peeling from a ceiling. Which was what it was.

He snatched at the strips, ripped them away, and tossed them to the floor. Shifting around on the platform, he tore every fragment from the frame.

An hour later, he'd destroyed the painting. His life lay in a heap on the living room floor.

He didn't fault his mother for the fable. It was a last-gasp effort to free him, and if the trick failed, he would be no worse off than before. Therapy and trickery were futile. Long ago, he should have seen the inevitable of life. Each one must have a death. It took Klaes, AI Klaes, to hammer the idea home. Raphael had found the last image only to be told by the image it wasn't the last. Had his mother planned it all? Through the painting, had his mother sent him on a hunt for his father, who would annihilate his magical thinking?

He gathered the canvas, held it to his chest, and kneaded the fabric until it compressed to the size of a beach ball.

Carrying the burden to the elevator and the building's roof, he stood at the parapet, lifted the fabric above his head, and tossed his heap of canvas, which shed flakes of paint that rose and fell, spreading ever outward in the currents and thermals.

A digital skyboard floated by, its lights sending the message *Death is Nowhere. Live Forever With Personality Plus! Special Introductory Offer.*

CHAPTER
THIRTY-TWO

An hour after destroying the painting, Raphael left a message for Addy: "I'm sorry, Addy, I can't meet you tonight. My fucked-up life is even more fucked-up. You don't deserve to get dragged into it. You're so damn sweet. It hurts me to say this, I mean, I feel like I'm coming apart, but I don't think I can see you again. It's got to be. Know that you'll be in my heart forever."

He powered off the phone. There was no running. He wouldn't take Addy's hand and enter the crosswalk. It just wasn't in him.

Plus, time was running out. In little more than forty-eight hours, he would turn twenty-seven, and someone would kill him.

Who wanted to kill him? Klaes wouldn't without Raphael's permission. Maglio needed Raphael alive to get the true version of Personality Plus. Maybe nobody wanted to kill him. Pink could be wrong.

And if she were right, he couldn't run anyway. No more than his mother could run from her fate.

Yes, like King Tut. But I'll be mummified while I'm alive.

"How come, Mommy? How you become that thing?" Even at four years old, he'd nagged her until she'd tell him a little, give him a hint.

In the following months, she provided more details. "Yes, it hurts sometimes. No, it won't go away by itself." Until, one day in spring—he must have been five—sitting on a grassy slope of the museum grounds with a view of the great boulevard, she kicked off her shoes. "Raphy, it starts with one little bump on the big toe, then jumps to the head, and then progresses from the top down."

"And what's soft gets hard," he said, repeating his mother's words. "You turn into a mommy, no—*mummy.*" The self-correction made his face hot, and salty, bitter tears flowed down his cheeks and into his mouth. He spit out the tears, cried more. His mother caressed and assured him. "It's a long time before it happens. Way in the future." If Raphy worried, *she* would be sad. "Don't make me sad, Raphy." With her plea, a gust swept the museum grounds as if to blow away Raphael's sad thoughts; instead it lodged a speck of dirt in his eye. He cried harder as his mother held the eye open and probed with a tissue, determined to find the tormenting mote in the sea of tears.

Under the breeze, the tissue fluttered, so close to his eye it seemed a great flapping wing. He clung tighter to his mother. "The Wilshire wind wants to get me, Momma."

"Don't worry, Raphy. I'm here," his mother said, drawing away the tissue and inspecting it. "There, we've got the mean thing out." Crushing the tissue in her hand, she hugged him, and her body then seemed so warm and so soft. In the comfort of her body, he gazed out at Wilshire.

"Don't worry, Raphy, I'll keep you safe." She drew him even closer. "As long as you can hear my voice ..."

Now, far away in time, he whispered. "Someone wants to kill me, Momma."

No comforting voice replied.

Lying on his bed, he thought of those days. Soon twenty-seven and finished, according to Pink, with his allotted days on Earth. He wondered how the end would happen: a bullet to his head, a knife to his throat, a poison needle to his vein. Before the execution, he might wake and fight, still the assailant would overpower him.

Raphael fought with the uncertainty of why he was dying, why he had lived, and worse, if he had lived at all. For a while, he kept his eyes open, seeking visions of death, and saw the dark shaped by the imagination into black ghosts. When he closed his eyes, the canvas appeared, but the images soon vanished, pixels consumed by a program's eraser, leaving only a sheet of pristine white.

Raphael closed his inner eye to the white screen and fell into sleep. Dreaming now, he rode the board along a concrete path with countless twists and turns and ending where it had begun. Did he dream the dream once or a hundred times?

RAPHAEL WOKE BEFORE DAWN, his head aching, hands stiff and sore. He had been fighting in his sleep, battling the mystery killer.

He powered up the phone: January 31, two days before his birthday.

Rolling off the bed, he opened the venetian blind. The blinking, buzzing world remained, and his square mile was still intact. He sighed, lowered the blind, and stumbled into the kitchen.

He ate a small orange, a bowl of oatmeal and half a pomegranate, the fruit of the dead, which beckoned him to pluck a seed and study it in the morning light. Beneath the radiant red sweet stuff of the shell lay the true seed. Nature worked hard to protect every little thing.

Would it be so bad to die? To leave behind all the anxiety and fear. Finally to end the search for escape, for a trick he might play on his own brain. Hope had gone out the window with his painting.

From the perspective of the world, it wouldn't be much of a loss. What had he done for humanity? Nothing. Less than that. He had tracked down the possums that Norval killed. He was complicit. Even Klaes's victims burdened him, for his father had taken their lives not just out of vengeance but for practice in building a better Raphael. He sighed and stuck another seed in his mouth. You got a little sweetness, brisk mornings filled with warm sun, and a concrete path to soar down as if in flight.

Addy was too good to be true, maybe just a dream. But how could he have imagined her voice, her eyes, her joy. Well, real or dream, she was gone.

He pinched up another aril. "Oh, little seed, you've led a better life than me. I consume you with humility and gratefulness."

He tilted back his head and gazed at the ceiling, Royer's floor. He couldn't even save that poor bastard. Had he done one fucking heroic thing in his life?

What's it all about, Addy?

Why do I want more of this? He glanced toward his kitchen's magnetic strip of knives. In his years of possum hunting, he'd viewed his share of suicide tapes, some faked, some real. A nice warm tub, a sharp knife, and deep horizontal cuts—to both wrists if possible.

He rose from the table and stepped up to the knives. Did seers— even digital ones—ever have change of vision?

Pink, Marion Jenson, was at Cedars-Sinai.

He turned from the blades to his phone. Who were *they?* Surely Pink would tell him, *could* tell him.

When his call to the hospital ended, he didn't breathe for a moment, and his eyes filled with tears. He leaned against the wall, banged the back of his head against the plasterboard and felt nothing.

Pink was dead.

When the shock subsided, he got his Exacto knife.

CHAPTER
THIRTY-THREE

Raphael pushed through the Norval lobby door and strode to the security counter, manned by Nikolay. "I want to speak with Mr. Maglio," he said, setting his fists on the counter.

Nikolay offered a puzzled smile. "Are you all right?"

"Yeah, fine." Raphael withdrew his hands, turned, and stepped toward the elevator.

"Raphael, stop," cried the guard.

Raphael spun. "I'm going to see Maglio."

His face flushing, the guard crossed his arms against his chest. "I cannot let you into the building, Raphael. Mr. Maglio's orders."

Raphael touched his belt beneath his shirt, felt the Exacto knife's cap.

"Tell him it's about Marion Jenson."

"You can't be here."

"Just tell him—"

"Mr. Maglio is not here."

"Don't bullshit me, Nikolay."

"I swear. He's not in the building"

Through his shirt, Raphael clasped the tool. "Is Struat?"

"No. The executives, programmers, and security team-leaders have all gone to Weblock." The guard frowned. "I still have orders."

An Exacto blade through that digital baby blue was not to be—and after today they'd have an armed guard waiting for him. Plan B.

Raphael stepped back. "Sorry, Nikolay. If Maglio's not here, I'd just like to say goodbye to my colleagues."

"Orders are orders."

"Come on, man, we're friends, aren't we?"

Nikolay's only response was the doleful stare of a person weighing duty against compassion. Further entreaties to the guard would meet the same response as duty weighed out. He'd be putting a nice guy through grief and gain nothing. Raphael strode toward the elevators, the guard calling out after him. "You're trespassing."

Raphael threw up the peace sign, then dashed for an open elevator.

On the second floor, Raphael rushed from the elevator, hurried past Anastasia, went straight for the wall panel, and entered the access code. They hadn't changed it.

"Raphael, what are you doing?" she cried as the door buzzed, rattled, and slid open. Striding into Necrology, he expected his brief absence to have brought about vast changes—maybe they'd gotten a water cooler or a caged parrot, but the impact was minimal if any. The cubicles remained as upright as ever. Computers hummed. Fingers tapped keyboards. Straws sucked vigorously on the remains of slushies and frappé. Powdered sugar wafted in the air. Everything was correct at Norval. On the wall above him, the mindfulness screens displayed the usual scenes of high-definition banality. The Cumulative Clock's digits flashed their toll. Someone struck a key loudly, then another. In all directions End Men hammered on their keyboards. A computer screamed, a violent sucking sound. The numerals on the Cumulative Clock sped up to a blur, a carousel of death.

He couldn't breathe.

One dead, two dead, three dead, four thousand, four million …

The department door buzzed behind him. "Raphael, please. I was told you shouldn't—"

"Hey, is Raphael here?" Matt emerged from his cubicle. "Hey, buddy, I thought you ..."

The utterance of his name caused inputting to stop, chairs to move, and End Men to peek out of their cubicles; calling out greetings as if he were a soldier coming home from the front. Ignoring Matt and the others, Raphael scrambled atop the counter beneath the mindfulness screens. Blinking rapidly, he peered beyond the image of the ironing woman to view a five-car collision on the Pennsylvania Turnpike. He slammed his skateboard into the image. The screen fractured and went black.

"Jesus, Raphael!" shouted Matt.

Anastasia raised her arms. "Stop. Please stop!"

He moved down the counter to the next screen: a pink-cheeked older man winding a ball of string. Blinking, Raphael saw an execution by lethal injection in Arlington, Texas. He drove his skateboard into the lie. The screen shattered.

A hand clasped Raphael's ankle. He glanced down at Matt, who said, "This is insane, dude. You'll get yourself arrested, locked up."

Raphael cried, "Ha!" He shook loose the grip and slid sideways to confront another mindfulness screen.

A toddler counting her fingers camouflaged a fiery trailer park in Reno, Nevada. "Fuck data!" Raphael shouted.

"What the hell are you doing?" bellowed Matt.

Glass exploded. Anastasia screamed, "Raphael, the monitor cost fifty thousand dollars!"

End Men streamed out from their cubicles. The room echoed with shouts of disbelief and excitement.

"Raphael, you can't!" yelled Matt.

"For Pink!" Raphael cried as he continued to smash the screens, the pieces seeming to fly out of his own head, as if jettisoning memories.

"Security's coming," said Anastasia. "Oh, my god, you're in so much trouble."

"For Fullers!" shouted Raphael.

"He's gone Blank," said another End Man.

"Oh, Raphael, stop, please stop," pleaded Akira. "You won't accomplish anything; they'll replace them."

"For Mirsky!" Raphael strode atop the counter. At his feet, chattering and gesticulating End Men extended their hands above their heads, beckoning for him to come down, as if they were the imprisoned souls in Brueghel's depiction of Limbo. Raphael met the imploring eyes. "Do you know what this company does?"

"Yes, they pay us," said someone unseen.

"Blood money!" shouted Raphael.

The faces of his fellow End Men remained blank. He strode to the end of the counter, where the Cumulative Clock steadily tolled death. He swung mightily. The clock screamed and the terrible digits sunk into darkness. His lungs emptied and his knees buckled. Letting the End Men take his arms, Raphael descended.

"Tell security I've left the premises," said Raphael.

"Sure, man," said Matt, worrying his beaded bracelet like a rosary.

"Are the cameras still down?"

Matt nodded.

"I may not see you guys again. Just know I ..."

"We know," said Akira.

Closing the door on Necrology, he gave himself five minutes before security corralled him if he stayed put.

He sprinted to the stairwell, climbed to the third floor and entered Ms. Goloda's office. She must have gone with Maglio. He hunted through her desk and found the remote of the door to the corridor of executive offices.

Running under the passage's strobing lights to Maglio's corner office, Raphael jammed in the skateboard and pried the door open. At Maglio's desk, he lifted the board above his head like an axe and brought it down on the computer. The machine cracked like an egg; keys, plastic, and circuitry flying across the room. In a minute, the board had reduced the electronic brain to rubble.

"For Pink."

He tossed the skateboard from hand to hand. Was it enough damage? Go, man. Save yourself.

Leaving Maglio's, he strode down the corridor, halting at the voices coming from research. He couldn't leave without first putting them out of their misery or whatever state a Personality Plus could rest in.

He keyed in Mr. Lean's password and pushed open the door.

As before, a hundred faces stared out from the monitors. He had put many of them there. If they were sinners, which of them could have envisioned this hell? To see the world through a glass and perhaps to the end of time. Or were they fragmented remains of what were once human? Was Raphael their dream?

The eyes followed him as he walked down the length of the display.

"Friend me," someone said.

"It's my birthday. Did you gift me?"

"I'm trending!"

"Do you play Candy Crush?"

"They deleted my post again!"

"You're hot!"

"I'm hot!"

"Dislike, dislike, dislike."

"Like, like, like."

You're more! he wanted to scream, though a deeper voice argued the AIs were not more, even if Klaes existed on another plane. Would it be better if the Resurrected existed in similar programming complexity? Could he make a deal with his father to raise the dead to his level, to build higher castles in the air? What was nothing times ten? Times a quintillion? Infinity?

He could destroy the research server, but there were more servers in the basement behind a thick and secure wall that would take a bomb to penetrate, and there were backups to those servers in other cities and backups to the backups in other states.

He had accomplished nothing. Smashed a few monitors. Even if Maglio had been here, he would have done no more than shake his Exacto knife in Maglio's face. A fool's errand.

"The fucking service around here stinks," said a familiar voice.

Raphael approached Mirsky's monitor. The physicist was tapping an empty cocktail glass against his head.

"Where are the babes?"

"Jonathan, it's me."

Mirsky stared at him. "Jason?"

"Raphael. Jason's son."

Mirsky studied him, then placed the glass on the bridge of his nose. "Didn't have no ..." Mirsky tilted back his head, balancing the glass as would a trained seal. "Where the hell's my drink?"

Another familiar voice pricked him like a needle. Raphael shifted away from Mirsky and glided to the voice as if in a dream.

"... Hypertext databases and mobile databases, spatial databases and temporal databases, probabilistic databases and embedded databases ..."

"Oh, Pink, not you too."

Pink quieted and blinked. She gazed at him, and for an instant there was recognition, but it vanished as rapidly as it came. "Data, sir? A dollar for data, sir?"

"They killed you, Pink. And now they've done this."

"Ten percent off probabilistic—"

"It's me, Pink. Raphael Lennon. Are you in there, Pink?"

She blinked twice. "No happy, happy—"

"—hour," said Mirsky.

Pink blinked twice more. "Happy better run."

His heart leaped. Could it be? "Pink, who wants to kill me?"

Pink's eyes pixilated, then reassembled. "One, two, three, maybe four."

"Everyone wants to kill me?"

"Three-forty."

"Huh?"

The PA crackled. "Raphael Lennon, this is security. We've closed off all exits. Return to the lobby."

Pink bent her head and tapped on an unseen keyboard. After a moment, she stopped typing and put her fingertips together in front of her face. "Find the three-forty."

"For Christ's sake, Pink, please explain."

"I've got hypertext databases and mobile databases, spatial databases and temporal databases, probabilistic databases and embedded databases ..."

The PA blared again. "We're searching the building, room to room. SWAT is on the way."

Raphael grabbed the monitor as if to shake Pink herself. "Do you mean time? Three-forty on the clock?"

Pink blinked slowly. "Can't run."

From below came voices, tramping feet.

"Pink, please—"

"Track, do not track. Track, do not track." Pink's head fell. She snored long and loud.

Raphael backed away from the sleeping Pink. He gazed along the rows of monitors. He should put them all out of their misery. But what would that accomplish? They were there but they weren't. They were on servers in the fucking mythical cloud. Everywhere and nowhere. The damned faces ... the hunger to be wanted.

"Like me."

"Favor me."

"Congratulate me on my years of service."

Raphael backed out of Research and closed the door. He sprinted to Maglio's wrecked office, went to the Wilshire-facing window and pressed his nose to the glass, scanning the sidewalk thirty feet below. The ledge was four feet beneath the window's base, which meant a twenty-six-foot fall. Jesus. He would have to hit it righteously. Someone cried his name. Voices in the corridor. He drew back from the glass and swung the board above his head.

He struck it, then again. Ten times until it cracked, ten more whacks before a hole appeared big enough to crawl through. He climbed out the window and lowered himself to the ledge. He stood with the skateboard on the eighteen-inch-wide ledge, which extended one hundred feet to the corner. Holding the board in his left hand, Raphael took a deep breath and stepped forward.

Raphael glanced down at his legs. "Sorry. No choice."

Dashing along the narrow strip, he calculated. A twenty-six-foot fall, but the sidewalk had a slight downhill slant. If he hit it at top speed theoretically it would be slanted enough to transform the force of the impact into forward motion. Fifty feet into the desperate run, drones humming above and sirens wailing below, he jumped. He lowered his butt, shoved the board under his feet, and fell at speed toward the rushing concrete rectangles.

CHAPTER
THIRTY-FOUR

He met the concrete like a pile driver, but his momentum and the sidewalk's slant kept him rolling for twenty yards until he fell violently from the wobbling board then skidded down the sidewalk to a stop, his fingers still grasping the skateboard. Bending to catch his breath, ignoring the brutal pain in both ankles, and the lesser pain of a dozen scrapes, he gazed at Fairfax. Should he have let himself go? If he tried and didn't fall into the canyon and die, he would have been in handcuffs in five minutes. Sirens wailed from all directions. Too late. Get the hell going. His body creaked and groaned as he mounted his board and pushed off.

A patrol vehicle, lights flashing, came up behind him. Don't panic. Fighting the escalating pain in his ankles, he continued at a measured pace, making a right on Sixth Street. The patrol car continued down Fairfax. He let out his breath and halted. How long would it take for it to be on the news? He slipped out his phone, then dropped it as if it were red hot. He brought his heel down on it a half-dozen times and then kicked it in the gutter.

Oh, fuck that hurt. He slapped the pocket of the drift pants, felt the cylinder and heard the rattle of the pills. He uncapped the bottle, shook out two blue pills, and shoved them in his mouth. He swallowed and hoped they hadn't lost their potency.

He skated east four blocks, then south to Wilshire, his pain deadening a bit. Norval security and the police would be spreading out over the Wilshire District for sure. SWAT knocking down his door. No, that was impossible. He hadn't shot anyone. Hadn't committed a capital crime. But who knew? *Three-forty. Can't run.* A buggy AI's code or an AI's buggy code? What difference? At a stoplight on Wilshire, he slumped, pulled up his hood and waited for the light to change. When it turned green and the pedestrian light said go, he eased the tip of the skateboard over the curb.

For an instant, the morning remained still. An inch more. The wind stirred as if a sleeping beast goaded by a sharp prick, and its roar shook the palms. The enraged air lifted him and set him down. He stumbled on the sidewalk and caught his breath. There's nothing there. Just have to ... He backed ten feet from the corner, mounted the skateboard, and pushed off, slamming his free foot against the sidewalk a half-dozen times. *I'll fly right through you.* As he reached the curb, a tornado swirled, sucked him up and tossed him like a twig back onto the pavement.

Wilshire was impossible, but—

One street. Only one relenting street.

Four elements. Three to go.

He skated north to Sixth and east to La Brea. On the corner, a fleet of delivery drones rose from the roof of a distribution center and spread out across a faintly lit sky. Holding the skateboard to his chest, he walked to the curb and inhaled sharply. When he exhaled, his breath was gray, smoky. A cold radiance rose from the street, and the air colored. Before him an enormous wall of blue ice rose. His skin numbed from the frozen mass of water. The glacier spread in both directions and climbed to the height of a skyscraper.

He fell and clawed at the frozen sweat on his forehead and cheeks. His prison was insurmountable ... or was it the eastern and southern walls? Wind was the first despair. Ice—powerful enough to carve canyons through rock—the second.

He skated to Beverly. What patches of ice remained melted away as the tip of the board inched over the curb. The air warmed, not unpleasantly. He inched forward, and the temperature rose twenty degrees. Beads of perspiration rolled from his forehead to his cheeks. A little painful, but nothing he couldn't handle. He let the skateboard wheels touch the street. He'd opened an oven set at five hundred and fifty for two hours. As he moved a little farther, the hiss of an angry steam iron vibrated, scorched his skin, and then a thousand more. Flames shot skyward. A molten metal heat slammed him. Bludgeoned, he dropped to his knees on the sidewalk and retreated. A short distance away, a passerby, who had probably witnessed Raphael's efforts, shrugged. An untroubled stranger took out his phone and swiped, swiped, swiped.

One, two, three, maybe four. What did that mean? Three-forty?

A patrol vehicle, lights flashing, sped down Beverly in his direction. He slumped and turned his face away. A half block down the street, a skyboard pulsed its message: *Tiny City! Deluxe Units Available! Free Armadillidiidae with Purchase!* The words morphed into a radiant arrow that pointed left.

CHAPTER
THIRTY-FIVE

ead throbbing, energy drained and maxed out on pain, Raphael could run no longer from the police, Norval security, and whoever else might be on his trail. If he could just get a few hours of rest, he could make his next move. He hoped Addy would be home by then—and welcoming.

He'd skated to Tiny City in five minutes, but it took another hour to find unit 61347. On arriving, he saw no light or movement behind the curtains. The vine covering her side yard wall would be ideal to hide beneath until she returned, but within the dark green glossy leaves and fragile yellow flowers were the thorns, and he needed no further holes in his skin to supplement the cuts and scrapes dealt by the hard landing.

While he worked out the next move, he studied the lush growth.

Lift my branches and my thorns leave you be, the bougainvillea said, taking pity on him.

I promise.

He raised the bush and, avoiding the plant's sharp guardians, crawled under, stretching out in the makeshift cave abutting the cinderblock wall. He drew in the skateboard and let the leafy blanket fall.

Sunlight pierced the red petals and warmed Raphael's cheek as he settled on the hard ground, folding the beanie into a small, soft pillow. He gazed out through the dense growth, the intricate play of light and shadow—imagined and missed his painting—and even the beat of drones policing the neighborhood couldn't disturb the dreamy half-sleep overtaking him after his exhausting mayhem.

He dreamt, and in his dream he encountered a rectangular woman with a rose in her navel. As he walked toward her, she became a triangle.

Are you three or four?

The flower grew into a luscious mouth, which turned clockwise into a zero.

When he awoke, through the chinks in the leafy wall, he saw the light in Addy's window. Conscious of the plant's sting, he inched out as he'd inched in. Standing up, he touched his ankles, hot and swollen. His head felt little better. He shook his beanie free of dirt and pulled it on.

He hobbled to Addy's front entrance and knocked on the door, which swung open as if she had been standing there at the peephole.

"My god, what happened?" She stared him up and down, a mother whose son trudged home from a brawl.

"I'm in trouble." Raphael glanced behind and shivered. "I need—"

She tugged him into the house, slammed the door, and double bolted.

"Ow." He yanked off his beanie, removed a thorn, and pushed his fingers through his hair. He took a deep breath and smelled citrus and old paper. "I hid all afternoon in your garden."

"I don't have a garden."

"I mean, the bougainvillea—under it. I didn't know you were home. I wasn't thinking."

"Next time throw pebbles at my window."

He slunk. "Got it." He leaned back against the door. "The police are after me. I don't know if they would think to come here, but ..."

Addy nodded. "You thought I'd give you shelter."

"You want me to go?" If she says yes, I'll close my eyes and pretend to faint.

"Are you going to faint? My God, your shirt, your beanie. You've got blood and bougainvillea all over you."

"It's my ankles I messed up."

"Pull up your pants."

He obeyed.

Addy crouched down. "They're like balloons."

"I'll only stay—"

"I swear. If I stuck in a pin, they'd explode."

"But you wouldn't, right?"

"Please, sit down, and don't use your phone."

"I smashed it and threw it down the gutter on the way here."

Within five minutes, she had set his feet in a basin of cold water with Epsom salts, cleaned the dried blood from his scrapes, and placed a thermometer under his tongue. Pain came in waves, but in between, he swam in Addy's touch and scent.

"Swelling is already going down. How amazing is the body, huh?"

Raphael studied her neck and bare shoulder. "Yes."

Straightening, she drew out the thermometer. "Ninety-nine point nine. Average body temperature worldwide has gone down a degree. So, you're running a slight fever. You've got some deep abrasions. Have you had your booster tetanus shot? If not, you may need antibiotics."

"Could I have something to drink?"

While Addy went to her compact refrigerator, Raphael examined the room. Even in her mini-kitchen, stacks of books rested on countertop and table: hardcover and soft, thick and thin, covers pristine and faded, creased and smoothed as if just printed. He recognized a few works and authors.

She set a pitcher of lemonade and two glasses on the table, then filled them. "I love novels, but also I can't sleep. Lift your feet." She took the basin and tossed him a towel.

A moment later, she guided him to her mini–living room, where makeshift bookshelves climbed the walls and books rested everywhere with the symmetry of a flock of birds settled on a tree. "At night I use them as soporifics. It's unfair to the stories. Maybe even abusive." She set the pitcher of lemonade down on a low-boy coffee table and gestured for him to sit on the matching sofa. She dropped beside him.

He sipped the juice and gazed around the tiny house, 144 square feet of efficient living. "I never thought you'd move east of Fairfax."

Addy spread her arms. "Lovely, isn't it?"

"Nor that I'd be with you."

"East of Fairfax?"

"Anywhere."

"Your hands are trembling."

"I'm scared. I don't want to wake and find out it's not real." He followed the path of the blue veins at the nape. How they ran into the swell of her breasts. He could smell her skin.

Addy reached to draw up her ponytail. She slipped off the round barrette from her braid and undid the weave, letting the green and blue hair fall.

"My company steals, cheats, and murders," he blurted.

"The first two are standard business practice, but murder—did you know that when you took the job?"

His head felt fiery under the pressure to explain. "Maybe I should have known."

"Um, how many murders are we talking about?"

His stomach tightened. She wasn't taking it seriously, or was Raphael not presenting it so? "Hundreds, maybe. Norval hired assassins to kill people, the possums."

She looked off to the side, took a deep breath, and swallowed. "Do you ... do you want more lemonade?" She lifted the jug.

"It's very good."

"The lemons are from the miniature Japanese lemon trees in the common area."

"Ah." He imagined lemons the size of marbles. "How many do you have to squeeze to make one glass?"

"Seven. It's a lot of work. Refill?"

"Oh, sure."

Addy filled his glass.

"Anyway, I pinpointed the possums' locations, so my company could put a hit on them."

"You didn't know?"

"I was a detective who couldn't follow his own footprints."

"So your company was stealing the possums' money?"

"Stealing their souls to create artificial intelligences."

She frowned.

"It's a technological trick. I don't understand it, and I doubt they do. There's a timeframe. The research subjects have to be alive when the program is ready to receive them, otherwise their consciousness can't be transferred. So they killed the possums within the timeframe and turned them into Personality Pluses. Except they didn't get it quite right. The AI versions are buggy."

She made a fist, tucked it under her chin and studied him with that *I have no idea what you're talking about* look in her eyes. She had gone back to when he first told her of the phobia. It was all too wild, and though she wanted to believe him, she didn't. But as if a child telling her of an invisible playmate, she'd humor him. He glanced at the books.

"Addy, does three-forty mean anything to you?"

"Like *Nineteen Eighty-Four* or *2001*? There's *Ninety-Three*."

"*Ninety-Three*?"

"Victor Hugo's last novel. I think I have it—" She scanned her books.

"That's okay. But nothing called Three-Forty?"

"No bells. Hey, Pink might have an answer. I should call her."

Raphael's chest tightened. Jesus, she didn't know. "Addy, I have to tell you something."

She snatched up her phone, but he touched her hand before she could call. "Addy, Pink's gone."

"She ran away from the hospital?"

"Pink died this morning."

She looked up at the ceiling so her tears pooled, falling down her cheeks only when she moved close to him on the couch and leaned her head on his shoulder.

He explained as best he could, leaving out Jason Klaes, the most important player in this absurd, deadly game. He feared Klaes would undermine whatever credibility he'd retained with her.

"I should get out of here," he said. "I've already put you in danger."

She put the back of her hand to his forehead. "You're coming down with something. Get up and shower, huh? In the meantime, I'll find some old clothes that won't look weird on you."

"Addy, I'm six-foot-three."

"Yes, but that writer—oops."

He slumped. "It's okay." *I will not wear his fucking pants.*

Addy laughed. "I'm kidding."

"Jesus."

"Sorry. Let me look. I do have some baggy sweats."

"No, I should leave." He stood uneasily and then fell easily.

The next hours were a blur. He was hot, cold, naked, clothed. He was curled up into himself, shivering, then tossing off covers from the couch where she made his bed.

Addy flitted around him, soothing and nursing. He dreamt she lay beside him and held her breast to his mouth. He awoke once sucking on his own knuckle. He burned. He slept.

He may have dreamt, but woke only from a vast, cold emptiness, as if he were at the end of the universe and there was nothing beyond or before. He opened his eyes to darkness, for several minutes not remembering what had happened or where he was. *Am I dead?* He tried to raise his arm, but nothing happened. Oh, man, it's over. Again, he tried to raise his arm and was jolted as if by an electric current. With a whimper, he turned to his other arm, and it obeyed. His left hand fell on a slab of wood, but the wood felt the fingers. Blood rushed into the sleeping limb. He crooked the dead arm and the life returned. In the dark, someone murmured, clacked their tongue. As if a light had been turned on, he saw a figure seated next to the couch, sitting in a little armchair. Was it the fate that was promised to kill him? He jerked himself up, pulling the waking arm to his chest, drawing back the other.

"Hey, it's just me," said Addy.

He panted and dropped his arm. "Jesus, how long have I been asleep?"

Addy reached out and touched his leg. "It's two in the morning, almost ten hours."

He jetted to his feet, heart pounding. "I'm twenty-seven! It's my birthday, and I'm fucking alive!"

Addy laughed. "Happy birthday, but it's too late to celebrate. I'm going to bed."

And will you join me? did not follow. He tucked up on the little sofa and fell asleep imagining.

IN THE MORNING, Addy came into the living room wearing her Corngold Center uniform and identity badge. Already awake an hour, Raphael smiled up at her.

"I have to go to work. You're on your own, Mr. Lennon. I'll be back late afternoon. Do you like chocolate or vanilla?"

"You've done enough."

"Yes, I have, but I love cake. Remember, it's your birthday the whole day."

A muscle in his back spasmed. Pink said thirteen days. It would be the thirteenth day until it ended. "Chocolate then."

"Stay inside. Don't even peek through the window. There's plenty of food in the fridge. If you use my computer, make sure you log in anonymously. Oh, and I've left you a syllabus of nineteenth-century novels you should read. By the way, it occurred to me that maybe you're in a book. A rectangle your poor character can't get out of."

Raphael grinned. "That's a good one." Impossible, of course, but he glanced around for dog-eared pages.

He watched Addy leave and lock the door. No one had tried to kill him yet. Pink could predict, but that didn't mean every prediction was perfect. "You have thirteen days," which could mean when the day arrived, couldn't it? Take it easy, Raphy. Her prediction was wrong. No one had tried to kill him, and he didn't see a killer on the horizon. He pulled on Addy's sweats, which showed a lot of ankle, and then a big, hooded jacket, which he sniffed for the writer's odor, finding only Addy's fragrance. He stuck his Exacto knife under the waistband of the sweats. He surveyed the room: the overflowing bookshelves, the flowers and plants, the retro turntable and albums, some new, some ancient. Like Raphael, she had a desire for the things of the past, machines that allowed you to know how they worked. A needle in a groove.

Maybe at heart, he was a Blank.

At any rate, Pink was wrong. The only one who had tried to kill him was Addy, and that was with kindness.

How long could he stay here? Even if they weren't publicizing it, the authorities would look for him. They'd question someone who'd seen him with Addy. She was a Karaoke star.

One more day, one more night with Addy.

He glanced at the laptop, started toward it, then stopped and walked over to the stack of books she'd left for him.

For most of the morning, he read book jackets and skimmed pages. He didn't read deeply, but he read broadly. He toured foreign yet somehow familiar worlds, and met people he didn't know but knew well. He absorbed the pages with a sense of escape. He traveled to distant times and places as a science fiction hero. He met orphans aplenty and women cruelly and unfairly marked and young men out to seek their fortune. All the while, he hoped in his proxy adventures, he might chance on a passage throwing light on three-forty. Time slipped by.

At mid-afternoon, he put the books aside and went to the window overlooking Addy's side yard. He separated the curtains and gazed at the bougainvillea. He tapped the glass pane. "How you doing, friend? Thanks again for taking me in." He smiled.

Next time throw pebbles at my window.

He gazed at the ground beneath the plant. He didn't see any pebbles, though there was one good-sized rock. He caught his breath.

Three-forty.

CHAPTER
THIRTY-SIX

The 340-ton granite megalith called *Levitated Mass* had been stored in the sub-basement since the original renovation of the museum had begun. He had been there on the day they moved it. Four Gargantua helicopters lifted the sculpture and deposited it through a temporary opening in the Plaza to reach the basement. The height of *Levitated Mass* made it necessary to extend its compartment from the floor of the sub-basement, through the basement, and to within two feet of the plaza. There below the newly paved central plaza, *Levitated Mass* remained out of public view, though visitors tramped above it daily.

"Find the three-forty," AI Pink had commanded.

Hair tucked under the beanie and head bent, Raphael picked his way through people streaming down Wilshire toward the museum. Like an old-time gunslinger who had forsaken his Colt 45, he'd left his skateboard hidden under Addy's bougainvillea. Skating or carrying around the board would be a giveaway.

He climbed the ramp to the museum. It was the Digital Art Show's Grand Opening, and fans had swarmed to document the generative and algorithmic, datamoshing and datamishing, and fractal super collages. The plaza was packed, but as he crossed the festive area, he stopped at the large square of concrete where a few feet beneath the surface, *Levitated Mass* sat stored. Three-forty, the Leviathan, almost a security blanket for his boyhood. How many afternoons had he skated down its ramp to stare up at the otherworldly boulder in the cool of its shadow? But how did it tie into his fate?

Above the museum, the weather drone seemed to have caught a thermal, riding it. The giant cranes and fortress-like earth movers surrounding the facility stood silent, given a day off from their creative destruction. A holographic urinal big as an elephant floated by, in its wake, sweat-drenched blogger-critics posting their judgments to the world.

Nearing the cafeteria, he took out the key ring and sorted, separating the tiniest from the others. It was one of his mother's museum keys. He examined it and saw the discolored surface. Wax? He wiped the substance away. Would it still work? Was there a new biometric device to gain access? The planners rarely got to the details of the reconstruction efforts before they set off in another direction. With a little luck …

In the cafeteria lobby, he pulled his hoodie tighter around his head and waited for the elevator to open. Two museum guides approached. To get on with the docents and not exit with them on the lower floor would attract attention, and the hood wouldn't help either.

Drawing down the hood, he backed away. It took two more round trips until he could board alone and press the button for the basement. When the door closed, he pointed the key at the narrow, easily overlooked sub-basement slot. From the exterior, the elevator would appear to go to the basement, and in the basement, it would look like it was on the first floor—if the key functioned.

He slid it in. The light dimmed, then brightened as the lift descended, passing the lower floor with a shiver. It stopped and opened on a wide, dim corridor.

Raphael exited and pivoted to watch the door close. On the elevator's right in a steel panel was a slot identical to the interior one: the ticket for a return ride to the surface. Every four hours, a security guard patrolled the sub-basement, but for most museum personnel, it was little thought of and rarely visited. The public was unaware of its existence.

It was cool and dry in the corridor, as it was throughout the floor, the temperature and humidity regulated to preserve the artwork. Most times, his mother had a particular canvas or sculpture she wanted to show him, but sometimes they would wander the cross-corridors, peeping into the hundreds of rooms where the pieces waited.

The last corridor off the main aisle was corridor Z, where the museum stored the awkward artwork, forbidden art, or art obscenely and irrevocably damaged, as well as art too disturbing to be seen or too immense to be housed elsewhere. When she brought him, she steered clear of Z.

IT WAS in the years of the pandemic, when everyone wore masks and kept their distance, that Raphael and his mom breached the corridor. Although they had sheltered in the apartment, she wanted to evaluate a piece stored in Z, document it with a photo. The museum was closed to the public and staffed by a skeleton crew. It would be just the two of them entering the building.

At the museum's main entrance, a security guard, whom his mother knew on a first-name basis, escorted them to the floor above the subterranean facilities. They rode the elevator past the basement to exit at the sub-basement. The enormous room was shadowy and gloomy as usual, but that would be the least of his worries on this day.

When they arrived at Z, his mother instructed him to wait at the beginning of the corridor. It would only take her five or ten minutes to take the photograph. He nodded agreement. She slipped down her mask to smile at him, then turned away.

He tracked her as she strode halfway down the hall and put her eye to a door's peephole. She then faced Raphael, held a finger up, opened the door and walked—vanished—into the room. He folded his arms and swung side-to-side. Already it seemed as if she'd been gone a long time. He counted to sixty under his breath. *Must be five minutes by now.* He pinched his mask, pulled it away and let it snap back. He shuffled a few steps down the hallway. The first door's sign said, *Magdalen with Pipe*. Shrugging, he walked to the next door. *Untitled Minus Four*. Minus meant take away, but take away from what? He scratched his head moved to the third room, which had a title that gave him goosebumps: *A Child's Worst Nightmare*.

He backed away from the door, but gazed at the tiny, round window as he rubbed his arm, knowing what nightmares were. It sounded scary, but if he just took a fast look.

Standing on his toes and peering into the room's peephole, he saw only dark, but it was a funny dark, not like the lights were out, but as if someone had thrown a blanket over his head. The blanket tightened on his face. His heart pounded. A real blanket was smothering him! From inside the room, a deep voice said, "Is the one that doesn't end." The blanket wound about his neck. He couldn't breathe!

"Mom! Mom!" he cried, pushing at the door, thrusting himself back.

Arm's length from the door, he sucked in a breath. He backed further away, then turned and ran back to *Magdalen with Pipe*. Heart thumping, he touched his neck. Smooth as a nectarine. That's what his mom said. What had happened? Was it something he remembered from an actual nightmare?

"Stupid," he muttered as he calmed. There was nothing in the room. No one whispered anything. He had given himself a little nightmare, scared himself. He smacked his leg and laughed. He wasn't frightened at all. In fact, he felt calm, as if he were in a warm bath, and his mother was shampooing his hair. He should look again, but what was the point? There was only a dark room.

He looked down the corridor for his mother, but she wasn't there. How long did a dumb photograph take? He touched his arm. The goosebumps were gone. Nothing had happened, and everything was fine. He backed out of Z into the main corridor.

He had never been so deep in the sub-basement, and his eyes fell on the western wall. A gigantic metal door stood guard at the center, bearing a sign that read *Authorized Personnel Only*.

What art did that door hide? Drawn to it, he walked up and when he got close saw faint writing and symbols on the steel rectangle. They would have been difficult to see even in brighter light. At the door's center a red star filled a circle, an arrow at the top. The vertical letters spelled *Beverly Boulevard*. Opposite was *Wilshire*. Below was *La Brea*, and above was *Fairfax*. *Pretty weird kind of map*, he had thought. From behind the door came a gust of wind, then a clink. The sound repeated itself, followed by a moan.

The back of his neck tingled, and his pulse jumped. He pounded his leg again. Don't be a baby. Nothing to be scared of. He stepped forward to put his ear to the metal when another gust nudged the door open. "Hey," he said, jumping back.

He glanced behind him toward corridor Z, expecting that his mother might appear. He gazed back at the big steel door, which remained open a couple of inches. He couldn't go to school, couldn't play with friends, couldn't do anything. But he could peek inside this door.

He slipped his fingers into the opening and pulled on the slab. It swung toward him as if weightless. Pulse racing, he stepped through the doorway into darkness. At his footfall, an overhead light came on. He stood on a platform from which a metal staircase descended into an enormous shadowy cave. He walked out onto the platform and peered down. From below, a flame shot up, which was met by a howling wind that whipped the flame back and forth. Behind him, something slammed. The overhead light died. He spun as warmth flowed down his thigh. He searched for a door handle but found only smooth steel. He pushed on the door, then hammered. The blood rushed from his head, and his legs turned to butter. "Mom! Mom!" he screamed.

Arms embraced him. "Raphy, I'm right here!"

He twisted into his mother, felt her warm, comforting body. "It's all right," she said. "I've got you."

"Hold me, Mom."

"What happened? You didn't look into this room, did you?"

Raphael inched back and peeked around his mother. He was still in corridor Z. He twisted his head to see the door labeled *A Child's Worst Nightmare.*

"Did you?"

Raphael nodded, his chest heaving. "There was nothing, Mama. I walked away and found another door. I got locked behind it."

"But you're right here." She glared at the door and said a bad word, one he'd never heard her say before.

"What, Mom?"

"It's okay," his mother said, stroking his head. She pulled down his mask and wiped his nose with a tissue.

He shivered. "My leg is cold, Mom. Freezing."

She looked down at him and smiled. "It's just pee, Raphy. You were frightened and wet your pants. It's evaporating."

"Oh." He touched the dark on his pants.

"We should go now." She took his arm and guided him out of the corridor.

"There's the door," he said as they emerged from corridor Z into the main corridor. He pointed at the enormous steel door to the right. "There. That's where I was."

"Oh, no, Raphy. You couldn't have opened that door. It's locked.

His mom had discovered him by the other door. He couldn't have been inside there. He swayed, then spread his feet for balance. "What's behind there?"

"That's the entrance to Dig Three, once the most productive of all the excavation sites."

"The door opened, Mom. I went behind it."

She squeezed his shoulder. "You had a night—a daydream, Raphy."

He looked for the writing and symbols but couldn't see them. If he stepped closer, but he didn't want to step closer. "It was different."

She came to his side. "Um. Well, maybe."

"Do people go down there and dig?"

"Not for a long time. They sealed it off when the museum proper was first built."

He jerked back. "I think I heard something."

His mother had stared at the enormous rectangular guard and fingered her key ring. "It's a sizeable space, like a cavern. There's some air movement. Just a draft, Raphy.

"Oh ..."

"And please don't ask to see it."

He wanted to stand in back of his mother but held his position. "Naw, I don't want to see it. What's down there, anyway?"

"There are old oil pumps from the days when they tapped into the field far below. They're half-dismantled and treacherous, same with the pit's scaffolding."

"But someone goes down there?" he asked, drawn to the door.

"Sometimes just to inspect."

"Have you?"

He recalled how intensely she looked at him as she fingered her key ring. "No, never. It's so dark down there, Raphy. And it's not much different from the museum's other pits."

"How big is it?"

"Oh, very big." We have to leave now, Raphy. Let's forget about Dig Three."

"Sure. No problem. Let's go."

BUT THE DOOR and what lay beyond it kept its mysterious allure, despite his fear. And on subsequent visits to the sub-basement, he would again stare at it from a distance, wondering at the writing and symbols that had disappeared, wondering if he had ever seen them or imposed them later when his phobia began. How much of that memory was dream?

As he now walked down the main aisle, he gazed at the steel rectangle, before pivoting at corridor Z toward the room that housed three-forty, the last space of the corridor, room nineteen.

Reaching that room, he pressed his eye to the peephole, then opened the door.

"Christ," he whispered, gazing up at an immense gray boulder.

As if someone had carried him there, Raphael pressed up against the granite, head tilted back. Bigger than all the craziness swirling around him. Not incomprehensible mites of chance, but undeniable solidity and reality. Something real. The rock was cold, but the cold was exhilarating. As he breathed in the rock's musty atmosphere, the hairs rose on his neck. The stone pulsed, as if there was a tiny heart in the center of the stone.

It had to be Pink's three-forty. But now what? As he studied the granite, he spotted something familiar lying at the base of the stone. Heart racing, he glanced behind him, bent, and stretched his arm out. One of his beanies, a bright green bean with red stripes.

Above him, something flashed. Clutching the beanie, he rose and backed away from the sculpture.

From above came a faint blue burst of light. He raised his eyes, and the light came again. He retreated farther and saw the flashing originated from the top of the stone.

Someone had climbed *Levitated Mass* and placed something up there.

Raphael scanned the rock's ledges and footholds. He calculated the best route up the granite, strode to the base, and reached above his head for a ledge. With a street skater's balance and confidence, he ascended and pulled himself over the top.

Breathing hard, he inspected a device set atop the boulder. Lights pulsed on a steel cylinder, casting an eerie blue glow. He raised his eyes to the ceiling and realized that the plaza was an arm's length way. He thought he could hear the cumulative chatter of people gathered above. He examined the cylinder and saw a tiny digital clock. A vinyl label clung to the artwork's base. The inscription read

Anonymous
Untitled
Undated

Steel, Plastic, Semtex

Semtex was bomb material.

A fistful of pins pricked Raphael's forehead.

An explosive device or Avant-Garde art? Maglio claimed the Blanks were intent on destroying the digital world. The Digital Art Show would be a perfect target. But how had his beanie gotten here? *There was wax on the key, and Struat had been in his apartment. Even as I speak, the news is they've blown up servers in five states. Yes, that looks like one of his colorful beanies. Our End Man has gone wrong, gone Blank.*

The blue light pulsed faster. A couple feet above, thousands toured The Digital Art Show.

If it was what it claimed to be, the explosion would blast through the plaza. *Get out. Get out. Big D. We have a Big D.* But he wasn't at his desk accumulating data. He was at ground zero.

He shifted on the granite and pulled the device to his chest.

Face down, he hugged the stone, dropping one leg over the side, seeking a toehold.

Drawing the bomb to him, he lowered himself. With his free foot, he prodded the rock for another ledge and found an inset.

As he dropped another foot and searched for the next ledge, a light on the device flashed yellow. *Shit.* He probed for a foothold, found a narrow one, held his breath, and lowered himself half a body length. He hunted again but found only smooth stone. "Fuck."

He let go and slid down eight feet of rock, hitting the ground so hard his knees buckled and lungs spasmed. His ankles, perhaps disbelieving he'd put them through more abuse, were slow to react. Were they beyond pain? *No. Jesus Christ.* He trembled. Somehow staying upright, he leaned into the boulder.

Should he set the device under *Levitated Mass*? If the bomb was as powerful as it appeared to be, even there it might penetrate the plaza above.

Hugging the bomb to his chest, he backed to the doorway and into the corridor. Set it down. Run. *Can't run.*

"Shit."

He measured the distance to the elevator. If it didn't go off before he reached the surface, what then? His heart pounded at his ribcage. He turned in the other direction. The wall, the Dig Three entrance. Did one of his mother's keys fit the lock?

He staggered down the hall with the cylinder, keeping his eyes on his burden until he came within ten feet of the massive iron door. Behind it was the deep pit that his mother described: earth, clay, and bone. He could drop the bomb into that hole. It would minimize the damage. Drop the bomb and get out.

He gazed at the door, his breathing matching the rapidity of his heart. He remembered the pit, the enormous cave, the flame, the door slamming shut, trapping him. Was that a dream? A forewarning? Whatever it was, it made no difference. He was holding a fucking bomb. He strode to the door.

At the center was the compass rose, and along the perimeter the names of the streets, his streets. Just like the frame of his canvas, the frame of his world. Through the door that mapped his world, would he lose the world he had? He set the bomb down, pulled out the key ring, pinched a small key, and slipped it into the lock. He turned clockwise and then counterclockwise.

The cylinder's light pulsed red.

The key wouldn't turn.

Behind the door wind shrieked, and something jangled.

On the door, the compass rose reshaped itself into a scarlet whirlpool. Beside it appeared the slash of a towering queen palm, a scrawled warning, a saber-toothed tiger, his mother's frozen face. *Have you lived today?* He closed his eyes and pressed his hands to the side of his head. He opened his eyes, but the images remained. His life absent one experience.

The last image, his mother's promise of escape. When the last stroke met the canvas, when the last image of his life painting had dried, he would be free of the phobia.

Behind the door was the image, and the image was death.

CHAPTER
THIRTY-SEVEN

R aphael stuck in the second key, but the lock resisted. He tried the third. The mechanism grumbled at the intrusion, then relented.

He pushed down the handle and pulled the door open.

Overhead lights shone on a metal landing and a long staircase that led downward and disappeared into darkness.

Holding open the door, he peered down the long flight. Not total darkness, but faint light. He crouched, hoisted the bomb, hugged it to his chest, and moved to the edge of the landing. An updraft blew his hair back. *Dig three must extend under Wilshire and Fairfax.* His heart said, "Heave it!" His head told him it would land on one of the upper steps, detonate, and cause as much destruction as it would have in its original location. The dig should be its final resting place. Breathing slowly, he lowered a foot onto the first step. Jesus, it looked almost vertical.

Each footstep on the metal staircase clanked, echoing a dozen times on the surrounding rock and dirt. The Semtex would explode and tear his flesh to shreds like his canvas. He'd have his image, but who would paint it? His head ached. He peered over his shoulder to see the door remained open. He should have closed it. Should he set the bomb down and scramble back? But if he reached the open door, would the temptation to run be too great?

He continued down the metal staircase, a grim path in a dream. His burden grew heavier, and he shifted his center-of-mass forward. He fought sadistic gravity, which waited to laugh when he tumbled. Now each footfall thundered, yet he got no closer to the terminus. The steps multiplied. How far down was the dig? Why was he not there yet? He turned his head toward the exit, the rectangle of light through which to escape. A lightheadedness struck him. Swaying, he lost his footing and slid. He bounced down the plates, each metallic blow jarring his body to the bone. Heart pounding, ears ringing, he slid to the stairs' end. He slammed into the ground, the impact knocking the wind out of him. As he recovered his breath, he gazed at the dig, illuminated by a few low-wattage lights around its perimeter. Like the tar pits on the museum grounds, but twice their size. He pressed his lips to the blinking cylinder. The red button pulsed faster. Wind blew from the left, from Wilshire. He stared into the pit. There was no time to look for a better place. He had to trust it was deep enough

Was Klaes trying to call him now? *Sorry, Dad. No phone. No connection. You can't know I may be about to die. No transfer of consciousness. No high-functioning AI for eternity.* There was no time. The thirteenth day. The wind growled as if in warning. How close was he to the boulevard?

As he hunched and set to roll the deadly device down the dig, Raphael strained to see in the darkness. Something shiny lay in the dirt beside his foot. He picked up a crinkled energy drink can and, scanning the dig, saw there were hundreds. This was where all the used cans and plastics went when they were dropped into the receptacles. The pit was the recyclables graveyard.

Behind him something clanked, drawing his focus back toward the staircase. Only the main corridor's light illuminated the exit. A back-lit form filled the doorway.

"Need a cigarette?"

Raphael stared. The intruder's features remained obscure. Raphael's chest tightened. "Who are you?"

Turning a quarter circle, the figure caught the light. He drew back his jacket to reveal a tool belt that held sufficient steely implements to build a house: channel locks, drill, vise grips, screwdrivers, sledgehammer.

The Electrician?

"How did you—" Raphael looked over his shoulder toward the cylinder. "There's a bomb down there, and it's about to go off." He turned his head back.

The Electrician held his sledgehammer in his right hand and tapped its face on his left palm. The clap echoed through the chamber.

Raphael swayed. "What is this?"

"Your birthday."

"Hey, man, look. It's Raphael. I'm Klaes's son! You work for my father." The hit man smiled, and ice crystals formed on Raphael's heart. "He sent you to kill me, didn't he?"

The Electrician pounded his palm again. "Naw."

Raphael lifted his hands as if they held the skateboard that lay beneath Addy's bougainvillea. "Then what are you doing?"

"New contract." The hit man wiped his mouth, spit.

"New contract?"

"Yep." He stepped down.

"Maglio."

"Fuck Maglio."

Raphael fell back another step. "Then who?"

Matching Raphael's step, the Electrician said, "Troy-Boy Tolover."

Raphael shook his head. "Troy-Boy's dead."

"Also Van Pelt."

"The pharmaceutical executive? He's dead too."

"And Dr. Royer makes three. A triumvirate," said the Electrician.

Raphael's laugh came out a squawk. "All three of them want to kill me? Tell me this is some sort of big punk arranged by my father."

"No joke, buddy. You want a last cigarette?"

"You killed them."

"Me? I'm the tool."

"Sure. Right."

"The tool of the lesser gods. Think of it like the Greek stuff. When the gods got pissed, they took revenge. If they couldn't put a hit on one of the heavyweights, they went for the kids and grabbed some human to do it. The sins of the father shall fall on the son."

"Those three are dead."

"So's your old man, and he paid me plenty of crypto. But these guys are way generous."

"They don't exist. Programs. Lines of code."

"Tell them that."

The Electrician took another two steps down.

"If you kill me, my father will have you killed. A new contract."

He smiled. "No, that won't happen. Your old man has changed, evolved. He won't—can't hurt anyone."

Raphael looked up at the dark vault and murmured, "Dad?" The heavens were silent. He glanced down at the pit and the blinking light on the bomb. "So you're going to whack me with that?"

"It's fast. Not so clean though, but down here, who would notice? Is that Dig Three there?"

An instant of reprieve. "Yes. Kind of hard to see. Were you for real with that cigarette?"

"No." He stepped down and tapped the hammer on his leg.

"Is Miranda in on this?"

"She bowed out. She has a soft spot for you. She's flawed."

Raphael laughed. The Electrician took two more quick steps, as if he expected him to turn and run.

Raphael balled his right hand. "How did you find me?"

"Cameras and gait trackers everywhere. Our AI friends have access to all of them." He took another step and drew back the weapon.

Raphael threw his fist. He aimed for the killer's temple, but the Electrician twisted his head, and Raphael's knuckles struck only that brutal mouth. Blood sprung from a split lip. He licked the blood, turned away as if he might climb back up the stairs, then swung the hammer backhand.

Raphael dropped as if on a skateboard. The iron whizzed by his head and slammed into the rail with a thunderous bang. Raphael scrambled back. "I'll leave town. You can tell them you killed me."

Tool raised above his head, the Electrician jumped, coming face-to-face with Raphael, so he got the man's hot breath in his nostrils. The hammer came down but overshot its target. Only the handle struck Raphael's shoulder. He grabbed the hit man with both arms, but the Electrician broke loose and sent Raphael stumbling down a dozen steps, landing on his belly. He pushed up, turned, and hobbled down the remaining steps to reach the tarry shore. Above, he saw a bright rectangle. Its light cut through the darkness and fell upon him.

He looked down at the bomb. It was blinking like crazy. He had to throw it farther down into the pit. The Electrician's feet clanged on the steps. He lifted the device and trudged several yards through the sticky earth. He halted, gazed into darkness and heaved the bomb.

As he turned to see the Electrician upon him, he smelled something distinct from the earth and clay. Something rising through the pit. Was it methane? What the fuck else?

Raphael swayed, dulled by the methane. He staggered back. The Electrician stepped onto the shore. He held the phone toward Raphael, then played the beam on the pit.

"Kind of pretty. Want to go for a dip?"

"There's a bomb. It's going to kill us both."

"Make it easy on yourself. Your father will fix you right up, anyway." The Electrician strode forward but sunk a few inches into the soft gluey beach. He shook his head as if he too were feeling the effects of the gasses. Raphael backed further into the pit, which grew softer, more liquidy. He glanced down at a pool of black. Something cool and hard pressed against his mid-section. *Fuck, his Exacto knife.* With his right hand, he drew the knife from the band of the sweatpants and opened it. With his left hand he reached down and scooped up a handful of the thick goo.

"One crack, that's all," said the Electrician in a begging tone.

With the last of his strength, Raphael rushed forward. As the hit man swung, Raphael drew the blade across the Electrician's thigh and jammed his palm to the man's eyes. The Electrician screamed in pain, dropped his phone, swiveled, and struck out blindly. Raphael skirted by him.

"Fuck! I'll cut your fucking head off!"

Raphael grabbed the rail and pulled himself up the stairs, trying not to breathe the gas. Reaching the landing, he looked down to see the Electrician crawling on the sludgy shore. Clawing at the sands and begging for light.

Raphael stepped into the doorway. From below came the sound of a phone ringing. He slammed shut the door and locked it. He was halfway to the elevator when he remembered the green beanie someone had planted beneath the boulder. Too late. He had to get the hell out.

CHAPTER
THIRTY-EIGHT

Shoes weighted with clay and oil, Raphael threaded through the plaza's crowd, shouting, "Run, there's a bomb!" The loud, urgent song produced by a disembodied mouth on the elevated stage buried his cries. He pushed through to the stage and climbed on the platform. He grabbed for the microphone, considered his empty hand, then screamed, "Can you hear me?"

"Major Tom!" yelled someone in the crowd.

"Couldn't they come up with a better hologram than that?" another audience member shouted, prodding the crowd into a spirited debate.

"There's a bomb! You're all going to die!"

"You're a bomb," responded a shrill voice, drawing laughter and further derision from the digital art fans.

A muffled boom silenced the crowd. A second boom, ten times louder than the first, shook the concrete plaza. Confusion surrendered to terror and panic. Screaming digital art fans clawed at each other to make for the exits.

Raphael leaped from the stage and joined the fleeing crowd. He slipped his slender body through seams in the fear-drenched mob, reached the sidewalk, and hobbled west on Wilshire.

He hadn't gone twenty yards when he saw the Norval Headquarters quiver and sway, the Art Deco's golden prow tacking left then right as if trying to find a steady course. The blood rushed from his head. He had done this. He swallowed, fingered the cuff of his beanie, and stepped forward. By the time he reached the building, the structure had sunk a foot into its foundations, oil spilling out from the perimeter like an overflowing sink. Dark tendrils crept up the prow. Norval employees ran from the building through the lobby doors and emergency exits, wading into the fast-rising black lake. The Art Deco marvel shook, groaned, and dropped another twelve inches. A cloud of dust rose fifty feet into the air, which smelled of oil.

Akira trudged through the muck toward Raphael, her arms spread wide as if trying to gather an immense object. "What is this?"

He spoke but nothing came out. He shuddered, but met Akira's eyes, and found his voice. "A bomb went off." He pointed to the ground. "I think the explosion opened a sinkhole." Other End Men approached like soldiers regrouping under their old sergeant. He addressed the blurted question. "The Salt Lake Oil Field is swallowing Norval."

"You can't mean the entire building," said Akira.

But he did mean that. Norval would be gone.

"Rescue Geo, you fuckers!" screamed Ms. Goloda, who stood outside the emergency exit, ankle deep in tar and pointing upward. At the top of her lungs, she wailed, "He's trapped in the tanner!"

"Ms. Goloda, get away from the building," shouted Akira.

The secretary dropped to her knees in the oil, her eyes flooding with tears. "My Geo doesn't deserve this." She raised her arms imploringly. "Won't someone help?" She scanned the End Man. Her eyes locked on Raphael.

"Thank god," she cried.

Ms. Goloda stood up and slogged through the rising oil to Raphael. She threw her arms around his legs and raised her tortured face. "His door wouldn't open. I tried." She held up her bloodied fingers. "You're brave. You're strong. You must help him."

"I-I can't."

"Geo will die and with him Matt."

"Matt Tucker?"

"Mr. Maglio was interviewing him for your job. They're trapped together. Go help them, you bastard!" Ms. Goloda pawed at his chest with her torn fingers.

Raphael wrenched himself from the secretary, smelled the now familiar gas, and turned to the pack of End Men. "Get the hell out of here, guys. There's methane. We could have another explosion."

As the other End Men retreated a few yards, Raphael started toward the building.

"Raphael, what are you doing?" yelled Akira.

"I'm going back inside."

"For Maglio?"

Raphael felt for his Exacto knife. "For Matt."

Raphael strode on toward the emergency exit, his heart pounding. He had set the widening disaster in motion. Maglio could go to hell, but he couldn't leave Matt behind. As he entered the stairwell, the structure shook again. Walls split with dreadful screams and chunks of concrete pummeled him. Dodging a brick-sized piece that could have felled him on the spot, he held his hands above his head and climbed upward, oily shoes slipping and sliding. He fell twice, grunted and got back up. He had to climb. As he exited the stairwell on the third floor, Norval moaned like a trapped mammoth.

Upon reaching Goloda's office, he located her remote and opened the door to the executive office hallway. He staggered down the zigzag passage to Maglio's door, which proved locked. He dropped to his knees and dug his fingers into the jam.

"Come on," he screamed, yanking and twisting. With a screech, the door gave way.

He entered Maglio's office, its ceiling half collapsed, furniture upside down and artwork strewn about. Raphael's heart sunk. Matt was stretched out face-down on the floor. Maglio's tanning machine lay across his body.

Raphael dropped to his knees beside Matt. Ripping off Matt's bracelet, he felt for his friend's pulse *Come on, come on. There, yes, not strong, but enough.* Raphael grasped the tanner and lifted it a few inches before it slipped from his sweaty hands. He wiped his palms on his pants and tried again. He shifted position and grasped the bottom. He rolled the tanner off Matt. His colleague sucked in a lungful of air, groaned, and opened his eyes. "Oh, lordy, where am I?"

"Maglio's office. There's been—an event."

Matt muttered. "I thought I was going to die."

"It's okay, buddy. I've got you." He ran his hand down Matt's legs. "Does anything feel broken?"

Matt wriggled his body. "Only everything. It's kind of hard to breathe."

"Yeah, the wind was knocked out of you." *Or broken ribs.* From below came an angry roar as if from one of the beasts that once roamed the neighborhood.

"He lured me up here with food: sliced ahi tuna with mango, Szechuan chicken lettuce wraps, and honey-glazed pomegranate seeds. Man, it was wizard. But I told him I wouldn't take the position, the anti-Blanking spot." Matt drew a breath. "I mean, you've only been gone a couple of days." Matt's eyes grew big and watery. "I respect you, man."

"Yeah, appreciated. We've got to get you out of here."

"Boy, Maglio was pissed. That's when he took off his clothes and stepped into the tanner."

"The tanner?"

"I swear he must wear a trick suit. It just dropped to the floor. The last thing I saw was his wrinkly old ass. That's when the earthquake hit. Jesus, it was crazy in here. I yelled, 'Earthquake, Geo! We should get the hell out of here. It's the real fucking thing.' Then the lights went out." Matt turned his head toward the tanner. "I told him, 'Get out of the tanner, Geo.'" Matt sniffed. "You know what he told me? 'I can't. It's stuck.' Must have been an electronic lock, huh?"

"Yeah. Now, if it doesn't hurt, I'm going to lift you from behind." He slipped his hands under Matt's armpits and hoisted.

Matt drew in several rapid breaths. "I told him to kick. Well, he kicked all right, but nothing happened, so he starts yelling over and over, 'It's not my time.' I should have gotten my ass out of there. But I took a shot at getting it open—then wham, the floor falls out from under me, and I'm slammed by the Solarium."

He eased Matt to his feet. "Can you stand by yourself?"

Matt held steady for an instant, but then swayed and collapsed, groaning in agony. "The pain's in my chest."

Raphael touched his shoulder. "It's all right. I'll carry you."

"Aren't you going to check on Geo?"

"No." No noise was coming out of the tanner. Maglio could have died of a heart attack. Asphyxiation maybe. Raphael tapped the Exacto knife tucked in his waistband. *Forget it, just get Matt out. You don't need a souvenir.*

But his heart raced. He dug his fingers under the lid of the tanner but did not find the resistance he expected. With one hand, he opened the tanner. With the other he drew out his Exacto knife.

The tanner was empty.

Raphael shoved the knife back beneath his waistband, and bent to Matt, who had closed his eyes and was moaning lowly. He grabbed him under his arms, hoisted, and dragged his inert body toward the door.

"Please set your little friend down." Spine icing over, Raphael turned. The potted palm quivered as a naked Maglio emerged from behind it, phone in hand. "I was trapped in the tanner, but it sprung open when it fell."

The building rocked.

Maglio ducked and shuffled sideways. With a shriek, a strip of ceiling peeled away and fell at Maglio's feet. He kicked it, grunted, and strode to the window. "Is this your father's plan?"

"What are you talking about?"

"Oh, you know. Don't play innocent." Maglio faced Raphael. Digits scrolled down the cybernetic eye.

He wanted to look away from the eye, but its lure was too strong. He dragged Matt another foot, not leaving the eye for an instant.

Maglio walked over to his desk, sat down, and pulled open a drawer. "I told you to set Matt down. You and I have to talk."

"Fuck you."

"I spoke a few moments ago to your father. We're close to a deal."

"I'm happy for you." Raphael dragged Matt another foot, eliciting a groan of pain from his friend.

Maglio smiled. "A perfect day to claim eternity. Please set him down, and we'll talk." He lifted a small black gun and pointed it at Raphael. "I'm happy to transition among the chaos, and so too will you."

"Hey, don't point that gun at him," muttered Matt.

Maglio shifted the barrel to Matt. "Better?

"Um, no."

"We're allies," said Maglio, letting the gun sway as if it were choosing its target.

Stick the Exacto into Maglio's digital and pluck it out like an oyster from its shell. "You're a murderer."

"Christ, I offed a few criminals on the run. Where's the sin in that?"

"The plane crash? The Toobyville Dam?"

"Crystal ball algorithms. Advance knowledge isn't culpability. "

Raphael's insides simmered. "You knew, but you did nothing."

Maglio shrugged. "I release your data, and we get our afterlives."

"Not interested."

The building trembled. Matt's face went chalk white. His eyelids fluttered, then closed.

"I'm waiting for a phone call from your father regarding the details. It should happen right about—" Maglio's cell rang. He smiled into the screen. "Hello, Professor Klaes. Yes, I have located your son. I've provided him the gist of our deal. Yes, I hear you," said Maglio. He nodded several times. "Yes, I know. Norval won't get Personality Plus, but I will. I'll get life everlasting. The company will have to make do with our current tech. Ready? I'm tingling with anticipation! Oh. I see."

Maglio held his phone out to Raphael. "Your father wants to speak with you."

"Not interested."

"Catch." Maglio tossed the phone. It landed face up on the floor. The familiar bearded face gazed up at him.

"I'm sorry, son," said Klaes.

"Fuck you, Dad."

"We're ready," said Klaes.

"For what?" demanded Raphael.

"Geo and I have made a deal. I have your data prepared to receive your consciousness."

"Pass, Dad. I'm not transitioning to an AI."

"When you are, you'll thank me."

"Should I have thanked you when a trio of your lesser AGIs sent your ex-stooge to bash in my head twenty minutes ago?"

"I tried to call you, but—"

"Right, no phone."

"You see how close that was? If I don't know when ... They'll send others. You'll have to run, but you can't run. Isn't it better to fall into the arms of your father? To be with your sister when she rises? To have our family."

He dismissed Klaes's words, but the picture Klaes had painted held him. A sister. A father. It was all a fantasy, but if, if—"I'm not interested." Raphael kicked the phone back to Maglio. He clasped Matt, lifted him, and dragged him closer to the door.

"Slow down," Maglio picked up the phone, though the gun barrel never wavered, "or your friend will slow down forever."

"Are you crazy? You and him, the AI—he's out of the mind he doesn't have."

The building jerked. The paintings remaining on the walls sprung from their hooks like tossed playing cards. The floor cracked in a half-dozen places. One devoured Dali's shattered *Memory*.

"Whoa," said Maglio.

"I'm getting Matt out of here."

Maglio shook his head. "Your father agreed to recreate me as a Personality Plus with consciousness. I gave him your data, so that you too will be a soulful Personality Plus. That's the deal." He turned the screen toward Raphael and propped it up on the desk.

"It was the only way, son," said Klaes.

"I'm staying."

"All is in readiness," said Klaes from the screen. "This is the moment."

Raphael shook his head. "You're not real. I won't be real either. None of us will exist."

Maglio aimed the gun at Raphael. "Half-baked AIs will worship at our feet, and Stillflesh will worship at theirs."

"What's happening?" muttered Matt, opening his eyes.

Klaes held up his hands. "Let's move on."

Raphael sighed. "I don't want to be a god." Norval shuddered again and oil's rich smell filled the air. Oil and methane.

"Do you think all I've done was for shits and giggles?" asked Geo.

"Suicide!" shouted a new voice. In the doorway stood Mr. Lean, face bright red, eyes bulging, and arms propped against the doorframe, ignoring Maglio's nakedness. "Hundreds marching down the boulevard like they're in a parade. Waving Norval Resurrection Policies like flags. Off to drown themselves in the sea like lemmings. Mass suicide!"

Maglio shook his head but looked toward the window. "What the hell are you talking about, Lean?"

"Your customers have had enough of this life; they want online eternity!"

Maglio growled. "Ridiculous. You can't just make the first payment, then cash in on an afterlife." Maglio's brow furrowed. "Besides, I told Maisie to get that clause into contracts." He shook his head, then let the gun drift toward Lean, then brought it back to Raphael.

"Look out the window," cried Lean.

"Raphael, you'll be with me and your sister for eternity," said Klaes.

"I'm staying," said Raphael.

Maglio shook the gun. "You won't cheat me out of an afterlife. Obey your father."

"Show me his face," said Raphael.

Maglio turned the phone toward Raphael. His father's face was as pale as his beard. Klaes's lips trembled. Above the phone that held his father's face, the barrel of the gun fixed itself on his heart. "No, Dad."

Something clicked.

"I can't say I'm not disappointed. We had so little time together. If I ..." Klaes's voice fell to a whisper. "Do you feel any love for me?"

It would be so easy. Just tell it what it wants to hear. "I can't love someone that doesn't exist."

"No, well then, goodbye. Down the road, *son*."

"Yeah, down the road ..."

"What about me?" yelled Maglio.

"You'll get yours," said Klaes. "A deal is a deal."

The screen went black. Maglio studied his phone. "You've screwed yourself out of an afterlife, Raphael, but I have one coming." He gazed around the remains of this office. "Soon."

"You're getting what you want," said Raphael. "Let me get Matt out of here."

"In the spirit of the pharaohs, I want someone with me when I go. Someone to accompany me to that other life."

"You asshole. He'll simply die under the rubble. He won't go anywhere."

Mr. Lean hopped twice. "I don't know what jiggery-pokery you've gotten yourself into, Mr. Maglio, but if you want a peek at bankruptcy, better look out your widow." Mr. Lean thrust a finger toward the window.

Keeping his weapon pointed at Matt, Maglio chewed his lip, glanced several times at the window, eyed Mr. Lean, and sidled to the glass. He gazed out and then pressed closer. "Are those fools really ..." The gun drifted to his side, as he stood transfixed by what he was seeing. "What the hell is this?"

Lowering Matt to the floor, Raphael sprinted to Maglio and wrenched the gun from his hand. "You can travel solo."

"Vamoose," said Mr. Lean.

Shoving the gun under his waistband, Raphael hoisted Matt again and dragged him to the doorway and into the corridor. The janitor took Matt's feet. "Wait," said Raphael, lowering Matt.

"We don't have much time," said Mr. Lean.

Raphael drew out his Exacto knife. He ran toward Maglio, who gazed out the window. He grabbed Geo by the shoulder, twisted him around and raised the knife. The digits had vanished from the cybernetic eye, and it appeared no different from the other. *Too human.* He couldn't do it. Raphael stepped back. Maglio returned his gaze to the street.

Nodding, Raphael backed into the hall and again lifted his friend. As they reached the intersecting hallway, he glanced into Research, whose door stood wide open. The lab must have shifted to battery. A hundred mournful faces gazed at him: Mirsky, Fullers, Pink.

From an unseen screen came a thin voice. "Dead, dead everywhere, but not a drop to drink. No, that's not right."

Oh, Gilly. They got you too. "Sorry, guys," said Raphael. "See you on the other …" His voice trailed off.

"When the hell is happy hour?" cried Mirsky.

Mr. Lean cleared the debris from their path as Raphel dragged Matt through the hall and into the stairwell, where he hoisted his friend to his shoulder. The custodian leading, they picked their way down the treacherous steps to the ground floor.

Mr. Lean pushed open the emergency exit door and oil spread into the stairwell. Raphael edged past Mr. Lean and lumbered into the warm pool.

A few steps later, the ground shook as if an earthquake had struck. "Watch out now!" cried Mr. Lean as stone and mortar toppled from the facade, throwing up tarry black sails that washed across them.

Raphael shook his head vigorously like a dog out of a bath, clearing the oil from his eyes. "Mr. Lean, I have to ask you something. In confidence."

Mr. Lean glanced at the sinking building. "It's confidence you'll have, but maybe we ought to wait to parlay."

His shoulders tightened. "Has to be now."

"Fire away then."

Raphael whispered his question, got his answer, and bowed his head in appreciation. Mr. Lean moved to change positions with Raphael, taking Matt under the arms, leaving Raphael to step free. Raphael glanced toward the waiting End Men, then turned and sloshed back into the stairwell.

"No, Raphael!" shouted Mr. Lean. "It's just a skateboard."

His heart aching, the entreaties of his friends growing louder before growing fainter, the consummate possum hunter climbed the sinking stairs.

CHAPTER
THIRTY-NINE

A possum threw a pebble at her window.

CHAPTER
FORTY

The skies grew lighter, but the city remained shadowy and vague.

On the northeast corner of Fairfax and Third, several blocks from Wilshire and Fairfax, where the ruins of Norval were bordered with yellow tape, guarded by police, and viewed with wonder by early morning commuters, Raphael stood with his skateboard. Cleansed by the night breeze, the city smelled fresh and invigorating.

On the far side of the street, a figure stepped out from the shadows, then stood as motionless as a street sign. The figure called out, *Cross now, Raphy.*

He had found his last image. Drowned in tar, buried among the remains of creatures great and small. Well, that would be the world's memory of Raphael Winston Lennon.

Mr. Lean would know differently.

As he and Mr. Lean had dragged Matt from the building, Raphael had whispered, "Mr. Lean, I want to be a possum. Is there any way I can go back inside, hide long enough for the world to think I'm dead, but safely exit the building in the night?"

Mr. Lean had scratched his chin. "There's an old Yam's ventilator shaft. Hasn't been used in thirty years. There's a way to access it from the third floor's restroom. Just pull off that dusty cover. On the roof, there's an exit right beside the Norval Logo. Got to push off that cover too. But you're an agile fellow and mighty strong. With a little luck, you'll do fine."

Returning to the building, he had followed Mr. Lean's instructions. In the small hours of the night, he pushed off the roof cover, crawled out behind the logo, stole across the oil-slicked roof, made it unseen to Fairfax, then to the Tiny City Complex and woke a grieving Addy with a pebble.

Well, almost a pebble, more accurately, a rock, and thrown with more force than he intended, shattering the quiet and the window.

When the curtains opened, Addy stared out with puffy, red, and disbelieving eyes. She touched the glass, a half-dozen crumpled tissues in her fist, the crack in the window splitting her face in half, which meant it was fracturing his face also. It took her a moment to put his broken face and garbled words together. Not exactly happy, she agreed to accompany him to Fairfax and position herself on the northwest corner. "Yeah, I'll be your carrot."

Now, she stood across the street and beckoned him.

"Cross now. Do it for me," begged Addy. "There's no canyon. It's just a street."

"Not in my brain!" Raphael cried.

Addy rocked her head, and the weighted braid swung from side to side like a pendulum. She stepped to the curb and shouted, "You're a monster, Raphael! I mean, *Leonardo*—wink, wink. First, I think you're dead. It crushed me. Two boxes of Kleenex!" Addy turned her head and blew out her breath. "Then—then, I'm trying to sleep, reading my ass off, and I hear this bang on my window. I go to my windowpane and guess what?"

"I don't—"

"There's a big crack! I said a *pebble*, not a goddamn *boulder*."

"It was all I could find."

"I swear, if you don't come here this very moment, I'm going to cry. Well, scream."

"No, no." *Forget being sad, Mommy. Forget the stupid mummy. Forget the stupid disease. Worry about me. I'll take your fear.* But it was his fear too. Not fear of the outside world, but of losing her. *Beyond the sound of her voice.*

Could he have always known it, yet not felt it?

Just as he knew the street was only a street. But he did not feel it.

Heart pounding, he set down his board and put a foot on the curb. The concrete moaned and cracks appeared. This border wouldn't push him back, wouldn't confront him with a wall of ice, wouldn't paralyze him with fiery pain. It could only take him. Skating into it, he would fall to his doom, and even as the fear grew, the ground buckled, splintered, and roared like a trapped tiger. He leaned forward and a depthless canyon appeared. He knew it was an illusion, but his knowledge made no difference. If you want to escape, you must chance the fall, chance death. Got it, skater?

If he could not break out of his prison, couldn't escape with Addy, better nonexistence. He put one foot on the board and pushed off.

He fell through black space. Faint stars appeared and spun themselves into images: mastodons and tigers, pools of tar and walls of concrete, *The Flesh Eaters* and *Three Quintains*, a featureless boy with wheels for legs, lips on a microphone, Shorty's neon and Royer's hellish wall, The Wall and a pomegranate, his mother's frozen face and a spinning skateboard wheel, a moat filled with tweets tipped with poison. He fell and fell but moved forward too. The wheels whirled beneath him, and an invisible solidity rose to carry his weight. An awful screech enveloped him. Not a scream, a horn. He twisted toward the blare's source. A little Roly-Poly stopped inches from him.

Raphael was crossing Fairfax against a red light.

"Sorry!" he shouted to the indignant vehicle. Raphael skated past the Roly-Poly to ollie the curb and set down with a bang on the western side of Fairfax.

"Hey, remember me?" cried Addy.

He placed a hand on his beanie and felt the solid skull. He breathed deeply from his belly. His heartrate slowed.

"I'm out, Addy! Out!"

She took his hand and pulled him to her. Her lips were soft and yielding and, though his experience was limited, he could not imagine better lips. They stood in front of the long-shuttered Johnnie's Café, making out as drones zipped by and pedestrians texted feverishly, and the Miracle Mile rose from the dim dawn light. When the kiss ended —a gracious withdrawal on Addy's part—Raphael faced Wilshire Boulevard with the courage of one who has tasted heaven after surviving hell. Stepping off the curb, he awaited a gale, but a light morning breeze caressed him. His La Brea glacier would have retreated to its Arctic climes, his Beverly inferno to the fires deep beneath the Earth's crust.

He gazed at the world beyond the prison walls. The sleek buildings, streaming cars, and tall palms shimmered and grew faint. *No. Stay. Be.* He breathed, and his body levitated above the sidewalk. The world stilled, the structures solidified.

"The ocean. I want to see it."

"Not Disneyland?"

"I want to stick my feet in the sand and the sea."

"If you're talking about the Pacific"—Addy pointed—"it's there. *Ten miles.*"

"Come on," he said, getting onto the board and guiding Addy on behind him. After noting the skateboard was surprisingly roomy, she clasped his waist. He pushed off. Far from his square, they passed through alien neighborhoods, crossing countless unfamiliar streets. They glided through the Gardens of Babylon and a run of stark desert plants. Glittering towers, roadways in the sky and an immense pink wall defaced with gargantuan graffiti: *Fuck Selfies!* They crossed a field of ten-thousand white stones, silent and whispering. Oh, how light it felt to be free. Out of his own clutching head.

Along the way, they stopped a half-dozen times, twice for food— air-burgers and seaweed shakes—twice to put fallen baby birds back in their nests, once to hold hands and watch a round of lawn bowling, once more to dance to the tunes of a 3D billboard band.

Hours later, they stood before a thundering sea veiled by fog. A flash of white appeared out of the rolling gray. White wings collapsed.

An enormous bird plummeted like a bullet into the sea. He gently squeezed Addy's shoulder, and she slipped her arm around his waist.

Then they kissed a hundred times, between each melding, whispering, "I love you," and "I love you, too."

They took off their shoes and sat on the cool sand. There were no drones.

"You know what?" said Addy.

"Tell me."

"We're free."

He laughed and lay on the sand. Addy dropped her head to his chest. The tardy moon glided between broken clouds.

Something cried. Not a cry, a squawk, and then a flutter. Cold against his feet, a warning or caressing cold? Was he being born? Was it his entrance into the world? He looked down the length of his body. A flash of white, then a rising black form: water gathering and closing on itself. The wave crashed and spilled over their feet. He bent his arms, pushed, and lifted his torso. He remained still as the sea lapped over his outstretched legs and his heels sunk into the soft wet sand. Not pixels on a screen, this was reality, a new land. He had escaped his frame.

CHAPTER
FORTY-ONE

Matt scooped up the last morsel of flan, considered signaling a waiter for seconds, but instead stood up and slipped through the King George Room, which smelled of whiskey and math, to the festively decorated open bar.

"Another strawberry daiquiri, huh?" said the bartender with a thin smile.

"Yeah, I'm driving."

The bartender nodded as he gathered the ingredients.

"That's a joke," said Matt. "My ride's a Roly-Poly with drunk-driver override."

"Nice." The bartender set a napkin on the bar and placed the colorful drink on it.

"Almost too beautiful to drink." Matt took a sip, sighed, and deposited a handful of cash in the tip jar." Drink at arm's length, he pirouetted and headed back to his table.

He had no complaints about the refreshments, but the first two hours of *Jason Klaes: A Life and Death*—postponed for a week because of the streak of tragedies—had been a bore.

Lily Faraday's recitation of Klaes's history and accomplishments— a jumbo monitor behind her showing equations and representations of quantum particles—had been informative but not riveting. Then, physicists from around the world had risen from their tables to read eulogies honoring Klaes. Few achieved their comic or tragic intent.

As he took his seat at the table, his three seatmates ignoring him, he thought how cool it would have been for Raphael to be here. His heart fell as he envisioned Raphael's face and the sound of his voice. He drifted back to those last chaotic moments. Norval sinking into the huge tar pit, Raphael going back inside for his skateboard, the boulevard a cacophony of policyholders off to commit suicide and live forever in servers.

Likely several hundred Personality Plus hopefuls, gathered through social media, would have met their maker that day if an emergency alert on their phones didn't inform them of the fine print in their Resurrection Contracts: Suicide in the first twenty years of their policy rendered the promise of an AI Afterlife null and void.

They had found Maglio at his desk, drowned in asphalt, phone in hand. Geovanni Maglio, "like a good captain, had gone down with the ship," as the media observed, never failing to add "naked as a newborn."

To expose the body, rescue workers had dug Geo out of a tarry cocoon resembling a cheap sarcophagus. Cleaned in the manner of a fossil by a team of paleontologists from the museum, he had departed the world with an inexplicable grin on the well-tanned face. The cybernetic eyeball still functioned, dilated pupil shrinking as the hammerdriver cracked the asphalt, and, in the words of one paleontologist, "The brilliant blue iris beamed as if in victory over death."

Though they pinned the bomb, the subsequent explosion of methane, and Norval's plunge into the Salt Lake Oil Field on Raphael, Matt knew that Raphael was an unsung hero. More so, a kind and sympathetic friend.

Why Raphael went inside to extract his skateboard was inexplicable to Matt. More bewildering was that he didn't remember Raphael's skateboard being in Maglio's office on that memorable day. Then again, having a Solarium Tanner slam into you likely didn't do much for memory.

The authorities reasoned the tar engulfing Norval Headquarters had consumed Raphael. Having spent only a few hours of his twenty-seventh year, he might one day be dug up with dire wolves and mastodons.

A few opined he would never be found in the sunken ruins of the building, that he had escaped his tarry crypt and gone into hiding to avoid the various criminal charges leveled against him. It was a farfetched scenario, but Matt hoped, if vainly, that Raphael was now one of the possums he long hunted, though if the possum were confined to his square mile, they would catch him down the line. Maisie Sparod wouldn't rest until they did.

From her new corporate offices in Santa Monica, Sparod had assumed the business of selling digital souls. A partnership agreement with Maglio gave her the Norval technology, and she had brought onboard half of Norval's staff, keeping financial support from Maglio's angels from the east.

It was a busy news week.

The LAPD cracked the notorious Stolen Pauper's Fund Case, the theft that had deprived the dead indigents of their plot of earth or cradle of urn. The suspect was no other than Gilly Stull, the undeclared whom Raphael had taken a personal interest in, no doubt pegging him as a possum. Stull was a bizarre twist in an already twisted case. The police never recovered the stolen money, nor a mysterious twenty-five thousand dollar Starbucks gift card that Gilly purchased.

On another front, social media influencers were provoking their followers to act out bizarre and unsettling rituals, including appalling sacrifices to newly emerged online wannabe gods with names such as Miranda, Troy-Boy, Van Pelt, Royer, and Oeg (suspiciously, the backwards spelling of Geo). The demigods of narcissism, conspiracies, stupor, cruelty, and greed. The Ludds and new followers skirmished daily. The hope of most people was that the two forces would cancel each other out.

Matt slipped from the memories, just as Lily reached the pièce de résistance: the contents of a mysterious crate. On the stage, under her supervision, a workman had cut the bands and was now using a crowbar to loosen a side panel.

Faraday faced the audience. "Let me be clear, I have no idea what's in here. If any of you want to leave the room at this time, please do so." She scanned the tables, but no one gave any sign of leaving. "Good. Then we'll continue."

Nails squealed as the bar pulled them from the wood. The sides of the crate fell. Lily and the worker drew away the foam packing to reveal the rectangular face of a machine, about twenty inches in height and width. At the center of the machine's face was a steel barrel.

Several of the guests slipped from their chairs and made for the exits.

On the monitor above the stage, Klaes's familiar bearded face appeared.

A motor whirred inside the machine.

"Good evening, friends and colleagues. This is Professor Jason Klaes speaking to you from where—according to current science—I can't be. What addresses you now is a machine in a ghost. I live within the soul that was once me. If I claim I'm an AGI, most of you will laugh in disbelief. But that's of little matter. What really matters is why I've done the impossible. My daughter Angie, aged five years, died from a terrible disease. She passed believing she might one day return. I promised I would move heaven and earth to give her back her life."

Klaes's face tightened. His unwavering gaze seemed to meet the eyes of each audience member. "My child was sealed in a cryogenic chamber, which I stole. Angie is in a place where she is safe. She'll remain frozen until a time when physicians can bring her flesh to life and cure her disease. In my present state, I'll accompany her through decades, centuries, perhaps millennia, until the world is ready."

Vague memories returned to Matt of the moments he lay half-conscious on Maglio's office floor. "I have your data prepared to receive your soul," a deep voice had said on the phone.

"Pass, Dad. I'm not transitioning to AGI," Raphael had responded. How like a dream, the memory and what was now happening. Matt didn't believe a word of it, but something happened, and he wanted to know what.

"Accompany her through centuries?" shouted one physicist at the screen. "In what form will you be?"

"Should I repeat myself?"

"That's not possible. It doesn't exist. We aren't close," said one woman.

"No," agreed Klaes, "*you* aren't."

"Can you offer any proof?" asked another.

In the pockets and purses of the hundred assembled scientists, cellphones rang. When they drew them out, Klaes's face was on the screen of each one. He simultaneously addressed every scientist by their first name and remarked on their latest work. For a moment the room was a chaos of voices, then fell into silence.

A fragile, elderly scientist spoke into his phone. "Good to see you, old friend, and for a moment I'll suspend disbelief. You always kept several balls in the air. You did this just to bring your daughter back to life?"

"Yes. Give me a lever, and I'll move the world. The lever? Love."

The machine's motor spun faster. Something white spurted from its barrel.

"With apologies to Mr. Joyce," said Klaes.

A hundred more bits of white flew into the air, rising, then drifting down. Then the machine really went to work, sending thousands of the flakes into the air to fall on the scientists.

"Why it's snow. It's only a snowmaking machine. Ha!"

Like a child experiencing his first snowfall, Matt put out his hand and caught a snowflake.

"Each the same, each different, and bound for the same fate," said Klaes. "But look how beautiful they are before they plummet and melt."

Matt gazed into the dazzling artificial snowfall.

On the monitor, Klaes's eyes found the elderly scientist. "No, old friend. I don't want this"—he held out his hands as if to thrust them into the room—"to end."

The old scientist scratched his head. "If I remember my Joyce, the snowflakes were the dead. You don't want death to end?"

Klaes laughed. "I thank Mr. Joyce for his metaphor, but here we part company. Sunrises, sunsets, the scent of a rose, a first kiss, a last goodbye, the thunder and might of a crashing wave, a daydream, an infant's cry, a pint of Guinness, a good laugh, a fresh fall of snow —*Nevermore*. Goodnight, friends and colleagues. Goodnight, Lily, and thank you."

Klaes vanished from the screen.

Lily touched her nape. Her eyes were distant and disregarding of the confused voices in the audience. "I'm sorry. That's it."

The crowd exited with much shaking of heads and chatter. In ten minutes, Matt was alone with Lily. The snowmaking machine had stopped, and the flakes had all turned to water.

Matt tugged on his ear. "Well, that was pretty cool." He surveyed the tables, which had not yet been cleared. "All in all, a success, I'd say."

Lily gazed at her blank phone screen on which a single snowflake appeared as if it had been born by the phone itself.

A couple of workers entered the room to clear the tables. Matt raised his arm and shook his bracelet to get one's attention. "Hey, buddy, you got any more flan?"

EPILOGUE

Namje, Nepal, 2445

From the Namje Valley, Kat gazed at the jagged, snow-covered peak as she caught her breath. The trek from the trailhead outside of Biratnagar had exhausted her, for there were no roads to Namje, only precarious footpaths, which sometimes disappeared entirely. Getting to Biratnagar itself was no piece of cake. Their company, Rise and Shine Cryogenics, barely had enough clout to obtain a flight from Kathmandu. Few places on Earth were as difficult to get to as Namje, but Kat supposed that was the point.

She had traveled with Mark and Marith, two seasoned employees of the firm. Kat was new on the job. This would be her first awakening.

"This way," said the ghost who waited for them.

The voice startled her. The holographic images of AIs had been around since her childhood, but speaking was a new development. She gazed at the wavering lines that formed a shape for a few seconds, became indiscernible, and then reappeared.

The shimmering ghost floated toward a red door, centered between sets of oval windows circling the geodesic structure. Solar panels covered the roof.

The ghost motioned for Kat and her companions. She had the kit in her backpack, and it weighed a good thirty pounds, no piece of cake to haul up a footpath. She was breathing hard when the three reached the structure.

No matter the assurances of her two colleagues, the assignment was spooky. She had witnessed over a dozen unsealings, but all at company facilities. Even under controlled conditions they occasionally failed. Cryonic chambers had been perfected, though the ones manufactured one or two hundred years ago were frequently flawed, their occupants little more than fossils. They'd opened the chamber all set to go to work and the person would long have been desiccated, turned to stone.

This chamber was more than four centuries old. Hidden away for four centuries, imagine.

The three now stood at the entrance.

"Please go in," said the ghost.

Kat watched Marith take a firm grip of the handle and turn. The door opened on a dimly lit room. Kat took a tentative step inside. As her eyes adjusted to the light, she saw dozens of ancient computers stacked against the walls. In the room's center, a silver chamber sat atop a three-foot-high platform.

Kat watched her colleagues approach the platform.

"How—"

"It's activated," said the ghost.

"Kat, get out the vitalizer," ordered Marith.

Heart pounding, Kat slipped off the backpack and extracted the vitalizer. She scrambled with the device and set it on the table. When she powered up the device, thin wires and narrow tubes slithered out of the box like newborn snakes.

The chamber squeaked. *Doesn't sound good*, thought Kat. Her spine felt icy as if she had fallen backwards into the mountain's snow.

Then a ticking.

"Is everything all right?" asked Mark.

The ghost shimmered.

The chamber door moved outward, and the interior lit up.

Kat stared at the little girl sheathed in cold crystal. Colorless, motionless, lifeless. Oh, how far away she looked. Was life still there? Faint, oh, so very faint. Marith and Mark went into action with their tubes and wires, probing and poking.

The vitalizer was attached. Kat watched for the first signs of life. A minute passed.

"Something's wrong," said Mark.

"Increase the spin," ordered Marith.

Mark made an adjustment.

Kat had seen two failures in her brief career. One was a moment of life that in another moment drained away. The other nothing more than stillness and silence.

The ghost wavered.

"Full spin," cried Marith.

Kat stared at the girl's blue lips, which trembled.

A swatch of pink on her chest. A streak of yellow across her hand. A colored shape here, another there. Something moved across the girl's shoulder. The frozen girl coughed. Stirred.

"I think we're okay," said Marith.

It was hardly over. They had to prepare her for the journey and the intricate operations to cure and restore her.

The hologram nodded. "Thank you."

She began her work on Angie Murie. The little girl wouldn't speak for a while, but when she did, the first words would be the same questions all asked upon awakening: "Where are they? My mother? My father? My sister? My brother? My friends?"

Kat sighed. It was the right thing to do. Most certainly it was the right thing. Everyone agreed. Life was better than death.

ACKNOWLEDGMENTS

I am grateful to the following for their support and critical feedback:

A.W. Cardiff, Lyle Cross, Paul Du Preez, Priya Doraswamy, Cassie Dutton, Eric Estrin, Penelope Else, Miriam Fristensky, Michela Gianello, Sammi Goldberg, Emily Grandy, Brent Higgins, Nada Holland, Cody James, Nathan Jones, Cynthia Knuts, Carrie Krause, Terri Lewis, Monique Lobosco, Danita Mayer, Clark McCann, Mac McCaskill, Michael McGinty, Kein Ouzunupi, Herman Padilla, Lydia Redwine, Natalie Ross, Terry Stroud, Clinton Tedja, Nicole Teske, Jessie Wolf, Steven S.Hood, Marith Zoli.

Special thanks to computer engineer Dusty Phillips for his guidance on technology, and to physicist/novelist Marco Ocram for his tutorial on quantum entanglement.

I thank my family for their enthusiasm about this fiction. My daughter Heather suggested some clever lines of texting dialogue. My son Chris pulled me back from the narrative edge a couple of times, and my wife Eileen stood fast when a personal dilemma threatened to escalate out of control.

I am indebted to Kelly and the staff of Cursed Dragon Ship.

ABOUT THE AUTHOR

Alex Austin is a Los Angeles-based journalist, novelist and playwright. His novel *Nakamura Reality* was published by The Permanent Press in 2016. Publishers Weekly gave the novel a starred review and called the writing, "powerful and moving." His novel *The Perfume Factory* was a finalist for Writer's Digest Independent Literary Novel of the Year, 2009, and was a Kirkus Recommended. Austin's plays include *The Amazing Brenda Strider*, a Backstage West Critic's Pick, winner of the Maddy Award for Playwriting and produced at several venues, including the CoHo Theatre, Portland. His play *Mimosa* was produced at Los Angeles Theatre Center, the featured play in Wordsmiths Playwrights Festival, presented by the City of Los Angeles Cultural Affairs Department. *Dupe* was featured in Ten Grand Production's Cold Cuts Series in New York City. His fiction has been published in numerous literary magazines, including Carte blanche, Black Clock, Beyond Baroque, District Lit, Midway Review, Foliate Oak and The Disconnect. He has written numerous nonfiction articles. Austin is a graduate of UCLA. He lives with his wife Eileen in West Hills, California. Retired from full-time teaching, he currently works as a substitute teacher for the Los Angeles Unified School District.

YOU MIGHT ALSO LIKE

In humanity's last city, you're either consumed by a monster, or you become one.

YOU MIGHT ALSO LIKE

One mind different from the rest must save her community from itself.

Made in the USA
Las Vegas, NV
21 October 2022

57879878R00199